HOLLY J. WOOD

DESERET
BOOK

SALT LAKE CITY, UTAH

Library of Congress Cataloging-in-Publication Data
Wood, Holly J., author.
    Invaluable / Holly J. Wood.
       pages cm
    Summary: When Eliza Moore begins dreaming about her great-grandmother, she comes to understand the significance of the eight Young Women values, and she finds her life changing for the better as she strives to live them.
    ISBN 978-1-60908-835-4 (paperbound : alk. paper)
       1. Young Women (The Church of Jesus Christ of Latter-day Saints)—Juvenile fiction. [1. Young Women (The Church of Jesus Christ of Latter-day Saints)—Fiction.
2. Mormons—Fiction. 3. Christian life—Fiction. 4. Conduct of life—Fiction.]
    I. Title.
       PZ7.W84943Inv 2011
       [Fic]—dc23   2011022423

Printed in the United States of America
Malloy Lithographing Incorporated, Ann Arbor, MI

10   9   8   7   6   5   4   3   2   1

For my children

ACKNOWLEDGMENTS

I'd like to extend my deepest gratitude to the wonderful people at Deseret Book. In particular, I'd like to thank Heidi Taylor and Lisa Mangum for their kindness, insight, and encouragement along the way (and for immeasurable amounts of patience with a "rookie" author!).

There have been so many incredible friends and family members who have shown me their love and support in this endeavor. I wish I had pages and pages to name each person individually, but suffice it to say—thank you, to each and every one of you (you know who you are).

My utmost expression of love and appreciation goes to my husband, Steve, for granting me the precious gift of time, for being "Super Dad," and for always believing in me. This book would not have been possible without you.

Finally, to my parents, David and Marilyn Rudd, for being the most amazing parents a person could ever hope for. Your unwavering examples of faith, love, and support have helped me in ways that I cannot adequately describe. Thank you so much—for everything.

CHaPTer

one

"Eliza! Honey, please hurry down for breakfast. I don't want you to be late for school again!" This was the second warning from Mom, and I knew better than to mess around with that tone of voice. I took one last glance in the mirror, then grabbed my lip gloss off the dresser and stuffed it into my backpack as I ran downstairs.

Mom stood by the stove wearing her usual morning attire: a velour leisure suit and slippers. Her brown hair was pulled back in a ponytail, and she was flipping French toast. I could smell the cinnamon she used as a special ingredient.

Argh! French toast was one of my favorites; this dieting thing was not going to be easy. I closed my eyes and tried to imagine myself wearing a stunning prom dress (that I had yet to find) and felt the resolve I needed to say no to the calories.

Just a few more weeks. You can do this.

"Go ahead and sit down. Breakfast is ready." Mom gave me a threatening look, and I wondered if it was a coincidence that she was serving my favorite breakfast.

Nope. After one glance at her, I could tell that she definitely knew about the diet; how did she *do* that?

"Thanks, Mom, but I don't have time today. I'll just take one of these." I tried to act casual as I searched the pantry for a flavor of granola bar I liked.

"Eliza, you need to *eat!*" She cast a desperate glance at my dad, who was sitting at the table finishing his last piece of bacon.

He reached over and picked up the glass of orange juice by my untouched plate and said, "It's the most important meal of the day, you know. At least drink your juice."

Mom sighed in exasperation—that was obviously not the kind of backup she'd been hoping for.

I smiled at Dad as I took the glass of juice, and he gave me a quick wink. Dad was more laid-back than Mom about most things, and, fortunately for me, a lot less observant.

I drained my juice glass, grabbed my bag, and headed for the door. I avoided Mom's glare, but as a peace offering said, "Sorry about breakfast. Maybe Courtney will want it." Doubtful, since my thirteen-year-old sister had yet to make her appearance this morning. "See you later!" And with that, I was out the door.

I stepped out into the beautiful April morning sunshine and headed for my car. Our neighbor was mowing his lawn and I could smell the freshly cut grass. To me that sound and smell always meant one thing—summer was on the way! For a moment I considered ditching school and heading for a park to bask in the sun all day, but that thought was short-lived. I knew the school would send a recorded phone message to my house that I'd been absent and then I'd be busted.

As I got in my car, I consoled myself with the fact that at least today was Friday. I turned on the ignition, blasted the radio, and headed for Jill's house.

Jill and I had been best friends ever since second grade, when her family had moved into the neighborhood a block away from my family. I tried to be patient as I waited in Jill's driveway, watching the minutes tick by with no sign of my friend.

Just as I was about to send her a text message, Jill came flying through the front door. She jumped in the car holding a half-eaten piece of toast in one hand and a mascara tube in the other.

"Sorry, I was trying to hurry," she said breathlessly.

"It's okay. It's not like this is our first time being late for school. Nice shirt," I added sarcastically as I backed out of the driveway. She caught my tone and smiled; she had borrowed that shirt from me last week.

Jill and I were about the same size and were constantly swapping clothes. We often went shopping together to make sure that we bought clothes *both* of us liked.

"Don't make any sudden stops; I don't want to poke my eyes out," Jill warned, flipping down the visor mirror and applying her mascara.

I had to hand it to her—even when she just threw things together at the last minute, she still managed to look good!

Although we were similar in lots of ways, our physical features were dramatically different: Jill was of Asian descent, with dark hair cut in a stylish A-line, dark almond-shaped eyes, and a flawless, creamy skin tone. Because of her striking features, she hardly had to wear any makeup. I didn't even know why she bothered with the mascara.

I, on the other hand, had fair skin, and it certainly wasn't always flawless. If I didn't wear makeup, I felt like my face disappeared. I had long brown hair, which I routinely highlighted to break up the monotony; my current highlights were a deep honey color. My height was a completely average five feet five, and although my weight would probably be considered average as well, I really wanted to lose ten pounds.

My one redeeming feature was my eyes. I had inherited my mom's strikingly bright blue eyes, and it was usually the first thing people noticed about me.

Jill was gabbing away about some TV show she'd watched last night while I inserted an occasional "Mm-hmm" and tried to focus on the road. She and I made a good pair. She was always bubbly and animated and never lacked for something to say, while I was a little bit shy and labeled as a "good listener." Jill made me go out of my comfort zone by suggesting fun and spontaneous things to do, and I kept her (or at least *tried* to keep her) from getting too carried away.

She was right in the middle of a sentence when her cell phone buzzed.

"Wow, lover boy's getting started early this morning. What has it been, like ten *whole* hours since you talked to him last?" I smirked.

She rolled her eyes at me and flipped open her cell phone. "Oh, he's sooo cute!" she gushed. "He says he misses me and he can't wait until lunch."

I made a gagging sound, but her fingers were already flying as she replied to his text message. I hoped she would spare me the details of whatever mushy message she was sending.

Jill and Nick Forrester had been dating since the beginning

of the school year. At first it had been fun to watch them become a couple and hear all of Jill's stories about what Nick said and how it felt to have a boyfriend (especially because neither of us had ever had one before), but after a few weeks, it started to get old, and I began to feel like I was losing my best friend. It didn't help that I'd never particularly liked Nick. He was always so clingy with Jill, almost as if he didn't have any life outside of their relationship.

And, yeah, I was a little bit jealous—jealous that Jill had a boyfriend and I didn't, and jealous that she spent so much time with him.

When she finished her text, she smiled at me and said, "He's gonna meet me by my locker before class. Isn't that sweet?"

I grimaced. "Thanks for the warning. I'll be sure to go in another direction." She smacked my arm, and I grumbled, "Just kidding, sheesh!"

We pulled into the parking lot and started searching for an open space.

"Wow, there's actually a spot toward the front, hurry!"

I looked to where Jill was pointing and lightly pushed down on the accelerator. I had gotten my driver's license only two months ago, and I prided myself on cautious driving.

Just as I was about to reach the blessed opening, a flashy red BMW came squealing around the corner and into our spot. I slammed on the brakes, and my tires screeched in protest.

Without missing a beat, Chelsea Andrews emerged from the offending vehicle and started walking toward the school with her signature runway model walk. She didn't even bother to glance back at us.

"Holy cow! We almost slammed into her!" Jill yelled. "You

should have just gunned it and ran straight into her *precious* little car. What a brat!"

I realized I was holding my breath, so I let it out and tried to relax my white-knuckled fingers from their death grip on the steering wheel.

Jill rolled down the window and yelled at Chelsea, "Watch where you're going next time, road hog!" But Chelsea had already disappeared through the front doors.

We found another parking space in the second-to-last row of the lot while Jill continued her tirade on the many faults of Chelsea Andrews. Secretly, I knew Jill was going off on Chelsea because deep down, she was jealous of her. I think *every* girl in school was jealous of her, and for good reason.

Chelsea had everything. She always wore the latest styles, which were frequently copied by her little swarm of friends. She was on the drill team, she was completely gorgeous (I mean like Barbie-doll gorgeous), and she always had a string of boys after her. To top it all off, Chelsea's family lived in a huge house on the hill, and she was known for throwing incredibly fun pool parties—which Jill and I had yet to be invited to.

Two weeks ago, she'd had a huge party for her sixteenth birthday, and her parents had surprised her with that brand-new BMW.

As Jill and I got out of the car, I looked at my own '89 Honda Civic hatchback and felt for the hundredth time that it wasn't fair. My dad worked in an office by Chelsea's dad, and I knew he made as much money—if not *more*—than Mr. Andrews, and yet they had a huge mansion and she got a brand-new car while I lived in a regular house and drove a lump of scrap metal.

I knew I should be grateful to have a car at all, but to add insult to injury, Dad had given me the car on the condition that I get a job and pay for the insurance myself. The only thing worse would have been riding the bus, so I had reluctantly agreed.

Jill snapped her fingers in front of my face. "Anybody home? Come on, I don't want to be late."

I pulled myself out of my personal pity party and picked up the pace beside her. As we were hurrying toward the school, she started unbuttoning her shirt.

"Um, what are you doing?" I asked in alarm.

"Don't worry; I'm not about to streak or anything," she said with a laugh. Underneath her shirt (or rather, *my* shirt), she was wearing a tight yellow tank top with a big purple flower and rhinestones on it.

"I don't remember seeing that shirt before," I said, trying to keep the surprise out of my voice.

Jill looked a little embarrassed. "Well, Nick and I went to the mall last night, and he saw this and told me it would look good on me. . . . And besides, this way I can get some sun on my skin before prom. You can borrow it whenever you want," she added in a hurry.

"Thanks," I said halfheartedly. She knew I would never borrow it. My mom was the Young Women's president in our ward, and she practically had the *For the Strength of Youth* pamphlet memorized. Sleeveless shirts were a no-no in our house . . . but it *did* look cute on Jill.

Maybe if I hid it under my clothes like Jill did . . . hmm.

Just then the bell rang.

"Oh, great, now I won't have time to meet Nick." Jill's lips pulled into a pout as we ran through the entrance doors.

CHaPTer

A few hours later, I walked out of my math class feeling like my head was going to explode. I did relatively well in all my classes—except math. Why did we need to take math, anyway? I couldn't imagine myself wanting to be in any profession that would require using a calculator with mysterious functions, so what was the point?

I walked through the halls toward my locker, surrounded by bright posters on the walls announcing prom: "This Year's Prom Theme Is 'One Last Dance.' Buy Your Tickets Today!" Although I thought the theme wasn't very original, I had to admit I was excited to be going to my first prom.

Jason Sorensen had asked me to prom on the very day they announced the date for the dance. He was a junior, and we'd met in a health class last semester. He was really nice, and I was flattered that he'd asked me.

What worried me was that I suspected he might want to be more than just friends. He was always searching me out at school, and lately I'd been getting secret notes in my locker that I was pretty sure came from him. But I wasn't sure if I liked him in that way, so I tried to keep all of our conversations casual and off the topic of dating. I didn't want to hurt his feelings, after all.

I reached my locker, and as I opened the door, a piece of paper fell on the ground. "Oh no," I mumbled under my breath as I picked up the note and slowly unfolded it.

Eliza,

   I just wanted to tell you that you look beautiful today. I always look forward to seeing your amazing smile.

   Your Secret Admirer

I swallowed hard and shoved the note into my bag just before I felt a tap on my shoulder.

"Hey, gorgeous, what's up?"

I turned around to see Jason's smiling face. "Um . . . not much. I was just on my way to lunch," I replied, trying my best to remain composed. I wondered if he was looking for a reaction to the note.

"Cool. I was headed to the cafeteria too. Mind if I walk with you?" His green eyes looked so hopeful that I couldn't say no.

"Not at all. How was your last class?" School was always a good, safe subject.

"Ugh, choir. Ms. Steele is really on one today. She made us sing the same line *over and over* until the tune was drilled into our brains. I'm gonna be humming 'All That Jazz' in my sleep tonight!" he moaned.

I laughed. "Yeah, that's pretty brutal. Hopefully she'll be in a better mood after lunch, because I have choir next."

"Oh, you've got nothing to worry about. You're one of her 'star students,'" he said with air quotes. "You could never be on her bad side." Jason smiled at me with an unmistakable hint of admiration in his eyes.

I felt myself start to blush, so I changed the subject.

"Thanks. So what are you gonna get for lunch today?" I attempted lamely.

Just then I caught sight of Jill and Nick waiting for me by the cafeteria doors. Nick had his arm around Jill and was whispering something in her ear while she giggled.

After taking one look at them I felt nauseated. In a moment of sheer desperation, I turned to Jason and blurted out, "Do you want to eat lunch with us?" I hadn't even given him time to answer my first question, but I knew I couldn't stand being the third wheel in the lovebirds' lunch party.

Jason's eyes lit up, and with unmasked enthusiasm he said, "Sure! I was just about to ask you the same thing."

I smiled at him. He had no idea what a favor he was doing me. "I usually meet up with Jill and Nick too. . . . Is that cool?"

Jason glanced toward where they were standing and in his usual congenial manner he replied, "Sure."

Jill and Nick looked up as we walked toward them, and Nick said, "Hey, Liza Lou, what took you so long today?"

I *hated* when he called me that.

"Sorry, Nich-o-las," I emphasized his full name, knowing that it bothered him. "I had to drop off some books at my locker. If I'd known *you* were waiting, I would have walked a little slower," I said with a smirk.

Jill glared at us. It frustrated her that her boyfriend and best friend didn't get along. "Okay, children, that's enough. Let's go get in line; I'm starving!"

"Jason's going to eat with us today," I said as nonchalantly as possible.

Nick was already pulling Jill by the hand toward the lunch line, but she flashed a smile over her shoulder. "Cool. How's it going, Jason?"

He smiled back. "Good, thanks!" He waved his hand in front of him, gesturing for me to go first.

He really is a nice guy. I bet he'd treat his girlfriend like a princess, I thought to myself.

I considered the sweet notes he'd left for me and how nice it felt to have someone act like you really mattered—not to mention the bonus of having a buffer between Romeo and Juliet. Maybe I'd been too hasty in deciding I didn't want to date him.

"So have you decided what you and Eliza are going to do for a day activity for prom?" Jill's voice snapped me out of my musings.

"Yeah, but it's sort of a surprise." Jason winked conspiratorially at her.

"Oh, I *see.*" Jill smiled at me, raising her eyebrows and signaling that she wanted to talk more about this later. She knew all too well about Jason's interest in me and my lack of interest in him.

I pretended not to see the look and continued loading my salad bowl with everything that looked edible and—more important—low-fat. Jill followed suit and began constructing her own salad masterpiece.

Nick looked at our trays in disgust. "Come on, Jason, let's go get some *real* food. These girls eat like rabbits." Jason laughed, and they both headed for the pizza and breadsticks I'd been trying hard not to smell.

"Eliza, *what* is going on? Did he invite himself to eat with you or something?" Jill whispered as we left the salad bar and headed toward the cashier. We each grabbed a chocolate milk carton (our single indulgence), and I handed my cash to the old lady behind the register.

"No, actually I invited him. He wanted to walk me to the cafeteria and . . . I don't know. . . . He's such a sweet guy." I felt like I was on trial.

"He *is* nice, and it's obvious that he completely adores you, but I guess I'm a little surprised. You've never been that into redheads, and you told me that you're not attracted to him. Did something change?" Jill stared at me quizzically, and then we both looked over to where Nick and Jason were standing.

Jason was average height, and he *did* have red hair, but not flaming red. Suddenly I felt a little defensive of him and tried to see him in a new light—he wasn't that bad looking! Granted, standing next to Nick didn't do him much justice, but I was willing to bet lots of girls thought he was cute.

I heard Jill sigh and looked over to see her gazing all dreamy-eyed at Nick.

"Oh, Jill, look at you! It's pathetic!"

She sighed again and shrugged. "I know. I just can't seem to help myself. He's so perfect! I can't believe I got so lucky."

"No way, *he's* the lucky one. You could have any guy you wanted." I looked at Nick, and from a physical standpoint I could see why Jill was so attracted to him. He was probably about five foot ten with blond hair (which was usually half-hidden by a baseball cap), hazel eyes, and tan skin, which I knew for a *fact* was compliments of the local tanning salon. He was constantly working out, and consequently he was fairly muscular, which he liked to flaunt by wearing muscle shirts. So, physically, yes, I could understand why she liked him, but personality-wise, I was still mystified by her choice.

The boys finished filling their trays and made their way toward us.

"I want to eat outside today. It's been ages since I've sat in the sun," Jill said.

We all agreed and made our way through the hall to the outdoor courtyard. As we reached the door and stepped outside, I stopped short, and Jason bumped into me.

"Oh, whoops, sorry!" I apologized and immediately began blushing.

"No problem, nothing spilled. Are you okay?" he asked.

"Yeah, um, it's just so crowded I wasn't sure where to sit," I said, trying desperately to cover up the *real* reason I'd stopped in my tracks. Luke Matthews was sitting just two tables away from where we were standing.

No matter where I was when I saw Luke, my body always had the same reaction: I would sort of freeze and start blushing. My heart would beat wildly, and I'd have to remind myself to breathe. It was almost as if time stood still. I'd had a crush on him since the first day I'd seen him, and I could still recall that moment with perfect clarity.

It had been my first day of high school and I was a total mess of emotions: nervousness, anxiety, and, most of all, excitement. I'd planned weeks in advance what I was going to wear. Ours was a three-year high school, but despite the sophomore orientation, I still had no clue where half of my classes were.

I was walking down the hall through a sea of students looking for room 213 when I accidentally tripped on someone's foot and landed flat on my face in the hallway.

"Oh, man, are you okay?" The words were said with sincerity by a voice so charming I had to see who'd spoken them. I looked up into a face so handsome my jaw dropped open.

A boy stood above me with his hand outstretched, and without hesitation I reached up and took it. As soon as I touched him, I felt an electric shock through my body. He pulled me up effortlessly, and I had to crane my neck to look up at him. He was at least six feet tall.

"I'm so sorry. That was totally my fault." He was looking at me intently, and as I looked into his eyes, I felt like I was in a trance. They were a beautiful shade of deep brown with specks of gold in them. They were, without a doubt, the most incredible eyes I'd ever seen, and in that moment I felt like I could almost see into his soul. It was like an out-of-body experience, and I wanted the moment to last forever.

"Are you okay?" the boy had asked again.

"Yeah, I-I'm fine. Thanks for helping me up. I guess I wasn't watching where I was going." I couldn't stop myself from staring at him as I took in every feature: the dark, wavy hair, broad shoulders, and a dimple in his left cheek when he smiled. He was smiling! At me!

"You must be a sophomore. Do you need help finding a class?" he asked kindly.

I felt relief surge through me. He was obviously not a

sophomore—more likely a senior—but perhaps he wouldn't be op-posed to dating one?

"Um, yeah. I'm looking for room 213. Do you know where that is?"

"Yep, it's up on the second floor, almost directly above where we're standing. My class is in the opposite direction, otherwise I'd walk you there." He gave me an apologetic smile that reached up to his eyes.

I felt like I was going to melt. "No problem, thanks for your help, uh . . ." I realized I didn't even know his name.

"Luke. And you are?"

"Eliza Moore." *Why am I telling him my full name? What is this, some kind of business meeting? He must think I'm such a dork!*

"Nice to meet you, Eliza Moore," he said with a twinkle in his eye. "I hope you have a good first day." And then he was gone, leaving me to relive that moment over and over in my dreams from that time forward.

"Where do you guys want to sit?" Jill's voice brought me back to reality, and I quickly started scanning the courtyard for an empty table. It seemed like everyone had had the same idea about basking in the sun.

I was about to suggest we go sit on the bleachers by the football field when Jason said, "Oh, look, there are four empty chairs over by Luke."

Gasp!

He was already walking toward the table and hadn't noticed the uncomfortable expressions on the rest of our faces. For Jason it wasn't so bad; he was a junior and on the soccer team with Luke. The three of us, however, were just puny sophomores who would be totally out of place at a table full of seniors . . . well, *almost* full of seniors.

Chelsea Andrews had parked herself next to Luke and was flirting her little heart out. Everyone knew she had her sights set on Luke as her prom date, and she was pulling out all the stops. I felt a jealous rage as I watched her lean toward him using what I knew she considered to be her sexiest, most serious expression while he was talking. She would laugh at various intervals.

Chelsea had flirting down to an art. How could anyone compete with *that?* My heart sank, and the hurt combined with the humiliation of being forced to sit by them was almost unbearable.

"Hey, Luke, what's up?" Jason said as he sat down at the table.

Chelsea threw Jason a smile but her eyes were full of venom. It was painfully obvious that she didn't like us encroaching on her space.

"Hey, man, are you ready for the game today?" Luke asked. I thought I detected a hint of relief in his eyes at Jason's interruption. Maybe Chelsea's tactics weren't as powerful as I imagined.

The rest of the table quieted down as everyone looked up at our arrival. I noticed a few raised eyebrows, but after it appeared that Luke approved of our presence, the conversations resumed, and Nick, Jill, and I all breathed a sigh of relief. Maybe this wouldn't be so bad after all. If only I could somehow manage to tune out Chelsea's incessant giggling.

Jason and Luke talked about soccer for a few minutes while I pretended to focus on eating. I loved listening to Luke talk. Everything about him seemed to have some magical quality. He seemed not to have even noticed me, and I wondered if he remembered my name or that day in the hall so many months ago.

By a stroke of amazing good fortune, I'd ended up having seminary with him this semester. It was my last class of the day and the one I looked forward to the most. Although Luke sat in a corner desk toward the back of the class and I sat toward the front, I still managed to glance back at him occasionally. Just being in the same *room* with him was special.

"So, Eliza, what are you doing tomorrow?"

I looked up at Jason from the cherry tomato I'd skewered with my fork. "Um, not much. I have to work in the afternoon. How about you? Do you have any fun weekend plans?" I was a little nervous about where this was heading.

"Well, actually, I was hoping maybe you could go out tomorrow night." Jason was looking at me, but Luke had turned away and was pretending not to listen, and I sensed that Jill and Nick were putting on the same act. Chelsea, on the other hand, was staring at me with a smug expression and even leaned forward, waiting for my answer.

Suddenly, the area around me was very quiet. In our school, asking someone out on a date was a subject everyone was interested in.

I hated being the center of attention. I could feel my face start to get hot as I blushed. I couldn't think clearly enough—or fast enough—to come up with an excuse, and the silence was getting a bit awkward, so finally I said, "Sure, what do you want to do?"

I could almost sense a collective sigh pass around the table. Apparently nobody wanted an uncomfortable date rejection to spoil their lunch.

"Well, a group of us were thinking about going bowling and then out for ice cream. Right, Luke?" He turned to Luke, and I felt my eyes widen in surprise. I had no idea they were *that* good of friends.

"Yeah, we're getting together around seven at my place." Luke kept his eyes on his tray and his tone was less than enthusiastic. Was he bothered that Jason had invited a sophomore?

"Oh, how fun! I *love* bowling!" Chelsea cooed as she batted her big blue eyes and gave Luke a stunning smile.

Jill's snort turned into a cough. I struggled not to laugh either because I knew we were both thinking the same thing: *Chelsea, bowling?* I was willing to bet she'd never set foot in a bowling alley before, much less put her perfectly pedicured toes into stinky bowling shoes.

"Who are you going with, Luke?" Chelsea looked at him with feigned innocence, as though it didn't matter one way or the other, but the hint was obvious.

Luke cleared his throat and now it was his turn to be in the spotlight. "Well, actually, I asked Whitney Dawson. Do you know her?"

"Oh, yeah, she's really . . . nice." Chelsea's face fell and there was an uncomfortable shift around the table. Apparently we were going to have an uncomfortable date rejection after all.

Jill whispered in my ear, "Maybe the princess doesn't get everything she wants after all, boo-hoo."

I smiled and nodded, but inside I felt crushed. Luke was definitely bothered about something, and I was afraid it was *me.* He'd been so nice to me that day in the hall, but obviously he didn't want to date sophomores. He was the only guy I'd ever heard of who had turned down Chelsea Andrews; most guys would give their front teeth to go on a date with her. I looked down the table at Chelsea and for a brief moment felt sorry for her; it would be so embarrassing to be rejected like that in front of everyone. She was daintily picking away at her piece of pizza and in between bites was chattering away to Luke as if the previous conversation had never happened.

Why doesn't she just wolf down a few slices? I'm sure her perfect size two figure never changes no matter what she eats, I thought bitterly. Just then she laughed at something Luke said and tossed her long blonde hair over her shoulder. Whatever pity I felt for her vanished.

I had to get out of there. I stood up and pushed my chair back with a bit more force than I meant to.

"Eliza, where are you going? The bell hasn't even rung yet," Jill asked. She, Nick, and Jason all looked up at me in surprise.

"I know. I just need to use the bathroom before my next class."

"Do you want me to come with you?" Jill probed. She knew something was up, and she probably thought it was about my date with Jason. I hadn't told anyone about my secret crush on Luke, not even Jill. I knew he was way out of my league; I didn't need Jill to rub it in.

"No, it's fine. I'll see you after school." I turned to Jason. "Thanks for eating lunch with me. I hope you have a good day." I reached for my tray, but he grabbed it first.

"Don't worry about that. I'll take it back."

"Thanks," I said, giving him a smile. I really appreciated all the little things he did for me.

He beamed. "No problem. I'll pick you up tomorrow around six forty-five?"

"Oh, um . . . sure." I realized how unenthusiastic I sounded, so I tried to brighten my tone. "Sounds great. See you then!"

I started walking toward the door when I heard Nick call out, "Bye, Liza Lou!"

I froze in horror, hoping Luke hadn't heard my nickname, but Nick was so loud I knew everyone had heard. Without turning around I said, "See ya, Nicholas," and escaped to the hall and headed toward the solitude of the girls' room.

My name had always been a sore spot for me. There just weren't that many *Eliza*s running around these days, even in Utah.

There had been a particularly bad day when I was in the third grade and some kids at school teased me, saying I had an "old lady name." I had run home and thrown myself on my bed, crying. My mom came in and asked what happened. I sobbed to her that I hated my name. She stroked my hair and told me that I was named after my great-grandma Eliza Porter, who was one of her favorite people. Mom said she'd always hoped to have a little girl so she could name her Eliza. I could tell I had hurt her when I said I hated my name, so I'd never brought it up again, but secretly, I wished I'd been the second-born daughter so Courtney would have been stuck with the name instead of me.

I was almost to the bathroom when I noticed Keira Davis sitting on the floor with her lunch tray balanced on her lap. She had just moved here from New Jersey, and even though our school was pretty big, she definitely stood out. Her clothes might have been in style on the East Coast but here they made her look out of place. She had short, spiky blonde hair and a nose ring, which gave her an overall "stay away" vibe.

Some of the girls in my seminary class had befriended Keira

when she first came to school. But after Keira expressed zero interest in going to seminary or reading the Book of Mormon, they'd dropped her like a hot tamale. Apparently, she hadn't been the "golden investigator" they'd been hoping for.

Keira looked up at me as if sensing my thoughts, and feeling embarrassed, I quickly glanced away and made a beeline for the bathroom door.

⁌

I leaned against my car and gloried in the delicious heat radiating off it. Finally, I'd made it to the weekend! I looked at my watch again and sighed in exasperation. Why did I feel like I spent half of my life waiting for Jill? I searched in my bag for my pink flip phone, pulled it out, and sent her a text: "Where R U??" I closed my eyes as I tried to let the stresses of the day melt away.

"Taking a nap?"

I opened my eyes and frowned at Jill. "Took you long enough that I *could* have. Why don't you ever reply to my texts?" I picked up my bag and walked around the car to unlock the driver's side door.

"Sorry, it's just so hard to say good-bye to Nick sometimes. I've been dying to talk to you!" She looked at me with a face full of excitement, and I smiled. It was hard to stay mad at Jill for long.

"Soooo, spill it, girl! Do you like Jason? He was so sweet to get your tray at lunch. And I bet he left you another note today, am I right?" I nodded, and she squealed in delight as she grabbed my bag and searched for the note. She unfolded it and read the words aloud, then sighed, "Oh my goodness, that is *so* romantic! You *have* to like him, Liza! If you two started dating then the four of us could double." She was bouncing with enthusiasm, and I had to remind her to buckle up before she got us both killed.

I shrugged. "I *feel* like I should like him because he's such a sweet guy, but . . . I don't know, I just don't feel any spark. Is that how it started with Nick?"

My borrowed shirt reappeared from the depths of Jill's bag and she buttoned it over her tank top.

"Not really. There were definitely sparks between us right from the start. But I've heard a lot of people start off by just being friends. Maybe that's the case with you two. Maybe you just need to give him a chance."

I thought about that for a minute. I knew Jill really wanted me to have a boyfriend because she knew I felt left out, but maybe she had a point.

I sighed. "Okay, I'll start thinking of him as boyfriend potential and see what happens."

"Awesome! You have to call me and give me all the details after your date tomorrow—" Her phone buzzed and, as usual, she stopped midsentence to read her text. I hated when she did that; it made me feel like our conversation wasn't as important as her ever-buzzing cell phone.

She smiled and giggled as she typed a response, and seemingly before she'd stopped typing, her phone buzzed again and the whole process started over. Some days I could ignore it and pretend like I didn't care, but today I really wanted to talk, and I knew she would text forever if I didn't do something.

I cleared my throat loudly and said, "Ahem . . . you were saying?"

She looked at me blankly, and then reality dawned and she

said, "Oh, sorry. I was saying you have to give me all the details after your date with Jason tomorrow night. I can't wait to hear how it goes." Although she was talking to me, she was still texting, and I knew she was only putting half of her thought process into the conversation, so I tried for a subject that I know would get her full attention.

"So, prom is only a few weeks away, you know. When are we going shopping for our dresses? I think I've finally saved enough to get a nice one."

That did the trick. Jill put down her cell and said, "Really? That's great! How much have you saved?"

"Exactly two hundred and forty seven dollars, and after my next paycheck I'll have almost three hundred."

"Eliza, that's incredible! Your dad is gonna flip! I bet he'll wish he never made you that promise."

My parents insisted that I buy my own clothes, but they were a bit more understanding when it came to special occasions. Dad had promised that he would match however much money I saved for my prom dress. I couldn't wait to see the look on his face when I revealed how much money I'd saved. Suddenly, I felt excited to get out there and find my dress.

"Why don't we go tonight?" I suggested. "We could go to the mall and then see a movie or something." I looked over at Jill hopefully, but as soon as I saw her expression, I knew she already had plans.

"Sorry, Liza, but Nick and I are going to a movie tonight." Her face was pained. "You could totally come with us. It would be fun." Even after all these months, she *still* insisted on offering me the pity invite. I wished she would stop doing that—for both our sakes.

"I thought your parents didn't want you to go on single dates with him yet. What are you going to tell them?" I tried to keep the bitterness out of my voice, but it was hard because I knew what she was about to say.

"Oh, I'm just going to say that we're going in a group. I'm sure my mom won't ask you about it—but you don't mind covering for me if she does, do you?"

Actually I do mind, I felt like snapping. Jill was fifteen and her birthday wasn't until July, so her parents didn't want her dating yet. They had made an exception for prom (which my parents would never have done), but I think they were a little more lenient with her because they worried that if they were too strict she would rebel.

I pulled into Jill's driveway and struggled with the clutch before putting the car in park. She grabbed her bag and looked at me, "So, do you want to come with us tonight?" Her phone buzzed in her hand.

"No, thanks. I think I'll just hang out at home." I felt my stomach twist at the thought. What was worse than spending a Friday night at home alone? I missed my best friend.

"Okay, well maybe I'll stop by and see you at work tomorrow or something. See you later!" She waved, but she was already looking down at her cell phone and typing with her free hand. I backed out of the driveway and cranked up the radio to drown out my thoughts.

◦◦◦

As I walked through the front door, I could hear the TV blasting in the other room. Courtney must be home. It was so unfair that she left for school after I did and she *still* got home before me! I peeked in the family room and saw her and her friend Alexis sprawled out on the sectional, watching a music video of a girl who looked around their age wearing a miniskirt and crooning about love as she stared seductively into the camera.

I tried not to laugh. What could a girl that age *possibly* know about love? I glanced at Courtney and wondered for a moment if she'd ever kissed a boy. It would be so embarrassing if my little sister kissed someone before I did. She was way too young to be kissing, but she was a cute girl, and I knew at least a few of the boys in the ward had crushes on her.

I envied her blonde hair and pretty brown eyes. When we were growing up, people commented on how adorable she was, and now that she was maturing, the compliment had changed from "adorable" to "beautiful." It was hard for me not to feel like the ugly sister sometimes, but I liked having a little sister, and for the most part, we got along pretty well despite the three years between us. With a pang of guilt, I realized I didn't talk to her as much as I should.

When she was younger, she used to drive me crazy with wanting to talk all the time and be involved in whatever I was doing, but lately she hung out with Alexis and didn't seem to notice me. I reasoned this probably meant she was getting older and didn't need me like she used to. She was probably doing just fine.

I headed to the kitchen to find a low-calorie snack. With effort, I bypassed the plate of freshly baked snickerdoodles Mom had left on the counter (man, she was *not* making things easy for me) and settled for some saltine crackers and a glass of water. Not wanting Mom to interrogate me about my eating habits, I took my snack and trudged upstairs to my bedroom.

I grabbed the MP3 player off my nightstand, put in the earbuds, and hit "love songs" on the playlist menu. I flung myself onto my bed and absently chewed at a dry cracker while I tried to think of Jason in a romantic way. But somehow my thoughts kept straying to someone else, someone with dark hair and amazing eyes . . .

I felt a tap on my leg and looked up to see Mom mouthing words, but all I could hear was, "mm es ol ooo aa?" I pulled an earbud from my ear and said, "What did you say?"

"I said, how was school today?" She smiled and sat down on the bed next to me.

"Oh. It was okay."

"How was choir? Did you get to practice your solo?"

"No, we practiced a different song today." *Over and over and over.*

"I went to the school today and bought our tickets for the con-cert. Dad and I can't wait!"

The choir concert was next Friday and Saturday night, and I was nervous about it. I had tried out for one of the few solos and had been ecstatic when I'd gotten the part, but after the initial excitement I had been filled with anxiety and wondered what I'd gotten myself into. There were few things I dreaded more than being the center of attention. What if I messed up? What if my voice cracked right into the microphone? I wished Mom hadn't brought it up; my stomach tied itself in knots just thinking about the possibilities for humiliation.

Mom saw the expression on my face and said, "Don't worry,

Liza. You have such a beautiful voice. It's a gift you've been given, and you'll do great."

"Thanks, Mom." Her words actually did make me feel better.

"So, what are your plans for this evening? Jill usually comes home with you after school. Are you heading over to her house later?"

I frowned. "No, she has other plans tonight."

Mom's face brightened, and she said cheerfully, "Great! We don't get to see you much on the weekends. Courtney and Alexis wanted me to take them to a movie tonight. Why don't you come with us?"

Yeah, that's just what I wanted to do: go to a movie with my mom and little sister on a Friday night. But what were my other options? Sit at home moping with my crackers and love songs?

"Which movie are you going to?" I asked in a noncommittal tone.

"It's an animated film, but it's supposed to be *really* good." I shot her a disbelieving look. "Okay, it's the only one in the theater rated PG, but it *does* look cute." I knew she added this last part to head off any protests I might make. I actually liked a lot of animated movies, but to be caught going to one with your family when you were in high school was social suicide.

At the moment, though, that was a risk I was willing to take. It hadn't been the greatest day of my life, and the last thing I wanted to do was be stuck at home, alone and bored. I sighed and said, "Okay, what time are we going?"

Mom beamed as she got up and walked to the door. "The movie starts at seven thirty, but I thought we might get something to eat beforehand. Where do you want to go eat? Piccolo's?"

Oh, no! She'd suggested my favorite restaurant nonchalantly, but she knew it was an offer I couldn't refuse.

"Sounds great," I said. I was defeated. When it came to those breadsticks, I was completely powerless. Mom's face was triumphant as she waltzed out my bedroom door. I could hear her humming all the way down the hall. I had to admit it, the woman was good!

cHapTer

three

"That will be $12.50, please." I took the man's credit card and swiped it. It had been a slow Saturday afternoon, and I was grateful to finally have a customer. I handed him back his card and placed the wrapped box of chocolates in a bag. "I hope you and your wife have a nice anniversary," I said. The man thanked me as he took the bag and then hurried off toward the jewelry store. I sighed and looked at my watch; only twenty-seven minutes until quitting time.

I worked at a candy shop in the mall called The Sweet Tooth, and because business was usually slow, I worked alone. I didn't mind it, though, because my boss let me do my homework when I didn't have customers. She even let me eat as much chocolate as I wanted, which was a definite perk (at least it *was* before I started my diet). The only drawback was the dorky red-and-white striped apron I had to wear, but if anyone from school walked by, I would duck down behind the counter and pretend to check inventory until they passed. All in all, it was a pretty good gig, and it was my ticket to a decent wardrobe—and hopefully a gorgeous prom dress!

The store bell rang and I looked up from my homework to see my boss, Cynthia, walking toward me.

"Oh, good, it's you. I was afraid it might be someone from school," I joked as I gestured toward my apron.

Cynthia laughed. She knew how much I hated the aprons. "Sorry, Eliza, but it's good for business. It gives the shop an old-fashioned feel; people like that. Speaking of things that are good for business, the mall is now requiring that we be open for a few hours on Sundays. I'll need you to take a Sunday shift at least once a month."

I looked at Cynthia in surprise. One of the reasons I had taken this job was because I didn't have to work Sundays, and she knew that. The look on her face told me that this was not negotiable, so I simply nodded and said, "Okay. I guess."

"Thanks. I know it's not what you want, but we all have to make sacrifices if this is going to work." She looked at me apologetically, and I wondered why this wasn't more upsetting to *her*. She was LDS too, but it almost seemed like she was excited about the prospect of better business instead of feeling bad about working on Sunday.

Oh, well, who was I to judge? I took off my apron and hung it on a peg in the back room. "Have a good night, Cynthia. I'll be here Tuesday at five o'clock."

"Thanks, Eliza. I'll post the new schedule soon. Your first Sunday will be in two weeks."

I nodded and walked out the door without saying anything. I knew my parents would hate having me work on Sundays and would probably want me to find a new job. But I really didn't want to find another job, and with summer coming up there would be fewer openings around. What a pain. Maybe I could convince them that one Sunday a month wasn't such a big deal.

⌒⤝

I was in my bathroom using the flat iron to smooth out the last few strands of my hair when I heard the doorbell ring. I glanced at the clock: 6:45 exactly. Apparently, Jason had a thing for punctuality. I quickly finished my hair and spritzed it a few times with hairspray. After applying a final coat of my favorite pink shimmer lip gloss, I grabbed a stick of gum and ran down the stairs just as my dad was calling, "Eliza, Jason's here!"

I entered the living room to see my parents on one couch and Jason on the other. He was sitting up very straight and seemed a little nervous, which was understandable because my dad was looking quite stern and fatherly at the moment. When Jason saw me, he stood up and smiled.

"Hi, Jason, sorry to keep you waiting," I apologized.

"No problem. I was just getting to know your parents." At this, he turned to them and said, "It was nice to meet you . . . and, uh, you guys have a really nice house."

My mom smiled graciously. "Well, thank you! It was nice meeting you too. I hope you have fun tonight. Maybe you can give Eliza some bowling lessons." She winked at me as I groaned.

Jason laughed and turned to me with raised eyebrows. "What's this? You mean you're *not* a pro bowler?"

I shrugged sheepishly. "For your sake I hope we're not playing on teams." I was neither athletic nor coordinated in any way, shape, or form—and that included rolling a ball on the floor.

Jason smiled in mock sympathy. "Don't worry, we can always ask them to put up the bumpers when it's your turn."

I rolled my eyes and grumbled, "Gee, *thanks.*"

We headed for the door and my dad cleared his throat loudly and said in his most intimidating voice, "Please have Eliza home by eleven o'clock."

Jason tensed as he turned around and said, "Sure thing, Mr. Moore."

I felt sorry for him, so I took his arm and pulled him toward the door. "Bye, Dad," I said, rolling my eyes a little. As I closed the door behind us, Jason gave a huge sigh of relief, and I couldn't help but laugh.

He laughed too. "I can tell your dad really loves you."

I hadn't thought of it that way, and I felt a little less annoyed at my dad. "Thanks for being so nice about it. He's really great, but he gets a bit carried away whenever I leave on a date."

"Well, if I had a daughter as beautiful as you I'd be protective too." He looked at me with that admiring expression again, and I realized with a slight tingle that I was still holding on to his arm. Trying not to be too obvious, I let go and walked toward the silver Chevy sedan parked at the curb.

"Is this your car?"

"No, it's my brother's, but he let me borrow it tonight. I'm saving up to get my own car. Not all of us are lucky enough to get cars on our sixteenth birthday." He looked at me in mock severity as he opened the passenger side door for me.

"Hey, have you *seen* my car? If you have a couple hundred dollars I'll be happy to sell it to you," I said.

"I'm just kidding. I think it's great your parents gave you a car, and I'm sure it's worth more than a couple hundred. Hondas get awesome gas mileage."

It was true; my car averaged forty-five miles per gallon, and I rarely had to fill it up. He closed the door and walked around to the driver's side. I looked back at my house and saw Courtney and Alexis peeking out at us from Courtney's bedroom window. I wondered briefly why Courtney hadn't come down to meet Jason; she always used to be so fascinated whenever I was going on a date.

We drove for a few minutes in semi-awkward silence. Jason fumbled with the stereo, asking what kind of music I liked. I told him that I was pretty much good with anything, which seemed to make him flustered. He continued scanning through songs, and I worried that he would keep scanning forever in search of a song I liked, so I claimed to *love* the next song that came on. Jason smiled, and we both relaxed a little.

"Have you ever been to Luke's house before?" he asked.

"No, I haven't." I couldn't keep myself from asking, "Are you and Luke pretty good friends?"

Jason nodded. "Yeah, all of us guys on the team are."

"Cool." I tried to sound casual, but I had to force myself to keep from prying further.

It turned out Jason didn't need further prodding, because the next thing he said was, "Yeah, he's hanging out with Whitney Dawson tonight, and I'm pretty sure he's going to ask her to prom. It would be cool if he did, because then they could be in our prom group. I told him he needs to ask someone soon because a girl needs time to find her dress, right?"

"Um . . . yeah." Suddenly I felt sick. I'd been so bothered by Chelsea at lunch the day before, that I hadn't even thought about

Whitney. Luke liked her, and he was going to ask her out to the most important dance of the year—and I was going to have to watch. I knew asking about it would only cause me pain, but I had to find out more information. "So, Luke talks about Whitney a lot, huh?"

"Not really. He keeps his feelings to himself. He's had a couple of girlfriends, but those relationships didn't last very long. In fact, since I've known him, this is the first group date that he's shown any interest in, so that's why I encouraged him to ask Whitney to the dance."

That little tidbit made me feel better. Maybe he *wasn't* totally head over heels for her. Maybe they were just good friends.

"Here we are," Jason said.

I looked through the window and admired the Matthews' residence. It was a spacious, plantation-style house with two stories and a wraparound porch. The driveway was lined with tall trees, and I caught sight of an old barn in the backyard. Set against the pale pink sunset, the house looked like something out of a home magazine. It was so inviting that I couldn't wait to see the inside.

Jason opened the door and said, "I meant to tell you that you look really nice tonight. I mean, you always do, but especially tonight." I smiled at the compliment and thanked him shyly. Apparently, the extra time and attention I'd spent on my wardrobe and makeup was paying off. "And don't worry if you're not a good bowler; nobody cares," he added reassuringly.

"Thanks. I've learned to laugh at myself, so it's not so bad. How many people are coming tonight?"

"I think there'll be four couples: you and me, Luke and

Whitney, Clark Sullivan and Becka Stanley, and Danny Johnson and Britney West."

Great. I was going to be the only sophomore, and to make matters worse, I didn't know anyone personally besides Jason and Luke. I hoped some of the girls would be friendly. It was a well-known fact that many of the junior and senior girls resented it when guys their age asked out sophomores.

We stepped on the front porch, and Jason rang the doorbell. Almost immediately, the front door swung open and a cute little girl with curly brown hair stood looking at us. She was eating a Popsicle, and I guessed her to be about eight years old. In between licks, she said, "Hi," and continued to stare at us.

Jason smiled at her. "Hey, Morgan. Is Luke home?"

Without answering his question, she turned around and yelled, "Lu-uke! Your friends are heeere!"

"Come on in! We're in the family room." Luke's voice echoed from down the hall. We walked past Morgan as she closed the door and followed us down the hallway. I turned around and smiled at her, and she smiled back shyly. I noticed she had the same dimple in her left cheek that Luke had when he smiled—adorable!

We walked into a large room with a beautiful fireplace and saw three other couples sitting on the cozy-looking couches. My heart sank when I realized we were the last ones to arrive. Luke and the girl who must have been Whitney were sitting closest to us and they both turned and smiled at us.

"Hey, guys, it's about time you showed up." Luke stood and jokingly punched Jason in the shoulder.

Jason laughed. "Sorry, I didn't know we were running on such a tight schedule. Besides, it's only a little after seven; I thought for sure Clark wouldn't get here until seven thirty, at least."

Clark scoffed. "Whatever, Sorensen! I'm always on time—well, usually." Everyone laughed, and I joined in, but I still felt uncomfortable not knowing everyone in the room.

As if reading my mind, Jason announced, "Guys, this is Eliza." Then he pointed around the room. "This is Luke, Whitney, Britney, Danny, Becka, and Clark." Everyone said "Hi," but I could feel Becka and Britney scrutinizing me, and the looks they were giving me were less than friendly. Danny had his arm around Britney, who was whispering something in his ear while she gave me a sidelong glance. I felt conspicuously out of place.

"Come on, guys, let's get going," Luke said. "Whitney has to be home early, but we should still have time to bowl a couple of games." The other couples stood up, discussing who would go in which car. Jason suggested that we ride with Luke and Whitney and that the other two couples take Danny's car. That arrangement was fine with me since I was definitely intimidated by Britney and Becka's glares.

As we walked around the couch, I saw Morgan sitting on the floor, where she'd obviously been eavesdropping.

"Hey, you little monkey!" Luke said when he saw her. She jumped up and tried to run away, but he caught her and tickled her mercilessly. She squealed and giggled in protest, which made the rest of us laugh. It was sweet to watch him interact with her. He was obviously a loving older brother, which I thought only made him more attractive. Luke finally let her down, gently swatting her on the rear before she took off like a shot down the hall.

"Is she your only sibling?" Whitney asked him.

"No, I have two older brothers. Skyler is married and going to medical school back East, and Tucker is serving a mission in Russia. Morgan is ten years younger than me. She's spoiled rotten, but she's a lot of fun to have around."

"I'm jealous. I'm the youngest in my family, and I always wanted a little sister," Whitney said with a hint of longing.

I had planned on not liking Whitney for obvious reasons, but being around her, it was hard *not* to like her. She was a genuinely nice person. She was shorter than I was, with strawberry blonde hair and a few freckles. I would have described her as cute rather than pretty, but she always seemed to have a smile on her face. It was easy to see why she had been voted senior class president.

We pulled up to Lucky Lanes bowling alley and piled out. On the drive over, Jason had kept me too busy talking for me to eavesdrop on Luke and Whitney, but I'd heard enough to know that he hadn't asked her to the dance yet. I hoped he would wait until he dropped her off to ask her. I was liking Whitney more and more, but I knew it would still hurt to see Luke dancing with someone else on prom night.

In the bowling alley, we were greeted by disco strobe lights and loud music. "Cool, I didn't know they did black-light bowling here," Jason said. I looked around and immediately wished I hadn't chosen to wear a white shirt. Under the black lights, it made me really stand out—and attention was the last thing I wanted when I tried to bowl.

We made our way to the front desk where the other couples were waiting for us. I saw Britney turn to Becka and heard her whisper, "Wow, look at her shirt. It's blinding me!" They both snickered. Pretending not to hear, I stepped a little closer to

Jason, wishing he could shield me from their cutting looks and remarks.

Our group was big enough that we decided to use two separate lanes, and I was grateful that we stayed in our same groups. That would put a little space between me and the two "evil stepsisters."

Jason paid for our games and handed me a pair of worn-out shoes with bright neon laces. He, Luke, Whitney, and I headed to our assigned lane. As luck would have it, the other couples had to use a lane a few rows away from us. I relaxed a little and focused on finding the lightest ball available. Jason came with me and after picking out a bright orange six-pound ball—which I was pretty sure was meant for kids—we racked the balls and began the game.

Whitney went first and got a strike right away.

"Yes!" she exclaimed and returned to her seat, where Luke was waiting to give her a high five. I smiled and gave her a thumbs-up, but inside my stomach was doing flip-flops. I'd secretly hoped that she'd join the "gutter-ball club" with me so I wouldn't look like such a fool, but those hopes were dashed after the first frame.

Luke went next and knocked down nine pins, acting disgusted that he hadn't picked up the spare.

Jason was up after Luke, and I tried to focus on his play, but I couldn't keep the dread from rising at the thought that my turn was next. I heard Luke and Whitney cheer and quickly joined in when I realized Jason had gotten a strike as well. I gave him a high five and tried to act casual as I stood up to get my ball. I stuck my fingers in the holes that were a little too small (this was *definitely* a kid's ball) and took a few steps down the lane.

Hoping for the best, I swung the ball but accidentally let go of it too soon, causing it to fly backwards. I heard a small scream of surprise from Whitney and then laughter. My face instantly grew red-hot. I turned around slowly, and having no other alternative, I laughed too.

"Is anybody hurt?" I asked as I retrieved the offending ball. They were all laughing too hard to answer, and from a few lanes over I heard more guffaws.

Clark yelled, "Hey! You're supposed to throw the ball *that* way." He pointed his arms toward the pins, which sent Britney and Becka into shrieks of laughter.

I smiled and shrugged, then turned to Jason and said, "I *warned* you that I was terrible." Looking at Luke and Whitney, I added, "You guys might want to back up a bit this time."

They laughed again, and Jason jumped to his feet. "Here, let me give you a few pointers." He stood behind me, reaching up to hold his arm under mine. "Okay, let's try it slowly. Bring your arm back, and then let it go right about . . . now."

I let the ball go and it rolled slowly down the lane, picking up four pins. I looked at Jason and smiled sheepishly. "Thanks. If you hadn't stepped in, I might have accidentally killed someone!"

He smiled back and for the first time I noticed how close to me he was standing. "My pleasure," he said before he turned around and walked back to his seat.

I noted with a twinge of frustration that I hadn't felt anything special when he'd touched me—only gratitude that he was trying to help. I waited for the ball to come back and tried not to notice Luke and Whitney, who were chatting away happily. Why was it so hard to focus on Jason when Luke was around? I didn't have a chance with Luke, while Jason was always so sweet and attentive.

I was pretty sure he would be my boyfriend if I gave the word, so what was stopping me?

I tried to focus my thoughts as I walked up to the lane again, and after remembering Jason's tips, let the ball go. I couldn't believe it when the ball glided smoothly down the lane and knocked down the rest of the pins. "No way!" I yelled in amazement as I heard the sound of cheering behind me.

Jason beamed. "Good job, Eliza! See? All you needed were a few pointers."

Luke winked at me. "Pretty impressive, Liza Lou. I think that's the fastest improvement I've ever seen."

My heart thrilled to hear him say my name—even if it was the nickname I hated—but I was surprised to see Jason throw a sharp glance over at Luke before he scooted a bit closer to me.

The frames filled up quickly, and before I knew it, we had already played two games. Jason had the top score in the first game, but Luke came out on top in the second. Whitney came in a close third both times. I, of course, was always at the bottom. Still, I was proud of myself for getting only a few gutter balls, and at least I hadn't seriously maimed anyone in the process.

The other couples in our group were still bowling, so Luke said we'd meet them over at the Tasty Freeze later.

As we drove away, the four of us joked about the wacky people who had bowled in the lane next to us. When we arrived at the ice cream parlor, I told Jason I needed to go wash my hands, which was really an excuse to check my makeup and make sure I still looked decent.

After reapplying my lip gloss and running a comb through my

hair, I headed out of the restroom and accidentally bumped into someone who'd been standing in the hall.

"Oh, excuse me," I apologized. The lighting was dim and it took me a second to realize who it was. Luke.

"No problem. Are you having fun?"

I tried to compose myself. "Yeah, it's been really fun. I've decided bowling isn't so bad after all."

He smiled, and then looked at me with a searching expression. "So, are you glad that Jason asked you out? He really likes you a lot. He talks about you all the time."

I felt like someone had sucked the air out of my lungs. I didn't know what to say. All I could think about was that Luke was standing next to me and that we were alone in a dark hallway. The last thing I felt like discussing was how I felt about Jason.

Luke watched me earnestly, waiting for my answer, and I suddenly wondered why he cared. Had Jason asked him to find out how I felt about him, or was Luke just making sure I wasn't going to hurt his friend? I wasn't sure how to respond, and I was surprisingly relieved to see Britney and Becka coming down the hall toward us.

"What are you guys doing back here?" Britney asked suspiciously, while Becka cast me an accusatory glare.

"Oh, I just wanted to wash my hands," Luke answered with a dazzling smile that clearly distracted both girls. "They always feel nasty after touching a bowling ball."

Taking the opportunity for escape, I slid past them without looking back.

I spotted Jason sitting in a large booth with his banana split and the fruit slushy I'd asked him to order for me. He waved and

then moved over so I could sit by him. "Is this what you wanted?"
he asked as I sat down.

"Yeah, it looks great. But do you want to split this?" I stared
helplessly at the monstrous cup before me.

"No, thanks, I have all I can handle with this banana split.
Besides, you could stand to eat a few more calories. What do you
weigh—like, ninety pounds?"

I gave him a withering look, ignoring his remark. Why were
guys so clueless when it came to girls and their weight? Jason
seemed to sense he'd stepped into troubled waters because we ate
in silence until the rest of the group arrived.

When Luke came back, he didn't look at me, and I carefully
avoided him as well.

All eight of us managed to fit in the booth, and for a while
the table buzzed with conversation. There were several minutes
of constant chatter, followed by one of those strange pauses when
everyone falls silent.

Danny broke the silence by looking over at me and asking
loudly, "So, Eliza, when are you gonna come watch Jason in action
at one of our games?"

I blushed as everyone turned to look at me. Was Jason trying
to get his friends to help us get together or something? What was
the deal?

I took a sip of my slushy. "I don't know. When's the next
game?"

"It's next Thursday, at home," Danny said. "Maybe if you
come, Sorensen will finally get his head in the game," he added
with a smirk.

"No, if she comes he'll be too distracted, and we'll lose for sure!" Clark teased.

"Whatever, you guys," Jason snapped, embarrassed.

I hoped to avoid answering Danny, but then Luke joined in. "Yeah, Eliza, I think Danny's right. I think you'd be good luck for our team. Will you come?"

He looked at me and there was something in his eyes that caused my heart to jump.

Without hesitation, I answered, "Yes."

Jason shifted beside me and the spell was broken. "Oh, great. Now if we lose, Eliza's going to feel responsible. Leave the poor girl alone!" he said, though I could tell from his expression that he liked the idea of my coming.

I gave him a reassuring smile. "No, seriously, I think it would be fun to come to a game. I hear you guys are doing really well this year."

The conversation turned to soccer and lasted until we were ready to leave. We said a quick good-bye to the other two couples, but Britney and Becka didn't even bother to acknowledge me as we left.

Luke started his Jeep and pressed a few buttons on the CD player. No one spoke for a few minutes as we listened to the music. Then suddenly I felt an arm around my shoulder. I looked up at Jason, and his face was a little too close to mine for comfort.

"I had a lot of fun tonight, did you?" he whispered into my ear.

Turning my face forward, I nodded and said, "Mmm-hmmm."

What was happening here? I tried to think of a way to get out from under his arm without being too obvious. I liked Jason and didn't want to hurt his feelings, but on the other hand, I wasn't sure I was ready to be his girlfriend yet.

I looked up to see Luke's eyes glancing back at us in the rearview mirror. His expression was unreadable, but I felt despair washing through me. I was sure that it looked like Jason and I were a couple now and any miniscule chance I'd had of Luke liking me was history.

Mercifully, Whitney asked Luke a question and diverted his attention. I wanted to cry. The evening had been going so well, but now I felt like a trapped rabbit. I realized with a sting that I'd allowed myself to have too much hope—I'd read too much into Luke's comments and looks. He was just watching out for Jason and making sure I wasn't going to hurt him; that was the only reason he'd paid attention to me at all. *Jason talks about you all the time*, he'd said. How embarrassing! It probably drove him crazy hearing Jason talk his ear off about someone as silly and insignificant as me.

"I'm really glad you're coming to our game on Thursday," Jason said. "Except now I'll be nervous."

I tried to laugh. "Don't be silly. Why would you be nervous? I'm sure you have lots of friends who come see you play." I emphasized the word "friends," and judging by the expression on his face, he seemed to catch my meaning.

Looking a little concerned, he began to protest, "But you're not just—"

"Hey, Jason, if you want, we can swing by Eliza's house and drop her off first instead of going all the way back to my place. That way she'll make it home before curfew," Luke cut in as he glanced back at us in the mirror again.

"Sure. Yeah, I guess we'd better." Jason sounded annoyed. He looked at me and added in a quieter tone, "But only because I promised your dad I'd have you back on time. You need to talk to him and try to get a later curfew." He winked.

I rolled my eyes. "Oh, believe me, I've tried! The man won't budge an inch; it's hopeless."

Luke seemed to have no problem finding my house, and in a few minutes we were parked at the curb where Jason's car had been just hours ago. Luke jumped out and pushed the seat forward so Jason and I could climb out.

Before getting out, I said, "Bye, Whitney. It was really nice to meet you."

She smiled sincerely. "Yeah! Maybe we can all hang out again sometime."

I accepted Jason's hand that he'd extended to help me climb down. Luke was standing to the side of the door, so I looked up at him and said, "Thanks for the ride and everything. You have a really nice Jeep . . . and house."

Lame! Was that all I could say?

He smiled that smile that put the gleam in his eyes. "Thanks. See you at the game on Thursday."

Jason reached for my arm almost a little defensively, and we started walking toward my front door. I didn't hear the car door close behind us, so I looked back to see Luke still standing by the car, looking a little impatient as he waited.

Jason followed my gaze and frowned, annoyed. "He could at least wait in the car," he said under his breath.

Thank you, Luke! I rejoiced silently as I realized I wouldn't have to endure an awkward doorstep scene. I wasn't sure if Jason would have tried to kiss me, but I wanted my first kiss to be special, and I knew I needed to sort out my feelings for him before that could happen.

When we reached the door, Jason leaned over and gave me a hug that lasted a few seconds longer than usual. "Thanks for coming tonight, Eliza. I can't wait to see you again on Monday."

I gently pulled away. "Yeah, thanks for asking me. I had fun." I reached for the doorknob. "Have a good night." I opened the door and turned to go inside, sneaking one last look at Luke. My breath caught in my chest, because even from this distance, I could see he was looking right back at me.

cHapter
four

I awoke to the sound of the Mormon Tabernacle Choir being broadcast on the speakers throughout our house. I grumbled and rolled over, pulling the pillow over my head. Mom liked to wake us up on Sundays by playing church music so loud you couldn't ignore it. Our meetings began at nine o'clock, so that meant one less day of the week I got to sleep in.

I groaned. Why was waking up so hard? Maybe I could fake being sick today. I pursued that train of thought for a few moments, but then I got that little twinge in my stomach that I always got when I was thinking of doing something I knew I shouldn't do. "All right, might as well get up and get it over with," I sighed to myself as I rolled off the bed. I knelt and said a quick, groggy morning prayer and then trudged to the bathroom.

I entered the kitchen at exactly 8:47 and saw Mom running around in her usual pre-church flurry. "Good morning, Liza! You look nice," she said in a cheerful tone.

"Thanks," I mumbled and opened the pantry door to find something quick for breakfast. I snagged another granola bar, which earned a scowl from Mom, and sat down at the table where

Courtney was finishing up her cereal. "Hey, Court, what did you and Alexis do last night?" I asked, remembering how they'd been spying on me through the window.

"Not much," she replied casually, but I sensed there was more to the story.

"Why didn't you come down and meet Jason? You used to like meeting the guys I go out with."

"Lexi and I were busy," Courtney replied absently. She was reading the back of the cereal box and had yet to make eye contact with me.

"Busy doing what?"

She shrugged, and I was annoyed at her lack of participation so I decided to drop it.

"Okay, girls, time to go." Dad appeared from the hall, and I admired how handsome he looked in his suit. He smiled at us. "Well, don't you two look lovely this morning?" Turning to Mom, he continued, "You better thank your mother. You got all your good looks from her." He reached over and gave her a kiss on the cheek.

"Thank you, dear, how sweet!" Mom gushed. She and Dad were always affectionate with each other. I hoped someday I'd have a husband who would treat me as well.

After throwing the granola bar wrapper in the trash can, I followed everyone out to the garage, where we piled into the family Suburban and headed off to church.

As I walked into the foyer, I spotted Jill, who had obviously been waiting for me. I smiled, and she waved her hand impatiently, beckoning for me to join her. She gave me a scowl and said, "What's the deal? Why didn't you call me last night and tell me about your date?"

"Oh, sorry, I totally spaced it!" I began to apologize, but then stopped. "Hey, wait a second! You can't get mad at me because *you* never came to see me at work yesterday. Busy weekend or something?"

Jill smiled guiltily. "I guess you're right, but you could have *at least* sent me a quick text. I've been totally dying of curiosity!" She arched her eyebrows dramatically. "So, what's going on? Are you and Jason an item now?"

I made a face. "I don't know. I'm totally confused! He's so good to me, and he's starting to act like my boyfriend, but—"

"Eliza! Courtney! Please come along to class," Mom called. "I'd like to start on time today."

I shrugged at Jill. "Guess I'll have to tell you after class." She sighed and followed me down the hall to the Young Women's room. I passed Courtney, who was talking to Nathan Adams (one of the deacons that I knew had a crush on her). He said something and she giggled, sounding too much like Chelsea Andrews for my liking.

"Come on, Courtney, you heard Mom."

She threw me a quick glare. "Co-*ming.*"

When had she gotten so sassy? I wondered.

Jill and I walked into the sunny room and found some seats nearest to the windows. I gazed around at the room Mom and her counselors had decorated profusely. A large poster with the Young Women theme was pinned next to the chalkboard and large, bright paper flowers with scriptures and quotes on them were taped all over the walls. Mom liked to go all out, and I knew she put a lot of time into her calling. She was giving the lesson today, and I'd seen her working on it all week. Secretly, I hoped she'd brought treats—that granola bar hadn't done much to fill my empty stomach, and it was threatening to grumble.

Courtney was the last girl to wander in, and I saw Mom give her a look that meant she was not happy with the tardiness. Courtney pretended not to notice as she slowly walked over to take an empty seat by another Beehive her age. Mom sighed, shut the door, and then, smiling cheerfully, she turned to all of us and said, "Good morning, girls! If you'll all quiet down, I think it's time we got started."

The chatter slowly died down, and for the first time, I noticed that Sister Owens had been playing on the piano. She played a few more bars and then finished, signaling that it was time to start. Mom smiled at her in appreciation. "Thank you, Sister Owens, for that lovely prelude music." Looking around the room at all of us, she said, "I hope that next Sunday we'll keep the talking down a bit more so we can enjoy the music and prepare for class." She smiled, and I knew that most of the girls would remember what she said and try to work on it next week. Mom had a gift for saying things without sounding too preachy, and most of the girls respected her for it.

We had the opening song and prayer, and after a few announcements, it was time to recite the Young Women theme. I hadn't been paying much attention until I heard a shy voice say, "P-p-please s-s-stand and recite the th-th-theme." A few girls giggled, and one of the leaders shushed them. I looked up to the front where Sierra Holbrook was standing. Her gaze was on the floor, and she fidgeted with the hem of her shirt. She wore glasses and had straggly brown hair that she usually wore down, covering half of her face. She looked absolutely miserable to be standing in the center of attention, and I felt sorry for her.

Being a little on the shy side myself, I understood how hard it could be to stand in front of a group like this. But add to that a speech impediment and it would be downright torture! Sierra had a stuttering problem, and it grew worse when she was nervous. She was a Mia Maid, and for the couple of years she'd been in Young Women, I'd never known her to accept when anyone asked her to do something that required her to be in the spotlight, like offer a prayer or lead the theme. She usually sat on the back row next to one of the leaders and didn't talk to anyone. I was surprised to see her up there today, and judging by her obvious embarrassment, I doubted if she'd ever do it again. The theme ended, and Sierra shuffled to her seat on the back row, followed by the whispers and giggles some of the girls made when she walked by.

"Poor thing," Jill whispered in my ear. I nodded and we both glanced back at her, and then returned our attention to the front, where Mom was beginning her lesson.

She stood by the chalkboard and pointed to the words she'd written in big letters: "Invaluable: valuable beyond estimation; priceless." She underlined the "valuable" part of the word and began talking.

"I know sometimes we repeat the theme without actually paying attention to the words we're speaking. I think if the prophet feels it's important enough for us to say it every week, then we should really focus on what it is we're saying. These values we talk about are truly invaluable, and they will change our lives if we will simply apply them . . ."

I tried to concentrate on Mom's words, but my mind kept

wandering to my date last night. What was Luke trying to pull? Why did he want me to come to their game this week? Why did he care if I liked Jason or not?

"And so, I hope this week we can make a goal to truly strive to 'accept and act upon these values' in our everyday lives . . ."

Did Jason think of me as his girlfriend now? At what point do you realize when you've got a boyfriend? Did I want him for a boyfriend?

"One way you might try to do this is to choose a value to focus on each day. It could be the subject of your scripture study and then you could pray for help on ways to apply that value. And of course, there's always Personal Progress . . ."

My attention wavered again as I felt something brush against my arm. I looked over at Jill and saw that she had her scriptures open, seemingly listening to my mom's lesson, but at closer glance, I saw that she was texting and using her scriptures to hide her phone. I felt a wave of annoyance and nudged her.

She looked up at me in surprise and mouthed, *What?*

I looked pointedly at her phone and shook my head disapprovingly.

"I'm almost done," she whispered and turned slightly away from me.

I tried to listen to Mom's words, but I couldn't stop feeling mad about Jill's behavior. It wasn't like I'd been paying that much attention, but at least I tried to *look* like I was. I knew Mom had spent a lot of time on the lesson, and if she saw Jill texting, it would really hurt her feelings.

Suddenly, the piano music started, and I realized it was time for the closing song. Jill discreetly snapped her phone shut, slipped it into her scripture bag, and picked up a hymn book off the floor in one fluid motion. I had to hand it to her—she was one seriously sneaky girl. If I hadn't been paying attention, I never would have noticed any of that.

After the closing song and prayer, we filtered out of class and down the hall to Sunday School. Jill was usually very animated and liked to talk with the boys in our class, but as the time passed, she seemed more and more withdrawn. After class, I pulled her aside. "What's going on? Are you okay?"

She grimaced. "I don't feel very well. I think I need to go home."

I looked at her in concern. "What is it, your stomach or something?"

She made another face and nodded feebly. "Could you find my mom and tell her I went home sick?"

I stroked her arm soothingly. "Sure. Do you want me to give you a ride home?"

She shook her head. "No, it's not very far. I'll be fine."

"All right. Call me tonight and let me know if you think you'll be going to school tomorrow."

She nodded weakly and walked out the door. I watched her for a few seconds and then headed into the chapel.

C ✄

"So, what's the deal? How are you feeling?" I asked. It was Sunday evening, and I was surfing the Internet while talking to Jill on the phone.

"Oh, I'm doing lots better. I think it was just something I ate for breakfast that made me feel weird. I'll definitely be going to school tomorrow."

"Good! I hate trying to find someone else to eat lunch with when you're gone."

"Well, *thanks* for the sympathy. I'm glad to know you were more concerned about who you'd eat lunch with than about your poor, sick friend!" She piled on the sarcasm, and I couldn't help but laugh.

"Sorry, I guess that did sound pretty selfish. It's just different for me than it is for you, because even if I'm not there you still have Nick."

"Yeah," she sighed dreamily. "Nick."

I instantly scolded myself for bringing up his name. I liked to avoid the Nick conversations as much as possible. I was about to change the subject when a message popped up on my screen.

"Hey, someone's trying to chat with me. I wonder who it . . ." I paused to check the screen. "Oh."

"What's the matter?"

"Nothing. It's just Jason. I guess he's online right now too."

"Aha!" Jill said triumphantly.

"What? It's not like this means anything," I responded defensively. *Did it mean anything?* I wasn't so sure. Maybe Jason and I were becoming a couple. Maybe he'd been on the computer, waiting for me to go online.

"Read it and see what he says."

With a hint of nervousness, I opened the message. "He says, 'Hey, how's it going?' What should I say?"

"Just tell him about your day, it's no big deal. Oh! Nick's calling on the other line, I gotta go. Good luck! I'll see you in the morning." Before I could say anything, she was gone, and I was left staring helplessly at the screen.

Taking a deep breath, I typed what I hoped was a very casual response:

> *Me:* Good. How are you?
>
> *Jason:* I'm great! I hope I'm not interrupting anything. Did you have fun last night?
>
> *Me:* I was just talking to Jill. Yeah, I did have fun, thanks again!
>
> *Jason:* I hope you weren't bugged by the guys. They can be a little annoying sometimes & I noticed Becka & Britney weren't very nice, but they're always like that so I hope you didn't take it personally.

I smiled as I read this. At least I hadn't been the only one to notice how mean they were.

> *Me:* No, I had a great time, I promise. ☺
>
> *Jason:* Good, because Luke and I were talking last night, and we thought it would be fun if we all hung out again sometime.

This was the opening I'd been hoping for!

> *Me:* Cool, did Luke ask Whitney to prom?

Please say no. Please say no.

> *Jason:* No, he totally chickened out! I told him he's a dork

and that he better not wait too much longer. A cool girl like Whitney will get asked by someone else pretty soon. That's why I asked you so early cuz I knew you'd get snatched up fast if I didn't.

Yes! I felt a huge wave of relief wash over me. I'd been worrying about if and when Luke had asked Whitney last night, but the fact that he *still* hadn't asked her probably meant that he wasn't going to at all.

Me: So, what do you think he's waiting for?

Jason: Who knows? He was acting kind of weird last night. After I told him he needed to ask her soon, he got all quiet and said he was thinking of not going this year. He gave some lame excuse about saving his money or something, so I said, "Dude, it's your senior year, you should totally go." We'll see what happens, but I was hoping they would be in our group because it seemed like you and Whitney got along pretty well & I really want it to be a special night for you.

Me: Thanks. . . . Hey, I gotta run, but it was nice chatting. I'll see you tomorrow.

Jason: Ok. You can call or text me anytime—I always have my phone on me. Have a great night, Eliza.

I sat back in my chair and thought about what Jason wrote. To my surprise, I felt faintly disappointed. I hadn't wanted Luke to ask Whitney to prom, but in preparing for the worst, I'd expected that he would. I'd even started daydreaming about seeing him in a tuxedo. The other thing I had consoled myself with was the fact that we would have been in the same group and I could have been near him—even if it was only for part of the evening.

I felt disgusted with myself; I wouldn't have been happy either way, and I knew the real reason was because *I* wanted to be his date. I was completely obsessed with a guy I didn't have the slightest chance with, and I was torturing myself over it.

But, the little voice inside my head whispered, *he took the time to talk to you last night, and when he looked at you, there was definitely something in his eyes.*

I smiled as I relived that moment in the hallway when it had been just the two of us. It had felt so natural to be close to him, to talk to him. Maybe . . . maybe there *was* something there. Maybe Luke hadn't asked Whitney to prom because secretly he wanted to ask someone else—someone who already *had* a date. My heart protested as I allowed the hope to glimmer and then burn with a bright flame. If I had even the slightest chance to be with Luke I would do whatever it took to be with him.

I glanced over at the latest issue of my favorite fashion magazine lying on the nightstand. The girl on the cover was gorgeous: totally skinny with perfect hair, skin, teeth, and makeup. She was wearing a tight tank top and short shorts, and she had her hands on her hips in a confident pose. I looked at her with envy. No guy on this planet would be able to resist a girl like that. And then I got an idea. I grabbed my cell and sent Jill a quick text.

Me: Hey, would you mind bringing that new tank top tomorrow? I want to borrow it—if that's cool.

I was prepared to wait a while for her reply because I figured she was still chatting with Nick, so I was surprised when my phone buzzed right away.

> *Jill:* Sure! I bought a couple of them, so I'll bring a few for you to choose from. See you tomorrow!
>
> *Me:* Thanks! See ya! ☺

I threw my phone on the bed and picked up the magazine, hoping to find some hot new tips for applying makeup. I wanted Luke Matthews to notice me and that meant I needed to look perfect tomorrow. Besides, what was one little tank top?

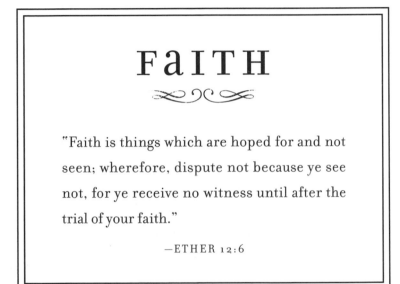

FAITH

"Faith is things which are hoped for and not seen; wherefore, dispute not because ye see not, for ye receive no witness until after the trial of your faith."

—ETHER 12:6

cHapтer

E liza? Wake up, dear."
       I rubbed my eyes, peering out at my bright room, and then I suddenly sat bolt upright. Had I slept in somehow? Why hadn't Jill called? Or Mom come to wake me up? As the room slowly came into focus, I realized that the light wasn't coming from the window. I did a double take and rubbed my eyes again, my mouth dropping open in disbelief. There, sitting on my bed as casual as could be, was my great-grandma Eliza Porter. She'd passed away before I was born, but I recognized her perfectly from the many pictures my mom had of her. She had the same wavy white hair, the same dimple in her right cheek, and, most noticeably, the same bright blue eyes my mom and I had inherited from her. She wore a simple white dress, and she smiled at me.

"Hello, sweetheart! I must say I thought you were never going to wake up! Ever since I was given permission to pay you a visit, I've been beside myself with excitement." She gazed at me affectionately. "My goodness, what a pretty girl you are! I couldn't be any prouder than to have you for my namesake." Then in a confidential whisper she added, "You know, your mother always was my favorite grandchild." She winked at me, and I realized that my mouth was still open and I forced myself to close it.

This *had* to be a dream, but I couldn't believe how real it felt. Great-grandma was still smiling at me, and I started to feel a bit self-conscious. It seemed to be my turn to say something, so I did my best to smile as I stammered, "I—it's nice to meet you, Great-grandma. Mom's told me lots about you . . . uh . . ." I debated whether or not it was polite to ask, but she seemed to read my thoughts and chuckled.

"You want to know what I'm doing here in your bedroom." Grandma grinned as I nodded. "Of course, of course! No need to waste time with my ramblings." She sat upright and assumed a serious expression as she looked me straight in the eye. "Eliza, *you* are a special soul. You're one of Heavenly Father's choice daughters, and I've had the privilege of watching you progress through your mortal journey thus far. You've made many wonderful choices in your life, and I'm very proud of you."

I blushed and looked down at my bedspread. I wasn't used to so much praise, but it still felt good to hear it, even if it was just in a dream.

"However," she continued, "I've noticed you're coming to a crossroads of sorts, and I'm concerned. You have a good grasp of right and wrong, and you've certainly been taught well, but I think that you're still struggling to see the big picture."

I looked at Grandma in confusion, and with a twinkle in her eye she said, "The easiest way to explain what I mean is to show you. Are you ready for an adventure?"

I raised an eyebrow and looked down at my pajamas, then up

into her excited face. She chuckled. "No need to worry about what you're wearing. Not where we're going, anyway."

I began to ask *where* exactly that was when something weird started happening. The walls of my room began fading away and for a moment everything was dark.

"Grandma, what's going on?" I asked in alarm.

"Don't worry. We're perfectly fine," she reassured me.

Although I heard her voice, I couldn't see her, and I felt strangely disoriented. The darkness was so complete that I couldn't even tell if my eyes were open, which bothered me, so I squeezed them shut.

"We're here. You can open your eyes now," Grandma said cheerfully.

I opened my eyes to make sure I hadn't lost her in a pit of blackness, and to my surprise, I saw that we were standing on a treelined dirt road that seemed to stretch on for miles. The sun was high in the sky, casting dappled shadows along the ground. Birds were chirping merrily from the trees, and I could hear a stream gurgling somewhere close by. I took a deep breath and felt exhilarated by the fresh, clean scent of everything. I circled around once, taking it all in and exclaimed, "Wow, this is beautiful! Where are we?"

"We'll get to that in a minute. I want to talk to you first." Grandma began walking down the road, and I followed beside her. She took a deep breath and asked, "Eliza, did you listen to your mother's lesson today?"

I was caught off guard by her question, and I scrambled to think back to church and what Mom had been talking about. Feeling slightly embarrassed, I shrugged. "Well, not really. My mind was sort of wandering and, um, I guess I wasn't really paying attention," I admitted.

Grandma gave me a half smile and nodded, as if I'd only confirmed something that she already knew.

"Your mother did an excellent job with that lesson, and there was a very important message in what she said. Allow me to review it for you." She gestured to a large boulder by the road, and we walked over and sat down. Grandma got that serious look on her face again. "Your mom talked primarily about the Young Women values and how important it is to apply them in your life. They were given to the Young Women leaders by inspiration as a standard to help guide you. I know at your age these things sometimes sound boring or unimportant. You have so many exciting things happening from day to day that it can seem like drudgery to think about subjects like this. But, Eliza, it is *crucial*." Her voice was quiet, but piercing, and for a moment even the birds seemed to be silent. "You must understand that you are living in a battle zone, and the fight for your soul is as real as the rock you're sitting on."

I felt the cold, hard surface of the stone beneath me and thought once again that I'd never had a dream this realistic.

"Distraction and subtlety are powerful tools the adversary uses on everyone, but especially on teenagers. Your lives are so filled with technology that sometimes I wonder how you can hear yourselves think! That's why I wanted to bring you to a place like this—away from all the noise and hubbub. This is a place where you can get in touch with your true spirit and, perhaps more important, with *the* Spirit. The Holy Ghost wants so much to be a part of your life, but he cannot communicate when there's a constant barrage of music and TV, or a cell phone demanding your attention."

I nodded. There was a lot of truth in what she said, but part of me bristled. "But, Grandma, not *all* technology is bad, is it? I mean, my mom is always using the Internet to help find material for her lessons. And let's not forget general conference. How would we be able to hear it if we didn't have the radio or TV?"

Grandma smiled a bit mischievously, as if she enjoyed my sudden defensiveness. "Gracious, no! Technology is a good thing. It *also* came by inspiration and enlightenment. However, like so many other things, it can be abused, and Satan knows just how to take something good and turn it into something evil. If all of God's children had perfect self-control and could discipline themselves to use these tools properly and not abuse them, it wouldn't be a problem. Unfortunately, too many adults, teenagers, and even children can't seem to turn off the television or pull themselves away from the Internet. And don't get me started on video games! Technology can be powerfully addicting, and it's a great challenge your generation faces." She paused and appraised me for a moment. "Let me ask you something. How many kids your age do you know who don't own a cell phone?"

I shifted uncomfortably as I struggled to think of someone. After a few seconds, I was still drawing a blank, so I tried to buy some time.

"Uh, my age *specifically*?"

"Well, even *around* your age if that makes it easier."

Still nothing. And it was obvious that Grandma could see right through my fidgeting.

"Well, okay, I can't think of anyone at the *moment*—but I've heard of some kids whose parents won't allow them to have one."

"Is there ever a time in school, other than during class,

when you can look around and *not* see someone texting or on the phone?" Grandma's questions were beginning to feel like an interrogation.

I twisted the hem of my pajama shirt uncomfortably. "So, you brought me here to tell me that cell phones are evil?"

Grandma sighed. "No, but the point is that they too often become a distraction that seems perfectly innocent, while it's subtly addicting. For example, how do you feel when you accidentally forget to bring your phone with you somewhere?"

I grinned sheepishly. "I feel naked and go nuts until I get it back again."

She nodded. "Anything that has that kind of effect on a person usually signifies a type of addiction." Noticing my discomfort, she smiled sympathetically. "I'm sorry if this sounds like an attack. I didn't sugarcoat it very well, but the fact is that this *is* part of the message I was sent to give you. I'm sure you've heard most of it before from adults who grew up in a much less technologically driven world, but there's a lot of truth in what they preach. People are losing essential bonding skills and family time. The art of face-to-face communication is declining, as well as a host of other problems we don't need to go into right now."

She looked at me earnestly. "Eliza, I only want to arm you with this knowledge. It's up to you how you choose to use it. All I ask is that you think about controlling the technology you use and not letting it control *you*. Time is a precious gift that should not be wasted. Once it's gone, it's gone—whether you spend it watching TV or actually *living life*."

I paused as her words sank in. The guilt of how much time I'd wasted hit me with the force of a steam shovel. I'd watched countless hours of TV in my life. In fact, I'd sometimes imagined that after I died and my life was replayed before my eyes, it would be like watching one, long show. That thought had seemed funny to me before, but not now.

"Well," Grandma said, her face brightening. "Enough on that subject! We're about to witness something truly special."

I looked around, but nothing about our surroundings had changed. "What's going to happen? Where are we?" I tried to keep the impatience out of my tone but the suspense was starting to get to me. It was unnerving to be in complete ignorance, and it annoyed me that Grandma knew but wasn't telling.

Grandma sensed my mood and scowled at me. "All right, spoilsport, I'll tell you where we are, but nothing else. You'll have to guess the rest." I smiled and raised my eyebrows expectantly as I waited for her to continue. "We are currently on a road in Harmony, Pennsylvania."

I jumped up. "*What?* Pennsylvania! You've got to be kidding! This is insane! What in the world are we doing here? Mom and Dad are gonna flip. Do they have any idea where I've gone or what's happened to me? We've got to get back right this min—"

"Slow down, Eliza, everything's fine. This is a dream, remember? You'll wake up back in your own bed, and everything will be exactly like it was before you fell asleep."

My breathing slowed and I sat down next to Grandma. Of course, how had I forgotten this was all a dream? This whole thing was crazy. I wondered if I would remember any of it when I woke up.

Grandma patted my shoulder and continued talking as if my outburst had never happened. "So, does the name ring a bell at all?"

"The name?"

"Harmony, Pennsylvania. Does that sound familiar?"

I scrunched up my eyebrows in thought. "It has something to do with Church history, right?"

Grandma smiled and her eyes twinkled. "Yes, you might say that."

Suddenly, I heard a faint noise coming from down the road: the unmistakable *clip-clop, clip-clop* of a horse's hooves. I strained my eyes toward the direction of the sound and could make out the outline of a carriage in the distance. A man and woman were sitting in the carriage, and as it drew nearer, I could see that they were in costume.

"Cool! Is this one of those places where they do reenactments?" I asked Grandma in a whisper, not wanting to be overheard by the strangers. Suddenly I remembered I was wearing my pajamas, and even though I was dreaming, I was still embarrassed.

In a normal voice Grandma answered, "No, what you are witnessing is real. We've taken a little trip into the past. You can do that in dreams, you know. And stop worrying about what you look like! We are here only as observers; these people can neither see nor hear us."

The carriage was drawing steadily closer, and to my amazement, I realized that the people inside truly didn't seem to notice us. The man had his arm around the woman, and she leaned her head on his shoulder. Her shiny brown hair was curled in tight ringlets and styled in a fashion that I knew I'd seen in a picture before. The couple was talking softly, and just by watching them a few moments, it was easy to see that they were in love. The man wore a hat and had his head tilted toward hers. He turned for a moment, and when I saw his face, I gasped.

"Grandma, I know who that is! Oh my goodness! Is this for real? Is that *really* who I think it is?"

Grandma laughed and clapped her hands, delighted by my re-action. "Oh, Eliza, I can't tell you how fun it was to see your face just then! Yes, that is indeed Joseph Smith, the Prophet of the Restoration. And as I'm sure you've guessed, that's Emma sitting beside him."

Awe settled over me. I was actually seeing the Prophet Joseph Smith, right before my eyes. I jumped up in excitement as their carriage passed by. "Oh, Grandma, can't we talk to them, just for a minute? There are so many things I'd like to ask; so much I'd love to hear!"

She looked at me sympathetically. "I'm sorry, sweetheart, but as I told you before, we're here only to observe."

My shoulders slumped, but I kept my eyes glued to the car-riage, which Joseph had pulled over to the side of the road a few paces away. He stepped down and tied the reins securely to a nearby tree. I noticed how young they both were; by the looks of them, they were not much older than I was. Joseph walked around the carriage, then reached up and took Emma's hand to help her down. He continued to hold her hand as they stood there, gazing at each other. He lifted her hand and kissed it and then led her off the road and into the underbrush.

"Come. You won't want to miss this," Grandma said as she stood and gestured for me to follow. We were about twenty feet from the carriage, and I wanted to jog to catch up so we wouldn't lose Emma and Joseph, but Grandma maintained a casual pace. "Don't worry, I know where they're going, and I want to give them a bit of a head start." I grudgingly obeyed, and we continued to stroll slowly along. As we drew nearer to where they had disappeared, I could see a small path beneath the trees and undergrowth. We pushed a few branches aside and entered what seemed like a fairyland.

The path widened and trees formed an archway above it. The sound of a stream was louder now, and birds and butterflies flitted about everywhere. A small squirrel darted across the path a few feet in front of us, and I laughed. I wished I had a place back home as beautiful as this to escape to when I wanted time alone. Something about being in nature made me feel closer to who I really was, and that I was a part of something important. I took a deep, cleansing breath, wanting to take this all in and remember it forever.

Grandma and I continued walking in companionable silence. She seemed to want me to have time alone with my thoughts, and I was grateful. Things seemed to be coming into focus in my mind. It felt like someone had removed a pair of foggy goggles from my eyes, and for the first time I could see things as they really were. I felt peaceful and happy, not worrying about boys or clothes or dances. I was just . . . me.

We reached a bend in the path, and as we came around the corner, I caught sight of Joseph and Emma standing by the stream. The tall grass was dotted with beautiful wildflowers, and the couple looked like they belonged in some magnificent painting, framed perfectly by their surroundings.

We were too far away to hear their conversation, but suddenly I didn't want to move any closer. I felt like this was a special moment, and I understood why Grandma had wanted them to have their space. Even though they couldn't see us, I knew it would feel wrong to interrupt whatever words they were sharing.

Just then, Joseph bent down on one knee, though he kept both of Emma's hands in his. My breath caught in my throat as I saw the adoring look he gave her and the look of surprise and joy on Emma's face as she wiped away a few tears and nodded happily. Joseph jumped up and swung her around, both of them laughing, as happy as I'd ever seen anyone.

I turned to Grandma, and she was dabbing her eyes with a handkerchief. She looked at me and sniffed. "Now, wasn't that worth coming here for? There's nothing like a sweet marriage proposal to get the tears flowing."

I giggled. "Oh, yes! It was beautiful. They seem so much in love, and I'm grateful you let me witness this. I hope that someday a man will look at me the way Joseph looked at Emma." I stared into space, all dreamy-eyed.

"Yes, it is important that you find a nice young man who loves you and who will take good care of you—but that's not the reason I brought you here today."

I felt a little embarrassed. "Oh, well . . . why did you, then?" Grandma looked back at Joseph and Emma, who were sitting in the grass with their backs against a tree. Emma rested her head on Joseph's shoulder, and he held her hand, their faces full of contentment. They were deep in conversation, and I imagined they were discussing the happy prospects of their future.

"When Emma agreed to marry Joseph, she knew it would not be easy. Because of his experience in the Sacred Grove, Joseph was already well-known in the community and openly mocked and persecuted for his testimony, but Emma believed him. She loved him, of course, but more important, she had *faith*. It was her faith that carried her through the many, many trials she would endure throughout her life."

As Grandma spoke, our surroundings began to get hazy, and the scene in front of us slowly changed.

It was nighttime. We were standing on a snow-covered road outside a house, but all of the windows were dark. Joseph sat waiting in a carriage, and Emma slipped out through the front door. She hurried to the carriage with a small bag under her arm. He helped her up into the seat and then climbed up and took the reins. Before starting off, he gave her a look that seemed to say, "Are you sure about this?" Emma smiled and nodded resolutely. Joseph flicked the reins and the horse walked forward quietly. I saw Emma look back at her home, just once, with tears in her eyes, and then she straightened her back and looked forward.

"Emma's father was against their marriage. Joseph asked Isaac Hale for his daughter's hand several times, but Isaac wouldn't relent. Joseph and Emma finally decided to elope, which is what you've just seen, but things were different back then. It was a very serious thing to go against your parents' wishes, and they didn't have phones or e-mail in order to keep in touch easily. When Emma left, it was with the full realization that she might never see her family again in this life. It was the first sacrifice she made by faith. If you can imagine yourself in the same situation, you'll understand it was a *big* sacrifice—and it was only the first of many.

"Emma lost several children. She was often alone while Joseph was away on Church business or when he was unlawfully imprisoned. She shared her husband's persecution for the gospel's sake and often feared for her own life as well as the lives of her family members."

As Grandma spoke, scenes began unfolding before my eyes, flickering past as if they were scenes from a movie that matched Grandma's voice. But it was much too real to be a movie. There was Emma, standing by grave after tiny grave, sobbing as if her heart would break, and I felt tears streaming down my own face.

Then, in another scene, she was in a home, walking the floors with a sick baby in her arms and looking exhausted. Her other children were in their beds trying to sleep, but all of them were coughing horribly, and Joseph was not there to help her. I wondered if this was one of the times he had been imprisoned, and I ached for her.

The scene changed, and I saw Emma, carrying two small children while her other two children clung to her skirts. It was winter, and their faces were chapped and red from the biting cold. They were walking across an icy river along with the other Saints.

Suddenly, I remembered the story of Emma crossing the Missouri River with her children while Joseph was incarcerated in Liberty Jail and the Saints were driven from Missouri. The scene was absolutely heart-wrenching! I longed to run to her and help with the children. I wanted to tell her everything was going to be all right.

Once more, our surroundings blurred, and the last scene came into view. Emma knelt beside a coffin, this one larger than the others. She cried bitterly, and I knew that it was Joseph inside. He had been shot and killed at Carthage Jail and had died a martyr.

"Oh, Grandma," I sobbed. "I can't take any more of this! Please make it stop! It's too terrible. How could anyone endure what she went through? It's not fair. It's just not fair." I fell to my knees and buried my face in my hands. My heart felt like it had been torn in two.

Grandma knelt beside me and spoke soothingly. "There, there, sweetheart. It's like I always say—no sense wastin' time and tissues over something like this. These things happened in the past. They're already done. I know it was hard on you, and I'm sorry, but believe me when I tell you there was a reason."

I sniffed and looked up, realizing that we were back on the dirt road where we'd started. I felt anger rise within me as I looked at Grandma. "What reason could you possibly have for showing me those awful things? To scar me for life? I don't understand why Emma had to suffer like that. It just doesn't seem right! She was the wife of a *prophet*—one of the most important prophets who ever lived. Why wouldn't Heavenly Father have treated her better?"

Grandma stiffened at this last remark, and I knew I'd gone too far, but I was mad and I wanted answers. She paused for a moment and then asked, "When does the 'happily ever after' happen in a play?"

I looked at her like she was crazy. What kind of a bizarre question was that? Wiping the tears from my cheeks, I shrugged. "I don't know. I guess it usually comes at the end."

She beamed. "Exactly! If it's a happy story and not a tragedy— none of that *Romeo and Juliet* nonsense—the 'happily ever after' *always* comes at the end, or in the third act. The second act usually contains the most conflict so that you wonder if the main character will ever achieve that desirable ending. Do you see where I'm going with this?"

"Um, kind of. Are you saying that even though Emma had a lot of trials, she was happy at the end of her life, and she felt like it was all worth it?"

"Not exactly—though Emma surely did have periods of joy in her life. What I'm saying is that the life all of us experience can be compared to a three-act play. The first act is our premortal existence, the second is our mortal life here on earth, and the third act happens after we die and receive our eternal reward. Emma Smith was an 'elect lady,' and because of her enduring faithfulness, her reward is greater than anything you can imagine. Her joy is full. So you see, you don't need to cry for her anymore.

"I know sometimes it's hard to understand from a mortal perspective why our Heavenly Father allows His children to suffer— especially when they are good people—but believe me, He knows each of His children and there is a reason for all of our experiences. Throughout the ages, it has often been those who are the most righteous who are the most severely tested. However, when they endure in faith, their reward is far greater than any of the suffering they had to endure."

In my heart, I knew what Grandma was telling me was true, and a feeling of peace came over me. I knew I would never forget those images from Emma's life, but at least I knew that she was happy now and would never have to suffer again.

"Thank you, Grandma, for bringing me here and teaching me all of this. I'll never think about Emma or the early Saints the same way again. They were so strong! It's a good thing I wasn't born back then, because there's no way I could have handled it."

Grandma stood up, placed her hands on her hips, and huffed, "Is that what you think? Eliza, you have no idea who you are or what you are capable of. Yes, those early Saints were strong, and they were prepared for the time that they were sent to—but you! You have been sent down in the very fullness of times, right into the heart of the greatest battle the world has yet seen. The early Saints faced extreme physical and emotional hardships, but you must fight a battle that is intense in a different way. Your world is teeming with filth and subtly destructive forces." Grandma had not spoken to me with such force before, and I was shocked into silence. Her gaze was piercing.

"What I want you to understand—what you *must* understand— is how special you are. You are vitally important to Heavenly Father. He loves you, and He has a plan for you. Although you don't remember, you prepared yourself to face all of these challenges and to fulfill the mission you've been sent here to do. The reason I'm here is to help you recognize the tools that will help you accomplish this."

She reached into the pocket of her dress and pulled out a small glass container no larger than a perfume sample. It appeared to be empty, but as I leaned closer, I saw a tiny, round pebble that was perfectly white inside the vial.

"Do you know what this is?" Grandma asked.

"It looks like a small rock or something."

"Actually, it's a seed. A mustard seed, to be exact. They're usually yellow, but this seed is special. Here." She reached for my hand and placed the tiny vial in my palm. I liked the cool, smooth feeling of the glass.

"Neat. What's it for?"

"Everything I showed you has significance. It's your task to figure out what the meaning is and how it applies to you."

"Great. That's all I need—more homework!" I mumbled sarcastically.

Grandma smiled and winked at me. "It's time for me to go. Ponder the things you've seen and heard. I'll be back again when you're ready."

Before I had a chance to say anything else, everything started getting fuzzy and then went black.

CHapTer

BEEP! BEEP! BEEP! I rolled over, frantically searching for the snooze button. I glared at the alarm clock through glazed eyes and tried to get my bearings. The offensively bright neon numbers displayed 6:45 A.M., my usual time for getting up.

I sighed and sat up, but I couldn't shake the feeling that something felt weird. After kneeling by my bed and hurrying through my usual morning prayers, I stumbled toward the bathroom. I turned on the faucet and grabbed my toothbrush. As I lifted the toothpaste tube, though, my mind started to clear and I suddenly remembered my dream.

It all came back to me with perfect clarity. I'd had strange dreams before, the kind that lingered through the next day, but I already knew that this dream had been different. It felt like something that had actually happened to me—something that was a part of me.

I realized the faucet was still running, so I shut it off and stared at myself in the mirror. After a few minutes of standing there like a piece of petrified wood, I decided the only thing to do was try to forget about it and go on like usual. I hurried through my morning routine, trying to make up for the minutes I'd wasted in my zombielike state. The rushing around seemed to help me feel more human again, and I started thinking maybe the dream hadn't been such a big deal after all—until I looked in my closet.

I remembered asking Jill if I could borrow her tank top, and last night that hadn't seemed like such a big deal, but now it did. I pictured Grandma's face and Emma's, and I remembered the way Grandma's words had felt true to me in a way that I couldn't deny.

I pulled on a pair of jeans and sighed as I yanked my pink-and-white striped polo off the hanger and put it on. The outfit was boring, and when I looked in the mirror, I started to doubt myself. *You have to compete with a lot of girls for Luke's attention. You'll have to look better than that if you want him to notice you. Boys want a girl who looks sexy. You look dull—and you could stand to lose a few more pounds.*

The thoughts came into my mind before I could stop them, and I decided I *would* borrow Jill's tank top. I had to do whatever it took to catch Luke's attention, and what was the big deal anyway? It wasn't like I was wearing a belly shirt and a miniskirt. I would just show a little shoulder.

Grandma's face kept popping into my head. What was with that dream? Was I losing my mind?

There was one way to find out. I hurried from my room and down the hall. A set of small stairs marked the entrance to the attic, and I took them two at a time.

Our house didn't have a basement, so the attic had become a catchall for our junk. As I entered the room, the early morning light filtered through a small window, illuminating the million tiny specks of dust floating in the air.

I squinted hard and could just make out the object I was

looking for. I walked a few steps and reached up to pull the string of the lightbulb hanging from the ceiling, and then continued quickly toward my destination.

In the corner of the room, hanging on the wall, was a large framed photograph of Great-Grandma Porter. I walked up to the picture, and chills ran over my arms as I stared at Grandma's face. The full force of my dream and all that had happened in it came washing over me as I stared into Grandma's eyes. This had been more than an ordinary dream—that much I knew. I ran my hand over the glass as if to convince myself it was really just a picture, and not Grandma herself.

A small creak sounded and I half-jumped, turning around quickly. Mom looked at me from the doorway.

"Eliza, what on earth are you doing up here? You're going to be late for school if you don't hurry." She looked at me quizzically, a slight frown on her face.

"I, um . . . I was just looking at this picture of Great-grandma." I struggled to think of something to say that would sound somewhat sane. "Do you think we look alike? We have the same eyes, and I wonder if I'll look like her when I get older." I glanced at Mom to see if she'd buy my excuse for why I was taking an early morning stroll through the attic. When she smiled and came to stand beside me I knew I was in the clear.

"I'll have to find some pictures of her when she was younger, but I think there definitely is a strong resemblance." She smiled fondly as she looked at the picture, and then she turned her attention to the dresser below it. "I don't know if I've told you this before, but when Great-grandma died, I inherited some of her possessions, including this dresser and several things in this corner of the room. It seems silly to keep it all, but I can't bear to part with it."

She ran her fingers lovingly over the dresser and then gasped as she looked at her watch. "Oh my goodness, look at the time! You really need to hurry or you're going to be late, honey."

"Okay, I'll be right down."

"I better get breakfast going." Mom hurried from the room, and I moved to follow, but my eyes lingered on the dresser. Knowing that it had once belonged to Grandma fascinated me, and I couldn't resist quickly opening the drawers. The first three contained nothing more than Grandma's old clothes, but as I opened the bottom drawer, a hard lump under one of her old dresses caught my attention.

I pulled the fabric aside and uncovered a small, intricately carved box. It looked like a music box, with a lid on top and little drawers on the side.

"Eliza, I hope you're hurrying; I almost have breakfast ready!" Mom's voice carried up from the kitchen.

"I'll be right down!" I called back, hoping she wouldn't be able to tell I was still in the attic. I'd be dead meat if she knew I was still up here. I quickly opened the lid to the box and a few unfamiliar notes escaped, threatening to blow my cover. It *was* a music box! I glanced inside before closing the lid and slamming the dresser drawer shut, vowing to come back when I had more time. I was halfway to the door when I realized what I'd seen.

Slowly, I made my way back to the drawer and opened it. I stared at the music box in disbelief, and carefully, as if I were afraid it would bite me, I lifted the lid once more. There, lying on red velvet lining, was a tiny glass vial containing a pure white mustard seed.

"Good morning, sunshine!" Jill seemed extra chipper as she climbed in the passenger seat. She didn't even wait for a response before chatting away, "So, I think we've been putting it off long enough. We need to go dress shopping *tonight*. The clock's ticking you know—only thirteen more days until prom!" She squealed in excitement, but after a quick glance at me she noticed my obvious lack of enthusiasm. She must have misunderstood my silence, because she immediately said, "So how did it go with Jason and the messaging last night? Is everything okay?" She touched my arm, and I snapped back to reality.

"Oh, what? Um, yeah, it went fine. We didn't chat very long. I think it will be . . . fine."

That wasn't the rambling response I'd usually give her on this topic, and Jill looked at me like I was from Mars. "Liza, is everything okay?"

"Yeah, why?"

"I don't know, you just seem distracted or something."

I considered telling her about my dream, but somehow it didn't feel right. At least for now the experience was something I wanted to keep to myself, so I decided to play dumb. "Sorry, I don't think I got enough sleep last night, and you know I'm not much of a morning person." There—true on both counts.

"Okay, but you *do* want to go shopping today, don't you?"

"Of course."

She beamed. "Great! Let's go right after school." She continued to describe her "ideal dress," but I couldn't keep my mind from wandering back to the dream. I drove to school on autopilot, and when we parked at the school lot, I turned off the ignition and reached in the backseat for my bag.

My hand was on the door handle when Jill stopped me. "Wait! Don't you remember?" She reached into her bag and pulled out three colorful tank tops. I recognized the yellow one, but there was also a red one with a stylish neckline and a dark gray one with lacy trim. They were all super cute, and I was sorely tempted by them. Jill pulled out one more: a plain white tank top with spaghetti straps. "You can layer this one underneath," she said. "Which one do you like best? I think you should wear the gray one—it would look great on you!"

I battled with myself inwardly and was about to cave when my hand brushed against the glass vial I'd tucked inside my pocket. The words from *For the Strength of Youth* came clearly to my mind: "Young women should wear clothing that covers the shoulder and avoid clothing that is low-cut in the front or back or revealing in any other manner." When I'd read those words before, they'd somehow seemed restrictive and old-fashioned, but when I heard them in my mind now I got goose bumps and knew that they had been written by a prophet and that they mattered. I had the courage I needed.

"Thanks for bringing those for me, Jill, but I changed my mind. I'm not going to borrow them."

She looked hurt. "Why not? Don't you like any of them?"

"I've just decided I'm not going to wear sleeveless shirts, that's all."

Jill smirked. "Liza, your mom is *not* going to catch you. You saw how easy it was for me to change in the car."

"I know, but I'm not doing it because of my mom." I left it at that and opened the car door, leaving Jill slightly frustrated and confused.

Before I closed the door, I heard her mumble, "Okay, *whatever.*"

She didn't talk to me the rest of the way across the parking lot. Once we were inside, she said she was going to meet up with Nick before class and disappeared.

C ∽

As I walked to my locker after class, I realized that I was largely a creature of habit. I walked the same halls every day, and I always waited until after math to go to my locker because my classes up until then were too far away. It was always such a relief to empty some of the insanely heavy textbooks from my bag and give my aching shoulders a break. I also liked stopping at my locker because lately there was often a note inside from my secret admirer.

I was in a hurry today because I knew Jason would appear at any moment. He'd sent me a text during my last class asking if we could eat lunch together again, and not being able to come up with a good reason not to, I'd agreed. But I didn't want him to show up while I was reading one of the notes, which I assumed he'd put in my locker again. I didn't know how I felt about Jason being my secret admirer, and I was doing everything within my power to avoid some kind of "define the relationship" conversation with him before I could clearly analyze my feelings for him.

I took a deep breath and opened my locker, immediately spying the small white piece of paper that had fallen to the floor at my feet. In a rush, I unfolded it and read the note.

Dear Eliza,

Some girls are pretty, but when you get to know them, they become less so. With you, it's different. I find that the more I get to know you, the harder it is to keep myself from thinking of you and wanting to spend more time with you. You are beautiful inside and out. I hope I can find the courage to tell you this in person someday, but until then, know you are always in my thoughts.

Your Secret Admirer

I looked around to make sure Jason was nowhere in sight, and then read the words again. It was the sweetest note I'd received so far, and while half of me cringed, feeling like I didn't deserve these words of praise, the other half of me was deeply flattered. Although I knew Jason liked me, I couldn't believe anyone could really think I was *that* beautiful. He made me feel like I was special—and I wasn't even sure if I wanted to be more than friends. I felt like kicking myself.

"Hey, sorry I'm a little late. I hope you weren't waiting long."

I folded the note and quickly stuck it in my pocket, my fingers touching the glass vial as I did so, and turned around. Jason's eager face was almost too much for me to handle.

"No, I just barely got here." I smiled. "Are you ready?"

We walked down the hall in silence, neither of us seeming to know what to say. I tried to act casual, pretending to be interested in watching the people around us. The halls were always crowded during lunch, and as I looked around, I noticed something that I'd never paid attention to before. Everywhere I looked, people were holding cell phones. I struggled to find someone, *anyone*, who didn't have a cell phone or earbuds in their ears, but I couldn't.

I was aware of my own phone in my back pocket, and my thoughts instantly turned to Grandma's warning about distractions. The more I looked around, the more I felt like I was in some kind of sci-fi novel. Were we so attached to our technology that we didn't even notice it taking over our lives?

I briefly toyed with the idea of shutting my phone off, but the very thought made me panic. I'd be completely cut off, and besides, what if Jill needed to get ahold of me or there was an emergency at home or something? No, I definitely wasn't ready to disconnect myself from the human race just yet. I began to feel uncomfortable and silently wished I'd never noticed the whole phone thing.

Jill and Nick were waiting for us in their usual spot, in their usual cuddly positions. Jill seemed to have forgotten about the tank top episode this morning, because after glancing at Jason, she flashed me an impish smile that said exactly what she was thinking: *So, eating lunch with Jason again, eh?* I knew I'd never hear the end of this, and I glared at her. Jason and I were starting to look like a couple, and if we kept eating lunch together, that's exactly what the gossip around school would be.

After collecting our various lunches—Jill and I dutifully sticking to our salads—we set out for the courtyard. Now that the warm weather had officially arrived, the courtyard was more packed than ever. As if programmed by radar, I instantly caught sight of Luke. My heart sank as I saw two girls sitting on either side of him. One was Chelsea Andrews and the other was Whitney. The rest of the table was completely full, as were all the other tables in the courtyard. We noticed some people sitting in the grass with their backs against the wall, so we found our own patch of turf and did the same.

Even from where I was sitting, I could see Chelsea was pulling out all the stops when it came to Luke. With prom less than two weeks away, her flirtations were borderline desperate. She was sporting a tight-fitting top with a deep V-neck and a short denim skirt. She had on strappy sandals that showed off her impossibly perfect legs, and every time she laughed, she flipped her long blonde hair so that it caught the sunlight and shone like gold. She was tan, she was gorgeous, and she looked like she belonged on a magazine cover.

I felt depressed and angry as I looked at her. *No one should be allowed to look that good—it's not fair!* I was ready to give up and head back to the cafeteria for some *real* comfort food, but then I noticed Luke. He seemed uncomfortable around Chelsea. He turned more toward Whitney, and I could see he would talk to Chelsea only when necessary.

He seemed to be hurrying through his lunch, and I watched in growing amusement as Chelsea seemed to slowly deflate, then pout. It was obvious that she wasn't accustomed to being ignored. After a few more minutes without success, she flipped her hair one last time and stood up to leave.

Once she was gone, Luke's relief was unmistakable, and he immediately seemed to transform back into his usual self as he chatted with Whitney.

"Wow! I think Queen Chelsea has *finally* given up on trying to get Luke for a prom date," I whispered to Jill.

She nodded and giggled. "Yeah, isn't it awesome? I don't think she's ever been rejected before." She grinned maliciously.

I should have known Jill had been watching the exchange as intently as I had been. She never missed an opportunity to mock Chelsea.

I tried to focus on eating my salad, but I couldn't seem to pull my eyes away from Luke and Whitney. From the way they were talking so easily, it was plain to see that they were friends. But could it be more than that?

I thought about how sweet and down-to-earth Whitney was. Although she wasn't annoyingly pretty like Chelsea, she still had nice features, and her personality seemed to make her shine.

I sighed as I gazed at Luke, and he must have sensed that someone was looking at him, because just then he looked up and our eyes met. I felt my face flush, and I hurried to look away, but there was no way I could hide that I'd been staring at him, and I knew that he knew it. I willed myself not to blush deeper, but as always, that only made my face get hotter. After a few moments, I glanced up from my salad to see if he had resumed his conversation with Whitney, but to my surprise, he was still looking at me. He gave me a half-smile that made his dimple stand out, and our eyes locked again. I felt that dizzying sensation like everything around me had disappeared and it was only the two of us here in the courtyard, sharing this moment together. My heart began thumping wildly.

"So, Jill says you guys are going dress shopping tonight." Jason's voice snapped me back to reality, and the spell was broken.

"Yeah, we're going right after school," I said offhandedly.

I felt Jason's eyes on me, and I knew it would be rude not to look at him while he was talking, so I reluctantly pulled my gaze away from Luke. Jason smiled and I smiled back, but I couldn't resist another quick glance back at Luke. He was getting up to leave.

"You'll have to be sure to tell me what color your dress is so I can get a corsage that matches."

"Okay, I'll let you know." My eyes trailed Luke as he walked through the door and disappeared. Seconds later the bell rang, signaling the end of lunch. Jason stood and held out his hand to help me up. I took it hesitantly and did my best to put most of my weight on my feet so he wouldn't think I was heavy.

"Wow, you need to start eating something more than salads. You're light as a feather!" Jason looked at me in concern. I was secretly elated by his comment, feeling like maybe all this dieting was paying off after all, but I wanted him to stop looking worried like that. I got enough of those looks from my mom.

I laughed lightly, but he still looked unconvinced.

"No, really, Eliza, I'm worried about you. You're really thin, and you don't seem to eat very much." He put his hand around my wrist as if to emphasize his point, and I tried to ignore the immediate impulse to pull away. "I think I better take you out to an all-you-can-eat buffet and try to put some meat on your bones," he said half-jokingly. While I was glad that he was lightening up, I sensed another date invitation coming on.

Feeling a stab of guilt, I pulled my arm away and said, "I better go. I have choir next, and I don't want to be late. Talk to you later." I didn't look back as I headed for the door; I didn't want to see his crestfallen expression.

After returning my tray to the cafeteria, I realized I needed to use the restroom and worried that maybe I'd be late for class after all. I absolutely *hated* being late. I hated the dirty looks the teacher gave me, and I hated having everyone's eyes glued on me when I was the last person to walk in the room. Vowing to be in and out of the restroom in record time, I pushed past some people and tripped on something. I heard an irritated "Ouch! Watch where you're going!" and realized that the *something* had actually been a *someone*. I looked down to see who I'd accidentally stepped on. The first thing I saw was the nose ring, and then the spiky blonde hair. I realized it was Keira Davis, the new girl.

What is she doing, always sitting here by the bathroom? I wondered in annoyance. I mumbled a quick apology and continued my mad dash to the restroom. Before slipping through the door, I looked back at Keira. She was sitting by herself with her earbuds in and was bent over a notebook, doodling.

CHAPTER

seven

Okay, guys, I want to try something new today. I'm con- cerned that some of you might not be making time to read your scriptures every day—do you remember the goal we made at the beginning of the year? Now I know you all have busy sched- ules, what with your favorite TV shows and video games and all," Brother Carlton, our seminary teacher, said sarcastically. This earned a collective moan from the class. "Just kidding. I know you have homework, extracurricular activities, work, and other *impor- tant* commitments you have to fulfill. So I've decided to take ten minutes out of our class time every day to let you study the scrip- tures on your own. And don't worry if you forgot to bring yours, we have plenty of extras here."

There was an excited shift to the mood that filled the room. Ten minutes of study time translated into ten minutes of *free* time during seminary!

"The one catch," Brother Carlton continued, "is you have to spend the time stud-y-ing." He stretched out each syllable for emphasis. "If I catch people talking or sleeping or doing home- work for other classes, then the deal's off. And of course, the same rule applies as always with cell phones. If I catch you with it, then what?"

He held his hand up to his ear expectantly and we all droned in unison, "Then you take it away." The note of exasperation was unmistakable.

He ignored the collective lack of enthusiasm and smiled cheerfully. "That's right! I just want you guys to realize the power the scriptures have to change your lives for the better. It's not easy to make time for them when there's so much else you could be doing, but there is little else that will have such a great impact on your lives. And there's a big difference between casually reading a few verses while your mind wanders and actually diving in and studying the words. Give it a try, and you'll see what I mean. Now if everyone's ready"—his eyes swept the room to make sure we all had our scriptures in front of us—"we'll begin."

Normally, I would have yawned at this assignment and spent ten minutes pretending to read while daydreaming, but today I felt excited. As soon as Brother Carlton had mentioned our study session, I'd had an idea.

I opened up my blue scripture quad and breathed in the familiar leather scent, then quickly flipped to the Bible Dictionary and searched for "mustard seed." I found an entry for "Mustard" with a brief explanation about how the seed grew to be ten feet or more and something about birds in the branches that ate the seeds. There were three scripture references in the New Testament, but after flipping through each of the verses, I felt slightly disappointed. The references were basically the same parable that compared the kingdom of heaven to a mustard seed and that, although the mustard seed was the least of all the seeds, it became the greatest among herbs. I thought about that for a few minutes, but even though I found it interesting, it still didn't turn on any lightbulbs for me.

Deciding to take a different tack, I flipped to the Topical Guide and resumed my search for "mustard seed." Again, I only found the word "Mustard" with the same three scripture references, but then there was another reference at the bottom that caught my eye. In excitement, I flipped to Matthew 17:20 and read: "For verily I say unto you, If ye have faith as a grain of mustard seed, ye shall say unto this mountain, Remove hence to yonder place; and it shall remove; and nothing shall be impossible unto you."

I felt goose bumps on my arms, and a warm feeling rushed through my entire body. As I stared at the word *faith*, I knew I had found my answer. I pulled the tiny vial from my pocket and stared at the seed inside for a moment. I read and reread the verse again, the glass vial warm in my hand.

I remembered the scenes from Emma's life, and I could hear Grandma's voice telling me that Emma had been a *faithful* woman, that it had been her *faith* that carried her through her trials. I read the last line of the verse again: "And nothing shall be impossible unto you." A new wave of chills came over me, and I felt tears come to my eyes. This was a special moment—a moment I knew I'd never forget. I closed my eyes and said a prayer of gratitude, thanking Heavenly Father for allowing me to have this experience and promising Him that I'd do my best to have faith—no matter what.

After closing my prayer, a thought came to me, and I flipped back to the Bible Dictionary and looked up the word "Faith." After reading through the definition once, I felt like there was so much to absorb that I started to read it again, but before I could finish the second time, Brother Carlton's voice interrupted my thoughts like a splash of cold water.

"Okay, time's up!"

I felt disappointed, but promised myself I'd study the definition before going to bed tonight. I placed the vial back in my pocket, keeping my hand over the tiny lump it made in my jeans.

The bell rang, and as I gathered my things, I felt someone's eyes on me. I turned to see Luke waiting for me by his desk. When our eyes met, he smiled, and my heart skipped a beat. Everyone else had filed out of the room, and I tried to act casual as I approached him.

"Mind if I walk with you?" His eyes held that searching look again, and I tried desperately not to get lost in them—and to remind myself to keep breathing.

"Not at all," I said, trying to sound calm, but I was already so nervous that my throat was dry. We walked a few steps together, and my mind raced to think of something clever or funny to say. Why couldn't I be more like Jill? She always knew the perfect thing to say to make a situation comfortable.

I was clamming up. I could feel my palms getting sweaty, and I was sure Luke would notice my awkward silence. He probably thought I was quiet, boring, *and* sweaty. It didn't get any worse than that!

"It seemed like you were pretty into your scripture study today. What were you reading about?" Luke asked.

I felt a huge rush of relief. He didn't seem annoyed or disgusted by me. In fact, he seemed friendly and sincerely curious. And his question meant that he'd been watching me in class. I tried to brush off the implications of that realization and focused on answering his question.

"I was reading about faith. Have you ever read the definition of it in the Bible Dictionary?"

"I don't think I have. What made you so interested in that topic?" There was a mild sparkle of curiosity in his eyes.

This was the tricky part. I knew I wasn't ready to share my experience last night with anyone, but despite that, I felt oddly comfortable talking to Luke. I felt like if I were to share it with him, he would believe me. I hadn't gotten that feeling from Jill, and when I realized that, I felt sad in a way I couldn't explain.

"Well, I just felt like it was something I didn't know much about. It's pretty fascinating actually. You should read the definition sometime—it really makes you think."

He gave me that famous little half-smile. "I will."

We had walked across the parking lot from the seminary building to the school, but he stopped a few paces before the doors and turned to face me.

"You know, I thought I was doing pretty well with my scripture study today. I mean, at least I was reading and trying to concentrate on the words, which was more than most of the class."

I laughed. Even in my deep study, I'd noticed that most people hadn't been reading at all.

Luke took the tiniest step toward me. "But then I noticed *you*, and I was completely humbled. You were totally into it. You looked like you were getting so much out of what you were reading. Almost as if ten minutes wasn't enough time. Watching you made me think, 'I want to be like that.'" He shook his head. "You're different from other girls, Eliza. What's your secret?"

My feet started tingling as I took it all in. Luke was standing mere inches away from me, and his eyes were locked on mine. I was about to answer that there wasn't any secret, that I wasn't different or special, except that deep down I *really* wanted him to believe I was.

"Luke, I—"

"*There* you guys are." Jason came striding up to us with a smile pasted on his face. He was acting like he'd expected to find us together, but it was obvious from his posture that it was a surprise—and not a welcome one.

He walked straight up to me and put his arm possessively around my shoulder. I noticed Luke stiffen slightly as he casually stepped back. Jason's message to back off was a little too obvious, and it irritated me.

"Jill was inside looking for you," Jason said to me. "She said she had something to tell you and wondered if I knew where you were. I was about to send you a text, but then I spotted you guys through the window."

Ah, just the opening I needed. I wriggled out from under Jason's arm. "Sounds like I better go find her then. See you guys later." I braved one last glance at Luke, but his eyes seemed to be trained on the sidewalk.

"Bye, Liza. Don't forget to call me when you find out about the dress!" Jason called. I waved and nodded at him, and then made my way past the exiting crowd to the nearest open door. Feeling like a fish swimming upstream, I glanced back at Jason and Luke. Their postures were more relaxed now that I was gone, and they seemed to be talking as friends. I tried not to notice all the girls who were checking out Luke as they walked by him. Standing there in the sunlight, he looked like some sort of model-superhero. I sighed in agony as I realized I'd never look good enough to be his girlfriend. With that depressing awareness in mind, I began my search for Jill.

I didn't have to search for long.

"Liza! I've been looking *everywhere* for you." Jill ran up to me in the hall with Nick trailing behind her. I thought I'd gotten used to them being inseparable, but sometimes it still bothered me. Like now.

"Jason told me you were trying to find me. What's going on?" I asked.

I recognized the guilty look on her face. It was the one she always wore when she was about to tell me something she knew I wouldn't like. "Well, it turns out Nick's little brother Colton has a baseball game this afternoon. I'd forgotten all about it, and I promised Colton I'd be there, so do you mind if we go shopping after the game?" She gave me her best puppy-dog pleading look, and I cut in before she could pout her lips.

"You *know* I can't do anything on Monday nights," I snapped. "That is, unless you want to drag my family around with us to go shopping for our family home evening activity." I threw a dirty look at Nick, whose apologetic expression was so fake it made my blood boil.

Jill's expression dropped. "Oh, right. I forgot it was Monday. What about tomorrow?"

"I don't know, maybe we could go for a couple of hours before work," I said curtly. "Have fun at the game. I'll talk to you later." I spun on my heel, not wanting to hear any more excuses or have any

more reasons to feel like once again, my best friend was choosing
her boyfriend over me.

C ✑

When I got home, the house was totally quiet. I peered into
the family room and couldn't believe my luck. Courtney and Alexis
were nowhere to be seen. It had become almost a ritual for them
to come straight from school to the couch, where they remained
fixated on their TV shows for hours. Now I had the TV all to myself
and could watch whatever I wanted.

I checked the kitchen to see if anyone was there, but again I
found no one. My eyes lingered on a plate of lemon bars set in the
center of the counter. Mom had been in a baking frenzy lately, and
I suspected she was going for the "cruel and unusual punishment"
method of destroying my diet. Unwillingly, I pulled my eyes away
from the treats and focused on the computer desk in the corner. I
hadn't checked my Facebook account in hours, and I wondered if
there were any updates.

I made my way over to the computer and logged on. After
opening my account, I saw that I had one new friend request.
I held my breath and briefly allowed myself to hope that it was
Luke, but as soon as I clicked on the link, Jason's beaming face
appeared.

Agh! I was beginning to feel a little claustrophobic. It seemed
like everywhere I turned, there was Jason! At least he hadn't texted
me again since this morning. Maybe he was waiting for me to text
him first. With that comforting thought, I accepted him as my
Facebook friend and clicked through the pictures on his profile
page. I couldn't help but smile as I scanned the photos. There was

a picture of him sitting on the grass with his arm around a golden retriever, and another picture of four, smiling redheads sitting on the front porch of his house. From the picture, I gathered that Jason had an older sister and two brothers, one older and one younger. Somehow, it made sense that he was a middle child, and that, judging by the picture, he and his siblings were close. There were a few soccer shots, and the final photo was the one he used for his profile picture. It was a headshot, and it was a good picture of him. Even on the computer screen, the sincerity in his eyes shone through.

I lazily scrolled down the homepage, reading the random thoughts and statements of people's minds, only pausing once or twice to comment.

I was about to log off when a face in the upper corner of the screen caught my eye. It was under the heading "People You May Know." It was Luke. Even in the tiny picture, his beautiful face made my stomach flip-flop. I clicked on his picture, and my hand hovered over the mouse as I stared at the link that suggested "Add Friend." It would be so easy—just one click. The thought of being connected to him in even that small way sent shivers down my back. We'd talked enough now that it wouldn't be weird for me to be friends with him online, would it? I wavered between taking action and doing nothing. The caption stated that we had sixteen mutual friends, so what was the big deal? *Just do it!* my mind screamed at me, but even as the thought came, I was logging off.

I felt partly frustrated with myself and partly relieved as I walked into the family room. If I didn't add Luke as a friend, then I wouldn't have to face the fear of him rejecting me, or worse— accepting me out of pity.

I flopped on the couch while simultaneously clicking on the TV with the remote. The TV was a good way to drown out my thoughts, and I flipped through the channels, searching for one of my favorite shows. Nothing good was on at the moment, so I found something I'd recorded and hit "Play."

Normally, I let my mind shut off and watched my shows in a half-stupor, but today something annoying kept happening. My thoughts kept returning to some of the things Grandma had said last night about technology and distractions. I tried to ignore those thoughts, but they lingered in the back of my mind until I finally gave up and turned off the TV. Almost instantly my mind quieted. In fact, everything was quiet.

As I sat there, my mind kept turning to Luke and the conversation we'd had today. I couldn't help but feel goose bumps when I thought of him and those few moments we'd shared after seminary. He had looked at me with such intensity that I couldn't put a name to the way it made me feel. What else would he have said if Jason hadn't interrupted us? Why was Luke acting like he was my friend anyway? Was he still looking out for Jason, or could there possibly be another reason?

"What are you doing?" Courtney and Alexis were standing in the doorway staring at me like I was some kind of mutant. I realized how strange I must look, sitting and staring at a blank TV screen. I'd been so absorbed in my thoughts that I hadn't heard them come in.

"Uh, I was just . . . thinking," I answered, somewhat absently.

"Well, would you mind *thinking* somewhere else? We want to watch our show," Courtney demanded.

"Okay." I stood up to leave, and I could tell Courtney was

surprised that she'd gotten away with sounding so bratty. I gave her a half smile as I squeezed past her through the door, but somehow I couldn't carry the smile for Alexis, who was still staring at me. I heard them whispering to each other as I made my way upstairs.

❧

Family night was, in my opinion, a total waste of time this evening. Courtney had forgotten she was in charge of the lesson, so she just read an article out of the *New Era*. I confess I've been guilty of doing the same thing, but for some reason tonight it bothered me. She'd spent all afternoon watching TV, and if she'd cut out watching even half of a show she could have prepared the lesson.

I remembered when Courtney used to love family night. After she got home from school, she and Mom would work together on the treat or whatever else she'd been assigned. She used to be so enthusiastic and eager about everything, but in the last few months, it was like she pulled a total 180. Ever since she'd become friends with Alexis, I realized.

As I brushed my teeth later that night, I felt a sense of satisfaction. I'd spent most of the afternoon doing my homework, and for once, I was caught up on my assignments. Ordinarily I procrastinated everything until the last possible opportunity, so having my work done ahead of time made me feel calm and organized. I changed into my polka-dot capri pajama bottoms and matching pink T-shirt and hopped into bed. I loved that it was warm enough to wear my summer PJs again!

I knelt on my bed to say my prayers, but before I closed my eyes, I noticed the mustard seed on my nightstand. All at once, I remembered a story from Primary about a little boy kneeling *beside* his bed to say prayers even though he was afraid there might be snakes on the floor. I hesitated for a moment, and then sighed and climbed down to kneel on the carpet.

After I was finished with my prayer, I realized that I had been more focused and sincere than I usually was, and that caused me to feel a warm kind of contentment. I wondered if it was because I wasn't half-falling asleep like I normally was while kneeling on the soft mattress. It was amazing that something so small and seemingly unimportant could actually make a difference.

I sat in bed, pulling up the covers over my lap, and felt a twinge of excitement as I reached for my scriptures on the nightstand. As I lifted the book, my hand bumped against my cell phone. Seeing it made me realize that I hadn't had any calls or texts in a while. Jill had been texting me less and less these days, so that wasn't a huge surprise, but Jason hadn't texted me either, which was a little strange.

I reached over and picked up my cell, ready to send Jill a text to see what she was up to, but then I realized something. I had my scriptures in one hand and my cell phone in the other. It was like one of those cheesy object lessons, but then I realized with perfect clarity I was demonstrating the point Grandma had tried to make last night. Exerting considerable effort, I switched my cell to silent mode and stuffed it in my nightstand drawer, where it would be out of sight. There. Now I could give my full attention to what I was reading. I smiled to myself when I thought of how happy that would make Grandma.

I had just opened up to the definition of faith when Mom walked in the room. She didn't hide her excitement at seeing me with my scriptures open, and I suspected she would hurry through our usual nightly routine so as not to break the magic spell. She came over, hugged me, and asked how my day had been, accepting my generic answer that normally she wouldn't have settled for. She beamed at me and turned on my reading lamp, then quietly turned off the main light and closed the door. I couldn't help but smile at her retreating figure. Parents were so easy to please when you thought about it.

I turned back to the definition of faith and read each line slowly, trying to internalize the principles being taught. After reading it several times, three ideas stood out to me. First, true faith had to be centered in Jesus Christ. And second, you couldn't let your faith lie dormant; you had to constantly work on it. And last, true faith led to action.

One phrase really jumped out at me: "Although faith is a gift, it must be cultured and sought after until it grows from a tiny seed to a great tree."

I picked up the vial with the mustard seed and marveled that if I had faith even this small, I could perform great miracles. If I could see my faith in the form of a seed, I wondered, just how tiny would it be? Would it even be visible? At least it was comforting to know that my faith was something I could work on and help grow.

As I looked at the radiant whiteness of the seed, I remembered Grandma saying that it was unique in its coloring. My eyelids grew heavy, and as I began crossing over into the realm of sleep, the last thing I pictured in my mind was the white flower decoration on the wall of the Young Women room.

DIVINE Nature

≈⊃ ℑℭ ⊂≈

"And I, God, created man in mine own image,
in the image of mine Only Begotten created I
him; male and female created I them."

—MOSES 2:27

CHAPTER

eight

Someone was gently tapping my shoulder. I opened my eyes, ready to scowl at my mom and beg for a few minutes more of sleep. But it wasn't my mom sitting there. I bolted upright and said simply, "You came back."

Great-grandma Eliza Porter smiled at me, and her brilliant blue eyes seemed to pierce my soul. "Yes, I came back. You learned more quickly than even *I* expected, and you are ready for your next visit. I'm so proud of you, Eliza." She gestured toward the glass vial on my nightstand, her eyes twinkling merrily. "I see you found the mustard seed. Tell me what you've learned about it."

I smiled, proud that I knew the answer. "It represents faith, which is something hoped for and not seen. True faith must be centered in Jesus Christ, and when someone really possesses it, it leads them to action. Living righteously increases faith. So does bearing your testimony and hearing the testimonies of others, and—"

"Very good, *very* good!" Grandma interrupted me enthusiastically. "You really *have* studied this principle, and I can see you've learned a lot. Do you know what impressed me the most?"

I shook my head.

"You were applying your faith even before you discovered what the seed meant. In fact, it's one of the gifts you've been blessed with, and you've had it all along! You just needed a nudge in the right direction, as we all do once in a while. I'm proud of you for choosing to follow the prophet and deciding not to wear that tank top, even though I'm sure it wasn't easy." She smiled at me. "You also made another good choice by not wasting a lot of time with mindless distractions. Wasn't it nice to finish your homework early and actually have time to listen to your own thoughts?"

My eyes widened in surprise. "Grandma, how do you know all of this?"

She laughed. "You can learn a lot from the hymns, Eliza. Have you ever heard the line, 'Angels above us are silent notes taking of every action'?"

"It sounds a little familiar."

"That's a line from the hymn 'Do What Is Right,' and believe me, it's true." She winked at me, but I felt slightly horrified.

Every action? My Primary teachers used to tell me, "Remember, someone is always watching." The phrase had seemed more like a scare tactic than anything, and I hadn't given it much thought, but to sit across from someone who actually *was* watching me was a whole different story! I was relieved that Grandma was recalling some of my better moments and not the time in fifth grade when I got in a catfight with Jenny Jorgensen.

Worrying that Grandma would do her uncanny mind-reading trick and see Jenny's mud-stained face, I quickly changed the subject.

"Grandma, those choices I made yesterday were pretty small,

especially after seeing what Emma went through. Would that really be considered exercising faith?"

Grandma's eyes lit up. "But of course, dear! The small, everyday actions in our lives are what truly enlarge our faith. It happens little by little, just like a seed grows slowly into a tree. However, there are times in everyone's life when something major happens to test their faith. Some people have more of these tests than others, but each person's trials and challenges are catered to them specifically. You can trust that Heavenly Father loves all of His children and has a purpose for each of them. He loves us so much that He sent His Son, our Savior, to suffer for us so that He could help us through the tough times. We don't ever have to go through these tests alone, and I want you to remember that when you are experiencing your own trials."

I felt that warm, tingling sensation through my body again. Tears stung my eyes, but I wiped them away quickly before Grandma could notice. She was looking at the seed intently. "Eliza, you've done a wonderful job discovering the significance of the seed, but you still haven't explained one thing: the color."

I looked at the seed, and then up at Grandma. The last image in my mind before I'd fallen asleep had given me the answer. "It's white because in the Young Women values, white is the color of faith."

Grandma beamed. "Exactly! Well done, Eliza. I think you're ready for your next lesson." Just as before, everything went dark around us. I waited patiently this time, knowing that the process would last only a few moments. Light began to chase away the darkness, growing brighter until the blurry edges of our new surroundings came into focus.

We were once again outside, standing in some kind of wilderness. Our surroundings seemed much more remote than they had in Pennsylvania. I couldn't see signs of human life anywhere. We stood on a grassy hill, and from the direction of the sun, I could tell that it was evening. There was a forest nearby, and I could hear the sounds of animals from the distant trees: birds calling to each other, crickets and other insects chirping, and the lonely howl of something I hoped was a coyote and not a wolf.

It was a beautiful area, but not knowing where we were was an unpleasant feeling. I turned in a full circle, taking in the landscape around us, but I still couldn't find any clues. Finally, I turned to Grandma with raised eyebrows. "Where are we now?"

Grandma's amused expression made me mad. I could tell she was the sort of person who enjoyed riddles and suspense, but I'd never had the patience for things like that. "We've gone back a long, long way in the history of the world. Or I should say, the history of *mankind*." She gave me a significant look as if I should know what she was talking about. "This excursion will be shorter than the last one because the lesson you need to learn is very simple. I brought you here to see someone, and then we'll be on our way."

I looked around once more. "Um, Grandma, I'm not sure you've noticed, but there isn't anyone *here*. We seem to be all alone."

"Things are not always as they seem. Remember, patience is a virtue."

It was obvious that she wasn't going to give me any more clues, so I did my best to be patient and wait for whatever—or *whoever*—was supposed to appear.

The sun slowly descended lower and lower until it was just above the horizon, creating a vivid assortment of pinks, oranges, and yellows across the sky. I sighed, wishing I had my camera here to capture this moment. Why was it that pictures never fully recreated what you saw with your own eyes? I'd taken dozens of pictures of sunsets, and they were never as beautiful in photos as they were in real life—but that didn't stop me from trying.

Grandma and I were sitting side by side in the grass, watching the last of the sun's final rays, when I heard a twig snap. I looked to the edge of the forest where the sound had come from and noticed a thin trail of smoke rising from somewhere in the trees.

My eyes strained to find whatever it was that had made the noise. I hoped it wasn't a bear. I had an irrational fear of running into a bear in the woods, and dream or no, I didn't want that fear confirmed. My muscles tensed when I saw a form emerging from the trees. We were close enough that I could see her clearly. It was a woman.

She was wearing deerskin clothes like a Native American might have worn in the frontier days, but she didn't look like a Native American. She had long blonde hair and fair skin—actually her skin was pretty tan, but I could tell it *would* have been fair if she hadn't been exposed to so much sun. She had a bundle of twigs under her arm, and her head was bent, scouring the ground for more wood. Her search was leading her back into the woods, so I stood and looked at Grandma to see if we should follow. She nodded and we set out together.

We followed the woman as she wandered deeper and deeper into the forest, collecting more wood as she went. I stayed silent, content to see if I could figure out who the woman was. I hadn't had a clear view of her face yet, and I was extremely curious to see what she looked like.

We lost sight of her for a moment when she walked around a thick stand of trees. We followed her and entered a clearing where there was a fire burning. A tall man with auburn hair and broad shoulders knelt by the fire, cooking some kind of meat. He was also wearing deerskin clothes, and his skin was tan as well. He looked up and smiled at the woman as she approached. She set her wood by the fire and then knelt to help him with their dinner. There was a cave behind them and a stream running nearby, and I couldn't help but think that this was where they lived. It seemed impossible, but it certainly appeared to be a dwelling.

Even though I knew the man and the woman weren't aware of my presence, I still whispered to Grandma, "Okay, I give up. Who are these people, and why are they all alone out here?"

Grandma's eyes sparkled. "Those people, my dear, are Adam and Eve—our first parents."

I gasped and stepped closer to look at their faces. Adam was tall and powerful looking. He seemed to carry a certain authority about him, and I wished I could hear him speak because I was certain his voice would reflect that power. He was the first man ever to walk the Earth—and here I was watching him make dinner over a fire. It was all too overwhelming!

I turned my attention to Eve, and once again my breath caught in my lungs. Though she was watching the fire, her face was turned toward me, and I was struck by her beauty. Even with a few dirt smudges on her face, she was gorgeous. After studying her for a moment, I realized that it wasn't necessarily her physical features that made her so stunning: she seemed to emit a glowing radiance from within. She was the "mother of all living." She was a *queen.*

I turned to Grandma, my mouth gaping open, unable to put my thoughts into words.

Grandma smiled and gestured to a log where we could sit and watch them from a distance.

"What you are seeing is the time just after Adam and Eve were cast out from the Garden of Eden." This immediately answered one of my questions. I'd secretly been hoping that this *wasn't* the Garden of Eden. I'd always imagined it as being sort of magical in its beauty, and although these surroundings were pretty, they weren't much different from places where I'd been camping with my own family.

"They made a temporary home here, but they will move again after the birth of their first child. As you can see, life was not easy for them. They had to struggle constantly for their food, shelter, and safety, but they *always* remained faithful to the Lord and sought for His guidance."

"Wow, I can't imagine living like this. It would be so lonely and hard. This is another example of faith, isn't it?"

"Indeed, faith was a quality that they both possessed, but that's not the lesson you're here to learn. Tell me what you noticed about Eve."

I looked back to where Eve was sitting by the fire, her head resting on Adam's shoulder. "She's beautiful. She seems to shine, inside and out."

Grandma nodded, a pleased smile on her face. "And do you know, Eliza, what makes her so beautiful?"

"Well, outwardly, I guess she's pretty because that's the way Heavenly Father made her, but inwardly, it's probably because she's a good person."

Grandma's eyes twinkled. "You hit it right on the nose! But do you know that it's often the *inner* beauty that people notice the most?"

I frowned. "Don't you mean *outer* beauty? That seems to be what people notice most."

Grandma shook her head. "Not at all. Think about some of your favorite movie stars or famous models, for instance. Their outward appearance is supposedly beautiful, but their lives are such a mess that they seem dark and unattractive when you take a good, hard look at them."

I thought for a moment of the famous people whose pictures I'd seen on the tabloids at the checkout stand. They often did appear sort of a mess, but I rationalized that was probably just the workings of the paparazzi or magazine editors.

And then, Chelsea's face popped into my mind. She was one of the prettiest girls in school, but because I knew how petty and mean she could be, she didn't seem that pretty to me anymore. Not in comparison with extraordinary women like Emma and Eve.

"I guess I see what you mean, Grandma, but it still seems like those are the people who get noticed the most and who can get anything they want." I thought longingly of Luke.

"That may be how it appears, but often getting everything you want only leads to trouble. Adam and Eve had to work hard, but hard work is a blessing. They were cheerful, and because they kept the commandments and the righteous counsel they were given, they received a great reward.

"The reason I wanted you to see Eve was to help you realize that each of us has been given a divine nature from Heavenly Father. We are all His children and have been given gifts and qualities from Him. We *all* have the potential to be beautiful. It's in our genetic makeup. Every young woman wants to be pretty, but once you focus on living a righteous life and recognize that you are literally a daughter of God, you'll know where true beauty comes from."

Grandma smiled patiently at my doubtful expression. "It sounds strange, I know. The world would have you believe that you have to constantly work to be attractive on the *outside*, but it simply isn't true."

"But, Grandma," I interjected, "we have to do *some* things about our outward appearance. Otherwise we'd all look like dirty slobs."

She laughed. "That's true. But just like with technology, there has to be moderation. There's nothing wrong with doing your best to look nice, but once you've gotten ready for the day, forget about your appearance and focus on others!"

Her face grew serious. "Your body is a precious gift—a temple, even. Take good care of it and don't waste time comparing it with other bodies. It is uniquely yours, and you are beautiful. And remember, anyone can turn a boy's head by showing off some skin—those aren't the kind of boys you want to be with anyway—but it takes *real* beauty to turn heads when you're modestly dressed. Don't ever sell yourself short. You are of royal birth."

Grandma reached down into the grass and plucked a flower I hadn't noticed before. It was a lovely shade of blue and fit perfectly into the palm of her hand. "Here is another reminder. You have many gifts and talents that you have yet to develop. Don't ever forget your divine nature. You, Eliza, like Eve, are the daughter of a king."

Grandma gently handed me the tiny flower. I was prepared

to shelter its small, delicate petals, but to my surprise, the flower seemed to be made of a hard substance like porcelain or glass.

Our surroundings blurred around us, and the last thing I remembered was the smell of the smoke from the campfire and Grandma's words echoing in my mind: *"The daughter of a king."*

CHapTer

As I got dressed the next morning, I noticed for the first time how loose my jeans were getting. I stood in front of the full-length mirror in my closet and examined my appearance. Before last night, the fact that my clothes were getting baggy would have made me extremely happy. After all, isn't that why I'd been half-starving myself these past few weeks? I'd wanted to look like one of the girls on the magazine covers or on TV, or like the skinny girls on the drill team. Now I felt differently. As I looked at myself, I felt ashamed that I'd treated my body so badly. My diet had been far from healthy. Jason was right; I was starting to get *too* skinny.

But you look good. And think how fun it will be to shop for a dress in a smaller size. Luke would never want to be with a girl who wasn't skinny.

I shook my head and tried to erase those thoughts that always came to my mind when I looked in the mirror. I knew that what Grandma had taught me in my dream last night was true. I'd felt it in my heart. I knew that my body was a gift and that Heavenly Father wanted me to be happy with it and take good care of it.

Taking a deep breath, I walked over to my dresser, picked up all of my fashion magazines, and dumped them in the trash. Then, with one quick turn in the mirror to make sure I looked okay, I grabbed my bag and headed into the hall.

All morning I'd been eager to return to the attic to search for the flower I'd seen in my dream. Finding the mustard seed may have been a fluke, but it seemed more than a coincidence that I would dream about something and then *find* it in the house the next day. Knowing how much Grandma loved games, I thought it only fitting she would leave me these little clues, and something inside me desperately hoped that the flower would be among her old possessions as well.

I searched through the dresser again as quietly as I could. Mom may have let my unusual visit to the attic slide for one morning, but I knew if she caught me again there would be awkward questions to answer.

I sorted through Grandma's old clothes and looked through all of the compartments in the music box—carefully muffling the music as I opened the lid—but the flower was nowhere to be seen. I didn't have much time before I needed to be down at the breakfast table, so I stood up and sighed in frustration. As I stared at Grandma's picture, I couldn't help but smile at the beaming face staring back at me from the frame.

"You think you're pretty clever, don't you, Grandma?" I said, wishing she could answer me. I sighed again and was about to turn away when something in the picture caught my eye. I gasped and took a step closer. There, pinned on Grandma's sweater, was a small blue flower!

I rushed down to the kitchen and found Mom in her usual spot at the kitchen stove cooking breakfast. I wanted to ask her about the flower right away, but suddenly, I felt a sense of gratitude and went over to kiss her on the cheek. "Thanks for making breakfast for us every morning, Mom. I really appreciate it."

She looked at me in surprise and nearly dropped her spatula. "Why, thank *you*, sweetheart. It's nice to feel appreciated. What brought this on?"

I shrugged. "I don't know. I guess I just feel bad I don't always thank you for all the nice things you do."

Her eyes started glistening, and I was afraid I'd gone too far. It didn't take much to bring on the waterworks with my mom. I hurried to change the subject before we had a whole emotional outburst. "So I noticed in Grandma's picture that she wore a little flower pin." Mom's eyebrows rose in confusion at this sudden turn in the conversation, and I tried to sound casual as I continued, "It looked kind of cool, and I wondered if you knew what happened to it."

To my enormous relief, Mom smiled and nodded. "Sure I do! It's on a shelf in my closet. The fastener is broken, and I've been meaning to take it to a jeweler to have it fixed for years now, but I haven't gotten around to it. I've never been one to wear decorative pins—are they in style now?"

I smiled at her innocent question, especially since it provided me with an excuse for my curiosity. "Sort of. Since you're not using it, would you mind if I kept it for a while?"

She beamed. "Of course not. I think Grandma would have liked for you to have it. Go ahead and get started on your omelet, and I'll be right back."

I picked up my fork, and before I knew it, Mom was back in the kitchen. "Here it is! A pretty little thing, isn't it? Grandma wore it often." She handed the small flower to me, and I tried not to let the overwhelming awe I felt show on my face. My fingers trembled slightly as I felt the familiar, delicate contours of the stem and petals on my palm.

"Thanks, Mom, this is really . . . awesome." The understatement of the century! I knew that if I kept staring at the flower Mom would suspect something was up, so after placing it carefully in my pocket, I looked at my plate and changed the subject once more. "This omelet smells really good. Do we have any salsa to go with it?"

"Of course. I've got some sausage here too, if you want some." I hoped her heart could handle the shocking change in my behavior, but she was smiling, so I took that as a good sign.

"Thanks, that sounds great." As I poured the salsa over my omelet, Dad walked into the kitchen. I pretended not to see Mom pointing at me and giving Dad a thumbs-up. Apparently, she'd been more worried about my diet than I'd realized. I wasn't about to go overboard and hog down everything in sight, but it sure felt good to be eating real food again. I literally sighed after my first bite and vowed that from then on, I would treat my body better.

C✖

"All right, everyone, let's take it from the top!"

We were standing on the stage in the school auditorium. With the spring concert approaching this weekend, we were holding choir class here every day this week to practice. Yesterday, we'd reviewed positioning and choreography, and today was the first time I would sing my solo in the auditorium. I tried to hide my nervousness by listening to the conversations going on around me. There was always an undercurrent of excitement in anticipation of a concert. Normally, I would have joined in on the chatter, but I was so edgy that I was afraid that if I opened my mouth, I'd vomit.

"Okay, places everyone. Soloists, do you have your microphones?" Ms. Steele's voice brought me back to reality. She looked at Gavin Stoll, who nodded, and then she turned her gaze to me. I held up the mic and nodded. Gavin had a solo in the first verse of the song; mine was in the last verse.

"Good luck!" I heard someone whisper from behind me. I smiled at my friend Melanie and mouthed a quick, "Thank you," before turning around again. I felt a momentary surge of pride at having been selected to sing one of the solos. Choir was a popular and competitive program at school, and it was an honor to be chosen from the many who'd tried out.

However, as the first chords of the piano rang out, that good feeling vanished, and all I felt was paralyzing fear. Singing in front of the class was bad enough, but it would be even worse when I was staring into the hundreds of faces on Friday night.

My heart sped up to a frightening pace, and my palms began to sweat. I tried to sing along with the rest of the class, but my voice was quickly drying up. Gavin gave an impeccable solo in his trained baritone voice, but I felt like I was hearing it through a tunnel. As the song continued, I knew that my turn was coming up—there was no going back. Frantically, I considered pretending to pass out, but I'd never been a good actor, and I knew that would attract more unwanted attention to me.

Suddenly, I heard Grandma's words in my head: *"You have many gifts and talents that you have yet to develop."* With my free hand, I reached into my pocket and pulled out the tiny flower, grasping it tightly. My other hand gripped the mic, and I slowly pulled it toward my mouth as I'd been trained. The spotlight turned its blinding light on me, and I began to sing.

ᒉ✆

"Great job on your solo today, Eliza!" Gavin called from across the parking lot.

"Thanks, you did awesome too!" I called back, blushing at his comment. I felt like I *hadn't* done a great job on my solo; my voice had cracked right at the very end, and I was sure everyone had noticed. I brushed off the embarrassing memory by laughing at myself and allowed that at least it was only a practice run. Ms. Steele hadn't said anything to me about it, which was a relief, because sometimes she really got after people, and she already terrified me. Now that our initial practice was over and I knew what to expect, I was confident that I'd do better the next time.

I tried to be patient as I waited for Jill beside my car. I felt a little depressed, and I wanted to analyze my feelings and figure out why. It didn't take me long to get to the source of it: for starters, Luke had been absent today. Whenever he wasn't in school, I felt deflated. Like it or not, he was my motivation for looking my best and (truth be told) for wanting to be at school at all. I hadn't heard any gossip about why he was absent, and I hoped desperately that he would be back tomorrow.

The second reason I was feeling bad was because of guilt over Jason. He hadn't tried texting me again since before lunch yesterday. I'd suspected that he was waiting for me to make the next move, and I was right; he hadn't left me a note today *or* tried to eat lunch with me. I knew that I needed to make more effort on his behalf, but I didn't know how to do that without sending the message that I wanted to be his girlfriend. I was afraid that if I gave Jason a little encouragement, he'd run wild.

"Hey, sorry you had to wait for me again. I'm so excited to go shopping!" Jill appeared by the passenger door.

I smiled at her as I tried to imitate her enthusiasm. I felt like saying, "Yeah, but it would have been *more* fun if we could have gone yesterday when we had more time," but I let it slide.

Jill didn't seem to notice, because as soon as we were in the car, she started talking. "Oh my goodness, I almost forgot to tell you! In my last class I heard the best piece of news I've heard all year. Guess who *isn't* going to get her dream prom date this year?"

There was only one person whose suffering Jill would enjoy this much, so it wasn't much of a guess. "Chelsea?"

"Yes! I heard that Luke Matthews isn't going to prom this year at all because he's going on vacation with his family or something. Isn't that awesome? You should have seen the way Chelsea was pouting in English today! I bet you a hundred bucks she'll have another date by tomorrow. I feel sorry for whoever the poor sap turns out to be; she's already turned down tons of guys since she was hoping Luke would ask her, so by now it'll be slim pickings!" Jill laughed crazily, and I smiled, but I wondered about what Whitney was going to do for prom—would she have a date by tomorrow like Chelsea? I felt sorry for her—and for myself—that she and Luke wouldn't be in our group.

Once we were at the mall, it was easier to share Jill's bubbly mood. It was great to actually be in the store, trying on dresses together. I had already secretly picked out the dress I wanted. It had been in the dress shop window for weeks, and from the time I'd first laid eyes on it, I knew I had to have it. It was a tangerine color with short sleeves and a sweetheart neckline trimmed with rhinestones. The bodice was satin and fitted at the waist. The skirt was full and had layers of iridescent tulle trimmed with satin ribbon. Rhinestones were placed decoratively on the bodice and skirt, which made the dress appear to shimmer under the lights. It was beautiful, and I couldn't wait to try it on.

I knew the store still had plenty of these dresses in my size because I checked their inventory every time I was at the mall—just in case I had to put one on hold. It didn't seem like they sold many, if any, of this particular dress, and I reasoned it was probably because of the price. The tag listed the price at a staggering sum of $435, which was more money than I'd ever spent on any one item. But with the money my dad had promised to match, I had more than enough. After weeks of seeing the dress in the window, I was ready to buy it.

"Okay, I'm coming out. Are you ready yet?" I emerged from the dressing room and saw Jill sitting on a chair, waiting for me.

"Oh, Liza, that dress is *gorgeous!* I love the color; I bet no one else will have an orange dress. It's so pretty! Come over to the mirror so you can see."

I smiled at Jill's praise. She was a great friend to go shopping with because she was always honest when it came to how clothes looked, and I knew I could trust her. I turned and followed her toward the full-length, angled mirror and almost gasped when I saw my reflection. The dress *was* beautiful, and I felt beautiful in it. It reminded me of when I was little and played dress-up, pretending to be a fairytale princess.

"Twirl," Jill commanded, and I obliged with a laugh. I was so excited and relieved to have found my dress that I felt giddy. Jill laughed with me and then said, "Okay, well this is so unfair! You found your perfect dress on the first pick, and I know it's going to take me forever to find one. You have to keep trying them on with me so I don't feel stupid."

For the first time, I noticed the dress that Jill had tried on, and I instantly felt sorry for not having noticed it sooner.

"I'm sorry, Jill, I've totally been hogging all the attention. Stand up so I can see your dress better."

"All right, but I've already decided it's not the one. It looked good on the hanger, but I hate the way it fits." The dress was a pale green satin with short sleeves and a drop waist. Normally, everything looked great on Jill, but this style was not flattering to her figure at all. We both returned to the dressing rooms and continued trying on dresses. Jill would leave the dressing room, continue her hunt, and return with more dresses for us to try on.

"Oh, I think this is the one! What do you think, Liza?" Jill asked excitedly as she stepped from the dressing room.

To spare her feelings, I tried to hide my disappointment. The red silk dress *did* look great on her, but it was extremely form fitting and low-cut in the back. The dress had spaghetti straps instead of sleeves. I thought she had wanted to try it on for fun, but the look on her face made me wonder if she might really buy it.

"I feel like red is my signature color, and I really want to feel, I don't know, *sexy* or something, I guess," she said as she looked at herself in the full-length mirror.

"Jill, you know your parents would never let you wear a dress like that. Besides, I think it's almost *too* bold—it takes the attention away from your natural beauty."

"Hold on a second. I have something I want to show you and then you can give me your final opinion." She clasped her hands and looked at me pleadingly. "Just try on that last dress I picked out for you, then I'll be ready."

I sighed and relented. "Okay, but we have to hurry because my shift starts in twenty minutes."

"I promise I'll be quick!" She darted back into her dressing room, and I hurried into mine. Shopping had been fun, but I was tired of all the zipping and unzipping that getting in and out of the dresses required. I looked at the last dress Jill had brought for me, surprised that I hadn't noticed it in the store before. It was a sky-blue organza with short sleeves and a fitted bodice that tapered into an A-line skirt. A black satin band trimmed the empire waistline and tied in the back, flowing down to the floor along with the skirt, with black beadwork and embroidery as accents. I looked at the price tag, prepared for a shock, but the price was even more surprising than I'd expected. The dress had been marked down to $175! I gasped and then hurried to undo the zipper and try it on.

"I'm ready, Eliza, are you?" Jill called.

I tied the ribbon and stepped out into the hall where I saw Jill, once again turning in front of the mirror, checking her appearance from every angle. She still wore the red dress, but she had found a matching red silk bolero jacket to cover up the straps and make it modest.

"What a great idea. That jacket looks so cute with the dress." I smiled at her encouragingly. "And the price is definitely a bonus." Jill's dress, including the jacket, was only $80. "I'm so glad you found a way to make the dress work. It looks fantastic on you," I said. She obviously loved the dress, and I was happy for her.

She beamed. "Thanks! I hope Nick likes it."

"No worries there. The poor guy will be drooling!"

She laughed and then seemed to see me for the first time. "Uh-oh, Liza. I think we have a problem."

My eyebrows rose in concern. "What's wrong?"

"I think I might like that dress even better than the orange one. It's completely, outrageously *gorgeous* on you!"

In my excitement for Jill, I'd forgotten all about my dress, so I quickly stepped over to the mirror. She was right, it *was* beautiful! "Well, I thought I had to have the orange one, but I agree—I love this! And it's so much more affordable. What would I do without you, Jill?"

She bowed dramatically, and we both laughed as we hurried back into our dressing rooms to change.

C✄

Work was slow for a Tuesday night. I had already cleaned the cabinets and the windows, plus finished my homework, and I *still* had an hour until closing time.

I reached for my cell, thinking maybe it was time to send Jason a text. I felt bad that he'd avoided me today, and I wanted to make sure he wasn't upset about something. I could use the dress shopping as my excuse for texting him—not that I needed an excuse— but it made me feel less silly. I wasn't used to being the one to initiate a text with a boy.

Me: Hey, Jason! I found my dress. It's blue.

Moments later my cell buzzed.

Jason: Cool. Thnx for letting me know. I was starting to worry that I was bugging you or something.

Me: What do you mean?

Jason: I don't know. I got the feeling you wanted more space.

I wasn't sure how to respond. While it was true that I wasn't sure if I wanted to be Jason's *girlfriend,* I didn't mind being his friend. I texted a quick change in the subject.

Me: Sorry! I didn't know I was giving off that vibe. What are you up to right now?

Jason: Watching TV w/the fam. It's hard to find a show my mom approves of. Watching a thrilling episode of *The Brady Bunch*—& if you repeat that to anyone I'll deny it to the grave!

I burst out laughing.

Me: LOL! Your secret's safe w/me. Unless I find a good reason to blackmail you.

Jason: Ha-ha, very funny. Still coming to our game Thurs?

Me: Yeah, if that's OK.

Jason: Totally! I really want you to be there. I hope I don't make a fool of myself.

Me: You'll do great, no worries. ☺

Jason: Thnx. So did you hear that Whitney and Luke won't be in our group after all?

Me: I heard he was going on a family trip or something.

Jason: Yeah, I told him he was a loser for skipping his last prom but, oh well. Our group will be small, but it'll be fun. I can't wait to tell you what our day activity is going to be—you're going to love it!

Me: No fair, making me all curious about it! When are you going to tell me?

Jason: All in good time . . .

Me: Argh! That's so lame, but I'll try to be patient . . . I guess. ☹

After a few moments' pause, I sent him another text.

Me: Well, it's time for me to close up the shop. See you tomorrow.

Jason: OK. I hope my *Brady Bunch* confession didn't scare you off.

Me: Pretty much.

Jason: I knew it!

Me: JK! No, I really have to go, but thnx for chatting.

Jason: See ya, Eliza.

Me: Bye.

I smiled as I closed up the store. My conversation with Jason had put me in a good mood. Maybe I wasn't interested in him as a boyfriend, but he made me laugh, and I hoped that if nothing else we would end up being good friends.

◦⚬

As I climbed up off the floor and into bed after saying my prayers, Mom came in the door.

"Hi, sweetie, mind if we talk for a while?"

"No, that's fine." I scooted over to make room for her to sit down on my bed.

"How was your day?"

"Long. I'm exhausted." I couldn't suppress the yawn that only served to emphasize my point.

Mom smiled sympathetically and leaned over to scratch my back like she used to do when I was little. I put my chin on my knees so she could reach my shoulders better and sighed at how good it felt. She smelled like lavender soap, and the comforting scent made me feel happy and relaxed.

"Did you practice your solo today?" she asked.

"Yep." Another yawn.

"How did it go?"

"It went okay, but I was a little nervous. I could have done better." I thought about the flower, which was now safely hidden in my nightstand drawer next to the mustard seed. "I think that maybe my voice is one of my talents, and it felt good to be using it. I'm sure the next time we practice, I'll do better," I said with quiet confidence.

Mom squeezed my shoulder. "I'm sure you will, honey. I'm glad that you recognize it as one of your talents, because it truly is a gift you've been given—along with many others, of course."

She reached over and gave me a hug. "I'm so proud of the person you're becoming. A lot of my friends complain about their crazy teenage kids, but I feel blessed to be your mom. You're really mature for your age, Eliza, you know that?"

"Thanks, I guess," I said with a shrug. I felt bad for accepting Mom's praise without revealing the true reason why I was changing—that it was Grandma's visits that had opened my eyes. I almost told Mom about my dreams, but I felt like it wasn't something that I could share easily or that I *should* share unless the Spirit told me to. These dreams had had a profound impact on me, more than almost anything else in my life, but they were also extremely personal, even sacred, to me.

Mom stood up to leave, but before she closed my door, I called out, "Love you, Mom."

She blew me a kiss. "Love you too, sweetie. Sleep tight."

While I was reading my scriptures, my cell buzzed. I realized I'd forgotten to turn it on silent like I'd planned to do when I read, and I was sorely tempted to put down my scriptures and see who was texting me. But I knew that if I wanted to gain anything from reading my scriptures, I had to devote some time to them—without distractions. I *had* to stick to my goal.

Without looking, I turned the phone to silent mode and stuffed it in my drawer. It took a few minutes for me to turn my mind away from the mystery text and back to my reading, but I finally succeeded and again immersed myself in my study. Even though it was a small thing, it felt good to overcome the magnetic draw of my cell. I felt like I was in control of *it*, and not the other way around. It felt good.

I had intended to check the message after I finished reading, but once I turned off my lamp, I was so tired that I decided it could wait until morning.

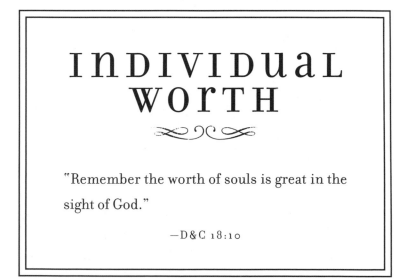

INDIVIDUAL WORTH

"Remember the worth of souls is great in the sight of God."

—D&C 18:10

CHAPTER

ten

Grandma and I stood in the courtyard of a palace. Until now, the closest thing I'd ever seen to a palace was the Sleeping Beauty Castle at Disneyland, but I knew that this was the real deal. This place made the Disney castle seem like a dollhouse by comparison!

Towering walls constructed of beige-colored stone surrounded us on every side. Tall columns adorned with brightly colored tapestries lined narrow paths leading in various directions, each made of intricately patterned stones. Everywhere I looked, I could see beautiful flowering bushes, but from the amount of dust covering the ground, I guessed that we were in a desert climate.

A wonderfully ornate fountain graced the center of the courtyard, and the sound of the trickling water was loud in the otherwise quiet room.

I turned to Grandma and, knowing better than to ask where we were, simply said, "This place is amazing."

She nodded in agreement. "This is the palace of Shushan, in the land of Persia. Can you guess why we are here?" She had that infuriating gleam in her eye, but I wasn't taking the bait this time.

"I have absolutely no idea, but I'm guessing that if I'm patient I'll find out."

Grandma gave me a shrewd look. "Not too thrilled with my guessing games anymore, I see." She sighed theatrically. "Ah, well! It will still be fun to watch your reaction as the events unfold." She gestured for me to walk with her down one of the small pathways.

After turning the bend around a large, ancient-looking olive tree, I spotted a small cluster of women gathered in a corner of the courtyard. They wore floor-length, long-sleeved dresses made from a pretty, lightweight material, which I guessed was a necessity for such a hot climate. Soft veils covered their heads, but I could tell that they all had dark hair.

As we drew nearer, I counted seven women, all standing in a semicircle with their heads bowed, facing the palace wall. It seemed strange, and I wondered what they were doing and why they were all so quiet. I stopped a few feet behind them, but Grandma nudged me forward. There was obviously something I was missing that she wanted me to see.

Feeling a little self-conscious, I slowly crept closer until I was standing right behind one of the women. I fully expected her to sense my presence, turn around, and demand to know what the crazy girl in her pajamas was doing! However, to my great relief, no one moved or acknowledged me, so I held my breath and peered over her shoulder.

To my surprise, I saw, seated on a small bench in the middle of the semicircle of women, another woman. Her head was bent over her clasped hands, and it was obvious that she was in the middle of a fervent prayer. Her eyes were closed with tears flowing freely from them, and from what I could see of her face, her expression was strained and pleading. I realized that the women surrounding her were also praying, and my heart went out to them. I wondered what the cause of their plea could be.

From the fine manner of the woman's dress, I guessed that she was a princess, or maybe even a queen, and that the other women were her servants, but I wasn't able to put the pieces together. I looked at Grandma, and she seemed to read the confusion on my face.

"Are you familiar with the story of Queen Esther?" she asked quietly.

"Is that who this is? I've heard the story before, but it's been a while. I know that there's a book about Esther in the Bible and that she was an important person, but that's all I can remember."

"You're right. The book of Esther is in the Old Testament, and she was a *very* important person. Let me give you a brief account of her story so you'll understand what you're about to see." Grandma's voice took on a narrative tone. "Esther was an orphan. She was raised by her cousin Mordecai, and they were both Jews. The king, of Persia found disfavor with his wife and divorced her. Then he sent out a royal decree seeking for the fairest virgins in the land so that he could choose one to be his new queen. Many people refer to this as the first beauty pageant ever recorded." Grandma chuckled, and I laughed too—it *did* sound a little like the Cinderella story.

She continued. "Many women were chosen from all over the kingdom and brought to the palace for a training of sorts. Esther was among them, and she quickly found favor with the king. I don't think you were able to see her face a moment ago, because if you had, you'd realize that she was uncommonly beautiful."

I glanced back at the group of women with renewed interest. I *hadn't* seen Esther's face clearly, and I was eager to get a better look.

"As you can guess, King Ahasuerus chose Esther for his queen, and he grew to love her. However, Mordecai warned Esther not to reveal to the king that she was Jewish. Mordecai himself worked within the king's household and knew the dangers that would accompany such a revelation.

"The king had appointed a man named Haman to be above all the princes and nobility in his court, and he commanded everyone to show reverence to Haman by bowing to him. But by Jewish standards, bowing to Haman would have been considered an idolatrous act, and so Mordecai refused to bow to him. When confronted by the other servants about the matter, he revealed that he was Jewish.

"Haman was furious at Mordecai's refusal to bow to him, but instead of going after Mordecai, he decided that all of the Jews in the empire should be killed. In a devious manner, he met with the king and led him to believe that the Jews were unruly and had to be exterminated. He offered the king a large amount of money for the royal treasury in order for the deed to be done, and the king agreed. A decree was sent out ruling that on a certain day all Jews— men, women, and even *children*—were to be killed. When Mordecai learned of the decree, he asked Esther to go to the king and reveal that she was a Jew and tell him that if his decree were to be fulfilled, she and all her kindred would die. In a very thought-provoking way, Mordecai posed this question to her: 'Who knoweth whether thou are come to the kingdom for such a time as this?'"

Grandma paused. "Now this may seem like a small thing to

ask—for a wife to talk to her husband—but things were different back then. Entering the court of the king without his invitation was a crime punishable by death. On top of that, Ahasuerus had not sent for Esther in thirty days, which was a sign that she might be losing favor with him. So, Mordecai was asking Esther to take her life in her hands by appearing before the king. She was understandably terrified!"

I raised my eyebrows and shook my head in disbelief, and Grandma nodded solemnly before continuing. "However, instead of refusing, Esther had great courage and faith. She told Mordecai to gather all of the Jews in Shushan and ask them to fast and pray for her, and she and her handmaidens would do the same. At the end of three days, she would go before the king, and in her own words, she said, 'If I perish, I perish.' What you are witnessing, Eliza, is the end of the three days. In a few hours, Esther will go in to the king."

I felt goose bumps on my arms as I looked at the group of women. Now I understood the tortured expression that had been on Esther's face. I couldn't imagine willingly doing something that might mean my own death. I felt sorry for her, but one thought was comforting. "But Grandma, the king doesn't kill her, does he? I think I would have remembered that part of the story if he did. She's going to be okay, right?" I wished that I could remember the details of the account better.

"We'll watch the events as they unfold, but there is a great lesson here I want you to learn. Along with great courage, faith, and obedience, Esther's story teaches a valuable principle—individual worth. Esther could have kept her heritage a secret, and she could have lied if she was ever confronted about it, but she didn't. She was willing to put her life at risk for the sake of others because she recognized that the worth of *each soul* is precious to our Heavenly Father. It was up to her to try to save her people, and she wisely turned to prayer and fasting so that she would be spiritually prepared for the enormously difficult task."

As Grandma spoke, I noticed that the women were beginning to stir. They were finished with their prayers, and the semicircle parted, leaving room for Esther to walk through. She stood, and for the first time, I got a good look at her.

The word that instantly came to my mind was "regal." She was tall and slender, and there was a certain grace in the way she carried herself. Her features were flawless. She had the lovely olive-toned skin and dark hair that the other women had, but her hair had a lustrous shine to it. Her eyes were large and bright from her recent tears, with finely arched eyebrows that framed them perfectly. She had thick eyelashes that I thought existed only on mascara commercials and that made her beauty even more exotic. High cheekbones were in perfect symmetry with her narrow nose, and a rosy, full-lipped mouth completed the masterpiece that was her face. Even by modern standards of beauty, she was stunning, and I could see why the king had chosen her for his bride.

With Esther leading the way, the group of women walked slowly down a path that led to the arched entryway of one of the palace quarters.

"They're going to the House of the Women to dress Esther in her royal apparel before she enters the court of the king. Come, you'll want to see this." Grandma and I walked quickly to catch up with the women before they disappeared through the entrance.

I watched in awe as Esther's handmaidens prepared her to

go before King Ahasuerus. They bathed her from head to foot (Grandma and I toured the lavish rooms during this part, but I did notice the oils and rose petals in the bathing water), then they dressed her in a gorgeous gown made up of yards and yards of burgundy silk. Next came her long, glossy hair. The handmaidens fussed over how to style it, finally pinning it up high on her head and allowing a few loose curls to escape here and there. The effect was very flattering.

I almost didn't want them to cover her hair with the lacy veil, but then I saw the jewels they were bringing out, and I was instantly distracted. An enormous gold necklace was placed around her neck, with matching gold-and-pearl earrings for her ears.

As the final touch, they brought out the royal crown. It was also made of gold and so finely crafted that I wondered how they'd managed to make something so intricate with the limited technology they had back then.

After the crown had been placed on Esther's head, the women stood back to admire their work. The overall effect was overwhelming, and I had to keep myself from bowing. She was a vision of royal magnificence. She was a queen.

One woman brought Esther a mirror; she glanced in it briefly, nodded in approval, and then returned it to her servant. Throughout the entire dressing process, Esther's manner had been as one preparing for the gallows, but I saw her gradually muster her courage.

She turned to each of her servants, hugging them and offering smiles of gratitude and encouragement. It was easy to see that they loved her in return, and it occurred to me that these women must have grown very close in the time they'd been together. It was touching to see their obvious affection and support for each other. They were here for Esther in her hour of need, ready to help in whatever manner they were able to.

Finally, Esther faced the door, signaling that it was time. She took a deep breath, pulled her shoulders back, and with her head held high, she moved forward, prepared to receive her fate.

I had expected to follow behind Esther and her handmaidens as they walked to the court of the king, but before I knew what was happening, Grandma had transported us to a huge, vaulted room. I was about to protest when she explained, "This is the inner court of the king's house. This is where Esther will come before him. I wanted you to see everything that transpires from this vantage point, rather than from behind Esther's escorts. Plus, this gives you a chance to look around at the grandeur of the court before the action starts."

I smiled in understanding and nodded. "Thanks, Grandma. You think of everything, don't you?"

She chuckled. "Well, I don't know about *that*, but I do my best." She pointed to the far end of the room where I saw a man who was clearly the king. Dressed in royal apparel and wearing an enormous crown, he sat on a throne that easily made him a foot taller than any of his servants. Guards and other men in various official-looking clothing flanked either side of the throne. The king seemed engrossed in a conversation with a man on his right.

"Who's that man sitting next to the king?" I asked in a whisper. I guessed he was some sort of noble since his seat was second highest to the king's, and even from where I was, I could see that he fancied himself as a very important person.

Grandma's eyes narrowed. "That is Haman, the wicked man responsible for all of this trouble."

I looked at him in disgust. "How could anyone be so evil as to want to destroy thousands of people—an entire nation—just because of his pride?"

She frowned sadly. "I know. It's difficult for me to understand too. The adversary has been around from the time of Adam, stirring up men's hearts to anger and hatred. It's essentially the opposite of what I told you before—while God values each soul and *all* are precious to Him, Satan seeks to devalue human life and its worth. He can never have a body, so he goes about whispering lies to those who will listen. And, unfortunately, Haman had open ears. He was so prideful and he valued his own life so much that slaughtering thousands of Jews meant nothing if it would soothe his injured feelings."

There was a loud, creaking sound, and I looked over to see the great doors of the court swing open. A sudden hush fell over the room as everyone turned to see who dared enter the court uninvited.

Esther appeared in the doorway, and I could almost feel the shock of the courtiers at her presence. I glanced at the king, and he seemed as stunned as everyone else, though any other feelings he may have had were unreadable in his stoic expression.

Still carrying that aura of calm courage, Esther proceeded to move a few steps further into the room, and then bowed before the king. One of her servants was shaking so badly that I thought the poor girl would faint, but Esther remained calm. All eyes were locked on the queen as she rose from her bow, awaiting whatever decision the king would make. I held my breath.

After a few moments of agonizing silence, the king arose, holding a golden scepter I had not noticed before. He held it out to Esther, and the whole room seemed to melt in a collective sigh.

Esther moved forward gracefully and placed her hand on the top of the scepter, and then she smiled sweetly at the king as he gestured for her to sit on the throne next to him.

Everyone resumed talking, and I blew out my breath. "Whew! That was totally nerve-racking! I was worried there for a second, but everything's okay now, isn't it?" I felt giddy with relief.

"Yes, everything's fine now. With the Lord's help, Esther managed to save her people. There's more to the story, but if you want to find out what happens, you'll have to read the account for yourself." She chuckled. "I was getting a little worried about *you* there for a second, Eliza. You were starting to turn a peculiar shade of purple from holding your breath. I'm sorry to have put you through the suspense, but a good nail-biter is fun to watch once in a while, don't you agree?"

Before I could respond, we were once again transported, and I found myself sitting on the sandy shore of a beautiful beach.

"Whoa, Grandma, a little heads-up next time would be nice. All of this fast change of scenery is giving me motion sickness!" I held a hand up to my forehead to illustrate my point. "What are we doing here? And where exactly *is* here?"

"I know this mode of travel is a little difficult to get used to, but believe me, it saves time," she answered with a smile. "This place doesn't hold any significance, other than its beauty. Just sit back and relax, and we'll have a quick chat before it's time to go."

I was only too happy to oblige. Living in Utah, I rarely got to see the ocean, and it felt wonderful to be so close to the water. I took a deep breath, reveling in the rich, salty smell of the air and the feel of the powder-soft sand enveloping my feet. The sound of the waves was soothing as I watched the sun dip lower and lower on the horizon, leaving behind drifts of pale pink and orange clouds. Palm trees dotted the shoreline, and as I looked around, I realized that we had the beach completely to ourselves.

Grandma seemed thoughtful as she sat beside me. She allowed me a few quiet moments to enjoy the breathtaking scenery before she spoke. "You know, Eliza, the lesson you are learning from this dream is one of the most important lessons of your life. When you study the mortal ministry of the Savior, you realize that He spent much of His time among those who were considered outcasts by their peers. The scribes and Pharisees mocked and scorned Him for associating with the kind of people He did, but of course, that didn't matter to the Lord.

"He is able to look past our exteriors and our flaws and into our hearts. Likewise, He has asked us to do the same. It's human nature to cast a quick judgment on others before we even get to know them. For some reason, most of us have a tendency to want to label others, and more often than not, that label is incorrect. If we could see all of our brothers and sisters as the Lord sees them—as His beloved children—there would be much less evil in the world."

She sighed. "Unfortunately, it seems that sometimes girls can be especially cruel by vocally criticizing others. Tell me, have you ever studied someone's face when they're gossiping?"

I was a bit puzzled by the question. "No, not really. Why?"

"The next time you hear someone gossiping, take a good look at their countenance. It's my personal opinion that when someone is gossiping or making fun of someone else, that person's own appearance becomes a little uglier. I think it is because gossiping, backbiting, and mocking are all things the adversary does, and when we participate in them, it darkens our countenances. Never participate in these things, Eliza. It may seem like a small matter, but the way we treat others in action and word—even if they can't hear us—greatly affects our spiritual growth."

I hung my head a little. Grandma's advice stung because I knew I had been guilty of gossiping on more than one occasion. Jill and I had a tendency to make fun of people (specifically Chelsea) more than we should. I think we mostly did it to try to feel better about ourselves in comparison to Chelsea—and also because she wasn't the easiest person in the world to get along with—but I knew now that I needed to stop.

"Along the lines of not judging others," Grandma continued, "I want to add a word of caution. Sometimes people get so carried away with not wanting others to *think* they're judgmental that they lower their own standards to prove a point. This is not what I'm talking about. If your friends invited you to a party where there would be drinking—which I hope would never happen because you should choose friends with your same standards—it wouldn't be wise to go to the party simply for the sake of proving to your friends that you don't judge them or that you want to be the 'good example.'

"Remember, in order to lift your friends, *you* have to be on higher ground. Stick to your morals, never compromise, and they will respect you for it." Grandma's face brightened. "Now, we're almost finished, but there's one last thing I want to talk about. In what way do you think you could apply the story of Esther in your own life?" she asked.

I thought back on the scenes I'd witnessed and felt a little stumped. Grandma had already pointed out the significance in the story about the worth of souls and of Esther's courage and faith. I knew she was looking for something more, but I wasn't sure what that might be.

"To be honest, Grandma, I think you already covered most of it. I know I can do better in not judging others and things like that, but Esther was a *queen*. She saved the lives of thousands of people. I don't see how that will ever apply to my life."

"It's true that you will probably never be in the position where people's physical lives are in your hands, but you can still be an instrument in helping to save someone spiritually. There are millions of people who are dying in a spiritual sense, and they need someone to help rescue them. The only way to be saved is through the Savior, but you can help them find the path back to Him. You will have opportunities in your life to share your testimony with others, whether by word or by example. I hope that when you are faced with those situations, you won't shrink from them, but will be as Esther was—steadfast and courageous."

Grandma reached into the sand and pulled out a beautiful red seashell. Like the other tokens she had given me, the shell was small and fit easily in the palm of her hand. The shell was perfectly round, and as she placed it in my hand, I noticed a circular pattern that started from its outer edge and continued inward until I could no longer see where it ended.

"Just as the shells of the sea are unique in color and design, each of us is unique. Yet, each and every one of us is precious to our Heavenly Father, and He loves and cares for us individually.

"The circular pattern on this shell seems to continue on forever, and it represents the limitless potential within all of us if we put our trust in the Lord. Never forget your worth, Eliza! Never forget the amazing potential that lies within you, just waiting to be set free! Once you begin to realize the great power that comes from putting your life in the Lord's hands, you'll want to help others realize their true potential also. That's the key to true joy. That's what Heavenly Father wants for you."

I felt the chills on my arms again, and a warm, happy feeling rushed through my body at Grandma's words. I knew what she said was true, and knowing that I was important, *really* important, and loved by Heavenly Father made me feel joyful in a way I couldn't describe.

Suddenly, I wanted everyone to feel as happy as I felt at that moment, and I began to understand what Grandma meant about helping others. I reached over and gave her a hug. "Thank you, Grandma, for everything. I promise I'll do my best to remember all of this and act on it."

She gave me a brilliant smile. "I know you will, sweetheart. I know you will."

I looked again at the tiny shell in my hand and traced its ridges with my finger. Stars were beginning to appear in the sky and I lay back on the sand to enjoy them. The rhythmic sound of the waves combined with the glittering canvas of purple sky above me made me feel drowsy and happy. I struggled to keep my eyelids open, not wanting this blissful moment to end, but after a few minutes, I couldn't resist any longer and I fell into a deep, peaceful sleep.

CHAPTER

eleven

D on't forget the test is tomorrow. It will be a comprehensive test, covering everything we've gone over in the last three weeks."

My stomach fell at Mrs. Bartlett's words. How could the test be tomorrow already? I was in no way prepared for a math exam.

I shoved my calculator and notebook into my bag. With shoulders slouched in defeat, I trudged out the door. As I opened my locker to exchange some books, a folded piece of paper fell at my feet.

In my despair over math, I'd forgotten to look for a note from Jason. He hadn't left one yesterday, and seeing one today made me feel secretly pleased. Texting him yesterday must have done the trick. I liked the way the notes made me feel. It was nice to know that someone thought I was special and took the time to tell me so.

I tried to ignore the gnawing guilt that reminded me I didn't necessarily return his feelings, and unfolded the paper.

Eliza,

The more I try not to think about you, the more I do. I know that I probably shouldn't feel this way for you, but I can't help myself. You have imprisoned me with your charms, and I only hope that someday we'll be able to be together and that I'll be able to tell you in person exactly how I feel. Until then, just know that you are incredible, and someone is thinking of you.

Sincerely,

Your Secret Admirer

I sighed as I placed the note in my bag. Who knew Jason was such a romantic? His feelings ran even deeper than I'd suspected. The floodgate of guilt finally opened, and I felt it washing over me. When I saw Jason's smiling face greeting me from down the hall, I dove in deeper, wanting to drown in it.

I forced a smile as I walked toward him. The look on his face was so enthusiastic that I vowed that I would like him—I *had* to like him—no matter how much my heart told me otherwise. He was too sweet and kind a person to hurt. I refused to break his heart.

When I reached him, he touched my arm affectionately. "Want to eat together today?"

I smiled. "Sure."

We walked down the hall and met up with Jill and Nick, falling into our usual routine—except this time I headed to the pizza line with the guys, dragging Jill along with me. She told me I was crazy to eat so many carbs and fats mere days before prom, but her protesting abruptly stopped when we reached the counter and the full force of the mouthwatering aroma overcame her. I almost laughed at the longing in Jill's eyes as the lunch lady placed the pizza on her tray.

"It's all right, Jill. Don't be so hard on yourself. We were practically starving before, and we both know that a few slices of pizza aren't going to make any difference. Go ahead and enjoy yourself."

She looked at me in shock. "I don't know where this new, crazy Eliza came from, but I like her!" We laughed, and after a stop at the cashier, the four of us headed outside. I was almost through the door when I glanced down the hall and saw Keira Davis sitting in her usual spot on the floor near the bathrooms.

A strong thought came to me to go talk to her, but almost as soon as it came, I pushed it away.

Talk to Keira? Are you kidding me? She was *not* the kind of person I felt like I could strike up a conversation with, and I was sure that she'd remember I was the girl who stepped on her yesterday.

I followed my friends out to the courtyard, and the thought came again. *Go talk to Keira.* It was quiet, but a bit more insistent this time, and I knew it was the Holy Ghost prompting me. I reached into my pocket, wishing the red seashell was there, but I hadn't been able to find it before school this morning. I would have to act without its comforting presence. I closed my eyes for a moment and took a deep breath.

"Hey, guys, I'll be back in a minute, okay?" I stammered. Jill, Nick, and Jason had already sat down at one of the tables, and they looked up at me in surprise.

"Where are you going?" Jill asked suspiciously.

"I'll be right back."

Not wanting to face any more questions, I spun on my heel

and headed for the hall. I couldn't believe my feet were actually moving me toward this total stranger so we could have a conversation. I had no idea what to say to Keira, but I kept moving, trusting the Spirit to guide me. I said a silent prayer before stopping next to Keira with what I hoped was a friendly expression on my face and not one of the sheer panic that I felt.

She was listening to her MP3 player, so it took her a few seconds to notice me. When she finally did look up, her expression was far from inviting. She pulled an earbud from her ear. "Can I help you?"

"Hi. You're Keira, right?" I couldn't believe I'd managed to get the words out.

"Yeah."

"Well, my name's Eliza, and I wondered if you'd mind if . . . if I ate lunch with you today."

She looked at me like I had aliens crawling out of my ears. "Uh, okay. . . . I guess."

I smiled and sat down beside her. "You moved here from back East, right?" She simply nodded and continued to eat her lunch. "How do you like it here?"

She snorted. "I totally hate it."

"Why?"

"Let's just say it's way different from where I came from. I'd go back to Jersey in a heartbeat if my mom would let me." She had an accent like I'd heard in movies, and I enjoyed listening to her talk.

"How come you guys moved out here? Was it for your mom's work or something?" I would have said "parents," but I gathered from her last statement that it was just her and her mom.

Keira seemed to look at me for the first time. I could tell she was trying to figure me out, wondering why a total stranger was asking questions about her life.

"Yeah. My mom works for the government, and she got transferred out here. She thought at first maybe it would only be temporary, but now it looks like they want her here permanently. I'm gonna try and graduate early so I can move back East for college," she said emphatically.

I could only imagine how awful it would be to have to change high schools.

"It would be tough to make a big move like that," I said sympathetically. She shrugged and looked at the ground. "Tell me what it's like in New Jersey," I said, trying to cheer her up. "I've never been farther east than Colorado."

"For real?" Keira looked at me in shock, and then proceeded to tell me all about her life in Jersey. She seemed happy to be talking about her memories there, and I was amazed with how easy the conversation was. I forgot about her nose ring and crazy hair, and I started seeing her personality. She was actually funny, and I liked how animated she was when she talked. I'd never met anyone like her before, and it was refreshing.

We'd been talking for about ten minutes when I sensed someone's shadow over us. I looked up to see Jill trying to hide her shock at seeing me chatting with Keira Davis, the *loner*.

"Hey, Jill, this is Keira." I smiled up at her.

They nodded at each other, each mumbling a "Hi," and then Jill turned to me.

"We were wondering what happened to you. I thought maybe you went to the bathroom, but then I realized you wouldn't have taken your *tray* with you. Are you gonna come back and eat with us?" She cast a furtive glance at Keira.

I caught Jill's look and turned to Keira. "Do you want to eat with us? I want you to meet some of my friends. They're all really cool."

She hesitated. "Nah, that's okay. I'm fine here."

I persisted. "No, really. I want to hear more about what it's like back East." I stood up and smiled as I offered her my hand. I wasn't about to take "no" for an answer. No matter how tough or standoffish a person seemed, I knew no one really wanted to eat lunch alone.

Keira gave me a half smile and took my hand. I turned to Jill and gave her a quick wink. We could read each other so well that I knew she understood the hint, and I was proud of how quickly she responded. She immediately started talking to Keira as though they had been friends forever. That was one thing I admired about Jill; she knew how to strike up an easy conversation.

When we walked into the courtyard, my heart skipped a beat. Jason and Nick were still sitting at our table, but now Luke was sitting with them, too! I tried to tamp down the excitement rising like a volcano in my chest at the sight of him. I was ecstatic that he was back in school today, but then I remembered my recent commitment to like Jason. I did my best to ignore the rapid-fire rate of my heartbeat in my chest as we approached the table.

"Hey, guys, this is Keira. She's gonna eat with us," I said as if it was the most normal thing in the world.

Jill sat down next to Nick and patted the bench beside her, motioning for Keira to join her. I sat on her other side as Jill introduced Nick, Jason, and Luke. Typical of guys, they were only mildly surprised by Keira's presence and readily accepted her into the group.

"I've seen that guy Luke before," Keira whispered to me once the conversations had resumed. "He's a total hottie!" My face must have given away the discomfort I felt at this statement because she quickly added, "Oops! He's not your boyfriend or anything, is he?"

I wish! I smiled and shook my head. "No, I'm going to prom with Jason." The fact that Keira noticed how hot Luke was reminded me how every girl in school had a crush on him—and how I didn't have a chance. But, I reminded myself, none of that mattered now that I was going to like Jason. *Jason, Jason, Jason,* I chanted to myself as if repeating his name in my mind would help me in my new quest.

"Oh, Jason's cute, too. Is *he* your boyfriend?"

"Not really. We're just good friends." I needed to redirect Keira's attention—and fast. "So, do *you* have a boyfriend?"

Her face broke into an instant smile. "Yeah, do you want to see a picture?" She flipped open her cell in lightning speed and showed me the image of a grim-faced guy wearing a sleeveless shirt and backwards baseball cap. If possible, it seemed like he had even *more* piercings than Keira did. "His name's Blake, and we've been together for a year and a half now."

I did my best to look impressed. "Wow, cool. You must miss him a lot."

She nodded and flipped her cell shut. "Yeah, but we text and e-mail all the time so that helps. Mom says I can fly back home this summer to be with him for a few weeks."

Suddenly, I realized how different our lives were: my mom

would drop dead before letting me spend a few weeks alone with a guy.

Keira pointed to someone a few tables away from us. "Do you know that girl over there?" she asked.

"*That* is Princess Chelsea Andrews." Jill's voice dripped with sarcasm as she joined our whispered conversation. It amazed me how she always seemed to tune in whenever Chelsea was mentioned.

Keira raised an eyebrow. "I hope she's not a friend of yours, 'cause she keeps pointing over here and laughing." She shook her head and called Chelsea a bad name under her breath.

Jill snorted and choked on her drink. I had to keep myself from laughing too. Keira looked contrite. "Oh, sorry. I forget Mormons don't say stuff like that. You guys *are* Mormons, right?" she challenged, but as if hoping we'd say no.

Jill seemed taken aback by the question, so I answered with a smile, "Yes, we're Mormons, and, yeah, we try not to swear if we can help it."

Keira nodded. "I thought so. It seems like *everyone* here is, but sometimes it's hard to tell. Our next-door neighbor is Mormon, but he's always out smokin', and he swears all the time!"

I laughed. "Unfortunately, not everyone acts like they should all the time. Sometimes a person may claim to be Mormon, but then they don't live what we're taught, and that can give people the wrong idea about our church. None of us are perfect, but the doctrine of our church is always the same."

"That makes sense. I'm a Catholic, but not super devout, if you know what I mean. Mom and I go to Mass every Christmas Eve and Easter, but that's about it. Your church seems a lot more involved—like you have *way* more rules than my church does." She raised her eyebrows as if to say she thought we were all nuts.

"I can see how it might seem that way, but we call our rules *commandments*—and we aren't forced to follow them. Everyone's free to choose for themselves whether or not they want to obey, but I know that my life is better when I choose to obey the commandments." I paused for a second and then continued hesitantly, "You know, if you ever have questions about our church, I'd be happy to answer them. Maybe that way it won't be so confusing."

Keira smiled ruefully, as if she'd been waiting for me to ask this question. "Thanks, but I already learned a lot about your church from this group of people who introduced themselves to me the first day. It was funny because after I told them I wasn't interested, they totally ignored me." She took in my embarrassed expression and quickly added, "But if I have any questions, I'll let you know, okay?"

I smiled at her and changed the subject. "Cool. So is your school back East going to have a prom?" I wanted to let her know that I still wanted to be her friend whether or not she was interested in the Church.

Jill had remained silent throughout the conversation about the Church, but now she jumped back in, wanting to know more about life in Jersey as well.

The guys had been involved in their own discussion throughout lunch, but now they were quiet and seemed to be listening to Keira, too. I looked up and caught Jason watching me, and I smiled at him, trying hard not to notice Luke sitting next to him.

Luke glanced up and our eyes met, but then he quickly looked back down at his food. Looking at my own tray, I realized that, with all the talking, I'd hardly eaten anything.

I began eating my pizza as quickly as possible while still trying to be discreet in case Luke looked at me again. The bell rang just as I was a few bites away from finishing, so I shoved the rest of the pizza in my mouth and stood up with my tray.

Just then, Chelsea waltzed by with her arm linked to Owen Black. He was a senior and the quarterback for the school football team. She laughed extra loud at something Owen said as she threw a haughty glance at Luke. Then she turned her attention to me.

"Wow, it looks like *someone* was hungry. You're supposed to *eat* it, not *wear* it, silly girl." She trilled with laughter at her own joke, and then Owen joined in as they walked past me.

I felt totally humiliated! What could Chelsea have been talking about? People were looking at me, and I heard more laughter.

"You've got a little sauce on your chin," Keira whispered to me. "Quick, here's a napkin."

I quickly wiped off my face, feeling the intense heat of my blush through the rough paper.

Jill looked at me apologetically. "Don't worry, it wasn't that bad. Chelsea was just being a brat, as usual."

I didn't dare look at Luke, but I could only imagine what he must be thinking. There I'd been, snarfing down my pizza like an ogre and getting sauce all over my face!

I quickly turned to Keira. "Thanks for the napkin. Will you eat with us again tomorrow?"

"You're sure you want me to?"

"We're sure," Jill affirmed as I nodded.

"Okay, then. Thanks." She smiled a little shyly.

"Great! See you tomorrow." I was glad Keira was letting us be her friends, and I was grateful that I'd followed the prompting to talk to her, but I was still mortified by the whole pizza sauce thing and felt like I couldn't get out of there fast enough!

I was dumping my tray in the cafeteria bin when someone caught my arm.

"I didn't get to talk to you much at lunch. Mind if I walk you to your next class?"

I looked into a pair of large, green eyes and said, "Sure, Jason. That would be nice."

CHAPTER

twelve

All through seminary, I tried not to glance at Luke. I was still embarrassed about what had happened at lunch, but I was worried that if I looked at him, I wouldn't be able to think about Jason the way I was trying to. When he had walked me to class after lunch, I'd been extra attentive to him and had smiled at everything he said. Now, if I could only get thoughts of Luke out of my head, I'd be set!

After the final bell rang, I took my time gathering my things. I wanted Luke to have a head start so he wouldn't think I expected him to wait for me like he had last time. I pretended to jot something down in my notebook, waiting until the room was quiet and I was sure everyone had gone.

"See you tomorrow, Eliza," Brother Carlton said.

"Yeah, thanks for class today." I smiled at him as I turned to leave, and then felt the smile freeze on my face. Luke was waiting for me by the door. I felt a mixture of surprise and delight at the sight of him. All thoughts of Jason instantly fled from my mind as I walked toward Luke.

"Not too eager to go home today, huh?" His eyes held that un-bearably charming gleam.

"Oh, yeah, I can't get enough of this place." I smiled, and he laughed as he fell into step beside me. "I heard you were sick yester-day," I said, trying to keep my tone casual. "Are you feeling better?"

Luke seemed surprised and a little happy at my question. He tilted his head and looked at me. "Yeah, I'm feeling a lot better. How did you know I was sick?"

"Jason told me."

His expression fell slightly. "Oh, right. That makes sense." He quickly changed the subject. "So, I didn't realize you were friends with Keira Davis. She seems pretty cool."

"We just became friends today, actually, but she *is* cool. I'm excited to get to know her better." I wondered if he was asking about her because he thought she was cute. A flame of jealousy flickered, but I quickly doused it by telling myself I had no right to feel possessive.

"It was nice that you ate with her. I've seen her eating by her-self in the hall for weeks, and it always made me feel sorry for her."

I cringed guiltily. "I have to admit that was part of the reason I invited her. But now that I'm getting to know her I really *do* want to be friends. I think I've had a tendency to judge people by the way they look, and that's something I want to work on." I hesitated, feeling a little embarrassed. "That probably sounds lame to you, doesn't it?"

He stopped walking and looked me in the eyes. "No. In fact, it sounds incredibly mature. I think that's something we all need to work on." He paused for a moment. "Did you know I'm filling out my mission papers?"

I felt my heart drop into my stomach.

Mission papers? Somehow knowing that he was so close to going on a mission made me realize how much older he was—and how after he graduated I'd probably never see him again. A sudden wave of depression overwhelmed me, but at the same time, I wanted him to know I was proud of him.

"No way! That's awesome! Are you excited?"

"Yeah, I've been waiting for this my whole life. What you said about not judging others made me realize that if I'm going to be a good missionary, that's something I really need to learn. But don't tell anybody about it yet, okay? I want to wait until after I get my call to tell people so I don't have to deal with everyone asking, 'Did you get your call yet?' or 'Where do you hope you'll be going?' and stuff like that." He grinned sheepishly.

I was thrilled that Luke trusted me enough to share this secret with me. I did my best not to read too much into it, but my heart was doing flip-flops! "Of course, I won't tell anyone. Thanks for letting me in on your secret. I'm really excited for you."

He smiled and took a step closer to me. "Eliza, I . . ." he began, but then his expression changed and he stepped back, his smile fading. "I hope you're still planning on coming to our game tomorrow. It would mean a lot to Jason."

At the mention of Jason's name, the spell was broken and I crashed back into reality. I was almost certain Luke had been about to say something else before he changed his mind. Without realizing it, he was toying with my emotions, and I wasn't sure if I could handle it. I wanted to shake him and demand to know why he looked at me the way he sometimes did and why he walked with me after class and told me his secrets. A guy as good-looking as he was couldn't go around messing with people's heads. It wasn't fair!

"Yeah, I'm still planning on it," I answered in a deceivingly careless tone. Suddenly I felt so irritated with him that I wanted to hurt him a little, to make him suffer the way he was making me suffer. I wanted to feel like I was in control of this situation and that the ball was in my court.

"Speaking of Jason," I continued somewhat haughtily, "he's probably looking for me. I'd better go find him." I felt a triumphant thrill at the flicker of disappointment in Luke's eyes.

"Oh . . . right. Well, see you later." He turned around and headed toward the parking lot. As I watched him go, I saw a group of cheerleaders pass him and collectively yell, "Bye, Luke!" He turned and waved at them, and they all giggled.

Ugh! Of all the stupid, crazy, idiotic things to do! I berated myself. The hottest, most popular guy in school had been talking to me, and what did I do? I brushed him off, all because of my silly hurt feelings!

I fumed at myself as I walked toward the school, not noticing Jason until I almost smacked into him.

"Hey, there you are! I keep waiting for you by your locker, but it seems like lately it's been taking you a while to walk from the seminary building to the school." His eyes swept the surrounding area suspiciously as though looking for Luke.

"Oh, sorry about that. The next time you're waiting for me, you should send me a text so I know," I said as nicely as possible but hoping he got the hint that I didn't expect him to wait for me every day. Granted, I was desperately trying to like him as more than a friend, but the thought of having to explain where I was at any given moment annoyed me.

"No problem. I was just wondering, um . . . if you had plans Saturday night after the final concert."

This was my chance to become Jason's girlfriend. If I said "yes" to a date, that would mean we would have gone out three weekends in a row—basically making our relationship official. I wasn't as excited as I hoped I'd be at the idea, but I was determined to stick to the decision I'd made earlier in the day. I was going to make this work!

"No, I don't have any plans. Did you want to do something?" I batted my eyelashes innocently.

He grinned and instantly relaxed. "Actually, yeah. A bunch of us were going to go to Danny's house afterward and watch a movie. His parents have this theater room with a huge screen—it's awesome!"

"Sounds like fun. I'm sure I'll feel like celebrating after my solo is behind me," I added.

Jason put his arm around me. "Believe me, Eliza, you have *nothing* to worry about. You're going to do great! I can't wait to hear you sing."

I let him keep his arm around me for a moment longer than I normally would have, trying to imagine what it would be like to have a boyfriend. After a few seconds, I felt awkward, so I pulled away.

"Well, I guess I'll see you tomorrow. I'm excited to come to your game."

"Yeah, I'm excited for you to be there too." He looked at me meaningfully, and I smiled and then quickly turned toward the safety of the school.

C ∽

"Are you up for some shoe shopping?" I asked Jill as we drove out of the school parking lot.

"Yes! Let's go right now. I want to look at some jewelry too. I can't wait to complete my outfit!" She rubbed her hands together greedily.

After a few minutes of talking about how we were going to do our hair and makeup, Jill turned down the radio. "So, can you believe Chelsea? I *told* you she was going to turn up with a date for prom as soon as Luke wasn't an option."

"Really? Who's she going with?"

She snorted. "Who else? Owen Black, the guy she was draped all over at lunch. I can't believe how tacky she is. It was totally obvious she wanted to make Luke jealous."

I glanced at Jill's expression, and something Grandma had said last night came to my mind. At that moment, Jill's normally beautiful face appeared . . . well, *less flattering* than usual. I remembered my resolve to stop gossiping about Chelsea, and although I felt the urge to bash the girl who'd caused me so much embarrassment, I knew I had to rise above it.

I cleared my throat. "You know, I actually feel kind of sorry for Chelsea," I began somewhat timidly. "Maybe she deals with stuff we don't know about. You never know what makes a person act the way they do."

Jill's face was incredulous. "*What?* Eliza, you can't be serious! The only thing that girl ever has to 'deal with' is which person she's going to make miserable on any given day. She's a total airhead with no heart at all." She threw me an accusing look. "How could you possibly defend her—especially after the way she humiliated you in front of everyone today?"

I stiffened slightly. "I don't know. I just think that maybe we shouldn't gossip about her so much. No matter how awful a person may be, it still doesn't give us the right to judge them when we don't know the full story."

Jill's eyes narrowed. "What is *with* you lately? It's like you're becoming this completely different person all of a sudden. I feel like I hardly even know you anymore." She shook her head. "Like what was the deal inviting Keira Davis to eat lunch with us without even talking to me about it first? We used to tell each other everything, but now I feel like I'm becoming some kind of stranger. And now, on top of everything else, it's like you've gotten all preachy about things." She looked at the floor. "I don't get you, Liza."

I felt anger swelling inside me. "Well, *excuse me* for trying to be a better person. I didn't realize that was some sort of crime. And where do you get off telling me that I'm making you feel like a stranger? How do you think *I've* felt ever since you got together with Nick? It's like you don't have time for me anymore, like I'm just there to fill in the gaps when he's not around. I'm always the third wheel, and I'm sick of it! I feel like I lost my best friend months ago."

Jill tossed her hair. "I thought that *best friends* were supposed to be happy for each other. You're just jealous that I have a boyfriend and you don't." She folded her arms crossly. "Just take me home. I don't feel like shopping anymore."

"Me neither," I snapped back, tears welling in my eyes. I pulled a U-turn at the next intersection and lowered my foot on the pedal, blazing past my typically moderate speed.

We both fell silent, but Jill flipped open her cell and texted the entire way home. I knew she was texting Nick—probably telling him all about our fight. I couldn't believe she could be so heartless! This was the first time I'd opened up and told her how much it had affected me when she got a boyfriend, and instead of being sympathetic, she'd only made me feel worse. Admittedly, I hadn't chosen the best time to express my feelings, and I probably could have done it in a more mature way—but still!

I pulled into Jill's driveway. Jill threw open the door and slammed it behind her. She ran to her house, and she didn't look back.

"What's the matter, honey?" At the sound of Mom's soothing voice, I finally broke down and cried. She put her arms around me, stroking my back and waiting until my sobs slowed enough that she could understand what I was saying.

"Jill and I had a fight." I sniffed and wiped at my eyes. "A really bad one."

"Oh, sweetie, I'm so sorry." Mom kept her arm around me but led me to the living room sofa. "Do you want to talk about it?"

"No, not really. She just said some things that really hurt my feelings, and then I . . . I said some things I probably shouldn't have either."

"That's too bad, but you know we all have fights now and then, especially with the people we're closest to. Why don't you give it a little time? You'll probably feel better in a few hours. Then maybe you'll feel like apologizing, and I bet she will too."

"Thanks, Mom. You're probably right." My breathing

returned to normal, and I wiped the remaining tears from my eyes. Mom smiled at me and stood up to leave, but just then Courtney and Alexis came into the room.

"What's wrong with you?" Courtney asked in a flippant tone. I noticed both she and Alexis were wearing black fingernail polish and, for some reason, that bothered me more than Courtney's attitude. Whatever happened to the sweet pink and red colors I used to paint her nails with?

"Oh, nothing. She just didn't have a good day, that's all." Mom winked at me, reminding me a lot of Grandma. "Don't forget about the activity tonight, girls. And, Alexis, you know you're welcome to come." She smiled and left the room.

Courtney looked at Alexis apologetically. "Sorry, I forgot it was tonight. Do you want to come?"

Alexis looked annoyed. "No, thanks. Let's watch TV until you have to go."

Courtney turned on the TV, and Alexis picked a show to watch.

I felt a renewed dislike for Alexis. I couldn't believe Mom let Courtney hang out with her. Judging by Courtney's drastic changes the past few months, Alexis obviously wasn't the best influence. She came from a family that I hadn't heard good things about. Her older brother was a junior at my school, and everyone knew he cut class all the time to go drinking. I thought about saying something to Mom, but I figured she already had a pretty good idea of Alexis's background.

Even knowing about Alexis's family, though, Mom always invited Alexis to join us for family prayer or scripture study if she was around (which was almost always), and more than once I'd heard her invite Alexis to church or to a Young Women activity, but she always refused.

I sighed and walked into the kitchen, hoping to grab a quick snack before heading to my room. To my surprise, I saw Mom bent over the table, working on something. I moved closer to get a better view and had to suppress my gasp. She held a hot glue gun in one hand and a handful of seashells in the other, which she was methodically gluing onto a small frame. Small piles of shells littered the table, and I immediately spotted the red shell from my dream. I'd spent precious snooze-button time this morning rummaging around in the attic looking for this shell, and here it was on our kitchen table!

Without thinking, I maneuvered around Mom and snatched up the shell as if afraid it would run away.

"Sorry for the mess," Mom spoke without looking up from her frame. "I'm redecorating the bathroom with a beach theme, and I remembered I had all of these shells I could use."

"Huh," I responded vaguely as my gaze remained transfixed on the circular pattern of the shell. I still couldn't believe I was finding these objects from my dreams—it was too bizarre! After I hadn't found the shell this morning, I'd worried that maybe there wasn't one, but here it was! I almost didn't dare ask the question on my mind, but I couldn't resist. "Where did all of these shells come from?"

Mom straightened up and sighed. "Oh, all over the place. I've collected them from different vacations we've been on, and some I think I got from my mom, who probably got them from her mom."

"Some of these might have been Great-grandma's?"

She nodded. "I'm sure of it. Grandma collected lots of things:

shells, rocks, postage stamps. It was sort of a hobby of hers." She smiled at me. "It seems like you've had a lot of questions about your great-grandma lately; I'm glad you're taking an interest in her life."

If you only knew! I tried my best to sound casual. "Well, I *am* her namesake, after all." I turned my attention to the seashell in my hand. "This red shell is kind of unique. Do you mind if I keep it?"

"Sure, honey." Mom leaned back over the frame and didn't bother to look up as she responded.

"Thanks!" I answered with more enthusiasm than I'd intended, but I was excited to have collected one more "value token."

I went back into the living room to get my backpack and heard Alexis and Courtney laughing at their TV show. Alexis's laugh annoyed me and I frowned.

I marched back into the kitchen. "Don't you think Alexis spends a little too much time over here, Mom?" I said in a somewhat huffy tone. "She's practically a permanent fixture on our couch."

Mom looked up in surprise. "That's not very kind, Eliza. Alexis's mother has to work long shifts at the hospital, and I told her that Lexi's welcome here anytime. I hope you'll try to make her feel as comfortable as possible when she's in our home. It isn't easy for her to have both of her parents working so much."

I felt for the seashell in my pocket and nodded somewhat contritely. Mom understood more about individual worth than I did, because apparently she saw something in Alexis that I couldn't.

⊂✄

A few minutes before it was time to leave for Mutual I sent Jill a text. Mom had been right; I was feeling better, and I wanted to apologize.

Me: Sorry about the things I said. I hate it when we fight. Forgive me? Are you coming to Mutual?

Jill: Forgot about Mutual. @ the mall w/Nick. Have fun.

I snapped my phone shut and tried to ignore the hurt that made my throat feel tight. Mom walked into the kitchen and saw me slumped over, staring at my phone on the table.

"What happened?" She sat down next to me, ready to offer comfort if I needed it.

"I sent Jill a text and apologized, but I don't think she's over it yet."

"Give her some time. I'm sure by tomorrow everything will be back to normal. Do you think she'll be at the activity tonight? It's always nicer to apologize in person when you can."

"No, she's not coming. I hope you're right about it being better tomorrow, because it's not like her to stay mad for long," I said, frowning.

Mom nodded. "Are you ready to go?"

"Yeah." I hesitated. "Mom, do you think after Mutual you could come with me to the mall to pick out some shoes for my dress?"

She looked ecstatic, but I could tell she was trying not to show how much she enjoyed the idea. "Of course, dear. But are you sure you don't want to wait and go with Jill?"

"I'm pretty sure she already went shopping without me." I didn't want Mom to feel like she was my second choice so I added, "Besides, it would be nice to have your opinion."

She beamed. "Well then, I'm glad our activity is a short one tonight. Let's go!"

༄

The cultural hall was filled with quilting frames and chatting girls. For the activity, we were tying quilts to give to a local women's shelter.

The other girls were already seated at their various quilts and were mostly clustered in groups of friends. I had been busy helping Mom cut yarn, but now that we were finished, I was ready to find a quilt and start tying. I scanned the room and felt another pang of sadness that Jill hadn't come. She and I always saved each other a seat, and it was nice having my best friend in the ward because then I never felt left out.

There was an empty spot by Courtney, but after the way she'd been acting lately, I decided it was better to steer clear of her.

I noticed a quilt in the back corner with only two people working on it: a Mia Maid leader and Sierra Holbrook. It was clearly the "outcast" table. The fabric wasn't as cute as the other quilts, and seeing Sierra sitting there, with only a dutiful leader at her side, was enough to break my heart. I didn't need to touch the shell in my pocket to know what I should do. I walked over to the table in the corner. "Mind if I work on this one with you guys?"

Sister Allen looked up at me and smiled. "That would be great, Eliza! Pull up a chair."

I chose a spot across from Sierra so I could talk to her more easily, and after I'd gotten into the groove of tying the yarn a few times, I asked her, "So, Sierra, are you excited for school to be out?"

She peeked at me through the tangle of brown hair covering her glasses, then quickly looked back down at the quilt and gave a slight nod.

Hmm, this is going to be harder than I thought. I tried a new tactic by asking a question that was not a "yes" or "no" answer.

"What's your favorite subject?"

Again she peeked at me shyly, her expression a blend of confusion and curiosity. I wondered how long it had been since someone her age had taken an interest in her. After a long pause, I decided she probably wasn't going to answer, and then, ever so softly, I heard her reply.

"My f-f-favorite subject is English."

"Really? Mine too! You're in ninth grade, right? Who's your English teacher?"

"Ms. Carmichael."

"No way! I had her for English, and she was awesome. I really loved that class." I was so happy to have gotten a response from her, and I wanted to keep the conversation going. "What book are you guys reading right now?"

"We're r-r-reading excerpts from *Romeo and Juliet*." Her answers were still quiet, but I could see she was letting her guard down. From there, our conversation took off, and we talked almost nonstop until the activity was over.

I noticed that the more comfortable Sierra got, the less she stuttered, and after a while, I didn't even notice it anymore. I also realized that behind that mask of dirty hair, she had very pretty features. She possessed a sweet personality, and I found myself hoping that we would become friends.

As we folded the quilt and packed up the frame, Sierra looked at me and said, "Thanks for talking to me and not making fun of my s-s-stutter."

I gave her a big smile. "No, thanks for letting *me* sit by *you*. I'm glad I got to know you better—and good luck with that essay you were telling me about."

She smiled back, and it was the first smile I'd ever seen on her face. The glow seemed to melt the unhappy, pinched look she usually wore, and I knew then that she definitely *was* a pretty girl just waiting to blossom.

Sister Allen caught my eye and winked appreciatively. I smiled back, but felt that the wink wasn't necessary, because I'd enjoyed talking to Sierra. Admittedly, I'd initially sat by her out of pity, but just like with Keira, now that I'd gotten to know her, I really *did* want to become friends. It was amazing the things you learned about people when you just took the time to talk to them.

❦

I lay in bed that night, staring at my new dress hanging on the closet door. It was dazzling, and Mom and I had found the perfect pair of black velvet heels to go with it. I daydreamed about twirling on the dance floor, my arms around the neck of my handsome date who was wearing a tuxedo. I imagined him holding me tight and sweeping me off to the garden to confess his love for me! I replayed the scene over and over again, but the problem was, every time I tried to imagine Jason, he somehow morphed into someone else—someone with dark hair and smoldering eyes. I couldn't stand it anymore and forced myself out of my dreams and back to reality.

Sighing, I flipped open my cell phone, but there was *still* no message from Jill. I set the phone to silent mode and placed it in my nightstand alongside the precious seashell. Despite my fight with Jill, it had been a satisfying day overall. I felt like I'd learned a lot about individual worth, and I was excited to tell Grandma all about it.

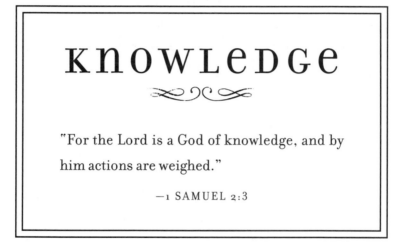

knowledge

"For the Lord is a God of knowledge, and by him actions are weighed."

—1 SAMUEL 2:3

CHAPTER

I felt like I was finally growing accustomed to Grandma's spo-
radic mode of travel. We stood in the hallway of a dank and
dingy building. I immediately recognized that this was the most
modern time period of all the places we'd visited so far, but judging by the furnishings and décor, I knew that it wasn't present day.

There were several rooms lining the hallway with various
noises emitting from them, mostly of children—and *unhappy* children from the sounds of it. I could hear a great deal of coughing
and crying. The overall atmosphere was extremely depressing.

"As you have probably already deduced, Eliza, tonight we will
be focusing on the value of knowledge. This is the almshouse of
Tewksbury, Massachusetts. The year is 1877, and we are here to
observe the remarkable life of Anne Sullivan. Does that name
mean anything to you?"

I looked at Grandma in surprise. "I don't believe it! You actually revealed to me all the facts about when, where, and *why* we're
here. What happened to all of the guessing games?"

Grandma sniffed. "I gathered from our last experience that
you weren't enjoying my little games, so I decided to spare you this

time. But I could always start them up again on our next outing if you'd like." She looked at me with hopeful eyes, and I was tempted to relent, but then I realized that two could play at this game.

"Well, we'll see. To answer your last question, no, I don't know who Anne Sullivan was. And what's an 'almshouse'?"

"Another word for it would be a poorhouse, where the homeless or needy were cared for. Anne's childhood was an extremely sad one. Her parents were poor Irish immigrants. Her father was an alcoholic, and shortly after her mother died from tuberculosis, he abandoned his children. Anne was only nine years old at the time. Anne's sister Mary was sent to live with her aunt, and Anne never saw her again. Anne and her brother Jimmie were sent to this almshouse, but due to complications from a tubercular hip, Jimmie died shortly after their arrival." I made a small, shocked sound, and Grandma nodded sadly. "And as if the weight of grief and loneliness was not enough, Anne was nearly blind due to an untreated bacterial eye infection."

As if on cue, a little girl emerged from the room near where we stood. Her ragged dress was hardly sufficient for the cold temperature of the building. She held a cane in one hand, and with the other, she touched the wall as she guided herself down the vacant hallway. The scene was so pitiful that tears instantly welled in my eyes.

"Oh, Grandma, this is awful. I never realized there could be such suffering in the world—and for a little child! How could she live under these conditions? Please tell me the rest of her story is happier!" I pleaded.

Grandma nodded. "Twice Anne underwent eye operations while staying at the almshouse, both of which were unsuccessful—leaving her already wounded soul even more broken and depressed." I groaned and covered my face with my hands, so she hurried on. "Then something happened that changed her life. After making a direct appeal to a state official who came to inspect the almshouse, Anne was given permission to attend the Perkins School for the Blind in Boston."

The scene before us changed, and we were in a clean, brightly lit classroom. I recognized Anne, now a young woman, sitting in the front desk of the class. I smiled as I saw how content she looked sitting there, completely engrossed in her studies.

"While at Perkins, Anne learned to read and write. She also learned sign language. Little did she know how vital that skill was going to be in her life . . . but we'll get to that later." Grandma winked conspiratorially. "Happily, also during her time at Perkins, Anne underwent a series of operations that almost completely restored her sight. She graduated valedictorian of her class in 1886, and the knowledge she had obtained opened the door for a better life than she'd ever dreamed possible."

I sighed in relief. "This is much better, thank you. What an incredible story! Imagine doing so well in school with hardly being able to see anything. It makes me realize how much I take for granted. I should be getting straight A's!"

Grandma laughed. "I'm glad you're learning from this so quickly, but there's more to the story."

Once again, the scene before us changed. We were standing in the garden near two people who were sitting on wrought iron lawn chairs. I immediately recognized Anne; she was wearing a lovely white dress, and her hair was pinned up in a flattering fashion.

Beside her sat a young girl who was holding Anne's hand, and Anne was speaking to her while tracing on her palm.

"Does the name Helen Keller ring a bell?" Grandma asked. The look on her face told me she'd be extremely disappointed if I didn't know the answer, so I was grateful that I'd paid attention in history class.

"Yes, it *does*," I replied confidently. "She was the woman who was deaf and blind, but she still accomplished a lot in her life. I think she even graduated from college, didn't she?" I paused as I began to put everything together. "Wait, this all makes sense now!"

Grandma seemed pleased. "You're absolutely right! Shortly after Anne graduated from Perkins, she received an offer to work for the Keller family as tutor for one of their daughters, Helen.

"As I said before, Anne's previous training in sign language was an extremely useful tool in teaching Helen to communicate. The two women became lifelong friends and companions. Anne even accompanied Helen to Radcliffe College and attended every class with her, spelling into her hand each lecture and assignment. When Helen graduated with a Bachelor of Arts degree, it was a huge accomplishment for both women. Although Anne didn't receive a degree, she had *still* received a college education, and much later in her life, both she and Helen were awarded honorary degrees from the Temple University of Philadelphia."

Grandma smiled. "So you see, knowledge was the key that unlocked a lifetime of wonderful achievements for Anne. She could easily have chosen to give in to her difficult circumstances as a young girl—I daresay many people would have in her situation. She could have lived a life in the slums as her parents had before her—but she never gave up! Although she had no one but herself to turn to for encouragement, she took hold of every opportunity she had to learn. And then she used that knowledge to help herself and others."

Anne's story gave me the chills. The woman who sat before me had lived an incredible life and had overcome unbelievable trials! I'd always known that a good education was important, but until now, I'd never fully appreciated just how *much* it could impact a person's life.

"I'm so glad her story had a happy ending. I can't believe I'd never heard of her before! I mean, I'm sure her name was mentioned when we learned about Helen Keller, but I guess I wasn't paying very close attention." I blushed. "But I promise, Grandma, I'm going to take my education more seriously from now on! I get decent grades, but I know I could spend more time studying than I do. I want to go to college."

Grandma beamed. "That's wonderful, Eliza! In my opinion, one can never have enough education. Obtaining knowledge is a gift, and it's a lifelong process. However, it's not just *secular* knowledge I wanted to talk about tonight. I have a surprise for you."

She winked mischievously, and before I knew it, the garden disappeared and we were standing in a church. The wooden pews were closer together than they were in our chapel back home. It seemed that every possible square inch of space was filled—and all with women in bonnets.

"All right," Grandma continued casually, as if we hadn't just time-morphed. "Please humor me and tell me if you can guess why we're here. I'll give you a few hints. We're in Utah, and these are all Latter-day Saint women." She pointed to the front of the room. "The woman standing at the podium is the reason we're here. And I'm *her* namesake."

I looked around the stuffy, crowded chapel at the women gathered. They were dressed in what I would describe as pioneer clothes: long-sleeved dresses and bonnets. Many were using fans to combat the oppressive heat in the room, but all were paying close attention to the woman who was speaking at the front.

As with the other dreams I'd had with Grandma, I couldn't hear what the woman was saying, so I studied her appearance. She was small and somewhat frail-looking, but I could see she took great care of her appearance. Her hair was arranged tidily under a crisp cap of white lace. From what I could see of her dress, it was nicely designed, and she wore a pretty gold chain around her neck. Her face was fairly stern-looking as she spoke, but I could see that she carried herself with a grace and dignity that the other women admired and respected.

"Well, you didn't give me a whole lot to go on," I said, looking at Grandma pointedly, "but I'm going to guess that this is a Relief Society meeting." I waited for confirmation from Grandma, and after she nodded, I continued. "And since you're her namesake . . . I'm going to guess that she is Eliza R. Snow."

"Oh, I think I made it too easy for you!" Grandma said with a smile. "You are exactly right, my dear. Serving under Brigham Young, Eliza R. Snow was called to be the second Relief Society president of the Church, and believe you me, this was no easy task!

"Eliza had been the secretary in the first Relief Society presidency, but the Society dispersed after Joseph Smith's martyrdom. Then, several years after the Saints gathered in Utah, the Relief Society was reorganized. It was Eliza's responsibility to reignite the flame of sisterhood in the hearts of the women, and she took that duty seriously. She visited many wards, testifying of the Prophet Joseph and of the importance of the Relief Society program.

"Eliza possessed an incredible intellect concerning things both secular and spiritual. Without a strong foundation of gospel knowledge, she couldn't have done what she did—but Eliza was prepared. She had an understanding of the scriptures and a love of the words of the prophets, so she was ready for this monumental calling when it came.

"Though she'd seen her fair share of trials, Eliza remained steadfast and continually applied her knowledge in the service of others. She had a gift for writing, and she made many great contributions to the Church, including writing the lyrics of some of our most cherished hymns. Something else you might be interested to know is that Eliza's younger brother, Lorenzo Snow, was eventually called as the fifth president of the Church."

This was all new information to me, and I must have looked sufficiently impressed, because Grandma smiled as she continued.

"I've always been proud to have been named after such an elect lady. I hope that after learning more about her, you will feel the same way too."

I looked up at Sister Snow with renewed respect and *did* feel a sense of pride in sharing the same name. "That's really cool, Grandma. I never knew you were named after Eliza Snow. And I am grateful I was named after *both* of you."

Grandma and I smiled at each other, and then she held out her hand to me. In her palm was a key. It looked both fancy and ancient—the kind of key designed to open a box of treasure. Its surface was a tarnished green color, and I held my breath as Grandma placed it in my hand.

"Remember that knowledge, of things both secular and spiritual, is the key that will open powerful doors in your life. It is a gift, and something you must always treasure."

I wanted to know where the key had come from and, more important, where it could be *found*.

"Grandma, this is awesome, and it would sure help me out if you'd tell me where to find it after I wake up. I've almost been late for school every morning looking for these objects—and being late will definitely affect my ability to obtain the amount of *knowledge* that I need." I smiled coyly, feeling proud of myself for coming up with such a convincing argument.

With an impish expression, Grandma returned my smile. "Oh, Eliza, if I just *gave* you the information you needed, where would be the fun in that? Besides, while searching for these tokens, you're learning another valuable lesson—that good things are worth *working* for."

Her eyes twinkled as my face quickly dipped into a pout. "But, but that's not—" I was about to say "fair," but everything around me was fading, and I knew that the dream was ending.

CHAPTER
fourteen

I awoke with a frown on my face. *Would it have been so hard for her to have given me a little clue—one tiny tidbit to point me in the right direction?* I sighed in frustration as I rolled over to look at my alarm clock. To my surprise, I still had twenty minutes until my alarm went off. Normally I would have smiled at my good fortune and rolled over to catch some precious extra sleep, but with a painful twinge, I realized that I'd probably awoken early for a reason. "Getting up earlier was *not* what I had in mind when I asked for help, Grandma," I grumbled.

Resentfully, I slid out of my warm bed and tiptoed down the hall toward the attic. Where was I going to find the key? I'd searched through all of Grandma's stuff several times already looking for the other tokens, and I'd never seen any keys.

I turned on the light and systematically began searching through the dresser drawers again. I took out all of the clothes and the music box and set them on the floor. No key. I went through some bags of old souvenirs Mom told me had belonged to Grandma, but with no luck. I stared at Grandma's photograph hopelessly, wishing a small key would suddenly appear on the faded print.

"You and your silly games!" I scowled at her. My shoulders drooped as I realized I would have to risk Mom's suspicion and ask if she knew anything about the key.

I began piling the clothes back into the drawers, but when I reached down to replace the music box, I noticed something—the music box had a keyhole! I'd been so preoccupied with what was *in* the box that I'd never taken much time to notice the outside. The lid wasn't locked, but if there was a keyhole, then it was reasonable to believe that there was also a key!

I dropped to my knees and lifted the music box onto my lap so I could take a closer look. Something on the bottom of the box brushed against my index finger—something that felt like metal! I lifted the box above my head, and my eyes widened. There it was, taped to the bottom of the box! The tarnished green key looked exactly as it had in my dream. I removed it and jumped up excitedly, waving the key in front of Grandma's picture.

"*Yes!* Who's the smart one now? Uh-huh, that's right—it's *me!*" I did a little victory dance, and then all at once I remembered something and stopped cold in my tracks. In thinking about the key and knowledge it suddenly hit me—*my math test!*

℅⸢

The pencil was slippery in my profusely sweating palm. The overwhelming sense of being in over my head weighed me down like an anvil. I couldn't believe I'd forgotten about my math test! I'd been so completely unprepared for it that I must have blocked it from my mind as a mode of self-defense.

All around me people were frantically scribbling down answers. I envied them. At least *they* had some sense of direction for how to work out these impossible problems! The test consisted of eight equations, and the blank piece of paper in front of me combined with the ever-ticking clock on the wall were constant reminders of how desperately I needed help.

But how? The figures on the test page looked like meaningless, archaic symbols. My mind felt numb, and with a sad sort of irony, I felt the tiny metal key in my pocket.

So much for my goal to excel in knowledge, I thought bitterly. I was going to fail this test, and consequently, this class. It would be a horrible blow to my GPA and would definitely jeopardize the possibility of my making the honor roll this term.

But maybe there's another way. The thought crept into my mind, and I allowed it to linger. I was so desperate that I was willing to resort to anything.

I looked over at Brad Collins. Brad was the brainiac of the class, and everyone knew that he willingly gave out his cell number to text answers to the tests we had. I'd often wondered why he did this, but had come to the conclusion that it was for popularity points. Many of the "cool kids" sucked up to him so he would help them out on test day. I had been ashamed when I'd entered his number in my cell, telling myself I'd never use it, but now I was glad I had it handy. I'd already noticed a few people were using his "help" by the way they sat in their chairs. Hiding a cell phone from a teacher was something we were all experts at. A small voice inside told me that what I was about to do was cheating and it was wrong, but I ignored it, rationalizing that everybody cheated once in a while.

I sent a message off to Brad, and moments later received eight texts with eight answers. As a precaution—and probably to ease his conscience—Brad suggested that I try to work out the problems by myself first, and also that I should get at least one of the answers wrong so the teacher wouldn't get suspicious.

After knowing what the answers were, I worked backward and was able to show the work on my paper. Two of the answers were tricky though, and I still couldn't figure out how he'd come up with the results he did, so I fudged on those and decided to accept the loss. A passing grade was all I was hoping for, after all. I sent Brad a text thanking him for his help, and I tried to ignore the sick feeling I felt at the smiley face he sent in reply.

The bell rang and I handed in my test, but that sick feeling followed me out of the classroom and down the hall. No matter how much I tried to ignore it, I knew I'd done something wrong. The key in my pocket felt like it weighed a ton. I wished I could turn back the clock and hand in a blank sheet of paper instead of the one I'd covered with someone else's work. Failing the test couldn't possibly have made me feel as bad as cheating had, no matter how much I rationalized otherwise.

Lunch was pretty quiet. Jill was barely civil to me, and it was clear something was still wrong between us. I'd tried apologizing again on the way to school this morning, but she'd just brushed me off and told me not to worry about it. I wished she would just yell at me or completely ignore me, because this false pretense that everything was fine was driving me crazy.

Keira sat with us again, and I was extremely grateful for her company. Once she got talking, she was able to fill the gaping void that Jill's bad mood created, and she also helped distract me from the gnawing guilt I was still experiencing over the test.

Jason and Nick ate with us too, but Luke sat at another table with some seniors I didn't know. My mind was so preoccupied by what I'd done in math that I hardly glanced at him more than once.

During choir and biology, I was distracted enough that I almost forgot about the test, but as soon as I walked into the seminary building it all came rushing back to me. The pictures on the walls of the Savior and the prophet seemed to sear my conscience, so I looked at the floor until I found my seat.

A substitute teacher came in and announced that Brother Carlton was absent today and that we would be watching a seminary video. Everyone brightened at this announcement, and I even heard a few quiet cheers. Watching a movie in class always seemed like "time off" from school, which was something we all looked forward to.

I was beginning to feel unusually tired, so as the movie started I laid my head down on the desk, and within moments I was in a deep sleep.

CHOICE AND ACCOUNTABILITY

"Wherefore, men are free according to the flesh; and all things are given them which are expedient unto man. And they are free to choose liberty and eternal life, through the great Mediator of all men, or to choose captivity and death, according to the captivity and power of the devil; for he seeketh that all men might be miserable like unto himself."

—2 NEPHI 2:27

CHaPTer

fifteen

I bet you're surprised to see me here. I must admit, I'm a little surprised myself." Grandma's face gazed at me with an inquisitive expression. "It seems the next lesson is needed sooner rather than later—and I think you know why."

I hung my head and scuffed my shoe on the ground, noticing as I did that I was wearing clothes in my dream and not pajamas. And instead of being in my bedroom, we stood in an empty classroom in what I assumed was the seminary building.

"Yeah, I think I do. You taught me about the importance of knowledge last night, and I totally blew it at the first opportunity." I looked at her in remorse. "The thing is, I was so busy yesterday that I completely forgot about the math test, and if I'd failed, it really would have affected my grades, maybe even my chances of going to college. So . . . I . . . cheated. I didn't know what else to do!" My chin began to quiver.

Grandma looked me in the eyes. "Eliza, you know that honesty is *always* the best policy. I understand that you were feeling a considerable amount of stress and that you acted in a moment of desperation, but that still doesn't change the fact that you made a mistake. Lying is a sin, no matter how much you try to candy coat it." She must have seen my anguished expression, because she softened her tone. "Regardless of how much we strive to justify our actions, there is a consequence to everything we do and every choice we make—good or bad. I'm afraid I'll have to illustrate this point, but let me warn you, this story is not a pleasant one."

I winced at Grandma's tone, but I didn't have long to wonder why she sounded that way.

Suddenly, we were standing in an ancient-looking bedchamber. It was dark and musty. I wanted to turn on a light to dispel the gloom, but the only light source available was a pathetic, flickering candle on a small table. A man was sitting on the edge of what looked to be his bed. He had long hair and a full beard, and his clothing was strange and robe-like. His head was bent, and his entire focus seemed to be directed toward the object he held in his hands. As we drew closer, I saw that the object was a crown. The man stared at it with an expression that was almost frightening. The longing and desperation was clear on his haggard face. I felt cold chills run down my spine, and I stepped back as my mind raced to place who this guy was and why I was getting such a creepy vibe from him.

I was about to ask Grandma to give me a hint, when the door to the room opened. It must have been nighttime, because there didn't seem to be any more light outside the room than inside it, but in the doorframe I could see the silhouette of a woman.

She stepped into the room, and after glancing at the man, she quickly rushed to his side. As her face caught the candlelight, I noticed that she was yet *another* beautiful woman. She was young and wore elegant silk robes. Her long, dark hair flowed about her shoulders.

However, when I looked closely at her, I noticed there was something different about her. Yes, she had striking features, and I was sure she would stand out in any room, but she was unlike the other women we had visited before. Where *their* beauty had seemed to radiate from the inside out, this woman seemed cold and almost cruel, causing my "creepy meter" to go up a few notches. She reminded me of those scary-looking supermodels you sometimes see on the pages of magazines. As stunning as they are, somehow you can just tell by looking at them that you'd never want to be in the same room with them—much less be friends with them.

I watched as the woman sat next to the man and stroked his arm and made a general fuss over him. Her expression appeared to be sympathetic, but in an over-the-top way that made you feel like it wasn't authentic. Although her actions were soft, her eyes glinted with a cunning, devilish gleam.

I shivered and turned to Grandma, who was looking at the couple with unmasked revulsion on her face.

"I'll make this as brief as possible, Eliza. I don't want us to be in this place any longer than we have to, so I'll dispense with the guessing games."

My curiosity was completely piqued by now; I'd never seen Grandma this serious before. "This man's name was Jared. His account is in the Book of Mormon, in the book of Ether. Let me clarify that he is *not* to be confused with the righteous Jared of the same book—the one with the famous brother. This Jared came along much later, and he was wicked to the core. The young woman sitting beside him is his daughter, and it's her story that we're here to discuss. To spare you from witnessing the horrific events that unfold in her life, this is the only scene we'll see, but I'll tell you her story.

"Jared was the son of Omer, a righteous king. He was jealous of his father's position, so he gathered a following and overthrew his father, putting him in captivity, and taking the throne for himself. While Omer was in captivity, he had two sons who became angry at what their brother, Jared, had done. They formed their own army and were successful in overthrowing Jared and reestablishing Omer in his rightful place as king.

"Jared was extremely bitter and sorrowful over his defeat. He'd had his heart set on ruling as king, and he was hungry for power. Which brings us to the scene before you. He had a cunning daughter who also thirsted for power and wanted to see her father returned to the throne. After all, if he was king then that would make her a princess. She'd already had a taste of the royal lifestyle and she craved more. So she came up with a plan and told it to her father. Listen."

For the first time in any of the dreams, I was able to hear exactly what the woman was saying. "Whereby hath my father so much sorrow?" she asked. "Hath he not read the record which our fathers brought across the great deep? Behold, is there not an account concerning them of old, that they by their secret plans did obtain kingdoms and great glory?

"And now, therefore, let my father send for Akish, the son of Kimnor; and behold, I am fair, and I will dance before him, and I will please him, that he will desire me to wife; wherefore if he shall desire of thee that ye shall give unto him me to wife, then shall ye say: I will give her if ye will bring unto me the head of my father, the king."

Grandma turned to me. "Did you catch all of that?" she whispered.

"I think so, but I hope I'm wrong. Did she just tell her dad that she wanted the head of her grandfather as a *wedding present?*" I whispered back, completely appalled.

"Yes, revolting as it is, you heard that part right. But there's something even more dangerous she's putting into motion here. Did you hear her talk about the 'secret plans of old'?"

I nodded, my eyes wide with horror as I contemplated how evil someone would have to be to come up with such a terrible plan.

"Those are the secret combinations you've heard and read about in the Book of Mormon. As the prophet Moroni explains, these combinations were what ultimately brought about the destruction of the entire Jaredite nation. They were works of darkness and authored by the very devil himself. Time and time again in the Book of Mormon we read of civilizations that were utterly wiped out because of these combinations. So you see, this woman was largely responsible for the destruction of many thousands, if not millions, of souls. She may not have been the one who actually did the murdering, but she made the choice to uncover the oaths and works of darkness and to put the idea into her father's head."

My mouth hung open in shock. "So did it happen? Did Akish kill Omer? Did Jared become king again?"

"You'll have to read the account in Ether for the full story, but I'll summarize a little to demonstrate the consequence of the actions of the daughter of Jared. In short, almost every part of her plan was put into action, except the Lord intervened and warned

Omer in a dream that Akish sought his life. Omer was able to flee with his family before Akish could murder him.

"Once Omer was gone, Jared took his place as king and gave his daughter to Akish as he'd promised. However, by this point, Akish had already begun the secret combinations. He thirsted for power, so he murdered Jared and then *he* became king. Ultimately, Jared's daughter was responsible for the death of her own father. She's not mentioned in the scriptures again, but as the story continues, Akish grew jealous of his son, likely *her* son, and he locked him up until the boy starved to death." Grandma's expression was somber. "This wicked woman had blood on her hands. And believe me, after she died, her reception on the other side was *not* a pleasant one."

I made a face. "Thank you for not making me see any more than this. I'm sure I would have been scarred for life!" I looked toward the door, wanting nothing more than to escape. "Can we go now, Grandma? Watching them sit there while knowing what's going to happen is making me feel sick to my stomach."

She looked at me closely. "You *are* starting to look a little green. I'm sorry to put you through this, sweetheart. We've seen all we need to see. Let's get out of here!"

I cast one last, disgusted glance at the woman before the dismal room disappeared. The ground beneath me turned rocky and uneven, and the fresh smell of pine cleared away the last of the stench that remained from the chamber.

We stood on a trail, about halfway up a mountain from what I could tell. The rocky edifice towered above us, its glorious peaks reaching into the clouds. Down below was an impressively steep canyon that was so deep I couldn't see the bottom of it. Although we stood a safe distance from the edge of the trail, after seeing the treacherous drop, I took a few steps toward the safety of the mountainside.

Grandma inhaled deeply. "Ah! It's nice to be outside again. Don't you love the feeling you get when you're in the mountains? There's nothing else like it."

"Yeah, and this is *some* mountain. I don't think I've ever seen one this big. I feel like I should be wearing climbing gear or something—that drop looks downright hazardous!"

Grandma laughed, but I still chose to sit on a rock as far from the edge as possible. She sat down beside me, and I wondered fleetingly how she managed to keep her brilliantly white dress from getting dirty.

"Eliza, why do you think I chose to tell you the story of Jared's daughter?" Grandma asked.

I scrunched up my nose. The memory of watching those horrible people plotting lingered like a bad taste in my mouth.

"Well, your visit today was unexpected—but if we're still on track, then that means you're here to teach me about choice and accountability, right?" I looked at her for approval, and she nodded, encouraging me to continue. "Jared's daughter made some really, *really* bad choices. And, like you said, the consequences for those choices followed her during her life and even after she died." I paused. "But here's the thing. I mean, all I did was cheat on a math test—which was definitely wrong." I rushed out these last words. "But did I need to see such an extreme example of bad choices? You don't honestly think I'm capable of committing murder, do you? I have a hard time squishing a spider!"

Grandma chuckled. "You do beat all, Eliza. Of course I'm not worried about that! But there's a reason why Moroni included this story when he abridged the book of Ether. He knew there were lessons in this story that would be beneficial to all of us. One of the main things we can learn from it is the far-reaching effects one person can have in society. In contrast to the other women we have previously visited whose works of righteousness blessed the lives of thousands, the choices made by the daughter of Jared brought countless people into darkness and destruction. So you see, the choices we make not only affect us, but also those around us—whether we realize it or not.

"Each of us makes countless choices every day, and every choice has a consequence. Think of it in terms of climbing this mountain. Imagine that your ultimate goal is to reach the top. When you make a good choice, you're able to climb upward, whether it's a small step forward for a little thing you did right, or a huge, bounding leap for a great act of goodness or charity.

"Conversely, when you make a bad choice, you move downhill. Sometimes it may be a backward step so small you hardly notice; other times it may be a grave sin that causes you to practically fall down the mountain. At any rate, you are constantly moving either forward or backward; there's no such thing as standing still.

"That is the beauty of this life, and it can be summed up in one word—agency. You have the freedom to choose which direction you will take, whether it's toward the mountain's peak or down into the depths of the ravine. All of us make bad choices now and then—not a single one of us is perfect—but that's where the magnificence of God's merciful plan comes into play. No matter how many times we make mistakes and no matter how far down the mountain we've fallen, the Savior is always there, waiting to help us back up again.

Let me repeat: He is *always* there. All we have to do is reach up to Him and allow the healing power of His atonement into our lives. Repentance is a miracle, and it's available to each and every one of us. That's the beauty of agency—that's the reason we're here."

As Grandma spoke, I knew that what she was saying was true, and I knew what I had to do. I felt a quiet confirmation of the Spirit at my decision and realized that the empty, sick feeling I'd experienced after the test was the absence of the Holy Ghost. Now that I knew what it felt like to be without His companionship, I never wanted to feel that way again. Suddenly, I was anxious to be done with the dream so I could put into action what I knew in my heart was the right thing to do.

"Grandma, everything you said makes perfect sense. I realize why you came when you did." I couldn't meet her gaze. "I really needed to hear this today."

She seemed to sense my change of heart, and she smiled. "You are such a special girl. I never doubted for a second that you'd do the right thing. I know you're ready to get back, but before you go, there's something I want you to see."

She held a tiny, orange hourglass on her palm, and I watched as the grains of sand began flowing from the top of the glass, through the narrow middle, and into the bottom.

"One of Isaac Newton's laws of motion states every action has an opposite and equal reaction. It's the same thing with choice and accountability. The sand moving through this hourglass represents the choices we make and the resultant consequences. Remember, while most of the choices we make are small and seemingly insignificant, they build up and eventually mold us into the person we'll become. Few people realize that the choices they make while they're young can affect them for the rest of their lives." She handed me the hourglass. "Make every choice count, Eliza, and eventually you'll make it to the top of the mountain."

⊂∽

"Do you think she's okay? I've never seen anyone so completely zonked out before."

It took me a minute to dispel the sleepy haze and get my bearings. Light seemed to scorch my eyes as I slowly blinked, and then sat upright. I heard a few snickers from behind me as the substitute teacher smiled at me.

"Phew, you're alive! I'm no expert, but I'd recommend you get a little more sleep at night, young lady. I was afraid we were going to have to leave you here until morning!"

I attempted to smile back at him while my face flushed. "Sorry about that. I didn't realize how tired I was."

He nodded sympathetically, and then returned his attention to the rest of the class, outlining the chapters in the Old Testament that Brother Carlton wanted us to read before tomorrow. With the spotlight mercifully diverted away from me, I was able to breathe again and collect my thoughts.

This experience had answered some questions I'd had about my dreams. I'd often wondered if they really *were* dreams or if I was physically being transported. Now I knew that, as Grandma had said, they truly were dreams, because I was pretty sure someone in the class would have noticed if Grandma had shown up and magically whisked me out of the room. However, I knew that they were more than just an average dream because I still couldn't explain how I was finding the value objects afterward.

The bell rang, interrupting my thoughts. I quickly jumped up out of my seat, anxious to head back to my math class and set things right.

I saw Luke sitting at his desk by the door, but I didn't allow myself to think that he might be waiting for me. He looked up as I passed by, and I couldn't decipher his expression. All he said to me was, "See you at the game."

My eyebrows rose in confusion. "The game? Oh, yeah. Of course! I'll be there. Good luck!" And with that, I was out the door and on my way. I said a silent prayer the entire way to my math classroom, asking for forgiveness and also for the strength to do what I knew was right.

I stopped outside the door and glanced in to make sure that Mrs. Bartlett was still there. She was sitting at her desk, sorting through a pile of papers. *Test papers*, I realized in dismay. I leaned against the wall for support, taking a few deep breaths to prepare myself. After saying one more quick prayer, I thought of Esther, and I stood up tall, squared my shoulders, and bravely walked into the classroom.

℃∽

"Well, Eliza, I must say I'm shocked. I was really pleased when I saw you'd passed the test; I know how much you've struggled this year." Mrs. Bartlett's expression was full of disappointment.

I looked at the floor and remained silent. After my full confession and apology, I didn't know what else to say.

She paused for a moment. "I *do* wish you'd tell me who was sending the texts, but I understand that you didn't come here to be a tattletale. Besides, I think I already have a pretty good idea who it is." She took off her glasses and rubbed her eyes. "You know, when I started teaching twelve years ago, cell phones weren't even an issue. Now, everything is different. All the students have them, and it sure makes life difficult for us teachers. This method of cheating isn't new—a lot of the other departments are having the same problem—but it's so discreet that we don't really know how to handle it anymore."

Mrs. Bartlett looked worn-out, and I felt sorry for her. It did seem like an insurmountable problem. Almost every teacher asked us to turn off our phones in class, and some had even tried to make us put them in a bin before class, but everyone just kept it on silent or said they didn't have one—including me. I realized with a twinge of guilt that I wasn't being completely honest in these situations and resolved to do better.

"I'm really sorry, Mrs. Bartlett. I didn't realize how frustrating it must be for you. I can't speak for everyone, but I promise I'll be more respectful about using my cell from now on."

She studied me for a minute, as if trying to figure out if I was being sincere. "I would be within my rights to give you a failing grade, but I'm really impressed that you had the courage to confess what you did." She shook her head. "In all my years of teaching no one has ever done that before. I'm going to let you retake the test tomorrow after school." She held up a finger in warning. "Keep in mind that this test will have different questions. I want you to study as hard as you can, and if you still can't come up with a pass-ing grade, I think we should discuss the possibility of a tutor. I'd hate to fail you so close to the end of the year."

I blew out a breath of relief. "Oh, thank you! I can't tell you how much I appreciate you giving me another chance. I promise I won't let you down."

She smiled at me and then waved a dismissive hand as she returned to the papers on her desk. "Good luck studying. I'll see you here tomorrow right after school."

I felt a thousand times lighter as I walked out of the classroom. It felt so liberating to be honest, and I couldn't believe she was going to let me retake the test! However, I knew that if I was going to be able to pull this off, I'd need help studying. I racked my brain trying to think of a person who'd be willing and able to come to my aid. One name came to my mind—and it just so happened he was the very person I was on my way to see play soccer.

CHAPTER

sixteen

"Over here, Eliza!"

I smiled and made my way over the bleachers to where Kelly Craig was sitting. Kelly and I had a few classes together this semester, and we'd become friends. Her older brother was on the soccer team, and I was grateful she was there. It was nice to have someone to sit by.

"Hi, Kelly! Thanks for saving me a seat." I sat down next to her, and she introduced me to her parents and her younger sister, who were also sitting with her. The bleachers were almost full, and I was pleased that the team was getting such great support. This was a big game for our school. So far we were undefeated, and if we won this game, it meant we would go to the state tournament this year.

The crowd buzzed with excitement that erupted into a cheer as the players made their way onto the field. Kelly and I clapped extra hard for her brother and for Jason as they came into view. Luke received the loudest of the cheers—mostly from girls screaming his name—as he took his place among his teammates. I didn't clap any louder for him, but that didn't keep my heart from wildly flip-flopping when I saw him in his soccer jersey.

I forced myself to look away and admire Jason instead. He was standing near the sidelines, and I saw him scanning the crowd. As soon as he caught my eye, a huge grin spread across his face, and he waved at me. I waved back shyly, feeling a little embarrassed, but pleased at the same time.

A family of redheads sitting on the second row had noticed the exchange, and they were talking as they looked up at me, which only served to embarrass me further. They were obviously Jason's family, and from what I could tell, they all seemed happy and friendly. His dad had a booming laugh I could hear from where I sat, and his mom beamed with pride every time she cheered for Jason. Meanwhile, his brother and sister kept poking each other and laughing as if they were close friends. After watching them for a few minutes, I found that I was eager to get to know them.

It was a close game. My fingernails were completely ragged from my nervous biting, but the tension was worth it because in the end we won! It was a huge victory! Everyone was on their feet, and some people even ran onto the field to congratulate the team.

After the frenzy died down, my cheeks ached from smiling and my voice was hoarse from yelling, but I was completely elated.

Kelly and I made our way down the bleachers and onto the grass. Jason ran toward me through the crowd, and before I knew what was happening, he grabbed me in a huge hug and swung me around. I squealed as my legs came dangerously close to hitting Kelly, and I tried not to mind how damp his jersey was from sweat. He put me down, and I laughed as I sought to regain my balance.

"Great job! You were awesome out there!" I exclaimed.

"Thanks! I think you *are* my lucky charm." He winked. "Come on, I want you to meet my family." He pulled me by the hand toward the group of smiling redheads. On our way we passed by Luke, who gave Jason a high-five.

"Good job, man. A bunch of us are going over to the Tasty Freeze to celebrate. Are you coming?" He only looked at Jason as he asked this.

"Sure." Jason turned to me. "That is, if Eliza wants to?"

"Um, I wish I could, but I have a math test I really need to study for." I wanted to add that I desperately needed Jason's help to study, but I didn't want to ruin his post-game celebration. "You go on ahead though. It sounds fun." I smiled encouragingly at him.

"Math, huh?" Jason said. "You know I'm pretty good at math. Do you need any help?"

I smiled sheepishly and blew out a big breath. "Actually, I *could* use some help. But I don't want you to miss out on all the fun because of me. Why don't you go to the Tasty Freeze—we can meet up after."

Jason looked at his watch. "Nah, it'll be too late if I go there first. Besides, I could stand to refuse an ice cream every now and then." He gestured to the non-existent paunch at his stomach. "Gotta stay in shape for the big game coming up." He turned to Luke. "Sorry, bro, looks like we're out this time."

Luke quickly looked at the ground and then back to Jason. "No, big deal." He gave me a half-glance. "Good luck studying."

"Thanks," I said, wondering why he was avoiding me.

"See ya." Luke nodded and then walked off toward a group of his friends.

I stared after him in bewilderment until Jason squeezed my hand and pulled me toward his waiting family.

"Everyone, this is Eliza. Eliza, this is my dad, my mom, Ben, and Freckle Face," Jason said as an introduction.

His sister stuck her tongue out at him and then approached me. "I'm *Christy*," she clarified, throwing Jason a dirty look. "It's nice to finally meet you. Jason talks about you *all the time*—Ow!" Jason punched her playfully in the arm as he blushed crimson. "Well, you do!" Christy insisted, and Ben nodded in agreement. Jason's dad laughed, but his mom saw Jason's embarrassment and hurried to change the subject.

We talked about the game for a few minutes, and then his parents asked me a few questions about where I lived and what I did for fun. Normally, I would have hated being the center of attention, but Jason's family made me feel so at ease that I didn't mind.

"Okay, that's enough interrogating for one day," Jason said. "I'm going to hit the showers and then Eliza and I are going to study for her math test. We'll see you later." We said our good-byes, and Jason pulled me toward the parking lot. "Do you mind waiting for a few minutes while I clean up? I'll be fast, I promise."

"No, I don't mind at all. It'll give me a head start on my study-ing. I'll just wait right here." I gestured toward the empty bleach-ers, and he smiled and nodded before running off to the locker room.

As I sat there, I thought about Jill and wondered if she'd minded that I hadn't given her a ride home today. I'd sent her a text explaining that I was staying for the game, but she'd never texted back. I was ninety-nine percent sure she'd gotten a ride with Nick—though she probably had him drop her off a block before her house so her parents wouldn't know she'd ridden with him.

I hated feeling the void that her friendship left, and I wanted so badly for us to be close again. I said a silent prayer asking that things between us could heal, and then I got out my math book and began to study.

⁂

We drove to my house and studied for an hour at the kitchen table until Mom came in and started getting dinner ready. She invited Jason to stay, and he seemed happy to oblige.

Courtney was staying at Alexis's house for dinner, so it was just me, Jason, and my parents. I wished that my Dad would act cool and relaxed like Jason's dad had been. Instead, he spoke very little and cast an "I'm watching you" glare at Jason more than once during the meal.

Mom came to my rescue by talking to Jason almost nonstop, and I made a mental note to thank her after he left—and to give Dad my opinion about his childish behavior. Why did he have to be so overprotective? If Jason didn't have such a massive crush on me, he would have fled the house hours ago.

After dinner, Jason stayed another hour, making sure I felt confident enough to pass the test. Surprisingly, with his help, I was beginning to understand the problems, and I finally felt like I was prepared. I walked him out to the front porch, thanking him profusely with every step, until he stopped and put his finger to my lips.

"No more thanking me, Eliza. Trust me—spending time with you is thanks enough." He leaned in, and for one paralyzing moment I thought I was going to get my first kiss, but he turned inches from my lips and kissed my cheek instead.

As he pulled away, he smiled. "Call or text me if you have any more questions, okay?" I was too stunned to speak, so I just nodded. "Good night." He winked and then turned and walked toward his car.

"Night," I said in delayed response, as I watched him get in his car and drive away. I stood in a half-trance, remembering how it felt when he'd kissed my cheek. The gesture was so sweet and unassuming; it made me feel warm all over to think of it. I looked up at the half-moon and sighed, listening to the crickets as they chirped.

Life was good! The carefree, joyful sensation I was experiencing was such a contrast to the empty, sick way I'd felt earlier today. I knew I wanted to make good choices so I could always feel this happy inside.

A car pulled up in front of our house, breaking me out of my thoughts. I recognized it as Alexis's mom's car, here to drop Courtney off. I headed into the house before Courtney could act embarrassed and ask me what I was doing by myself on the porch.

I walked into the kitchen to find Mom and Dad sitting at the table, eating brownies and milk. They had stopped talking abruptly as I walked into the room, and the concerned looks on their faces told me something was up. I grabbed a brownie and sat down beside Mom.

"What were you guys talking about?" I asked suspiciously.

They shifted uncomfortably, and for a frightening moment I was worried they'd been talking about Jason and me. The thought seemed ridiculous! After all, we'd only been on a few dates, and it wasn't like he was my boyfriend or anything—at least not yet.

Dad cleared his throat. "Nothing that you need to be concerned about, honey. I was just telling your mom that the Foxglove Mortgage Company went under today. They've been extending loans to people who never should have qualified for the money, and I'm afraid the consequences have finally caught up to the company—and to the people."

He turned to Mom. "Grant Andrews came to see me at my office today. The poor man was completely distraught. It seems that he was already deeply in debt, and now that he's lost his job, he's not sure what he's going to do. He admitted that his family has grown accustomed to having nice things, and this is going to be a major challenge for all of them."

"Oh, dear," Mom said sympathetically, as she placed her hand over Dad's.

He nodded. "It was awful. He was almost in tears saying he should have followed the prophet's counsel to get out of debt. He said he meant to work on it, but he never got around to it. Worldly goods were just too important to him, and he always wanted to have the nicest and newest of everything. He told me it was like an addiction. If someone he knew bought a nice car, he had to buy one that was nicer." Dad shook his head. "It's something we're all susceptible to, I'm afraid. Once the desire for *things* gets into your system, it's insatiable. You'll never have enough because there will always be something better out there."

He sighed. "I felt so sorry for Grant and his family. I encouraged him to meet with his bishop and discuss his options, but beyond that I didn't know what else to say. We'll have to keep his family in our prayers."

Mom nodded, but personally I felt a little mystified by Dad's sympathy. Sure, it was sad that the Andrews family was having financial struggles, but hadn't they brought it upon themselves because of greed? I couldn't imagine praying for Chelsea Andrews, the girl who had everything and who'd made my life miserable on more than one occasion. As far as I was concerned, they got what they deserved, and part of me was even a little bit glad that Chelsea was finally going to learn a lesson!

I considered sending Jill a text; she would be ecstatic over this juicy piece of news. I flipped open my cell, but at the last second remembered what Grandma had said about gossip and closed it again.

As Mom and Dad continued talking, I finished my brownie and chugged down a glass of milk. After all the cramming I'd done for the test, I was beyond tired.

"I think I'll head up to bed now," I said with a yawn.

"I think I heard Courtney come in," Mom said. "Let's say family prayer first, okay?"

We walked into the living room where Courtney was watching TV and simultaneously texting on her phone. She acknowledged our presence with a scowl and wordlessly flipped her cell closed as she knelt down beside us on the carpet.

"Did you get any studying done at Alexis's house tonight?" Mom asked, taking the remote and turning off the TV.

"Yeah," Courtney muttered. Her head was already bowed, clearly impatient to get prayers over with.

Mom and Dad exchanged glances, and then Dad asked me to

offer the prayer, reminding me to pray for the Andrews family. I
cringed at the request, but tried to sound sincere as I prayed for
Chelsea's family. The words felt strange on my tongue, and I knew
it was because in my heart, I really wasn't sincere.

After our prayer (and despite a few tired protests), Mom read
a chapter from the Book of Mormon aloud. When she was done,
we gave each other hugs, and I started to head up to my room, but
then I saw Dad going into his study. I wanted to talk to him about
his treatment of Jason, so I followed him.

He sat down at his desk and turned when he saw me enter the
room behind him. "I thought you were headed up to bed, sweetheart." After one look at my face, he asked, "Is something the
matter?"

"Yeah, kind of." I paused. Talking to my dad about boys was
not a comfortable topic, but for the sake of my future dating life,
I knew I had to say something, so I plunged in. "Dad, the way you
treated Jason tonight was totally embarrassing! You've got to back
down a little or word will get out that you're a nutcase and no one
will dare ask me out!" I'd meant to sound calm and mature, but
that flew out the window as soon as my emotions took the reins.

Dad smiled as he thoughtfully placed his hand under his chin.
"Hmm, you mean all I have to do is act scary, and I don't have to
worry about you dating anymore? I had no idea it was that simple!"

"*Da-ad!*" I wailed in frustration.

"Okay, okay." He held his hands up in surrender. "I didn't
think I was *that* bad"—I rolled my eyes in exasperation—"but I
promise I'll try to be a little more civil with your friends that are
boys."

I smiled and gave him a hug. "Thank you! That's all I ask."

"Notice that I did not say *boyfriend*. If you get a boyfriend, that's a whole other story." He rubbed his hands together fiendishly.

I sighed. "You're impossible. If I die an old maid, I hope you know that I'm holding you personally responsible."

Dad laughed, and I turned around with every intention of walking haughtily out of the room when something on his bookshelf caught my eye. The light glinted off a piece of glass wedged slightly behind one of his books. I moved closer and had to stifle a gasp when I realized what the object was—the hourglass! With trembling fingers I moved the book aside and carefully picked up the small token.

"What have you got there?" Dad asked, and I turned around to face him, keeping my expression composed.

"Oh, it's just a cute little hourglass. I'd never noticed it before." I held the item up for his inspection. I couldn't take my eyes off of it!

"Oh, yeah. I'd forgotten all about that. I think your mom put it in here when she was decorating the office." He came to stand beside me so he could observe the object more closely, and it took every bit of my willpower to hand it over when he reached for it. "It's kind of a neat little thing, isn't it? There's something fascinating about an hourglass."

"Mm-hmm, it's really cool." My fingers itched to snatch it back from him, but I knew that would be rude . . . and suspicious. I had to go about this in a diplomatic way. After Dad replaced the hourglass on the shelf, I continued to admire it.

"Was there anything else you wanted to talk about, hon?" he asked as he sat back down in his chair.

"No, not really. I was just sort of wondering . . ."

He looked at me expectantly.

"Well, I wondered if—since you'd forgotten about this hour-glass—would you mind if I kept it for awhile?"

"Sure, go right ahead," Dad said, turning his attention to the papers on his desk. I quickly picked up the hourglass and started for the door.

"Thanks, Dad."

"No problem."

I breathed a huge sigh of relief as I made my way into the hall, but then Dad's voice stopped me in my tracks.

"Oh, wait a second, Eliza."

I swallowed as I poked my head around the doorframe, my heart in my throat.

"Make sure you take good care of that. I think it belonged to your great-grandma."

❧

I smiled as I brushed my teeth—another token found! This one had practically jumped out at me, and it was a good thing! I'd been afraid I was going to have to spend hours looking for it, and I was already worn out from all the studying I'd done tonight.

I was thinking about Jason and the kiss he'd given me on the cheek when my cell phone buzzed. I wondered if it was Jason, but my heart skipped a beat when I saw that the text was from Jill. Maybe she'd decided to start talking to me again! I quickly scrolled through the message, which didn't take long because it was only a dozen words long.

Jill: Don't worry about picking me up tomorrow. Nick's driving me to school.

Tears stung my eyes as I read the words over again. Why was Jill acting like this? We'd had fights before, but they'd never carried on this long, and certainly not after one of us apologized. It had hurt when I'd taken second place to Nick, but now it was as if she was trying to cut me out of her life completely.

I looked down at the charm bracelet on my wrist. We'd given each other these bracelets when we were eleven years old as a symbol of our friendship, promising that we'd wear them every day. My little bracelet was something I cherished, and wearing it felt as natural as my own skin. Now, it felt like nothing more than a silly, meaningless trinket.

I unclasped the bracelet and stuffed it in the back of my sock drawer, where it would remain out of sight. After wiping the tears from my eyes, I went through the motions of prayer and scripture study, but my heart wasn't in it.

I heard Mom open the door to wish me good night, but my lamp was already off, so she quietly closed it again, leaving me alone to wallow in my sorrow.

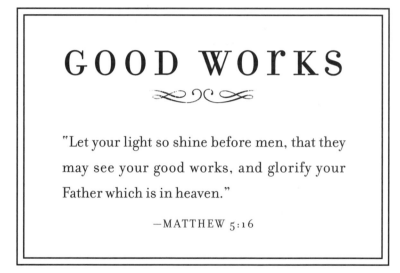

GOOD WORKS

"Let your light so shine before men, that they
may see your good works, and glorify your
Father which is in heaven."

—MATTHEW 5:16

cHapTer

seventeen

My eyelids felt puffy, and my eyes burned as I struggled to open them.

Grandma sat on my bed and smiled at me, just as she had the very first time she'd visited me in my dreams.

"You've been crying. Is everything all right?" She looked at me in concern.

I nodded and smiled sadly. "It's funny—earlier tonight I felt completely happy. I knew I'd done the right thing by being honest about the test, and everything seemed to be going so well. I felt as light as a feather—like I could do anything! But then something happened right before I went to bed and everything changed like *that*." I snapped my fingers. "It's crazy how fast things can change."

"Do you want to talk about it?" she asked softly.

"Oh, Jill and I had a fight a few days ago, and she doesn't seem to want to forgive me. I feel like we're growing apart, and I don't know what to do about it." My lower lip began to tremble. It was painful to talk about my feelings, and I felt a fresh wave of tears coming on.

Grandma smiled sympathetically. "Life is full of ups and downs. I know this may sound cliché, but it really *is* like a roller coaster. Making good choices doesn't ensure that your life will be easy, but if you try your best to live righteously, you will have those precious glimpses of perfect happiness—times when you *know* you're on the right track. You got a taste of that tonight. Those are the moments you must remember and hold close when things get tough.

"You and Jill have been best friends for several years, and I can understand how upsetting it must be to have something like this come between you. It may not provide much comfort now, but I'm sure things will work out very soon, and you'll be as close as ever." She winked at me reassuringly. "In the meantime, I have the perfect remedy for dispelling the blues, as they say. I realize that our lessons have been coming at a rather whirlwind pace, but are you ready for another adventure?"

I sniffed and nodded. I was ready for *anything* that would keep me from crying again. My head ached, and my throat scratched like I'd swallowed a bucket of sand. Overall, I felt like a soggy, wrung-out mess! Sometimes crying was satisfying, but the after-effects were always unpleasant.

I stood up with Grandma as the room transformed around us. Noises of all kinds immediately began assaulting my ears: car horns, people yelling, and the general ruckus of what I could only imagine to be hundreds of voices all clamoring around me. Even before the scene unfolded, I knew we were going somewhere extremely crowded.

As things started coming into focus, I saw that we were standing on a dirt street teeming with people. They all had dark skin and hair, and many wore clothes that were somewhat tattered and filthy. I'd never seen so many people on one street before. I was happy that this was a dream, because I was sure if I'd been here in reality, I'd have been crushed by the constant flow of humanity.

The few cars scattered along the street told me that this was the most modern time period we'd visited yet, but somehow everything still seemed old. Well, *old* wasn't the right word exactly—more like, extremely shabby.

I was, however, still acutely aware of the smells around me, and they were none too pleasant: strong spices intermingled with the overpowering stench of body odor. The combination caused my stomach to roll in protest.

A group of women passed by us wearing long dresses and veils over their hair. I noticed that each woman had a red dot in the center of her forehead, which ignited the figurative lightbulb above my head.

"Grandma, I know where we are—this is India!" I was delighted to have guessed our location before Grandma had said a word.

"Right you are, my dear! This is Calcutta, India, one of the most densely populated cities in the world, and, sadly, there are large portions of the city suffering from extreme poverty. The year is 1986, and we are here to observe a woman whose life was truly remarkable. Follow me."

We entered a building on the side of the street, and once inside, I realized it was a hospital of some sort. Cots lined every conceivable space, and each cot was occupied by someone suffering in one manner or another. The sights, sounds, and smells were completely overwhelming. I'd been in hospitals before, but this was totally different. It was obvious to me that the number of people who needed care far surpassed the number of staff on hand.

The staff consisted mostly of women, tirelessly moving from cot to cot to offer assistance. They wore white dresses and white shawls over their heads, with a border of blue stripes edging the material.

"Those are Catholic nuns rendering service to help these poor souls. The task seems insurmountable, doesn't it?" Grandma asked.

I nodded my head. "Yes, it does! I can't imagine how they can look after this many people. Even while we've been standing here, more people have come in for help. How do they keep going? I'm exhausted just thinking about it. They need a bigger staff."

"Indeed that would be helpful, but these women are volunteers, and finding additional help is much harder than you think." She signaled for me to follow her. "Come with me, and I'll show you what motivates many of these women to keep going, despite the challenges."

I walked behind Grandma into another wing of the hospital. This room was filled with children, many in cribs, and some babies were so tiny they couldn't have been more than a few weeks old. My heart broke at the sight of them and tears overflowed onto my cheeks. The babies were so small and helpless; I wanted to gather them all up and bring them home with me.

"It's so hard to watch this and not be able to do anything about it," I complained to Grandma.

"The fact that you *have* the desire to do something is wonderful; it shows that you have charity in your heart. Fortunately for these little ones, they had someone very special watching over them, a woman whose entire life was devoted to charity and good works." She gestured to a tiny, hunched figure standing beside a child's bed a few rows from us. If not for her nun's garb, I might have mistaken her for one of the children because of her size, but one look at her kind, wrinkled face told me she was quite old.

Grandma smiled. "Eliza, meet Mother Teresa."

"Oh, wow! I've heard of her before. She's pretty famous, right?"

"*Was*. She passed away in 1997. And yes, she was known worldwide for her incredible dedication in caring for the poor and needy. Let me give you a brief summary of her life.

"Mother Teresa was born in August of 1910, in Macedonia. She found her calling very early in life. At the tender age of twelve, she felt of God's love and desired to become a missionary so she could share that love with others. When she turned eighteen, she joined with an Irish group of nuns who were training to go to India. She had a few months' training and, once she arrived in India, she took her initial vows and became a nun.

"For several years, she was a teacher in a high school convent in Calcutta, but the extreme poverty she witnessed outside of the school compelled her to take action. She received permission from the Catholic church to leave teaching in the convent school and work among the poor. She began a school for the children who lived in the slums, and with no money to aid her, she relied entirely on the Lord for help. Soon volunteers joined in her cause, and eventually funds began to pour in, which enabled her to broaden her work."

Grandma paused and her eyes twinkled. "What began in that tiny school was like a spark that gradually grew into a huge, flaming fire. Mother Teresa was tireless in her dedication to the poor and desolate. Despite the difficult tasks in front of her, she kept serving, one person at a time. Her Christlike service was an inspiration to hundreds—and then thousands.

"In 1950, she was granted approval from the Catholic church to start her own order called the Missionaries of Charity. The main goal of this organization was to love and care for those who had nowhere to go and no one to turn to. That order is still working today, and it has spread throughout the world. In 1979, Mother Teresa was awarded the Nobel Peace Prize. She has also been awarded numerous other awards throughout her life for her humanitarian efforts.

"The extent of people affected for good by this woman is no longer counted in thousands—but in millions. Her mission was one of love, and she devoted her life to spreading good works and lifting the downtrodden."

I had been watching Mother Teresa in wonder as Grandma spoke. She sat beside a small boy and held a damp cloth to his forehead. She smiled at him with such love and compassion that it melted my heart. He looked into her face and smiled back, touching her arm and nodding at something she said. Her very presence seemed to bring him strength and peace, and I knew the smile on his face was something I'd never forget.

"Oh, Grandma, what a privilege to be able to see a moment in the life of such an incredible woman!" I looked down at my hands. "I have to confess though, it makes me feel sad when I think of all the things she did with her life, and how insignificant my life has been in comparison."

"But that is the beauty of this lesson, Eliza. Mother Teresa taught us that the power of good works lies in our everyday actions. She said, 'In this life we cannot do great things. We can only do small things with great love.' Don't you just love that statement? It reminds me of the scripture in Alma that states that 'by small and simple things are great things brought to pass.'"

Grandma smiled. "So you see? There will be times in your life when you'll have the opportunity to do great acts of service, and while those things are important, it's the little, everyday things we do to help others that sometimes have the farthest reaching effects. Never underestimate the power of a simple smile or a listening ear. It may not always seem like it, but even serving your own family can have a great impact."

I pondered this as Grandma continued. "When speaking of the Savior and His teachings, one word always comes to my mind, and that word is *love*. From the scriptures, we know that 'charity is the pure love of Christ.' It's His desire for us to learn to serve each other and to be instruments in His hands to help others. Do you remember our visit to Eliza R. Snow and how we talked briefly about the Relief Society?"

I nodded. "Of course."

"Well, in a few years you'll be able to join that great organization, whose motto is 'Charity Never Faileth.' The Relief Society is an inspired institution, and it is truly amazing what women can accomplish when they work together. You'll have many opportunities to serve others when you become a part of Relief Society—you're going to love it!

"However, the Relief Society is just one part of the many programs our Church has to help those in need. There are welfare and humanitarian efforts going on throughout the world that are orchestrated by members of our faith. And don't forget that when you pay fast offerings and contribute to things like the Perpetual Education Fund, you are also contributing to this great work."

She sighed happily. "I must confess that good works is my favorite value to talk about. I can't say enough about the importance of serving others; it brings you close to the Savior like nothing else can. When you serve others, you are truly serving Him. Imagine what this world would be like if we all understood that truth!"

I smiled at Grandma's enthusiasm; her face positively glowed with excitement.

"Just *talking* about helping others makes you feel good inside," Grandma said. "But it feels even better when you put the talk into action. Look—even the *color* for the value is cheerful."

She handed me a small, unlit yellow candle. It was short and thin, the kind of candle that would fit perfectly in a tiny candlestick. I felt the smoothness of the wax as I twirled it between my fingers.

"This candle represents the light you spread when you participate in good works," Grandma said. "Remember, even a tiny flame can dispel darkness. And no matter how small the spark, it's still capable of starting a large fire."

Her eyes were piercing as she looked at me. "Eliza, *you* have the potential to do great things in helping the Lord with His work. I noticed the way you looked at your hands when you felt like you had not accomplished much, but if you're willing, those are the *very* hands which will be instruments of service. Pray often for guidance. The Spirit will direct you to those in need, and as you act on those promptings, you'll bless not only the lives of others, but your own life as well."

I took one last look at Mother Teresa and, silly as it was, blew her a kiss. It was an honor to have caught a glimpse of her amazing life—and it motivated me to want to help others as well.

Just before the dream began to fade, I looked down at my hands again and thought about what Grandma had said.

CHAPTER

Word was all over school before second period: Chelsea Andrews had broken off her prom date with Owen Black just *one week* before the dance. She had offered no explanation, and Owen was completely heartbroken. Everyone speculated over the reason for the breakup. Did she have another date in mind? Had Owen done something to make her mad? Was she still upset about not being asked by Luke? The texts flew as everyone analyzed the situation. This was the biggest piece of gossip since midterm, and rumors buzzed about like flies.

I had a pretty good idea why Chelsea had canceled her date, and I was fairly sure it wasn't because of Owen. After what I'd learned last night about her family's financial situation, I was willing to bet that she hadn't bought her dress yet, and now that the money train from her dad had come to a crashing halt, she had no way of getting one.

A tiny thought crept into my mind, but I immediately shoved it right back out. Dream or no dream, there was *no way* I was going to help Chelsea! The nasty part of me still felt like her family was getting what they deserved, and if Chelsea couldn't go to prom it was the result of her own unchecked excesses. Let her sell her precious car, or auction off some of her designer clothes on eBay. I was sure she could scrounge up the money from *somewhere* if she had the proper motivation. Besides, the good works I'd learned about last night had been toward the poor and needy—not girls who lived in mansions. I would do my part of kindness by not spreading what I knew about her dad. I smiled and feeling justified, let the subject drop.

"May I take the hall pass, please?"

Biology was almost over, and I'd tried to wait to use the bathroom, but suddenly my bladder warned that waiting was no longer an option.

Mr. Norman glanced at the clock and gave me a withering look, but finally conceded. "All right, but please make it fast."

I shot out of my seat before he'd finished his sentence and grabbed the wooden pass from its peg. I darted down the hall to the bathroom; however, once I was inside, the sight before me almost made me forget why I was there.

Chelsea stood at the mirror, sniffing and trying to apply makeup to her reddened cheeks and nose. She startled with embarrassment when she saw me.

I looked away and pretended not to notice her as I headed into the stall. Normally, I would have waited until I heard her leave before reemerging, but class was almost over, and I was in a rush.

She was still working on her makeup when I walked over to wash my hands. To my surprise, she looked over and gave me a sort of apologetic smile. I reached for a paper towel and smiled back in what I hoped was a reassuring way, and then left. No words had been spoken between us, but somehow in those smiles, we'd exchanged something. She knew that I wasn't going to gossip about seeing her crying, and I knew that she was trying to apologize for the way she'd treated me.

It had been an unexpectedly pleasant moment, and my heart felt lighter as I realized I was already forming a plan.

⌁

"Okay, pencil down please."

I'd just finished the last equation as Mrs. Bartlett walked over to my desk and picked up the test.

"I'll save you the agony of waiting and grade it right now, okay?" She smiled at me, and I nodded my head, blowing out a big breath.

"That would be awesome, thanks." I drummed my foot and chewed my fingernails as I watched her go over each problem. After five minutes, she looked up at me.

"Would you like to know how you did?" Her stoic expression offered no hints, and I felt my stomach tighten into a pretzel.

"Yes, please!" I closed my eyes and braced myself for the worst.

"You got a B+. Great job! That means that if you do well on your final, you'll pass the class."

"Oh my goodness, I can't believe it!" Without even thinking, I ran over to her, wanting to give her a hug, but I stopped when I reached her desk. She laughed and stood up, holding her arms out to give me a quick hug.

"You should be proud of yourself—for telling the truth and for studying so hard. Remember, if you have trouble in the future, you can always come and talk to me, that's what I'm here for." She smiled at me.

"I will. I promise. Thank you *so* much for giving me a second chance."

I felt as light as air as I left the classroom. School had been out for almost forty-five minutes, so I was surprised when I turned down the hall and saw Jason standing there.

He waved at me. "How'd it go?"

I ran toward him and gave him a huge hug, which he gladly returned.

"Whoa! That good, huh?" He laughed.

I pulled away from him and proudly held up the paper.

"No way—a B+! That's awesome! I knew you could do it."

"Yeah, well I couldn't have done it without your help. Thanks so much for studying with me."

"Anytime, but, if you *really* want to repay me, you could agree to hang out with me after tonight's concert," he said slyly.

"Aha! So your charity comes with a price," I teased.

"Only when the reward is too irresistible to ignore." His eyes were playful, but there was an underlying sincerity in them that made me blush.

I tried to lighten the mood. "Okay, but you *do* realize that would mean hanging out with me two nights in a row. Do you think you can handle that?"

He took my hand. "Absolutely. A group of us are going to Luke's tonight to play pool and Ping-Pong and stuff. Is that okay with you?"

Ack! Why was Luke always involved in our activities? Was he purposely trying to torment me?

"Sure, that sounds great," I said, trying to maintain an enthusiastic tone.

"Sweet! Do you mind if I walk you to your car?"

"That would be nice."

He continued to hold my hand as we walked down the hall, somehow making things seem official. *Congratulations, Eliza,* I thought to myself. *You have your first boyfriend.*

♾

My car rattled violently before wheezing to a stop beside the gas pump. I patted the dashboard consolingly. "You just take it easy for a few minutes."

I climbed out of the car and was about to hit the PAY OUTSIDE option on the keypad when a thought came to me. I pushed the PAY INSIDE button instead. After fueling up, I ran into the service station and found what I was looking for—a king-sized candy bar. Placing the chocolate on the counter, I told the cashier I also needed to pay for pump 8. With that taken care of, I got back in the car and, after a few frightening failed attempts, started it up and zoomed toward the bank.

Once back home, I selected a couple of cards from Mom's never-ending supply of greeting cards. I chose two that had cute designs on the cover but were blank inside, and I hurried up to my room. I had only a few hours before I had to be back at school, so I had to move fast. The first card I wrote was for Courtney.

Courtney,

Thanks for being such a great little sister. I want you to know that I'll always be there for you, and if

you ever need anything, let me know. I miss hanging
out with you and hearing all about what's going on in
your life. You're the best! I love you! ☺
     XOXO,

               Eliza

I sealed the card and wrote her name on the envelope. I
grabbed the candy bar and headed for her room. I knocked even
though I knew she wasn't there. After waiting a few seconds, I went
in and placed the card and candy bar on her bed. I smiled when I
pictured her reaction. I'd chosen her favorite kind of candy bar,
and I hoped that my note would brighten her day.

I glanced around at the posters on her walls and realized that
I hadn't been in her room in a long time. She was into different
bands and movie stars now, and it made me feel bad that these
changes had happened without my even noticing them. Suddenly
I felt like a stranger in her room, like I was imposing, and something about that seemed wrong.

I hurried out of her room and closed the door, looking both
ways down the hall before running back to my room.

The next card was a little trickier to write. I sat for several
minutes trying to think of what to say, but nothing was coming, so
I decided to keep it short and simple.

Chelsea,
     This is for your prom dress—or whatever else
you need.
     Sincerely,
               Your friend

I tried not to cringe as I placed two, crisp one hundred dollar bills in the card and sealed it. If I'd had time, I would have typed the note to ensure total anonymity, but I doubted Chelsea would recognize my handwriting, and time was of the essence. I scribbled her name on the front of the envelope and grabbed my car keys before I could talk myself out of my plan.

I drove up the hill to the Andrews' residence and parked my car half a block down the street from her house. Creeping stealthily up their long driveway, I carefully scoped the landscape for a good hiding place.

After making sure the coast was clear, I ran up to the door and balanced the envelope on the doorknob. Feeling a surge of panicked adrenaline, I rang the doorbell and then bolted down the steps and around the corner. I hid behind a large tree, my heart pounding in my chest. I held my breath and strained my ears to listen.

I heard the front door open, and I waited for several seconds, imagining someone was looking around to see who the visitor had been. I finally heard the front door close again, and I waited a few more seconds before leaving the safety of the tree and peeking around the corner of the house. I could see the front porch clearly. The envelope was gone. Mission complete!

I crouched down as much as possible and dashed out of the yard and down the drive. A warm, peaceful feeling overcame me as I reached my car, and I recognized the Spirit letting me know that I'd done the right thing.

I smiled as I drove home. Sure, it had been a lot of money, but Chelsea needed it more than I did right now. I realized that doing something nice for someone I didn't like had somehow miraculously healed my heart. All the bad things I'd felt about her had melted away and all that was left was kindness.

I said a quick prayer, thanking Heavenly Father for this wonderful lesson and for the promptings I'd received. I also thanked Him for helping me do well on my math test. The list of things I was grateful for seemed to keep growing, and I prayed all the way home. By the time I pulled in the driveway, I felt so happy I thought my heart was going to burst. Grandma had been right— about everything. I looked up at the attic window and grinned. *Time to find that candle.*

C ✑

Piles of clothes lay strewn about me as I looked at my watch. I'd been through Grandma's things so many times now that I felt like I knew her old wardrobe better than I knew my own. The candle was nowhere to be found, and it was time for me to get ready for the concert.

Maybe this value token will randomly appear like the last one, I thought hopefully as I began piling the clothes back into the drawers. I'd grabbed the last sweater when I noticed something. I held the sweater up and examined it for a moment, and then looked up at Grandma's picture. It was the same sweater she was wearing in the photograph!

I turned the soft white fabric over in my fingers and smiled as I thought of Grandma wearing it. "This must have been one of your favorites, huh?" I asked as I looked up at her picture.

Just for fun, I slipped the sweater on over my shirt and wrapped my arms around myself as if giving Grandma a hug. Laughing at the silly gesture, I moved to take it off when suddenly

I felt something lumpy in the pocket. I closed my eyes and reached down, hoping it wasn't something nasty like old dentures, but to my surprise my fingers closed around a thin, waxy object—the candle!

I quickly pulled it out. "Grandma, you old rascal! I never thought to look in your pockets!" I remembered her saying that good works was her favorite value, so it made sense that she would keep this token close to her heart.

As I looked at the candle more closely, I saw something that I hadn't noticed in my dream last night. Written on the side of the candle in tiny letters were the words *Let your light so shine.*

I turned to Grandma's picture and smiled. "I will, Grandma. I promise."

CHAPTER
nineteen

W e're so proud of you, honey. You did great!" Mom said, hugging me.

Dad reached out and put his hand on my cheek. "For a minute I thought it was an angel singing up there. You looked and sounded absolutely beautiful," he said.

"Oh, Dad." I rolled my eyes but smiled at him, secretly pleased by his comment. "Thanks so much for coming." I turned and impulsively gave Courtney a hug. "You too, Court. Thanks for being here."

She hugged me back awkwardly and didn't look me in the eyes when she said, "Sure. You sounded really good."

I was a little hurt that she seemed so standoffish, but then I reasoned that she probably hadn't gotten my note yet.

"Hi, Mr. and Mrs. Moore! Didn't Eliza do a great job?" Jason appeared by my side, and although he was talking to my parents, his eyes never left me.

"She certainly did. And I enjoyed the numbers that your choir performed, too," Mom said. "Eliza said that you're going over to a friend's house now, is that right?"

Jason smiled. "Yeah, we're just going to go play some games and stuff." And then after a quick glance at my dad, who was frowning, he added, "But don't worry, I'll have her home by eleven o'clock *sharp.*"

My dad acknowledged this with a grunt and slight nod, and I saw my mom discreetly elbow him in the ribs. "Well that sounds like fun! You two have a good time."

I smiled at her, thankful to have at least *one* sane parent. "Thanks, Mom. See you later."

Jason and I walked toward a group of after-choir stragglers, mostly the people going to Luke's house. Luke, however, was nowhere in sight.

"So, what am I going to have to do to get your dad to like me?" Jason asked once we were out of earshot.

"Well, I think all you'd have to do is change yourself into a girl, and then the two of you would be *best friends,*" I said, trying to keep a straight face.

"Ha-ha, *very* funny." He rolled his eyes. "Seriously though, the man *hates* me, and I need to get on his good side."

"Why?" I asked in feigned innocence.

"*Why?* I'll tell you why." He turned to face me and his voice dropped so that only I could hear. "Because I'm crazy about his daughter, and I want to spend as much time with her as possible. I have to be honest, though; I don't blame your dad for being protective. When I saw you in that dress, I almost broke out in a sweat. You look incredible!"

I blushed furiously, happy to know that he thought I looked pretty. I was wearing one of my favorite dresses. It was a little on the formal side, but not enough that I couldn't wear it to church.

It was a black satin, tea-length gown with a lace overlay and bead-work on the empire-waist bodice. It was my "little black dress," and I wore it whenever I wanted to look extra nice.

He shook his head. "I don't know what I'm going to do when I see you in your prom dress. Maybe we should have an oxygen tank on hand—just in case."

I smacked his arm and laughed. "Whatever!"

C ∽

We headed to Luke's house and found several cars already parked in the driveway. I tried to quiet the flutter in my stomach at the thought of seeing Luke again. He and I had barely spoken since that day outside the school, and I still felt bad about the way I'd acted that afternoon. We had shared something special that day, and I felt like we'd bonded in a way I couldn't explain. I hated this new awkwardness that had come between us.

I'd looked for him in the audience tonight, but the stage lights were too bright to see much past the first few rows. I wondered what he'd thought of my solo, and I couldn't help but hope that he liked my dress as much as Jason did.

Jason! It seemed like it took great effort to remember to think about him whenever Luke was near. I scolded myself and then turned my focus on Jason. He was holding my hand as we walked up to the house, and I realized that it was beginning to feel natural now, but I still couldn't drop the nagging worry about what Luke would think when he saw us this way.

Jason rang the doorbell, and after a few seconds, Luke's mom answered the door. She seemed to be about ten years older than my mom, but she still had an air of youth about her. Her hair was dark, like Luke's, and her warm, brown eyes conveyed kindness. She had a welcoming aura about her, and I liked her instantly.

"Hello, Jason, it's nice to see you. Who's your friend?"

"This is Eliza Moore. She's been here once before, but I didn't get the chance to introduce you that night," Jason explained.

Sister Matthews smiled at me, and the wrinkles around her eyes and mouth were evidence that it was an expression she wore often. "It's nice to meet you, Eliza. The kids are all in the game room if you want to head up there."

I smiled in return. "It's nice to meet you too, and thanks for letting us hang out at your house—it's beautiful!" I was surprised by my own words; normally I was shy in the presence of adults I didn't know well, but something about her made me feel right at home.

"Thank you! We really enjoy it here." She leaned in and added in a whisper, "But don't look too closely at anything because I haven't dusted in a week!" Jason and I laughed. "Have fun, you two." She winked at me and then walked down the hall toward the kitchen, which was emanating the rich smell of chocolate chip cookies. My mouth watered as I realized that in my rush this evening I'd forgotten to eat dinner. I hoped that some of those cookies would make their way up to the game room.

"Hey, guys!" Danny yelled as we entered the room.

People were everywhere. Some kids were playing pool, Ping-Pong, or air hockey, and others had spread out on the extra large sectional sofa. At least half of the kids were still dressed up from the concert, and I was glad that I wouldn't stand out in my dress.

A sizable group had congregated around a table covered with cookies, chips, soda, and a deli tray with rolls. *Jackpot!* After spotting the food, my eyes (and my stomach) couldn't focus on anything else.

"Do you mind if I go get some food? I forgot to eat dinner, and I'm *starving*," I whispered to Jason.

"Not at all, that's what it's there for. Come on." He pulled me to the table and loaded up his plate, allowing me to feel free to do the same. I noticed a few girls at the table widen their eyes when they saw how much food I was piling on, but I was too hungry to care.

Jason and I found a spot on the edge of the sectional and dug in. I looked around the room to see who I knew. Danny, Clark, Becka, Britney, and Whitney were all there. I was a little surprised to see Whitney, but she was happily talking to Alex Bedford. She caught my eye and waved. She said something to Alex and walked over to where we were sitting.

"Eliza, you did a great job tonight! Are you going to try out for Sound Harmony?" she asked enthusiastically.

I was overwhelmingly pleased to receive a compliment from Whitney both because she belonged to the Jubilee choir—the top choir in our school—and because she was one of Ms. Steele's favorite students.

"Thanks, Whitney! You did an awesome job, too! I always look forward to watching you guys perform." I sighed. "As for Sound Harmony, I've thought about it, but there are so many girls planning on trying out that I don't know if I should even bother."

Sound Harmony was the all-girls junior choir, and I secretly longed to be a part of it.

Whitney shook her head. "Do it. You have an *amazing* voice! I'm sure you'll make it, and I wouldn't doubt if you made Jubilee the next year." She smiled at me encouragingly. "It's too bad we won't be in your group for prom, but hopefully I'll see you at the dance."

"Yeah, that would be great! Are you going with Alex?" I asked.

She beamed, and I could tell that she liked him even more than I'd thought. "Yes, he asked me a few days ago." She glanced at him briefly, and her eyes were dreamy when she looked back at me. "I'll talk to you later, but remember what I said about tryouts."

"Thanks, I will." I felt like I was on cloud nine. Whitney had given me the confidence boost I needed, and even if I didn't make it in Sound Harmony, at least I wouldn't have the regret of not giving it a shot.

"She's totally right," Jason said. "You *have* to try out. I can't believe you'd even think you wouldn't make it. You have the most incredible voice I've ever heard and Ms. Steele loves you."

I blushed. "Thanks, that's really sweet of you to say. I'll try out next week, and we'll see what happens."

At that moment, Luke appeared at the top of the stairs, carrying a two-liter bottle of soda in one hand while balancing a tray of cookies in his other hand. He looked as if he were used to hosting parties all the time, and it made him all the more attractive.

After he'd set everything on the table, he turned around and almost immediately caught my eye. I looked away quickly, embarrassed to have been caught staring. I tried to cover it up by sweeping the rest of the room casually, but I couldn't help but glance at him out of the corner of my eye.

A few girls I didn't recognize instantly flocked to Luke's side, and by the way they touched his shirt I imagined they were complimenting his clothes. I had to admit, he looked extra handsome tonight. He had changed out of the formal suit he wore for senior choir and into a brown hoodie and jeans. The clothes were casual, but somehow he made them look like they could be featured in a magazine ad.

I was beginning to feel that absurdly jealous feeling as I watched the girls fawn over him, so I diverted my attention elsewhere. I ate all the food on my plate, and after my second cup of soda, I realized I was in desperate need of a bathroom break.

"Hey, Jason, do you know where the bathroom is?"

"Yeah, down that hall, second door on the left."

"Thanks. I'll be right back." I stood up and took my plate over to the trash can, which happened to be right next to Luke and his adoring fans. I kept my eyes on the floor, not daring to look up as I dropped my plate into the black plastic lining, but I felt a pair of eyes watching me.

"Hey, Liza, you did a great job tonight." Luke's warm voice sent shivers down my spine.

I looked up into his gorgeous brown eyes. "Thanks, you did too." I couldn't help but notice that the faces of the two girls next to him had suddenly become menacing. The looks they were giving me screamed, "Back off!" so without saying another word, I turned and walked down the hall toward the bathroom.

After using the restroom, I was about to turn back down the hall toward the party when I spotted a balcony at the other end of the hallway. It beckoned to me with the bluish cast of moonlight, and I decided that since the door was already open, I wouldn't be imposing if I checked it out.

I was a few steps from reaching the door when I heard voices and stopped dead in my tracks.

"Chelsea, you should have told me. I totally would have understood."

"I know, Owen, and I'm so sorry I wasn't honest with you in the first place. I guess I was embarrassed that my dad lost his job, and I didn't want you to feel sorry for me. When I got that money today, I thought for sure it was from you. You *promise* it wasn't?"

"I wish I could say that it was, but I swear I had no idea what your family was going through."

"Huh. Well, hopefully someday I'll found out who it was so I can thank them. It was one of the nicest things anyone's ever done for me. I tried to get my dad to take the money, but he insisted that I use it for my dress . . . so, if you can forgive me, I'd love to go to prom with you."

"Chelsea, you know there's no one else I'd rather go with," Owen said. "Listen, is there anything I can do to help you? It must be really tough to go through something like this."

"That's sweet of you, but no. It's time for me to grow up, I think. I'm going to sell my car and get a job. Hopefully that will help to pay off some of our bills, and my dad is already applying at different companies. It's going to be hard, but we'll get through it."

I couldn't believe this was the same Chelsea Andrews talking! She sounded truly sincere and even—dare I say it?—*humble.* I felt a fresh confirmation that I'd done the right thing by giving her the money, and I hoped she'd never find out it was from me—the secrecy was the fun part.

I was about to turn around and quietly make my way down the hall when Chelsea and Owen suddenly emerged from the balcony doorway, almost bumping into me.

"Oops! Sorry." Owen had his arm around Chelsea, and they steered around me. Chelsea gave me a brief smile, but neither of them seemed to suspect that I'd heard their conversation.

I smiled back. "No problem." After they left, I made my way out onto the balcony.

I inhaled deeply. It was a perfect spring evening. A soft breeze caressed my cheek and carried the heavenly scent of lilac. It gently blew the tender limbs of a willow tree that stood sentry in the backyard.

I spotted a bench swing and sat down to enjoy the peaceful moment. I closed my eyes and thought back over the happy events of the day.

"I see you found my favorite hangout. Mind if I join you?" Luke's voice startled me, and my heart began a rapid staccato as he sat down by my side.

"Not at all. It's beautiful out here," I managed.

"Yeah, it is. Lots of times, this is where I come to do my homework or to just sit and think." His voice was soft and thoughtful, and I felt goose bumps on the back of my neck as I sensed how close our bodies were. I tried to think of something to say, but my mind was blissfully blank. With anyone else, it might have been uncomfortable, but somehow the silence felt relaxed with Luke.

After a few moments, he turned to me. "I've never seen you in a dress before. You look . . . um . . . really nice." He sort of winced as the words came out, and I wasn't sure how I was supposed to respond.

"Uh, thanks. I see *you* didn't waste any time in changing out of your suit. When you're a missionary, you're going to have to get used to wearing one, you know," I chided him playfully, trying to smooth over the awkward moment.

He laughed. "That's a good point. I guess I'm just trying to enjoy my casual clothes while I still can." He got an excited look in his eyes and lowered his tone confidentially. "I should be able to submit my papers in a few more weeks."

"Awesome!" I was genuinely happy for him and couldn't help but wonder where someone like Luke would end up serving.

Then, he unexpectedly reached over and placed his hand on mine. His touch sent an electric shock running up the length of my arm and into every part of my body!

"Eliza, I'm glad I have someone like you that I can tell these kinds of things to. I—" Before he could say anything else, I snatched my hand out from under his and stood up.

"Sorry, I . . . I think I better get back into the party. Jason— h-he's probably wondering where I went." My voice stuttered in confusion, and Luke looked up at me in a mixture of panic and remorse.

"No, please, just wait a second . . ."

But I had already turned around and was headed back down the hall, my mind racing a thousand miles an hour.

Never in my entire life had I felt this way before, and my instinct was to run! Luke had touched me once before, back in the hallway on that fateful first day of school—but this had been different. This time he hadn't touched my hand to help me up, but of his own choice! I knew from that moment that my heart was in serious danger.

I already felt physically pained from leaving him, and every cell in my body shouted at me to run back and apologize—to do *anything* that would bring me close to him again, but I fought the impulse and kept my feet moving back to the game room. I needed more time to sort through my feelings before facing Luke again. I was practically Jason's girlfriend, for crying out loud! I needed to calm my frenzied heart. Surely his touching my hand had just been a friendly gesture. He must think I was a complete maniac for running away! But I couldn't be his friend in the way that I was sure he wanted; not when being in his presence made me feel so entirely out of balance. I'd need time to carefully guard my heart before I could offer him friendship, and *only* friendship. Yes, time was what I needed. Time would solve everything.

I entered the game room and saw Jason sitting in the same spot on the sofa. He was watching some people playing tennis on a video game, but his face looked somewhat concerned. As soon as he saw me, the concern melted away and he smiled.

"Hey, I was about to ask one of the girls to check on you. Are you all right?"

"Um, not really." The noise and commotion from the room was making me feel more confused, and I kept looking over my shoulder anxiously for any sight of Luke. It would be humiliating to face him again so soon after my freak-out on the balcony, but even worse was the thought of him seeing me with Jason—especially if Jason wanted to hold my hand again.

"I have a really bad headache. Would you mind taking me home?" I begged.

He jumped up. "Sure. Do you want me to ask Luke for some Tylenol or something?"

"No, that's okay. I just want to go home and lie down," I said truthfully.

"All right, let's go." Jason gently took my arm, leading me through the crowd and out of the house. He checked my face in concern every few seconds and kept asking if there was anything he could do.

I reassured him that I was going to be fine, that it really wasn't a big deal, but the scene on the balcony kept running through my mind. Each time I thought of it, I was more shocked and embarrassed at myself, and a flood of tears crept dangerously close to the surface.

Jason pulled into my driveway and gave me a quick good night hug. Then he waited until I'd gone into the house before he finally left.

It was a little past 10:15 when I walked through the front door.

My parents were in the family room, sharing a bowl of popcorn and watching an old movie. They looked up at me in surprise.

"Home already?" Dad asked incredulously. The expression on his face was one of unmasked enthusiasm. I could practically read the thought running through his mind, *Maybe this Jason guy isn't so bad after all!*

Mom, however, was more perceptive. "Is everything all right, sweetie?" she asked, setting down the bowl of popcorn.

Her genuine concern almost caused me to unleash the tears, but I put on my best game face and smiled feebly. "Yes, I just had a headache so I felt like coming home."

"I'm sorry, honey. Is there anything I can get you?"

"No, I'll be fine. I think I'll take a shower and go to bed."

"That's a good idea." Seemingly satisfied by my answer, she picked up the popcorn bowl and Dad restarted the movie.

I had headed for the kitchen when Mom spoke again. "Don't

forget that Dad and I are leaving early in the morning. We'll come in to say good-bye before we go and give you any instructions you might need."

"Oh, right. Okay." I actually *had* forgotten that Mom and Dad were leaving on a trip tomorrow.

Dad sometimes had to travel for business, and occasionally he would take all of us with him. Now that I was old enough, though, he and Mom trusted me to stay home with Courtney so they could have a night away once in a while.

I usually looked forward to their trips for weeks in advance. The feeling of being in a house with no parents totally thrilled me. Normally Jill would spend the night when my parents were out of town, which made it seem more like a party. I felt a twinge of sadness as I remembered how we'd stay up half the night eating junk food and watching movies until we both fell asleep on the floor. Courtney would usually join us too, excited to be hanging out with us. Thinking of Courtney, I suddenly wondered if she'd gotten my surprise.

When I reached my bedroom door, I looked down the hall and heard music coming from her room. She *must* have gotten my note by now. Despite all the junk on her bed, there was no way she could have missed the king-sized, shiny wrapper.

I entered my room hopefully, expecting a little thank-you note on my bed or an acknowledgment of some sort, but everything was just as I'd left it.

I sighed as I retrieved the yellow candle from my backpack where I'd stashed it and placed it gently in the nightstand drawer with my other special keepsakes. Maybe my nice gesture to

Courtney hadn't made a difference, but at least I knew I'd helped Chelsea, and that felt good.

I stared at the objects in my drawer, noticing that I was beginning to acquire quite a collection. Just two more to go and the collection would be complete. I wondered distractedly what those items would be, but my nagging thoughts kept trying to force me to think about something I was trying to forget. I rubbed my eyes wearily and made my way to the shower.

My cell phone buzzed, and I flipped it open to find a text message from Jason.

Jason: Hey, I hope your headache is better. Can't wait to hear you sing again for Sat. concert. Or for our date after. ;) Sleep tight!

I smiled, but didn't feel up to replying, and I was grateful he'd ended his message in such a way that I didn't have to.

As the hot water enveloped me, I finally relaxed and released my thoughts, allowing myself to think about tonight's encounter with Luke. I tried to dissect meaning from every word he'd spoken and each gesture he'd made—especially the last one.

Did he have any idea what he'd done to me by taking my hand? Maybe he was a touchy-feely kind of person and physical contact was natural to him. Maybe he held lots of girls' hands.

The thought was like poison in my bloodstream, and I immediately rejected it. I'd never seen him touch another girl before, not even in a friendly, joking kind of way, and I *knew* he wasn't a player.

This allowed only one other solution, but it was so preposterous that I immediately shook my head to banish the thought. Luke

would *never* be interested in me as more than a friend, and allowing myself to hope would only cause me incredible heartache.

Besides, I wasn't a player either, and Jason and I were all but
officially dating—one good "DTR" session and we'd be a couple. I
had a feeling that the opportunity for "defining the relationship"
would come on prom night; maybe I'd even get my first kiss. I
simply couldn't allow my thoughts to dwell so much on Luke. It
wasn't fair to Jason, and it wasn't fair to my unprotected heart.

Still, I couldn't help but wonder what would have happened if
I hadn't run off when I did. What had Luke wanted to say to me? I
remembered the pained look in his eyes, and I wanted to slap myself for being so rash. He had been in the middle of thanking me
for listening to him, and one touch of his hand had made me bolt
like a crazed rabbit. I couldn't imagine what he must think of me.
Part of me hoped that I'd never have to face him again, while the
other part of me hoped desperately that I *would* face him again—
and soon.

InTeGriTY

"Till I die I will not remove mine integrity from me."

—JOB 27:5

CHAPTER

twenty

Bodies were everywhere, strewn over the floor of what appeared to be a royal court. It amazed me that after all the experiences I'd had with Grandma I could *still* be surprised by my surroundings, but this was the most shocking scene we'd come upon yet. The sight was eerie, and I turned to Grandma with frightened eyes.

"Please tell me these people aren't all dead, because if they are, you've completely scarred me for life!"

Grandma smiled reassuringly. "No, they're not dead. Take a good look around and tell me if you can figure out what we're witnessing here. I'll give you a hint: this story is told in the Book of Mormon."

I was too relieved about the fact that I wasn't witnessing a cavernous coffin to be mad at Grandma for playing the guessing game. Besides, I knew the stories from the Book of Mormon pretty well and was confident I could figure this one out.

I studied the people's clothes, which were mostly animal skins and hides fashioned into various apparel. At the front of the room there was a man lying on a bed with fur blankets around his still form. He was the most ornately clothed, and the feathered and jeweled headdress near his head made it clear that he was the ruler of whatever land this was.

A woman lying on the floor near his bed was dressed in a similar way, with the addition of an impressively large necklace and gold bracelets on her arms. I assumed she was the queen, and I racked my brain for a story which contained a king and a queen in the Book of Mormon.

The other people in the room all appeared to be servants, and they all had brown or bronze-colored skin—all except one.

A large, muscular servant stood out from the others both because of his dress and because of his skin tone. It was easy to tell that he was not native to this land, and I puzzled over this fact until something caught my eye.

A servant woman was kneeling in the back of the room, observing the scene before her with tears in her eyes. Although she was crying, I soon realized they were tears of joy. Her countenance was lit up with a glorious smile as she bowed her head in prayer. She knelt for several moments, and then she stood up and fled from the room.

I looked at Grandma, trying to disguise my bewilderment. Something about all of this was familiar, and I *knew* I'd heard this story before, but I couldn't quite put my finger on it, and that made me feel irritated.

"So, any guesses yet?" Grandma teased. I could tell from her delighted expression that she knew I was stumped but that I wasn't about to give in.

"Just give me a few minutes. I know I can figure this out!" I snapped as I returned my attention to the foreigner. Something told me that he was the key to unlocking this mystery.

In my head, I quickly went through each book in the Book of Mormon, thinking through every story I could remember that mentioned a king. It was the book of Alma that finally gave me my answer.

"I've got it!" I yelled triumphantly, momentarily forgetting my natural inclination to speak quietly around all of the resting figures on the floor. "This is the story of Ammon and King Lamoni, isn't it?" And then, after seeing Grandma's nod, I couldn't help but rub it in. I danced merrily in a circle around her chanting, "I got it ri-ght, I got it ri-ght, ha-ha-ha-ha-ha-HA!"

Grandma chuckled and then asked, "All right, Miss Smarty-pants, then can you tell me the name of the woman who went running from the room a few moments ago?"

I stopped dead in my tracks. "Her name? Does it even *mention* her name in the scriptures?" I asked incredulously.

Grandma theatrically placed a hand over her heart and assumed an expression of false shock. "You mean to tell me you don't know? Tsk-tsk!"

"Oh, come on, Grandma! I don't have all the names in the Book of Mormon memorized. I bet not even my seminary teacher knows all of them by heart."

"Well, this is a name you *should* know, because this woman is the reason we're here. Her name was Abish, and she was the queen's servant."

I said the name a few times, liking the way it sounded as it came out of my mouth. *Abish.*

"After her father received 'a remarkable vision,' as the scriptures tell it, she was converted to the Lord. She held this testimony close to her heart for many years and secretly remained faithful until the time came to act on her faith. Of all the servants of King Lamoni, she alone knew what was taking place when the king and all of his court fell to the earth. The Lord had prepared her, and she was ready.

"After witnessing what happened here in this room, she was overjoyed because she knew it was the power of God. She thought that if she could gather as many people as possible to come see what was happening, they would also become converted."

While Grandma spoke, people began gathering in the court, and it wasn't long before a large crowd had assembled. They all seemed to be incredibly astonished at the scene that lay before them.

Unfortunately, it wasn't long before an undercurrent of conflict swept through the group as they debated over the cause of what they were witnessing. With hatred burning in their eyes, many men repeatedly pointed to Ammon in accusation.

One man in particular seemed to be seething with uncontrollable rage. All of a sudden, he drew his sword and rushed toward Ammon's still frame. I gasped in shock and horror, wanting desperately to intervene in some way, but moments before the man reached Ammon, he stopped as if he'd hit a brick wall and fell to the ground.

There was complete silence in the room as a man went over to check on the fallen swordsman. He looked up at the crowd and shook his head, confirming that the man had died.

Immediately, the room erupted into shrieks and outcries. Confusion, fear, and anger all created an atmosphere of chaos as the people tried to figure out what was happening.

In the midst of the turmoil, I saw a woman push her way to the front of the crowd. It was Abish, and she looked completely distraught and heartbroken. Tears streamed down her face as she watched the spirit of contention overtaking the crowd. She had gathered these people with the intent of leading them to the truth, but they were blind to the hand of God.

I watched her bow her head in earnest prayer, and then she did something remarkable. She wiped her tears, and with head held high, she began walking toward the queen. Some watched her, waiting to see if she would be struck dead as the last man had been, but many others were completely unaware of her, arguing among themselves.

Abish stood beside the queen. Reaching down, she took her by the hand and immediately the queen stood up. Her countenance was glorious! She praised God and spoke many words while several people in the crowd watched in amazement.

The queen then took King Lamoni by the hand, and he also stood, his face radiating pure joy. After a few moments, he saw the arguments that were taking place among his people. He instantly went to them and began quieting their disputes, preaching the gospel to any who would listen.

I couldn't help but watch Abish as all of this was taking place. The happiness had returned to her face, and she continued to move quietly about, helping and serving whoever was in need, all the while giving thanks to the Lord for this great miracle.

"So," Grandma whispered, "do you think you'll be able to remember her name now?"

I nodded resolutely. "I had no idea what a special person she was! Why have I never paid attention to this part of the story before?"

"Abish is just one of the many examples of people who go quietly about, staying faithful and doing good works with little or no recognition. In the eyes of her people, she was merely a servant, but in the eyes of the Lord, she was much, much more. He knew her heart, and He knew that when the time came, she would not fail Him because she possessed something special—integrity." Grandma looked at me pointedly, and I smiled. I should have remembered that this was the value we were focusing on tonight.

She continued. "Can you imagine the courage it would have taken to remain faithful for so many years when you were the *only one* who believed in the true gospel? Can you imagine how frightening it would be to attempt to touch the queen when you'd just seen a man struck dead for coming within mere feet of Ammon?" She paused, emphasizing her next words. "Oh, yes, Abish had integrity, and there's a great lesson to be learned from her story."

The walls began to fade, and I knew we were done visiting this scene. I looked once more at Abish and smiled, wishing she could see me and that I could thank her. It was strange that I could feel a bond with a woman who'd lived thousands of years before me, yet somehow it seemed like if I'd lived back then we would have been friends, and that thought made me happy.

The room disappeared around us, and Grandma and I now stood on a long gravel road that seemed to stretch for miles. The terrain around us was completely flat and barren, reminding me of what the Midwest must have been like during the Dust Bowl. In fact, standing there, I felt almost as if I were Dorothy and this was the legendary Yellow Brick Road.

Just as I was about to begin singing a rendition of "Somewhere Over the Rainbow," Grandma's voice broke through my thoughts and saved me from myself.

"You know, Eliza, when it comes right down to it, integrity is a simple concept. It means staying true to the things you know are right, regardless of what others may think or say. It's putting your beliefs into action and truly *living* the gospel, not just claiming to be a member of the Church.

"Having integrity is like telling someone you're going to walk down this road until you get to the end of it, and then starting out. It might seem easy at first, but when the tornadoes come or when you see people you love heading off the path, claiming they've found a better way, it gets a little tougher to keep the goal in sight."

She bent down and picked up a rock. It was a deep shade of purple and perfectly smooth. "However," she continued as she handed it to me, "if you stay the course and keep moving down the path, eventually you'll get to the end, where you'll find a reward so great you'll know it was all worth it."

I squeezed the rock in my hand as I looked down the seemingly endless stretch of road. It appeared daunting, not being able to see the end from where I stood, but I figured that's where Grandma's lesson on faith came in. If you could see the end when you began, then it wouldn't require any faith to get started.

"I think I understand what you're trying to say, Grandma." A rush of sadness overwhelmed me as I suddenly realized that we had only one more value to discuss. "Will you still come to visit me after the next dream? I'll really miss you if you don't."

Her expression saddened a bit as she smiled. "No sense wastin' time and tissues worrying about that now. Just remember what you learned tonight, and I'll be back again when you're ready."

I wanted to stay with her, but slowly the warmth of Grandma's smile was replaced by the warmth of my bedspread, and I was fast asleep.

CHAPTER

"Wake up, sweetie." Mom's gentle voice aroused me from deep slumber, and I squinted against the early morning sunlight. "Dad and I are leaving in a few minutes, and I wanted to make sure you didn't have any questions before we go."

I blinked and sat up in bed. "Um, I don't think so. Unless you have certain rules for Courtney."

My parents had established a few set rules for when they weren't home, and I knew them by heart. Rule number 1: No boys allowed in the house. Rule number 2: No throwing wild parties (which couldn't really happen unless rule number 1 was broken). Rule number 3: Be home by curfew.

Mom sighed. "Actually, I'd like you to keep an eye on Courtney while we're gone. She's been acting so different lately, and I'm worried about her. If it's not too much trouble, I'd like you to send her a text every so often asking where she is and what she's doing."

She patted my knee. "I know you have a busy day, but I'll feel better knowing you're checking in on her often. I didn't want her to be lonely tonight, so I told her Alexis could stay over. Courtney knows the rules, but call me if anything goes wrong, okay? In fact,

call me tonight when you get home and let me know how everything is going." She sighed again, her brow wrinkling with concern. "Maybe I shouldn't go with Dad today. I just have this feeling
like something's wrong."

I placed my hand on her arm. "Don't worry, Mom. You and
Dad deserve a night away. I promise I'll check in on Courtney a
lot—I'll even text her every hour if you want me to. Everything will
be fine. You guys go and enjoy yourselves."

Conflicting emotions passed across Mom's face as she
struggled to decide. It was obvious she really wanted to go with
Dad, and after I gave her another squeeze and a smile of encouragement, she relented. "Okay. I guess it's only one night. Thanks,
sweetheart. I'm so lucky to have a daughter as trustworthy as you."
She gave me a hug. "Don't hesitate to call us anytime. And I left the
address and phone number of our hotel in Denver, just in case,
but I'll always have my cell with me, and—"

"Come on, Vivian!" Dad appeared in my doorway. "Eliza's a
big girl now, and she can handle this. If we don't leave now we're
going to miss our flight." Dad walked into my room and smiled
at Mom playfully before kissing her cheek. I gave him a grateful
wink, and he leaned down to hug me good-bye. "See you tomorrow, captain. You're in charge of the home front until we get back."

"Aye-aye, sir!" I saluted, and he saluted back, then took hold
of Mom's hand and marched her out of the room.

"Are you sure you don't mind us missing the concert tonight?"
I heard her call from down the hall in a last attempt to guilt herself
into staying.

"I already told you, it's fine! You were there last night *and* you
taped it. Get out of here already!" I said in exasperation.

"Okay, love you!" Now her voice was coming from the stairway.

"Love you too!"

After a few moments, I heard the luggage rolling on the kitchen floor, followed by the door closing. Amazing! They actually left. I smiled as I thought of Mom and her worries, but then I heard the music blasting from Courtney's room. I hoped I wasn't getting in over my head when I'd promised everything would be fine.

Courtney was definitely going through some sort of phase, and I still couldn't understand why. I thought about Grandma and the advice she'd given me and decided I would try to get closer to my sister by continuing small acts of service.

Skipping down to the kitchen, I poured myself a bowl of cereal and then one for Courtney. After placing her bowl and a glass of juice on a tray, I made my way up to her room. I knocked on her door, but her music was still blasting, so I entered before waiting for an answer. She was sitting up in her bed with a magazine in one hand and her cell phone in the other. Texting Alexis, no doubt. She didn't bother to look up as she said sarcastically, "Thanks for knocking."

I did my best to maintain a cheerful disposition. "I did knock, but I guess you couldn't hear it over the music." I stepped over to her stereo and turned down the volume a few notches. "I brought you some breakfast. Are you hungry?"

Courtney glanced up from her magazine and looked at me for the first time. I might have imagined it, but I thought I detected a hint of surprise in her eyes.

"Yeah, I'm kind of hungry. Thanks." She set down her things

and took the tray from me. I sat on the edge of her bed, and after a few mouthfuls she asked, "Why are you being so nice to me all of a sudden?"

"I just realized that I haven't talked to you in a long time, and I miss you. Mom and Dad left a few minutes ago. What are your plans for today?"

She shrugged. "I dunno. Alexis is coming over in a little while, and I guess we'll figure something out when she gets here."

I nodded. "I'm sorry I won't be around much today. I have to work, and then I have the concert and a date after that, but I'll check in on you to see how things are going, okay?"

Courtney instantly looked annoyed. "You don't have to babysit me. I'll be fine."

"I know. I just don't want you to feel like I don't care, and besides," I added authoritatively, "Mom asked me to."

"Mom asked you to check on me?" she asked suspiciously.

"Yeah, you know how Mom is." I smiled and shrugged, trying to smooth down the irritation I could see in Courtney's eyes. I looked around her room, searching for a way to change the subject, when something on her dresser caught my attention. It was a black velvet drawstring bag, and as soon as I saw it, I remembered—Courtney collected rocks!

"How's your rock collection coming?" I moved to the dresser and picked up the bag as casually as I could. "Mind if I take a look?"

"Huh?" She was once again absorbed in her magazine, and she looked up in irritation. "Oh, yeah. I haven't collected rocks for a long time. It was a stupid hobby."

I winced a little at her words. She used to love spending time outside and collecting things. What was happening to my little sister? Since she didn't seem to care one way or the other, I turned my back to her and opened the bag. As the contents spilled onto my palm, I was immediately disappointed. There were several rocks here, but no purple stone.

Fighting to hide my disappointment, I was about to return the rocks when I felt a hard lump at the bottom of the bag. Somehow I'd missed one! I quickly turned the bag upside down and heard a soft plop as the object fell onto the carpet.

The purple stone! Smiling triumphantly, I picked it up and inspected its smooth surface. Grandma would be so irritated to know that I'd found it this fast!

But I hadn't won yet. The rock still belonged to Courtney. I replaced the rest of the stones in the bag and placed it back on the dresser, and then turned to her. She was already annoyed by my presence so I knew I had to keep things short and sweet.

"Hey, Court, since you're not collecting rocks anymore, do you mind if I keep this one?"

She put down her magazine and looked at me suspiciously. "Why?"

"I don't know . . . it's pretty. Where'd you get it?"

"Mom gave me that one. She said it used to be Great-grandma's so I thought it was special. It was one of my favorites." She eyed the stone in my hand, and for one terrifying moment, I thought she wasn't going to let me keep it.

"Well, if it's special to you . . ." I unwillingly moved to put the token back in the bag, but Courtney sighed.

"You can have it, if it means you'll leave me alone."

"Thanks. Sorry I bothered you." I was deeply hurt by

Courtney's rudeness, but I realized I used to treat her the same way when she came into my room.

I turned to leave, but Mom's words kept ringing in my ears and so I stopped at the door. "Courtney, are you okay?" I asked timidly.

"I'm fine!" she snapped. "Why does everyone think something's wrong? I'm the same old Courtney I've always been. I don't get why everyone's freaking out lately!"

I nodded and mumbled a quick "Sorry" before stepping into the hallway and closing the door behind me. I took a deep breath as I heard Courtney crank the volume on her music to a deafening roar.

One thing was for certain—the girl in that room was anything *but* the same old Courtney.

⸎

"Thanks for coming in. Have a nice day!" I smiled at the woman who walked from the store, clutching her bag of chocolates as if they were a precious treasure.

It had been a surprisingly busy day, and I was glad, because it had helped keep my mind off what I was about to do.

Butterflies raced in my stomach as I heard the store bell ring and looked up to see Cynthia striding in. She smiled at me and gave me a thumbs-up as she pointed to the line of shoppers waiting to buy candy. In no time at all, she donned her apron and came out to help me. We were busy for twenty minutes straight until the last customer finally left, allowing us a few moments to relax.

"Whew! Has it been like this all day?" Cynthia's expression was hopeful.

"Yeah, I've never had such a busy Saturday," I confessed.

"Wow! Thanks for staying a few minutes extra to help with the rush. I'm really impressed with how well you handled all of those customers without losing your cool."

"Thanks. I'd stay longer to help if I could, but the concert starts soon, and I can't be late."

"Oh, you better get a move on then." She smiled.

"Okay." I walked to the back room and hung up my apron, almost deciding this conversation could wait until another day, but after glancing at the schedule on the wall, I knew it was now or never.

I grabbed my purse and headed back to the counter. I glanced at the door, making sure there weren't any customers around. "Um, Cynthia, can I talk to you for a second?"

"Sure, what is it?" She turned and faced me with her full attention, a manner she had which I found enormously intimidating.

"Well, I've thought a lot about this, and I want you to know how much I've appreciated working here, but I'm not going to be able to work Sundays."

Cynthia looked down briefly in disappointment and then back up at me. "Are you sure about this, Eliza? You've been such a great employee that I was about to offer you a raise."

The look on her face made me feel like I was being stupid, and I considered backing out. *Besides, a raise would be so nice!* I shifted uncomfortably and put my hands in my pockets, instantly feeling emboldened by the glassy stone at my fingertips.

"Yes, I'm sure. This is something that's really important to me. I'll work my two weeks though . . . if you want me to?" I ventured. This was the first job I'd ever quit, and I wasn't sure what the proper procedure was.

Cynthia sighed and shook her head. "All right then, if that's what you want. I'd like you to finish out your two weeks so I have time to post the job and find a replacement for you."

"Okay. I'll see you next week then." I turned and rushed from the store, not wanting to prolong the awkward moment any longer than necessary. I felt a ping of disappointment. I'd secretly hoped that Cynthia would make an exception for me and allow me to stay on without working Sundays, but that obviously wasn't going to happen.

Stronger than the feeling of disappointment, however, was the wonderful and peaceful feeling that I'd done the right thing. I'd stood up for my beliefs, and regardless of what the temporal consequences might be, I knew that Heavenly Father was proud of me. Finding another job would be inconvenient, but finding integrity was something much more valuable.

℮ ⚶

"Okay, guys, quiet down, the movie's starting." Clark's voice boomed.

We were all gathered in the theater room in the basement of Danny's house. I sat next to Jason, sharing a box of chocolate-covered mints with him. The concert was over, thank goodness! My solo had gone well, and I was proud of my performance, but it was definitely a relief to have it over with now.

Knowing that we'd be watching a movie after the concert, I'd brought a pair of casual clothes to change into, and I leaned back comfortably in the sofa. Glancing at the various couples around the room, I was painfully aware of Luke's absence. We'd seen him after the concert, and Jason had invited him to join our group, but he'd mumbled something about having other plans.

I'd tried to get him to look at me so I could smile or somehow convey an apology for my behavior last night, but he'd completely avoided my eyes. Adding to my misery was the devastatingly handsome way he looked in his suit. The mere sight of him had caused me to feel almost faint. He looked like he belonged in the starring role of some chick flick, yet there was no trace of the arrogance that often surrounded actors or models. He had somehow miraculously managed to be unaware of his good looks, which only served to make him all the more appealing.

"Have you seen this movie before?" Jason asked, snapping me out of my daydreaming.

"Um, I'm not sure. Which one is it?" I hoped the guilt I felt from thinking about Luke wasn't obvious on my face.

"It's called *The Fever of Love,* and I think it just came out on DVD."

"Huh . . . no, I haven't seen it. Have you?"

"Nope."

I'd seen previews for this movie, and I knew it was rated PG-13. Instantly, I felt a knot forming in my stomach. My parents didn't allow us to watch a PG-13 movie unless they'd seen it first and given permission. This was the first time I'd been faced with the situation of having to explain that on a date. What made it more intimidating was that no one else in the room seemed to be the least bit uncomfortable.

I couldn't help but notice Becka and Britney sitting with their dates. They'd been giving me dirty looks all night and whispering and laughing to each other. I imagined how they'd ridicule me if I were to confess that I wasn't comfortable watching this movie.

I began to feel uneasy as I tried to decide what to do, and that feeling only intensified once the lights were turned off and the movie began. Jason put his arm around me, and I tried to relax, but his touch only served to confuse me more. I decided I would wait and see what the movie was about before saying anything. After all, maybe it wouldn't be *that* bad and all my worrying was for nothing.

After the first few scenes, however, I knew that this was not the type of movie my parents would approve of. The language was crude, and it wasn't long before an extremely offensive bedroom scene came on. I felt sick inside, and I looked around to see if anyone else was reacting as I was, but no one else seemed bothered. I turned my eyes away from the screen and contemplated just closing my eyes for the rest of the movie, but the sickening feeling persisted.

"Jason, I need to go," I whispered.

He turned to me. "Is everything okay?" he asked.

"Yeah. It's . . . it's just that this movie makes me feel kind of uncomfortable. Do you mind if we go do something else?"

His expression was a mixture of surprise and relief; he was obviously feeling the same way I was. "Sure, let's get out of here." He took my hand and stood up, heading for the door. "See you later, guys," he said to Clark and Danny over the booming of the surround sound.

"Are you leaving already?" Clark asked.

"Yeah, we're not really into this movie. We're gonna go play miniature golf. Anybody want to join us?"

I smiled at Jason in admiration, not believing he had the guts to speak up like this in front of everyone. Clark looked slightly offended, but I saw a few people shift uncertainly as if they weren't sure what to do. After a few moments though, no one spoke up so Jason and I left alone.

Once we were in the car I turned to him and said, "Thanks for being so understanding about that. I really appreciate it."

Jason frowned. "No, thank *you* for having the nerve to say something. That movie was trashy, and I was feeling the same way, but I was too chicken to do anything about it."

"I was proud of the way you told Clark how you felt, and how you invited others to come with us. That took some serious courage!"

"Nah." He smiled sadly. "It's too bad no one else came. I thought Danny would at least offer to put in another movie, but no such luck. I guess he just wasn't blessed with the fortune of being raised watching shows like *The Brady Bunch.*"

I laughed at Jason's playful sarcasm and felt the calm, happy reassurance that I'd done the right thing by walking out of the movie.

"So, is miniature golf really okay?" Jason asked, raising an eyebrow at me. "I just said the first thing that popped in my head."

"Sounds great. But I have to warn you, my golfing skills aren't much better than my bowling skills," I confided.

"That's fine with me! The best part of bowling with you was giving you the lessons." He winked mischievously as he began driving, and I felt my face flush crimson.

"I better send Courtney a text to make sure she's doing okay," I mumbled as I dug around in my purse for my phone. I needed something to distract me from my embarrassment over his flirtation, so I pretended to concentrate hard on the text. Jason turned up the music, and to my relief, he began talking about his excitement for the upcoming state soccer tournament.

I listened while waiting for Courtney's reply. She'd dutifully responded to my texts throughout the day, and it never took longer than a few seconds to get her replies. As the minutes ticked by, however, she still hadn't responded. I sent her another text, and another. Finally I called her, but the phone rang and rang until I got her voice mail. Why wasn't she answering?

By the time we arrived at the miniature golf course, I felt a distinct impression that something wasn't right. As with the movie, I tried to rationalize the feeling away, but it persisted. I knew I needed to go home and check on Courtney—and soon.

"Jason, you're going to think I'm crazy, but Courtney hasn't replied to my texts, and I feel like something's wrong. Do you mind if we go to my house and check it out? I *promise* I'm not always this wacko, but I'm worried."

Jason instantly backed the car out of the parking lot. "No problem, Eliza. If you feel like something's wrong, we should go check on her, especially since your parents are out of town."

I breathed a sigh of relief and touched his arm. "Thanks so much. I can't believe how nice you're being about all of this."

"Hey, like I said before, just *being* with you is fun for me. We could watch paint dry, and I'd have a good time." His eyes twinkled, and I was grateful for his ever-positive attitude.

A few dim lights flickered from inside the house as we pulled up to the curb.

"Good, it looks like she's home." I was relieved to know where Courtney was, but the feeling that something was wrong persisted. I turned to Jason. "I'm not supposed to let guys in the house when my parents aren't here, but just in case it's an intruder or something, would you mind coming in with me? I'm pretty sure my parents would approve in this situation, and as soon as we make sure things are okay, we'll leave."

Jason nodded soberly, seemingly already prepared to summon his defensive skills in case I was right. We walked up to the front door, and I opened it quietly, terrified of what I might find.

Nothing could have prepared me for the sight that was before me.

From where we stood I could see clearly into the family room, where the lights were dimmed and four young people sat together on the couch. A movie was on, and Alexis and a boy were kissing on the couch, while Courtney and Nathan Adams sat on the other side. Nathan had his arm around Courtney, and all four of them held cans of beer.

I gasped, which instantly startled everyone. Nathan dropped his beer can, spilling liquid all over Mom's rug, and leaped from the couch in one swift move.

I marched into the room. "Courtney Christine Moore!" I yelled. "What is going on here?" I couldn't keep the hysteria out of my voice, and I saw my little sister crumple, hiding her face in her hands. The two boys attempted to escape by squeezing past me, but I caught Nathan by his sleeve. "You better tell your parents about this, or I'll tell them when I see them tomorrow. And if I *ever* see you touch my little sister again, you'll live to regret it, understand?"

He nodded, and fear flooded his eyes as he realized just how serious I was. The smell of beer all over his shirt caused my stomach to roll so I let go of his sleeve, allowing him to bolt out the front door, followed closely by Alexis's friend.

I turned to Jason, who was standing behind me in shocked silence. "Jason, thanks for coming with me. I'll call you tomorrow, but right now I need to deal with this, and it's probably best if you're not here to see it."

He must have seen the fire blazing in my eyes because he nodded and quickly made his way to the door. He told me to call if I needed anything, and then hastily retreated to the safety of his car.

I spun around to face Courtney and Alexis again, trying to think of what to do next. Courtney looked humiliated and terrified as she sat hunched over on the couch, but Alexis wore a bitter scowl, and I could tell that she was simply annoyed.

"I'm going to get a rag to clean up this mess, and when I come back, I expect to hear a full explanation." I walked over and picked up the beer cans, relieved to find that at least two of them were nearly full. I was shaking as I walked into the kitchen and poured the beer down the sink and then threw the cans in the trash.

What could Courtney have possibly been thinking? It was like she was completely out of control! Mom had been right to worry. How could we not have noticed that things were so bad? These thoughts flew about in my mind as I got some rags and carpet cleaner and made my way back to the scene of the crime.

Just before entering the room, I paused and said a silent prayer. Now that the initial shock and anger were wearing off, I was sincerely afraid for my sister, and I didn't have a clue how I could help her. I asked Heavenly Father to help me to know what to say and how to react in this situation. In those few moments, I poured out my soul to Him, and almost immediately I felt the sweet assurance of the Spirit. I felt a sense of peace. I knew that Heavenly Father was aware of what was happening, and that He would guide me by the Spirit. With renewed strength, and relying on faith that I would be guided, I entered the room.

I was a little surprised to see that neither Alexis nor Courtney had moved an inch while I was gone. I'd half expected them to make a run for it as soon as I was out of sight.

I turned off the movie and started cleaning up the rug. I tried to open my mind to the promptings of the Spirit. After a few minutes of complete silence, and after I'd done as much as possible to salvage the rug, I sighed and sat down on a chair facing my sister and her friend.

"So, Courtney, why don't you tell me what happened here tonight."

Courtney's eyes widened, and she was obviously caught off guard by my calm tone. She'd probably been expecting more of the scream-fest I'd displayed earlier.

"Liza, *please* don't tell Mom and Dad about this!" she begged. "I swear this was the first time I've ever tried beer, and I've never brought boys in the house before, either. . . . I promise I won't ever do anything like this again, just please, *please* don't tell Mom and Dad!" She was almost hysterical as tears came to her eyes, and I couldn't help but go to her and put my arms around her. She began to sob while Alexis continued to glare at me from her seat on the couch.

"Okay, calm down, Courtney. I'm not worried about Mom and Dad right now—I'm worried about *you*. Court, you *know* that drinking is wrong— and *illegal*—and you *know* that you're not sup‐ posed to date until you're at least sixteen, much less be alone with a boy in the house. I don't want you to feel bad because you got caught; I want you to realize what a special person you are and that by making these bad choices you're damaging your spirit and al‐ lowing Satan into your life. I want you to feel sorry because this is a dangerous path, and it's not what Heavenly Father wants for you."

"Oh brother!" Alexis mumbled, rolling her eyes.

Trying hard to rein in my temper, I turned to her. "Is there something you'd like to say, Alexis?"

She scowled at me and then to my astonishment, unleashed her anger. "Yes, there's something I want to say. I am *so* sick of all these Mormon rules about what you can and can't do! There's nothing wrong with taking a sip of beer now and then. My dad has let me have a sip of his wine before," she sassed. "All we were do‐ ing was watching a movie with a couple of guys; it's not like we were doing drugs or having sex or something! You Mormons think that anything fun is evil, and I hate sitting here and watching you make Courtney feel bad about something that's not even a big deal."

My mouth hung open in stunned silence. I had *not* seen this coming! However, it was obvious that Alexis was nowhere near be‐ ing finished.

"I have an older brother in college who's done tons of re‐ search on different religions. He says that there's *no way* anyone in their right mind would believe in Joseph Smith if they knew the truth. He says that your whole church would fall apart if they actually taught you the truth about everything.

"He says you're all just a bunch of blind believers and that you only stay in the Church because that's all you've known your whole lives and that no one takes the time to study the real history. He says that the leaders of your church even tell you *not* to go looking into what they call anti-Mormon literature because they're afraid you'll actually find out the truth—"

As Alexis continued speaking, I felt something building within me, something I hadn't even realized was there until that moment.

Looking directly into her eyes, I quietly interrupted, "Alexis, what you're saying isn't true. I'm sure your brother is really smart and that he's a good person, but what he's taught you or led you to believe simply isn't right."

She snorted and began to protest, but I held up my hand calmly. "Knowing that the gospel is true or not isn't something that can be proven by theories or research. Otherwise it wouldn't involve any faith, and *faith* is what the Lord requires of us.

"Sure, Joseph Smith was a man, and he had his faults—I'm sure he was the first to admit that—but I know that Joseph Smith was a true prophet of God because I've felt it in my heart in a way that I can't describe. I know it more than I know anything else in this world. And because I know he was a prophet, I know that this Church is true. And *that* knowledge is the most precious thing I possess. I have read the Book of Mormon, and I've had the same witness through the Holy Ghost that it's true. It's true—all of it! Living the gospel has brought a joy and meaning to my life that I never could have imagined."

Alexis folded her arms across her chest as she listened to me.

I smiled at her. "The best part is that you can have this knowledge too if you really want it, Alexis. The invitation is open to everyone to find out for themselves; that's the beauty of it! You don't have to rely on what your brother says, or what I say, or what anyone else says, because if you really want to know, you can follow the steps and find out for *yourself*!" I felt the words flowing from my mouth without even realizing what I was saying, and I knew it was the Spirit, helping me tell Alexis what she needed to hear.

Her face softened a little, and I could tell that she was really listening, and more important, *feeling* what I was saying to her.

"She's right, Lexi." Courtney stood up and then moved to sit down next to her friend. She put her arm around Alexis. "I know the gospel is true too. I've felt it in my heart. I'm sorry I've been a bad example to you, and I hope you'll forgive me. I had no idea you felt this way about our church, but I promise that what Eliza said is true."

Courtney shrugged. "I've heard negative things about Joseph Smith before, and even about our prophet today, but I always get a confused, dark, sick feeling when I hear things like that. It's totally opposite from the way I feel when I read the scriptures or hear someone's testimony. At those times I feel warm, peaceful, and happy, and I just know that what I'm reading or hearing is true. It's not easy to find your own testimony, but it's so worth it!"

She looked down at the floor and continued, "I felt sick and empty inside when I agreed to have those guys over, and even *worse* when you brought those beers from your house and I took a few sips. The Holy Ghost kept warning me that I was making mistakes, but I chose to ignore those warnings because I wanted

Nathan to like me—and I didn't want you to make fun of me." She looked guiltily at Alexis. "But now I wish I'd been a better example to you. Lexi, you are my best friend in the whole world! I want you to have the gospel in your life because I know it will bring you so much happiness, just like it has brought happiness to me when I've chosen to follow it."

I was stunned to see tears slowly falling down Alexis's face. Courtney also seemed surprised by her friend's sudden display of emotion, and we all sat for a few moments in silence.

Alexis finally wiped at her tears and began quietly. "My mom used to take me to Primary when I was little, but then we just sort of stopped going. I think it was hard for her to go to church without my dad or brothers there, and she wanted Sundays to be a family day. I missed going to Primary, and I felt left out when all the other kids were doing Church activities and stuff."

Courtney jumped up to get Alexis a tissue. She accepted it and dabbed at her eyes. I thought maybe she was done opening up about her past, but she twisted the tissue in her hands and continued speaking. "It seemed like everyone around us was Mormon, and it made me feel like there was something wrong with my family—like people judged us for not going to church. I guess I started feeling bitter, and I didn't ever really think about whether or not the Church was true. It was easier to listen to my brother and accept what he said about it. But I think deep down my mom still believes it's true. She tries to act like she's moved on with that part of her life, but there are times when I catch her crying or with a certain expression in her eyes, and I think she's never really stopped believing." She looked at Courtney and then at me with tears in her eyes. "I want to know. I want to find out for myself if it's true like you say it is. So what should I do?"

Courtney hugged her, and then I sat down beside her and hugged her too, and we all laughed behind our tears.

I grabbed the box of tissues and passed them around again. I sat back as I thought about her question. "Well, first I think we should get you a Book of Mormon to start reading. We have a few extras so that won't be a problem, and we can mark some of our favorite passages and write our testimonies in it . . . if you want us to?"

She smiled and nodded.

I grinned. "Okay. Well then, if you want to, Courtney and I would love for you to come to church with us tomorrow. That way you can meet the missionaries and see if you feel comfortable having them teach you more about the gospel. They'll be able to answer your questions better than we can, but we'll be right beside you through all of it. Don't ever hesitate to ask us anything either. We'll do our best to answer any questions you might have."

Alexis looked at the floor and seemed a bit nervous about my invitation, and I worried that maybe I was rushing things. I was about to apologize and explain that I hadn't meant for her to feel pressured, when she unexpectedly raised her head and smiled.

"Okay. What time does your church start?" For the first time since I'd known her, Alexis looked sincerely happy. Courtney and I exchanged quick, relieved glances, and then Courtney went on to explain what time church was and what Alexis could expect there.

I was amazed at the change in the atmosphere in our home! When I'd first arrived, there had been a tangibly dark feeling, but now that darkness seemed completely dispelled and had been replaced with a beautiful, calm environment.

I told the girls I was going to the kitchen to get us a snack, and as I made my way there, I said a prayer of sincere gratitude to Heavenly Father. I'd had no idea where our conversation tonight was going to lead, and I shuddered to think of what might have happened if I hadn't prayed for guidance and instead had continued to yell and scream. Undoubtedly, I would have only made Courtney and Alexis mad, and the real root of the problem would never have been addressed. Courtney would likely have continued being withdrawn and moody, and Alexis wouldn't have had the opportunity to find out more about the gospel. It felt like a miracle.

As I gathered some cookies and a bag of potato chips, I debated whether or not to tell Mom and Dad about what happened when I called them tonight. After weighing the options, I decided it would be better to wait until they got home. Telling them now would only upset them and ruin their one night away. Besides, I would be home with Courtney and Alexis for the rest of the night to make sure there weren't any more problems.

However, somehow I knew they'd both had a change of heart and, for now, the worst was over.

CHAPTER

S he hadn't come.

I woke up Sunday morning, and it took me a few minutes to realize that Grandma hadn't visited me the night before. At first I felt slightly panicked. Had I done something wrong? Had I not tried to live with as much integrity as I should have the day before? Deep down I knew that the answer to my questions was "no." I knew that I'd tried my best to have integrity. In fact, of all the values so far, I felt like I'd applied this one more in one day than I had any of the others.

Why hadn't she come? I lay in bed pondering, until I heard a soft knock on the door. There was only a moment's pause before it opened and Courtney appeared.

"Liza, can I talk to you?" she asked timidly.

"Sure, what's up?"

As I looked at her, it was plain to see that she was feeling humble and very, *very* nervous.

"Well, it's about last night. How I took a few sips of beer, and how I broke the rules by letting boys in the house," she began.

I nodded, but couldn't stop the question from escaping my mouth. "Did you and Nathan, like . . . kiss or anything?"

She shook her head emphatically. "No, we didn't, but I was planning on it. He wants to go out with me, and he's *such* a popular guy in school. And most people my age have already had their first kiss." She brought herself up short from these rationalizations and looked at the floor. "But that's not what I was going to say."

I tried to hide my shock and disappointment at this confession from my thirteen-year-old sister, but she obviously had something else on her mind, so I forced myself to wait until I had heard everything.

"It . . . it's just that our Beehive class is supposed to go to the temple to do baptisms for the dead this week—and I'm not sure if I'm still worthy to go." Tears began to fall down her cheeks, and I quickly collected her in a hug.

"Courtney, I know this is going to sound scary, but I think the only thing that will make you feel better is if you talk to the bishop about it. I can't tell you what he'll say, but I know that he is a good man and he's there to help us. If you want, I can go to the bishop's office with you during church to help you make an appointment."

She sniffed and nodded. "Thanks, that would help. But are you sure it's serious enough that I need to tell the bishop about it?"

Courtney's face was fearful and strained, and I wished I could give her an easy answer, but I knew I wasn't the one who could properly judge in this situation.

"One of the questions we're asked during a temple recommend interview is if we keep the Word of Wisdom. I'm not sure what the bishop will decide, but I promise that if you're completely honest with him, he'll help you in the repentance process so you won't have that sick, guilty feeling anymore." She nodded, and I smiled, giving her shoulders another squeeze. "I feel like I'm getting the old Courtney back. And I'm *so* proud of you! You're doing the right thing. As you repent, you'll be able to feel closer to the Savior and to feel His love for you. It won't be easy, but it will be so worth it!"

A feeble smile crept across Courtney's lips, and she nodded. "I know you're right. Thanks for being so supportive." Her smile grew even bigger. "Isn't it exciting about Alexis? I hope she feels comfortable with us at church today."

"Me too. Did she call and ask her mom if it was okay?"

"Yeah, she called this morning and said her mom sounded surprised, but didn't seem to have a problem with it."

"Cool!"

Courtney nodded and then jumped up. "We better hurry and get ready so we're not late. It's weird not having Mom here to rush us around like a bossy hen."

I laughed as she closed the door, then got out of bed and headed for the shower.

♋

My head was full of thoughts as I drove to school Thursday morning. I switched off the radio so I could sort through the tangled mess of ideas and emotions running through my mind.

I thought back to Sunday, still grateful for how well everything had worked out. Mom and Dad had taken the news about what happened with Courtney and Alexis surprisingly well. Mom said she knew something was wrong and felt guilty she hadn't been there. I pointed out that if she'd been home we might never have realized how bad the situation had gotten. Courtney and Alexis would probably have made the mistakes somewhere else, and we might never have found out.

However, Courtney didn't get off the hook without punishment. She was grounded for two months, with the exception that Alexis could still come over to our house. Mom and Dad also took away her cell phone indefinitely, which was the biggest blow to her, but I silently agreed with them for doing it. None of us had had any idea that Courtney was thinking about starting a relationship with Nathan.

I couldn't help but smile when I thought of Nathan's contrite face on Sunday. His mom had approached me in church and apologized profusely for what had happened. She seemed almost in a state of shock, and I did my best to reassure her, but I felt sorry for her all the same.

Fortunately, Courtney hardly seemed to acknowledge Nathan's presence anymore. She and I had a heart-to-heart talk about boys and dating, and although I knew it wasn't easy for her, she agreed with the things I said. She wanted to be a better example for Alexis, and she knew that the guidelines for dating in the *For the Strength of Youth* pamphlet were inspired by the prophet.

Courtney had been able to meet with Bishop Howard right after church. She'd told me that the appointment had gone really well, and she was grateful she'd gone. Although she didn't give me all of the details, she said that the bishop had been loving and kind, and she felt like a weight had been lifted off her shoulders.

Just by looking at the difference in her countenance, I knew that Courtney was experiencing a change of heart. I was so relieved to feel like I was getting my little sister back!

Alexis went to all three meetings, though she was a little shy and quiet. We introduced her to the missionaries before sacrament meeting, and she seemed genuinely excited to meet with them to find out more about the gospel. Her mom had agreed to let her take the discussions at our house. Her dad had also consented, but only after a great deal of begging from Alexis.

She had already met with the missionaries twice this week, and the Spirit had been strong each time. Alexis seemed completely receptive to the missionary's teachings, and our entire family was excited by her progress. We were hopeful that when the time came, she would accept the invitation to be baptized and confirmed a member of the Church. This was the first experience I'd ever had with someone investigating our church, and it was inspiring to see the light and happiness apparent in Alexis's face as she began to find her own testimony.

The whole episode with Courtney had shaken my parents though, because after taking her cell away, they'd decided that I needed to "check in" my phone at nine o'clock every night.

Even though they returned it to me in the morning, I knew that if my parents had tried to enforce that rule a couple of weeks ago, I would have resisted with a furious tantrum. However, Grandma's visits had changed my heart on the subject. I knew they were just trying to protect Courtney and me from making bad choices, but since I'd already been turning off my phone at night, it wasn't a hard transition. Besides, the only person I used to text or call at night was Jill, and she still wasn't talking to me.

Jill.

I frowned as I tried to think of a way to mend our broken friendship. She hadn't been at church on Sunday, and her mom said that she wasn't feeling well again—which personally I found a little fishy. Jill hardly ever got sick . . . at least she never used to. It seemed like one more way she had changed, and I missed her terribly. There were so many things I wanted to talk to her about, so much going on in my life that I wanted to share with her.

For example, tryouts for Sound Harmony had been yesterday, and the results would be posted after school today.

Plus, Jason had left yesterday for the state soccer tournament in Southern Utah. The big game was today, and I wished I could be there, but between work and the tryouts, it hadn't been possible. I'd wished him luck before he left, and he sent me texts throughout the day, which made me feel better—until he told me that he and Luke were roommates.

Luke hadn't looked at or spoken to me since the night I'd fled the balcony. I had intended to walk with him after seminary and apologize for everything, but now every time the bell rang, he was the first one out of class. His obvious avoidance hurt more than I dared to admit. Each time I felt the pain in my heart from missing him, I berated myself for having ever entertained a hope that he could actually like me. He had only tried to be my friend, nothing more, and yet I ached for him constantly.

In quiet moments, I would replay over and over in my mind our last conversation together, only I changed the ending. Instead of running off, I sat down and listened intently while he confessed that he secretly had a crush on me and that he wanted me to be his girlfriend.

I'd stay in this daydream until it hurt too much, and then I'd force myself to face the reality that he'd probably never speak to me again.

I shook my head angrily as I got out of my car and headed toward school. Something else was bothering me, too. It had been five nights since Grandma's last visit.

After the first night of her absence, I'd thought for sure she would come the next night, but again, I'd woken up disappointed. By now I was beginning to wonder if she was coming back at all. I'd never really had a chance to say good-bye, and already it felt like the dreams had been a figment of my imagination. I had to keep opening my nightstand drawer and looking at the value keepsakes to convince myself that I hadn't made it all up.

The truth was, I missed Grandma, and more than that, I felt like I *needed* her. Without the lessons and objects she gave me to carry in my pocket, I felt lost and alone.

As my mind whirled with these thoughts, I entered the school doors and headed for my first class.

Jason had promised to call or text as soon as the game was over, so I was surprised when I heard someone yell from down the hall: "Hey everybody, we won! We took state!"

An eruption of cheers followed the announcement, and I smiled as I joined in the excited clamor. Surely Jason would text me any second with the good news. I was so excited for him, Luke, and our school!

I put some books away in my locker and closed the door, a little disappointed that I hadn't received a note today. I knew it was silly to have expected one while Jason was gone, but it had been a busy week for him, and he hadn't left me a note since last week. I hadn't realized how much I'd looked forward to those little pieces of paper until they stopped coming.

"There you are!" Keira's pixie-like face beamed at me from the side of my locker. "What are you doing standing here? Aren't you dying to find out about tryouts?"

Once again I was grateful that I'd followed the prompting to talk to Keira. She had been a source of strength and support to me since my fight with Jill. I was beginning to realize that while I thought I'd received the prompting so I could help *her*, in reality, she was helping me every bit as much.

"Of course I'm dying to know, I've been nervous all day, but I'm also scared to find out."

Keira laughed at my expression and pulled me along by the elbow.

"Come on, scaredy-cat. Let's put you out of your misery!"

I followed her obediently, but my stomach twisted in anxiety. She marched me up to the line of girls who were gathered around the audition results posted to the choir room door. I waited for a break in the crowd before timidly making my way to the paper. The names were listed in alphabetical order, so I scanned down the list. I couldn't believe what I saw.

"I made it!" I squealed as I turned to Keira. A few girls around me offered their congratulations, and Keira gave me a hug.

"I knew you would! I don't know what you were ever scared about. Your voice totally rocks!"

We made our way down the hall, and Keira shared in my enthusiasm as I bubbled over, the words of surprise and excitement spilling out of me faster than should have been humanly possible.

The feeling of having achieved something I'd dreamed of gave me a sense of total euphoria. After saying good-bye to Keira, I said a silent prayer of thanks as I made my way to my car. Not long after turning on the ignition, I got a call from my mom, wanting to know the results.

The thrills returned again as I shared my news and listened to my mom shriek excitedly. She promised to call my dad at work right away. I heard Courtney cheering in the background, which made me smile. This was turning out to be a great day!

It wasn't until I was sitting alone at work that I realized I still hadn't heard from Jason. The game had been over for hours, so I sent him a text asking how everything went. I was sure that he'd just gotten caught up in the excitement and forgotten to let me know, so when I received a reply a few minutes later, I gasped in shock.

Jason: This is Christy. Jason broke his leg. He's at the hospital right now getting a cast. He's going to be fine. He says he'll call you.

I sat in complete silence, reading the words over and over again to make sure I hadn't misunderstood. Jason broke his leg? Unthinkable! Was this some kind of sick joke? Was Jason trying to break up with me two days before prom? I felt physically ill as I typed a reply.

Me: Christy, thnx for letting me know. Tell Jason I hope he's OK. How did it happen? Is he still going to be able to come home w/the team tomorrow?

A few seconds later my phone rang. I flipped it open and was instantly greeted by a clamoring of sounds.

"Hello?" I answered uncertainly.

"Hi, Eliza, this is Christy. I had to wrestle the phone away from Jason."

I heard a slurred voice yelling in the background. "Gimme that phone, Chrishty. I'm jusht fine!"

"Um, is he okay?" If I hadn't recognized Jason's voice, I would have thought this was a prank call.

Christy giggled. "Yes, he's fine, but he's pumped full of about a thousand kilos of pain meds right now, and he's not exactly . . . coherent." She covered the receiver and said, "Hush, Jason! You're in no position to talk. I *promise* I'll tell you everything she said later."

Another frantic shout ensued. "I'm sho shorry, Elizha! Tell her I'm shorry, Chrishty!"

I felt sorry for Jason, but I had to stifle a giggle as I listened to his slurred speech. I heard a door close and suddenly the background noise was gone.

"Sorry about that," Christy said, sighing in exasperation. "He was getting so worked up that I had to leave the room. Anyway, about your question, Jason broke his leg during the game when he collided with a guy from the other team."

I gasped. "No way. How awful!"

"I know! It was a total freak accident. Jason's leg was underneath him when the other kid landed on top of him. Fortunately, it was toward the end of the game, so Jase didn't miss much. But it's still a bummer." She paused as if uncertain what to say next. "Anyway, he's going to be fine, and he'll come home with us tomorrow, but he made me *promise* to apologize for what this might mean for your prom date. I think he'd be calmer if he knew you weren't upset. Are you going to be okay?"

I felt awful to know that he was worrying about how *I* felt when he was the one with the broken leg.

"I'm totally fine! Please tell him that he doesn't need to worry—things like this happen." Despite my noble attempt at sounding sincere, tears began forming in my eyes. I had to cut this conversation short before my shaky voice gave me away. "If it's okay, I'll stop by tomorrow after school to see how Jason's doing. Please tell him not to worry one bit about prom and to just take it easy."

"Thanks, Eliza, that's really sweet of you. I'll tell him you'll stop by tomorrow. See you then!" she said cheerfully.

"Bye."

I snapped the phone shut in a stupor. In a matter of a few minutes, all of my planning and daydreaming about prom had come to a crashing halt.

Part of me held a glimmer of hope that Jason would still be able to go even with the cast on his leg, but the more realistic part of me acknowledged that there was a good chance he wouldn't be able to move at all for the next few days. I knew it was selfish to be thinking of my own disappointment when Jason was in physical pain, but I was sixteen after all, and this was supposed to have been my first prom.

Cynthia entered the store, and I carefully wiped at my eyes to hide any evidence of tears.

"Hey, Eliza, how was work tonight?" she asked.

"It was pretty slow. I think we only had about eight or nine customers come in." I headed for the back room to hang up my apron and grab my purse. Since I'd given my notice, things had been a little awkward between Cynthia and me, so I tried to keep my conversations with her brief.

As I was walking out, she called, "Your last day will be next Thursday. Does that work?"

I turned around. "Sure, that works for me. Have a good night."

"Eliza, hold on a sec."

I looked at her in surprise. Was she going to let me stay on without working Sundays?

"I just wanted to tell you that I'm sorry I can't let you work here without working Sundays, but I also wanted to tell you that I really admire you for sticking to your standards like that. I'm pretty sure I wouldn't have had the guts to do something like that when I was sixteen." She shook her head. "I obviously don't have the guts to do that *now,* but I wanted to let you know that I'm impressed by your determination. I'll let you know if I hear of any job openings, and I'll be happy to write you a letter of recommendation if you need one."

I was stunned by Cynthia's words. In all the time I'd known her, she'd never opened up to me like this.

"Thanks, Cynthia. That really means a lot to me. I'll miss working with you too. You've been a great manager." We smiled at each other, and then I waved and walked out the door.

What a crazy day! Cynthia's kind words had helped me push away the sadness about prom. As Grandma would say, "No sense wasting time and tissues" over something I couldn't control anyway. Tomorrow I would talk to Jason and figure out what we were going to do about prom. Until then, I was determined to focus on the things that had gone right today, because when I stopped to think about it, I had plenty to be thankful for.

CHAPTER

twenty-three

"Wow! How did you know I've been craving a milkshake all day?" Jason sat on the couch in his living room with his leg propped up on an ottoman.

"Lucky guess." I smiled as I handed him the milkshake and sat down next to him. "I have another surprise for you, too." I pulled a flat, wrapped object from behind my back and handed it to him.

"What's this? You didn't need to get me anything."

"Just wait till you see what it is," I said, smiling at him mischievously.

He tore open the paper and laughed. "No way! Just what I've always wanted—a Brady Bunch DVD!" I laughed as he jokingly stroked the DVD case as if it were a treasured object. "Mom will be so pleased."

"I saw it in the store and thought of you," I teased.

He rolled his eyes but smiled. "I'm surprised you even bothered coming over here after what happened." His smile faded as he looked at me.

"Oh, Jason, knock it off! You keep talking like this is your fault. I feel bad enough that you're stuck wearing a cast, but it makes me feel worse to hear that you keep blaming yourself. There will be other proms. It's no big deal."

I reached out to take his hand, and he shifted uncomfortably. Something was bothering him.

"I wish there was some way I could still take you, but the doctor said I have to stay off the leg for a few days," he explained apologetically.

"I know, and it's okay. I promise." He looked so sad that I wanted to throw my arms around him and make him believe that I really wasn't disappointed. I looked down at his cast and noticed the signatures on it.

"I see you have a fan club. Mind if I add to it?" I picked a marker from the assortment scattered on the coffee table and searched for a space to add my name. I recognized a lot of his team member's signatures—particularly Luke's. He'd written, "Tough luck, man, but you played awesome! Get well soon."

As I searched for an empty space to make my mark, I tried to think of something creative to write. Signing things like casts and yearbooks always made me feel a bit intimidated. It was hard coming up with something witty and original on the spot, but I felt extra pressure because as Jason's almost-girlfriend, a simple "Get well soon" hardly sufficed.

After a few moments' hesitation, I decided to be a bit daring. I uncapped the purple marker and wrote, "Casts are sexy—wear it with pride!" followed by a heart and my signature. I felt a bit uneasy using the word "sexy," and I secretly hoped his mom wouldn't see what I'd written.

Jason read what I wrote and laughed out loud, which made me feel like the risk was worth it.

We talked for a while, and I noticed that no one from his family ever came into the room. It seemed a bit strange that a family as friendly as his would be absent while I was there, but I assumed they were all busy.

Jason looked a little tired, and I decided it was time to let him rest.

"I better go," I said, "but is there anything I can do for you before I leave?"

His anxiety seemed to increase, and he looked around the room as if making sure no one was listening.

"Actually, yes. There is something I want to talk to you about." He turned and looked at me straight in the eyes. "Eliza, you don't really want to be my girlfriend, do you?" he said bluntly. It was more a statement than a question, and I stared back at him in complete shock.

"Wh-what are you talking about?" I felt my palms begin to sweat.

"I've been doing a lot of thinking these past few days. I don't know how to say this, but it's just . . . for the past week or so you've been *acting* like my girlfriend, but sometimes I feel like that's all it is—an act." He shook his head as he took in my hurt and confused expression. "Don't get me wrong! It's not like I think you've been leading me on, or anything like that. You're one of the coolest girls I know, and I'd like nothing more than for you to be my girlfriend. In fact, I'm completely flattered that you'd even consider *me* for a boyfriend, but I can tell by the look in your eyes and the way you act that you'd prefer if we were just friends. Am I right?"

I looked down at my hands to hide the shame I felt. *How did he know?* I couldn't believe I'd been so easy to read all along! I felt like a total fool, but I knew that now was the time to be honest.

Without meeting his eyes, I slowly nodded. "Jason, you're absolutely right, and I'm so sorry." I looked up at him apologetically. "You are such an amazing guy, and I *really* wanted to like you, but you deserve someone who will be as awesome to you as you've been to me. I know it sounds totally cliché, but I hope we can still be friends."

He smiled somewhat sadly and reached over to give me a hug. "You can count on it."

I couldn't believe how cool he was being about the whole situation, and I marveled once again about what a great guy he was. After a few seconds, he released me, and I stood up to leave. "Do you want me to come over tomorrow night and keep you company or something?" I hated that he would be stuck at home in a cast on prom night, and it wasn't like I had plans anymore either.

Jason shook his head and seemed to smile to himself. "No, I don't think that would work out."

I felt like he'd been about to say something else, but I decided to let it go. He probably needed a little space before we started being "just friends."

"Okay, well, take care of yourself. Let me know if you need anything."

He nodded, and we looked at each other with an understanding that this was more than a normal good-bye; the chapter of "Jason and Eliza" had come to a close.

As I walked toward my car in the chilly spring evening, I couldn't help but feel a little sad. My first serious relationship had only lasted about a week—what did that say about my dating future?

I walked into the kitchen and plunked my keys on the table, barely aware of my surroundings.

"How did it go?" Mom was sitting at the table and looking at me with an anxious expression.

"He's going to be okay, but, as I expected, there's no way he can make it to prom."

"Oh, honey, I'm so sorry! This must be really hard for you." She took my hands and pulled me down to sit in the chair beside her. "Tell you what— why don't you and I do some 'girl time' to-morrow? We can go shopping, get massages and pedicures, and gorge ourselves at whatever restaurant you choose for dinner. Maybe we can even catch a movie. How does that sound?"

I smiled weakly at her. It was sweet that she was trying to make me feel better, and I wanted her to know I appreciated it.

"Sure, that sounds really fun."

She still looked a little worried, and as much as I wanted to reassure her that everything was fine, I just didn't have it in me. I was dangerously close to crying, and right now, escape was my best option. "I think I'll head upstairs and take a nap. It's been a long day."

Mom patted my hand. "Okay, sweetie."

As soon as I entered my room, the first thing I saw was my prom dress, all beautiful and sparkly, hanging from my closet door. *Maybe I'll get to wear it next year,* I thought, trying to be posi-tive, but the tears were already flowing freely down my cheeks. Turning my music up loud to cover the sound of my sobs, I flung myself onto my bed and let the floodgates open.

I wasn't even close to being done with my crying session when a knock sounded at my door.

"Liza, there's someone here to see you," Mom called loudly. With my music turned up, I hadn't heard the doorbell ringing. I moved swiftly to the door. There was no way I wanted to see anyone right now, and I was sure that as soon as Mom got one look at my face she'd politely tell the visitor that I wasn't feeling well.

By the time I opened the door, however, Mom had already vanished, and I was left without a choice. Irritated, I ran to the bathroom and quickly applied some makeup to disguise the fact that I'd been crying. *Who could possibly be visiting me out of the blue on a Friday night?* I wondered. After a few moments of fiddling with my makeup, I sighed and headed downstairs. It was as good as it was going to get.

I entered the living room, and there was Luke Matthews, sitting on the couch in *my* house! He smiled and stood up, causing my pulse to quicken at an alarming rate. Mom made an excuse about needing to check on dinner and walked past me toward the kitchen, winking at me discreetly as she walked by.

"Hey," Luke said rather shyly, looking at me.

"Hey," was all I managed in reply. I wanted to melt into those chocolate-brown eyes of his. I stood for a few seconds before I regained my senses. "Do you want to sit down?"

"Sure, thanks." He sat back down on the couch, and I sat in the recliner facing him. He looked at his hands and cleared his throat, but didn't say anything.

I tried to think of something to say to break the silence. I didn't want him to think I didn't want him here, especially since I'd never had the chance to apologize for the other night. "It's so awesome that you guys took state," I finally said. "I really wish I could have been there."

Luke smiled. "Yeah, it's too bad you couldn't come. It was amazing to be a part of something like that!" His eyes dropped to his hands again. "Except of course for the part when Jason broke his leg. I felt really bad for him. Maybe if his lucky charm had been there it never would have happened."

He smiled slightly as he spoke, but now I was the one looking at the floor, a steady blush rising to my cheeks. Was he here to talk to me about Jason? It would be absolutely humiliating to admit that Jason had just dumped me!

"I was never really his lucky charm," I mumbled. Wanting to change the subject, I grasped at another topic. *Might as well get it off my chest*, I decided. "Luke, about the other night at your house. I'm really sorry I ran off like that. I'm not sure what I was thinking. I . . . I was just caught a bit off guard, I guess." I looked at him apologetically. I knew it was a lame excuse, but I'd die a thousand deaths before admitting the reaction his touch had caused in me.

Now it was Luke's turn to look uncomfortable, and he waved a hand. "Don't worry about it; that was totally my fault."

I wasn't sure what to make of that comment, and Luke shifted a little on the couch before seeming to determine something.

Looking at me intently, he said, "Liza, I came here to ask you . . .

My stomach filled with butterflies, and I held my breath as I waited for him to continue.

"I know Jason can't take you to the dance tomorrow, and I wondered if . . . if . . . you'd be willing to let me take you instead."

Kaboom! It felt like a giant bomb went off inside my body!

Could I really have heard him right? I shook my head slightly in confusion and squeaked, "You mean . . . like to prom? Tomorrow night?"

Luke smiled sheepishly, and I could tell he felt embarrassed. "Well, yeah. I know it's pretty lame to ask on such short notice. I hope you don't mind."

Mind? Was he *crazy?* It was all I could do to keep from jumping up and doing a happy dance in the middle of the floor! Luke was looking at me anxiously, and I realized I hadn't given him an answer.

"Of course I'll go with you!" I tried to tone down the excitement I was feeling, but it wasn't easy. When the look of relief crossed Luke's face and he grinned, revealing his gorgeously white smile, my excitement bordered on hysteria.

"Cool! If it's all right with you, we'll be going in the same group you would have gone in with Jason."

His words brought me up short, quickly killing the euphoria.

Jason. I felt a lump in my throat as realization dawned.

"So, Jason knows you're taking me?"

Luke averted his eyes. "Yeah. He offered to let me buy his tickets for the dance and the . . . other stuff." Noting the expression on my face, he hurried on. "Liza, we don't have to go in the same group if it bothers you. I just thought we would since I know everyone in that group and since I didn't have enough time to plan something else, but I don't want you to feel uncomfortable." He frowned, a worried look in his eyes.

"No, no, it's totally fine!" I plastered a happy smile on my face. "It will be great." At least Luke had had the decency to not say to my face what we both knew—that Jason had *asked* him to ask me to the dance. He was going to be my "pity date" to ease Jason's conscience. I felt completely humiliated, but Luke was watching me closely so I maintained the cheerful façade.

After a few moments of silence, he stood up. "Well, I guess I better get going if I want to be able to find a tux. If it's okay, I'll pick you up at eight in the morning for the activity. Sorry it's so early, but trust me, it will be worth it!"

I smiled and nodded. "What should I wear?"

"Jeans and a long-sleeved shirt with a jacket should be fine. And you'll want to wear a pair of comfortable shoes, not sandals. Oh! And don't worry about eating breakfast beforehand." Luke smiled mischievously, and I couldn't help but feel a little thrill of excitement. Even if this was just a pity date, it was electrifying just being in his presence!

I walked him to the door, and we said a brief good-bye. I watched him start down the steps and was about to close the door when a thought came to me.

"Wait a second!" I blurted out. Luke stopped and turned toward me. I felt a bit childish, but I couldn't resist asking the question that I knew would make him squirm. "Aren't you supposed to be going out of town with your family this weekend?"

I'd expected him to look contrite, but Luke just grinned and shrugged. "Change of plans," he said innocently before he turned and continued walking towards his Jeep.

Hmph! I really thought I'd had him there. For one horrifying moment, I wondered if his family had changed their vacation plans so Luke could escort poor, sad, little me to prom. I quickly pushed the thought away; it was too awful to contemplate.

I closed the door and leaned against it, letting out a sigh. Pity date or not, I was going to prom with *Luke Matthews*. There wasn't a girl in school who wouldn't give her front teeth for that chance, and on top of that, I'd be darned if I'd spent $175 on a dress to let it sit there collecting dust on a hanger!

⊂✄

That night Courtney helped me pick out what outfit I should wear for the day activity, and then she and I discussed how I should do my hair and makeup. We talked and giggled together, bonding in a way that we hadn't done in a long time.

When I finally got into bed, I was sure I wouldn't be able to sleep. It had been such an amazing day—and there was so much to look forward to tomorrow!

However, almost as soon as my head touched the pillow, I was swept away into a deep slumber.

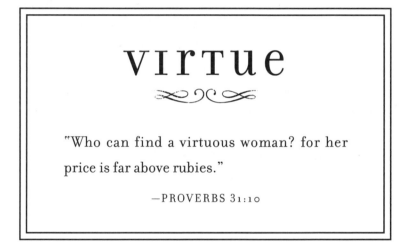

virtue

"Who can find a virtuous woman? for her price is far above rubies."

—PROVERBS 31:10

CHAPTER
twenty-four

I'll bet you've been wondering where I've been."

I startled awake to find Grandma smiling down at me.

"Grandma!" I sat up in excitement. "You came back! I was worried you wouldn't come again."

She laughed. "I was waiting until the time was right. I've been watching you, Eliza, and I'm so pleased with the choices you've been making! I knew that these visits wouldn't be wasted—not with someone as special as you are."

"I'm so glad you're here. I was beginning to feel a little lost without your help."

"Nonsense, child! As you may have already guessed, this will be my last time visiting you for a while, perhaps forever—at least in this life. But you must know that you'll always have guidance when you need it, and from a far more remarkable source than me—you've been given the gift of the Holy Ghost! As long as you're worthy, the Spirit will always be there to guide and direct you throughout your life.

"Along with that precious gift, you also have your parents, teachers, and leaders to give you counsel. And don't forget the many other resources available to you, including the scriptures and the *For the Strength of Youth* pamphlet. Not to mention the Personal Progress program!"

I thought guiltily of my Personal Progress book that had been lying untouched for weeks on my dresser.

Grandma continued, "Once you understand the potential these things have to help you, you'll realize that you never really *needed* my visits or the little objects I've given you." She smiled at me warmly. "Be that as it may, I want you to know that I've cherished our time together, and I'll continue to watch over you. There'll always be a special place in my heart for my beautiful great-granddaughter."

I felt moisture in my eyes as Grandma cleared her throat and sniffed.

"Now, enough of this blubbering! We have a very special person to visit." Her eyes held that familiar twinkle. "Are you ready?"

I smiled back through my tears and nodded. "I can't wait."

"Good, then here we go!"

As had happened so many times before, the room began to fade around us. I tried to capture the strange sensation of it all, knowing that this would be the last time I would experience it. Colors and images seemed to whirl as my mind filled with anticipation. Who would this last woman be?

The ground became solid beneath my feet as the new scenery came into focus. We were standing on a gentle slope of a grassy hillside. I looked down the hill and saw a city constructed of small stone buildings.

If I squinted hard enough, I could make out the shapes of

people moving about on the streets, but here on the hill everything was peaceful and quiet.

My attention turned to a small stand of olive trees near us, and that's when I saw her. A young woman knelt beside the gnarled trunk of a tree, leaning against it for support. She wore a simple dress with a shawl draped over her dark hair, but nothing, not even the simplicity of her clothes, could have disguised the beauty that radiated from her.

She stared straight at Grandma and me, but her gaze moved past us, and I knew she was unaware of our presence. Words could scarcely begin to express the magnificent power that surrounded this woman. Her face held an expression of complete wonder, and there was a glorious light in her soft eyes. In fact, her entire face seemed infused with light, and it was this brightness that magnified her already lovely features and made her the most beautiful young woman I'd ever seen. She appeared to be the very embodiment of meekness, love, and purity. Watching her as she knelt beside the tree, I knew she was no ordinary person.

I looked at Grandma, desperate to know who this young woman was.

Grandma's eyes filled with tears as she reverently whispered, "Eliza, this is Mary. The mother of the Son of God."

I caught my breath. Tears flowed freely down my cheeks as I humbly gazed at one of the most important women ever to walk the Earth. I had seen several depictions of Mary in pictures and movies, but none of them had come close to accurately portraying the majesty of this woman. It was evident that we were close in age, but she had the grace and nobility of a queen.

I couldn't keep from staring at her. Out of all the incredible women we'd visited, I was most in awe of Mary. The scene seemed too reverent to ruin with speech, so I stood silent and motionless beside Grandma. We watched Mary for several minutes, until she arose from her place and began walking quietly down the hill toward the city.

Grandma made no move to follow, so I watched as Mary's figure grew smaller and smaller, eventually disappearing into the throngs of people moving about on the streets.

I dabbed the last remaining tears on my cheeks and noticed Grandma wiping her own eyes.

"What you witnessed here was very special," Grandma said. "Mary had just received the message from the angel Gabriel that she would give birth to the Messiah, and she came here to ponder over all the things she'd heard." Grandma shook her head in amazement. "Can you imagine what feelings must have been passing through her heart? What thoughts were in her mind? I can scarcely fathom how overwhelming it would be to have the knowledge that you were the one chosen to be the earthly mother of Jesus Christ, the very Savior of the world!"

Her words struck me, and chills ran over my arms as I thought of Mary's calling.

Grandma was silent for a few moments, and then she turned to me. "So, my dear, I think you know the value that we're here to learn about. With that in mind, tell me your impressions of Mary."

I found it hard to put my feelings into words. "Oh, Grandma, I don't know where to start! Mary was completely beautiful in every way. I had no idea that someone so incredible could be human; she seemed more like an angel. I . . . I can't seem to express what it was like to be around her, you know?"

Grandma smiled. "Yes, I know what you mean. Mary was truly a unique woman, a 'chosen vessel' of the Lord. She possessed several amazing qualities, but the one we're going to focus on is purity. Or in other words—virtue.

"Among other things, it was because of Mary's exceptional purity that she was chosen to fulfill the calling she received. I'm sure you've heard the scripture that says a woman's virtue is more precious than rubies?"

I nodded.

"After seeing Mary, do you see the truth in that scripture?"

"Yes! A ruby would be *nothing* in comparison to Mary's beauty." I paused in contemplation. "It was so much more than her outward appearance, though. Her radiance seemed to come from inside of her."

Grandma beamed at me. "Exactly!" She took my hand and suddenly we were being transported again. I'd hardly had time to figure out what was happening when we were suddenly sitting on a bench in a *very* familiar place.

I gazed up at the spires of the Salt Lake Temple, trying to orient myself to this rapid change of scene. The temple grounds were covered in beautiful flowers, and somehow I knew we were back to the present day, but there was still something unusual about our setting. It was dusk, and a gorgeous sunset filled the sky—but Grandma and I were completely alone.

Even in the quietest of times, there were usually lots of people walking around Temple Square, but right now everything was completely still. I'd never been able to see the Salt Lake Temple in this type of setting; it was so peaceful!

Grandma sat beside me on the bench, and she spoke softly to

maintain the serenity of the moment. "There's not much I need to teach you about virtue. By now you've read the *For the Strength of Youth* pamphlet, and you've had enough lessons in church to know what you need to do to stay morally clean and pure."

I nodded, and she continued, "Keeping yourself personally pure is not an easy task in the world you live in today. The earth is teeming with sexual sin—it's practically everywhere you look: on TV, in magazines, in music, on the Internet, with texting, and tragically, in the lives of millions of wayward souls.

"Satan has successfully turned society's logic into accepting sexual sin as normal and even good. To put it simply, Eliza, the destruction of personal purity and virtue is Satan's main goal. It's where he puts all of his time and energy when tempting the youth."

Grandma's face was stern. "The adversary uses subtle and seemingly harmless temptations to deceive even the brightest Latter-day Saint youth. People sometimes send inappropriate pictures of themselves in text messages or post them on their Facebook pages, and far too often people text or e-mail words they would never dare say in person. Pornography, in all of its ugly forms, is *never* acceptable and *always* corrosive to the soul. Once these thoughts or images are put into the mind, it's extremely hard to get them out. Young men are especially prone to these temptations, and I wish the young women of the Church could understand what a powerful influence for good they can be! By dressing modestly and holding steadfast to virtuous principles, they can help the young men honor their priesthood and even encourage them to work toward serving a mission.

"Tragically, there are young women who are intentionally provocative in their dress in order to catch a young man's attention, and even some who might discourage a young man from serving a mission. Such a girl may claim that she loves her boyfriend too much to be without him for two years, but in reality her feelings are purely selfish. *True* love means wanting what is best for another person—no matter the cost."

I pondered Grandma's words as I gauged how strong my feelings were for Luke. Did I care for him enough to put his interests ahead of my own? It was silly to think about it when I wasn't even in a relationship with him, but I couldn't help myself.

Grandma's voice broke through my thoughts. "Love and physical attraction are among the most powerful feelings given to us by Heavenly Father, and He expects us to use those feelings wisely as part of our test here on earth. If we 'bridle our passions' and follow the commandments the Lord has given us, we prove our love and devotion to Him. It's not an easy thing, but it's not supposed to be easy. Tests are meant to be challenging.

"Eliza, someday you'll experience the joyful feeling of being in love, and that's something very special. However, the more you date, the more you will realize how difficult it can be to stay morally clean—hold fast! Follow the guidelines you've been given, and don't try to see how close to the edge you can get before slipping off. Satan knows you and he knows your weaknesses; don't think that you can outsmart him. He's been around a long time and is just waiting for the opportunity to lure you close enough to the ledge so that, before you know it, you're falling."

Grandma paused and looked me directly in the eyes. "The next thing I'm going to tell you is extremely important. You've had the privilege of seeing Mary, the mother of our beloved Savior. Jesus Christ overcame the world by taking upon Himself each and every one of our sins and weaknesses. Without His merciful atonement, we would all have been lost because all of us are subject to sin."

Grandma's eyes filled with tears as she stated resolutely, "Eliza, don't *ever* feel that you are not worthy of repentance, no matter what may come. There is nothing you could do, no sin so great, that it cannot be overcome by Christ's redeeming love. If you remember nothing else from my visits remember this: repentance is for *everyone*, and it is real."

Grandma motioned for us to stand, and then she swept her hand toward the temple. "Make *this* your goal, Eliza! There is no blessing sweeter than being married and sealed in the House of the Lord. The Lord loves you more than you can comprehend, and He wants you to be happy. You and those born to your generation are part of the great 'youth of the noble birthright.' You were prepared to come at this time to the Earth, and you are special! Never underestimate your potential, for with the Lord's help, nothing is impossible."

She smiled. "Remember the examples of the women we've visited. Hold fast to the values of faith, divine nature, individual worth, knowledge, choice and accountability, good works, integrity, and virtue. In the end, you will see that it was all worth it!"

Tears were streaming down my face as I gazed at the glorious beauty of the temple. Its brilliant walls glistened with the last rays of the setting sun, and right then and there I made a commitment that this *was* my goal—no matter what.

Grandma's words had struck me powerfully, and I sensed that she would soon be leaving. More tears flowed as I tried to memorize the sight of her; I never wanted to forget her face.

"I love you, Eliza, my precious, precious great-granddaughter," Grandma whispered.

"I love you too, Grandma. I'm going to miss you so much!" Before my last words were spoken, everything suddenly went dark.

Just as my mind was surrendering to the inevitable deep slumber, I heard a faint echo of Grandma's voice. "No need to miss me, I'll always be close by."

CHAPTER
twenty-five

I was awake before my alarm. Normally, after one of my special dreams with Grandma, I slept so soundly that a herd of elephants couldn't wake me, but this morning was different. I awoke recalling all of Grandma's words with perfect clarity, and with sadness, because I knew that I would never receive another visit from her.

I felt a twinge of panic when I realized that she'd forgotten to show me what the final value token was, but then I remembered she'd said that the objects weren't really necessary. I didn't need to have something tangible to hold to know what I was supposed to do.

Still, it would have been nice to finish off my collection, I thought regretfully.

I reached over and opened the music box on my nightstand, listening to the melody that I now knew by heart. After telling Mom how much I admired Grandma's music box, she had agreed to let me keep it, and I'd put all of the value tokens inside.

Sighing, I lay back on my pillows and wondered what our activity was going to be today. I wanted to be excited about hanging out with Luke, but the real reason for his taking me buzzed around me like a pesky wasp. I was "pity-date girl," and everyone in our group would know it. Why else would someone like Luke ask out someone like me?

⁓

"Okay, is everyone ready? One . . . two . . . three!"

The blindfold was stripped from my face and I heard my own gasp mingle with the excited shrieks and giggles of the other girls. There were four couples in our group: Clark and Britney, Danny and Becka, and two others I'd never met, Joey and Marina.

Marina was a junior, and although she seemed a little shy, I could tell that she was a nice girl, which was more than I could say for Britney and Becka, who'd been glaring at me from the moment I'd entered Clark's family Suburban.

Before we'd left this morning, the guys had insisted on blind-folding each of us so as to maintain the secrecy of the event. I'd felt mixed emotions about that. Not being able to see made me self-conscious, but it was also a relief to have a break from Britney and Becka's mocking looks, which undoubtedly would have accompa-nied their constant whispering.

"So, what do you think?" Luke's question snapped me back to the present.

"It's awesome, I can't believe it!" A huge smile spread across my face as I looked again at the surprise.

Hovering close to the ground in the meadow before us was a giant hot air balloon!

"You probably won't believe this, but I've always wanted to

ride in one of these." I couldn't hide the excitement in my voice as I watched the balloon crew prepping everything for our ride.

Luke blew out a sigh of relief and grinned. "I'm so glad! I was hoping this would be a *good* surprise. Some of the guys were worried their dates might be afraid of heights."

I glanced around and noticed that Becka and Britney did indeed look more nervous than excited. I felt sorry for Clark and Danny, who were trying to coax their dates into going for the ride. Surely they'd spent quite a bit of money on this activity, and I thought it would be a shame if it went to waste. Although I had to admit I wouldn't particularly mind if they didn't go up with us.

After a few minutes, the pilot stepped forward to give us all instructions. The guys had already secured the necessary permission slips from our parents, but we had to add our signatures to the liability waiver as well. Admittedly, I was a bit uneasy after reading everything that could go wrong, and I had a little more sympathy for Britney and Becka, who were nearly hysterical by now.

After the pilot and crew spoke with them, however, they seemed to calm down, and they finally signed the waiver. Now there was nothing else to do but take flight!

I felt an electric shock radiate up my arm as Luke took my hand and helped me into the balloon. I might have imagined it, but it seemed that he let his fingers linger a few moments longer than necessary before letting go, which set my pulse racing.

Don't go imagining things! I reprimanded myself sharply, but I couldn't keep my heart from thumping into my eardrums. I tried to distract myself by watching the crew go to work.

As the rope released and the burner lit the magnificent envelope, we began to lift off the ground. Becka and Britney squealed, clinging to their dates for dear life. Luke looked at me and raised an eyebrow. His expression was so comical that I turned around and stifled a giggle. He also turned, so that we were both facing outward, and we watched in silence as the ground fell farther and farther away.

"This is amazing," I breathed.

Luke nodded. "Definitely one of the coolest things I've ever done."

I stole a glance at him, and butterflies immediately hit my stomach. He was wearing a hoodie and a pair of jeans, but he looked so incredibly hot! We stood mere inches apart, and as much as I tried to ignore it, I was getting goose bumps along my arms just being near him. He must have sensed my eyes on him, because he turned and looked at me, our eyes locking for one heart-stopping moment before I shyly looked away.

"Hope y'all brought your appetites with you this morning!" the pilot said cheerfully in his thick Southern accent.

For the first time, I noticed the large picnic basket on the floor. Joey and Marina immediately began looking through the assortment of breakfast foods and then made a place to sit and eat.

Britney and Becka were still sniveling in a manner that made it clear they were just doing it for attention, but since they were ignoring the food, Luke and I made our way over to it.

"Do you mind if we eat standing up?" I asked him as we carried the delicious-smelling food back to our spot. "I don't want to miss a minute of this."

He chuckled. "I was thinking the same thing." There was an intensity in his eyes that made me feel like blushing, but again I scolded myself.

You've read one too many romance books. Calm down!

We ate our breakfast mostly in silence, watching the beautiful scenery around us and listening to the pilot's narrative. I looked up at the bright, citrus-colored stripes of the balloon and felt an overwhelming sense of joy. The thrill of this ride, being next to Luke—it was all so incredible! I wanted to capture the moment forever.

I was still staring at the balloon when I felt Luke's gaze on me. He was smiling, and his eyes seemed to ignite with the reflection of the burner's flame. I felt a smile spread across my face as our eyes met, and in that moment we seemed to communicate dozens of things without speaking a single word. Suddenly, we were sharing some kind of silent connection that I'd never experienced with anyone else. The sensation was so powerful I had to grab the rim of the basket for balance.

All too soon, we were descending back to solid ground. We thanked the pilot and crew and began walking back toward the Suburban.

Luke lingered for a moment, and when I turned back, I saw him hand the pilot a check along with what I could tell, even from where I was standing, was a generous tip.

We all piled back into the Suburban, and everyone seemed to be on a high from the thrill of the ride. Becka and Britney continued their drama about how scary the whole "ordeal" had been, but I was too glad to have the attention off me to be annoyed.

The drive passed quickly, and before I knew it, we had stopped at the curb outside my house.

The guys had planned an early activity because the other girls had hair appointments and wanted plenty of time for their primping. My mom and Courtney were planning on helping me with my hair and makeup, so I had plenty of time to kill, but I figured it wouldn't hurt to get started early anyway. Hopefully the better I looked tonight, the less people would feel sorry for Luke for getting stuck with me.

Luke jumped out of the car and held the door open, taking my hand to help me down.

"See you at six." He flashed a smile and winked at me.

"I'll be ready." I grinned back at him and tried to keep my voice steady; I was all too conscious of his hand still holding mine.

After a few moments, he let go, and I walked quickly up the steps to the front door. What was this guy trying to do to me? If the simple touch of his hand had me in near paralysis, what was going to happen to me when his arms were around me at the dance?

C ∽

"There now, just . . . about . . . perfect!" Mom finished fussing over the final curl and stood back to inspect her handiwork.

"Oh, *wow!*" Courtney sighed. "Liza, you look gorgeous!" She grabbed the hand mirror off Mom's dresser and gave it to me. "See for yourself."

I turned in the chair and held up the mirror so I could see the back of my head. "It looks awesome!" I squealed. Mom beamed, and Courtney clapped excitedly.

I stood up and gave Mom a hug. "No, seriously, it's completely beautiful!" She had twisted my hair up into a series of loose barrel rolls. A few strands of my hair curled into soft ringlets around my face. As a finishing touch, she'd interspersed a few sparkly rhinestones that dazzled as they caught the light.

"Well, let's make sure it's going to hold—cover your eyes."

I placed a protective hand over my eyes as Mom sprayed what felt like a quart of hairspray onto my hair before finishing it off with a spritz of something that added extra shine. When she was finished, I was sure not even a tornado could move this hairdo masterpiece!

I walked over to the full-length mirror for a final inspection, twirling all the way around to make sure everything was satisfactory.

Courtney giggled and talked animatedly about how pretty I looked, while Mom took pictures like a crazed paparazzo. I had to admit, staring at my reflection in the mirror, I truly felt like a princess! I was so grateful I'd decided to go with this dress; it was completely elegant.

Mom had also done an excellent job applying my makeup. She knew some special tricks for accentuating the eyes, and I was almost startled by how attractive the effect was. For the first time, I felt like I was pretty enough to go out with the hottest guy in school. Butterflies filled my stomach as I looked at the clock and realized that Luke would be arriving any second.

As if on cue, the doorbell rang downstairs. Courtney and Mom shrieked in delight and fled the room. I knew they wanted to be in the living room to see Luke's expression when he first saw me in my dress. My heart began to race as I waited a few moments and then descended the staircase.

As I entered the living room, I tried to keep my jaw from dropping open. Luke in a tuxedo was more handsome and dashing than any guy had a right to look! His eyes lit up, and a huge smile spread across his face when he saw me.

"You look absolutely beautiful!" he said as he took a few steps forward, his eyes never leaving my face.

My mom and Courtney were beaming, obviously ecstatic with his reaction. I was happily surprised to see my dad smiling at me too. Mom had warned him not to ruin my special evening, and it was a huge relief to see that he was being civil with Luke.

"Here's your corsage. I hope you like it." Luke removed a delicate gardenia corsage from its plastic container and carefully slipped it over my wrist.

I breathed in the flower's delicate aroma and smiled. "It's gorgeous; I love it!" Gardenias were now *officially* my new favorite flower.

"I have a boutonniere for you too." I turned toward the kitchen, but Courtney was one step ahead of me.

"I'll get it!" she chimed as she skipped to the fridge and returned with admirable speed.

"Thanks, Court." I smiled at her as I opened the box. It took me a few awkward moments to pin the white rose to Luke's lapel, and we were both laughing by the time it was finally in place.

"Okay, you two, I want to get a couple of pictures before you go," Mom said.

"You mean more than the hundred or so you've already taken?" I teased. She had been snapping photos almost the entire time, pausing only occasionally to comment about how nice we looked.

"Oh, those were just candid shots. Come stand over here by the fireplace for a nice, posed picture."

I looked at Luke apologetically, but he was grinning.

We humored her and posed for at least a dozen more pictures

before I insisted that we'd better get going. I hugged each of my family members, and then Luke followed me out the door, pausing to tell my dad he'd have me home by midnight. I looked back in time to see Dad smile and nod in appreciation.

Way to go, Luke! I was glad I'd told him my curfew ahead of time and extra glad that my parents had allowed me an additional hour for this special occasion. I didn't want to be the only person who had to be home by eleven on prom night.

As we walked out into the fragrant April evening, Luke stopped and looked at me again, shaking his head.

"What I said before wasn't right. You look more than beautiful—you're radiant."

The look in his eyes made me blush, and I wanted desperately to believe him, but part of me still wondered if he was just being nice for Jason's sake.

"Thanks. You look really"—*insanely handsome, painfully attractive, smokin' hot!*—"nice too." It was a lame attempt at a compliment, but I couldn't reveal how attracted I was to him.

As we walked down the sidewalk, I noticed his Jeep parked at the curb and stopped short.

"Is this our ride?"

"Yeah, sorry it's nothing fancy. Is that okay?" He looked nervous.

"Of course, it's perfect!" Suddenly I felt a little silly. "For some reason I was expecting that we'd all be riding in the Suburban together."

He smiled as he held the door open for me. "We decided it would take too long to go to each house and wait while everyone took pictures and stuff, so we're all driving separately and meeting up at the restaurant." He held out his hand to me and said, with a teasing look in his eyes, "Don't worry. I know it's not easy to ride alone in a car with a guy like me, but I promise I won't bite."

My blush intensified at his words, and goose bumps raced up my arms at the sudden gleam I caught in his eyes. As was my habit, I tried to deflect attention from my embarrassment by changing the subject.

"So, where are we going for dinner?"

"You'll find out soon enough." He winked mysteriously and closed the door.

My heart thrilled with the way he was flirting with me. As I watched him walk around to the driver's side, I had to pinch myself to believe that this wasn't a dream.

We drove for a while, talking comfortably as if we were old friends. I found myself letting go of my worries and enjoying the flow of conversation. Luke seemed relaxed, and I noticed for the first time that he had a great sense of humor. I found myself laughing so much that I felt almost giddy!

Why had I never noticed these things about him before? I'd always assumed he was quiet and unreachable because of his good looks, but sitting here beside me was a Luke I felt completely comfortable with—a Luke I knew I could be friends with.

I enjoyed our conversation so much that I hadn't paid attention to our whereabouts until Luke pulled into the parking lot of a restaurant nestled in a canyon just above Salt Lake City. I'd heard of this place before, and my mouth began watering as Luke opened the door for me and I caught a whiff of the food wafting over from the restaurant's open door.

"M'lady." Luke bowed dramatically and reached for my hand

to help me down from the Jeep. I giggled and accepted his hand gratefully. Getting in and out of a Jeep while wearing heels was no small feat, but I was glad he hadn't tried to borrow a fancy sports car or rent a limo. I had a special fondness for his Jeep, and riding in it made me feel more comfortable somehow. Besides, sitting up higher meant he had to help me in and out, which gave me multiple opportunities to touch his hand.

"Looks like the others are already here," Luke commented as he glanced around the parking lot.

I'd been hoping that we'd arrive before Britney and Becka so I wouldn't have to endure their nasty looks when we walked in, but I guessed the sooner I faced the music, the better.

"Have you eaten here before?" Luke's question helped distract me from my worries.

"No, but I've always wanted to. Just *smelling* the food is making me hungry!"

He laughed. "You're in for a treat. The food is awesome, but just wait until you see what they have for dessert."

"I can't wait!" I had to keep my stomach muscles tight to prevent it from rumbling at the mere suggestion of dessert!

A hostess led us into a large, elegant dining room lit with candles and encased almost entirely by windows. The view of the mountain scenery was breathtaking. I was so engrossed by the beauty of it all that I didn't notice the rest of our group until Luke was pulling out a chair for me.

"Glad you two could make it!" Danny teased.

"How long have you guys been here?" Luke asked as he sat down beside me.

"Only about an hour or so," Joey said with an exaggerated look at his watch.

Marina playfully swatted at his arm. "Don't listen to them! We got here no more than fifteen minutes ago, and we just barely sat down." She smiled at me. "Eliza, your dress is beautiful!"

I beamed at her, enjoying the faint Spanish accent in her voice. "Thanks, I love your dress too! That color is so pretty on you."

Marina wore a gown of buttery yellow satin that flattered her dark hair and olive skin tone. I silently counted my blessings that she and Joey were seated opposite us, thereby deflecting the sneers that were already coming my way from the two sour grapes at the end of our table. I'd risked a quick glance in Britney and Becka's direction, but their faces were so full of mocking contempt that I quickly looked away again. It would be no use to compliment them on their dresses; their expressions had been so awful that I hadn't even noticed what they were wearing.

Dinner was indeed fantastic, and Luke and I ended up getting along so well with Joey and Marina that we spent most of the meal talking with them. When it was time for dessert, I was worried I hadn't left enough room in my stomach—but one look at the decadent marble chocolate cheesecake with raspberry sauce told me that I'd find room or die trying!

Luke and Joey laughed at Marina and me as we moaned, joking about how they would have to roll us out of the restaurant after all of the food we'd consumed. I laughed as well, but I was grateful to find that I'd shared enough of my dessert with Luke that I wasn't painfully full when we stood up to leave.

"Here, you better take my arm . . . just in case," Luke teased, revealing the dimple in his cheek as he smiled.

I was only too happy to oblige.

"Thanks, I wasn't sure I was going to make it." I smiled back at him, ignoring the tingling in my legs that shot right up my spine as my arm entwined with his.

We all headed to our individual cars and caravanned to the state capitol, where the dance was being held. The night already felt magical, but when I walked into the grand room of the capitol, I felt like a princess entering her first ball.

The room was magnificently decorated, and the special lighting created an ambience of enchantment. Couples dressed in tuxedos and beautiful gowns were scattered all across the large dance floor. The whole sight was thrilling—my first prom!

"Let's get our pictures *first*, before anyone gets all sweaty." Britney's nasally voice broke the spell, and I realized in horror that she was looking pointedly at me. It was obvious that I was the "anyone" she'd been referring to.

"Yeah, let's get it over with." Clark looked embarrassed by Britney's comment and began pulling her toward the line for pictures. Becka threw me a fake smile and then tugged on Danny's arm, forcing him to follow her as she caught up with Britney. Joey, Marina, and Luke all pretended not to hear Britney's insult as we followed the other couples. Marina began talking about the decorations, and Luke took my arm again.

I may have imagined it, but his jaw seemed to be clenched, and I felt completely humiliated. Here he was, the best looking guy in school, stuck with a sweaty little sophomore! I felt sure that my face was shiny or something, otherwise why would Britney have said that? I tried to force the blush from my face before it was our turn for pictures, but of course that only made me blush more, and I started to feel moisture at my armpits. Suddenly the room felt stuffy and claustrophobic, and all I wanted to do was get out of there.

We posed for a group shot, and then Luke and I had our single dance photo taken. The photographer posed us somewhat awkwardly, with Luke standing slightly behind me, his arm on mine. Normally I would have been ecstatic to have him standing so close, but we both seemed a little uncomfortable, and all of my attention was focused on not sweating.

After the photos, we walked out onto the dance floor. A fast song was playing, and I began to feel a bit dizzy.

"I need to use the restroom. I'll be right back," I said quietly.

"Is everything all right?" Luke looked at me in concern.

"Yeah, I'll only be a few minutes." I turned and rushed through the crowd, not wanting him to look at me again until I could be sure that I wasn't the shiny-faced freak I was imagining.

As I pushed through the crowds of couples, I spotted Jill and Nick dancing. Jill had her back to me, and they were several couples away, but I felt a stab of sorrow at the sight of her. She and Nick were practically glued together, and Nick was resting his chin on her bare shoulder. Jill wasn't wearing her bolero jacket, and seeing her dancing in her revealing red dress made me feel like she was a complete stranger; the Jill I'd grown up with would never have worn something like that. In fact, she would have made jokes about a girl wearing a dress like that—so obviously trying to be sexy and seductive.

I turned away and continued toward the bathroom, but I couldn't erase the image of Jill's glaring red dress from my mind.

It would have been so fun to get ready for the dance together, to tell Jill all about what happened with Jason, and now about Luke. She didn't even know I was here with Luke! I wondered if she would see us together tonight and what she would think about it. Maybe her curiosity would get the better of her and she'd finally talk to me again. Jill never could hold back her curiosity for long.

The thought gave me hope, and I found myself smiling as I entered the ladies' room. I went straight to the mirror to inspect my face and was filled with immense relief to see that my makeup looked as flawless as when Mom first applied it. My face was a little flushed, but there wasn't a trace of shine on it.

Thank you, Mom! I inwardly applauded her fantastic cosmetic skills and turned to head for the door once more, when two unwelcome faces appeared before me. Britney and Becka blocked my way, and instead of moving to let me by, they advanced, pushing me farther into the bathroom.

By the looks on their faces, I could see this was the opportunity they'd been waiting for—to get me alone and helpless. I was grateful there were other girls in the restroom as witnesses in case Becka and Britney decided to whip out their claws and inflict a mortal wound.

"So," Becka sneered, "it's too bad Jason broke his leg. That must have been *so* devastating for you." The look of false pity on her face was almost laughable. "And now this whole thing with Luke . . . Well, I must say you're dealing with it extremely well, but don't worry—it will be *our little secret.*" Becka said the last part in a stage whisper. She had put on such a dramatic performance that the restroom fell silent and the girls around us began to watch with interest.

"I-I don't know what you're talking about," I stammered. "What thing with Luke?"

"You mean you don't *know?*" Britney exchanged an overly shocked glance with Becka and then took my hand in pity. "Eliza, Jason felt so bad about breaking his leg that he *paid* Luke to bring you here tonight."

A collective gasp sounded all around me; Britney had made sure to speak loud enough for everyone to hear. I felt the room start to spin and a sickening lurch in my stomach as I stumbled toward the door.

"I feel so bad," Britney's sarcastic words echoed off the walls and followed me out the door. "I *totally* thought she knew."

Tears stung my eyes. I needed to escape. Now. I looked down both ends of the hallway, but people were everywhere. I rushed to the closest door I could find that would lead outside.

Stepping into the cool night air, I quickly closed the door behind me and leaned against it for support. After glancing around to make sure I was alone, I covered my face with both hands and let out a shaky breath. It was taking every ounce of effort to keep the tears from falling down my face.

I remember Luke had said something about buying Jason's tickets, but I must have gotten it mixed up. Luke hadn't paid Jason; he had been paid. Paid to take me to the prom. This wasn't a pity date after all. This was worse.

What was I going to do? I had never been so humiliated in my life! The thought of going back in there and facing everyone was unthinkable. Undoubtedly the word would have spread like wildfire

by now. The thought of facing Luke was even more painful. I'd actually *believed* that he liked me; how could I have been so blind?

I swallowed the lump in my throat and considered my options.
There weren't many. I decided I could call my mom to come pick
me up and then send Luke a text explaining that I'd left. Surely he
didn't deserve an explanation from me considering what he'd done.

I pulled out my cell, but I felt completely conflicted. I knew
what I had to do.

Finding a quiet corner along the building, I bowed my head
and silently poured out my heart to Heavenly Father. I couldn't
keep the tears from flowing as I expressed my pain and pleaded
for help and comfort. I felt depressed and alone, but as I continued my prayer, I felt the warm companionship of the Spirit fill my
soul with peace.

Glimpses of the dreams I'd had suddenly entered my mind.
Once again, I saw the remarkable women whose lives were filled
with light and purpose. I heard Grandma's voice, telling me that I
possessed a divine nature, that I had individual worth, that I was
the daughter of a king.

As all of the memories and thoughts came flooding back to
me, a slow smile spread across my face. I thanked Heavenly Father
for reminding me of the incredible lessons I'd learned in those
dreams. I was His daughter, and I knew He loved me. I had no reason to be ashamed!

After expressing further gratitude, I asked for help with what
I was about to do and closed my prayer. Taking a deep breath, I
lifted my chin and squared my shoulders. It was time to put my
newfound confidence to the test.

CHAPTER

twenty-six

As I walked back into the hallway, I immediately spotted Luke waiting a short distance from the girls' restroom. He had a worried expression on his face, and with a start, I realized that he thought I was still in there. Ten minutes ago I would have been mortified to have him think I could take so long in the restroom, but as it was, I found the situation slightly funny.

He didn't see me coming, so I walked up to his side and touched his arm.

Luke smiled in relief when he saw me. "Oh, there you are! I was about to have someone go in and make sure you were okay." He looked at me closely, and then paused. "Is everything all right?"

I ignored the genuine concern in his eyes. It was going to take all the strength I had to keep from completely losing it, and I was determined not to let him see the hurt I was feeling.

"Yes, everything's fine, but I think you'd better take me home now. Or, if you'd prefer, I can have someone come pick me up." I tried to keep the edge from my voice, but it was difficult.

Luke's eyes narrowed in confusion. "Eliza, what's going on?

Something's wrong. Why won't you tell me?" He put his hand on my arm, and suddenly my temper flared.

For the first time, I met his eyes. If he insisted on continuing this charade, then I was going to have to be blunt. "I know about what happened. About how Jason *paid you* to bring me here tonight," I stated coolly.

Luke's eyes widened in surprise. He gave a short laugh, "What? Where on earth did you get a crazy idea like that?"

I looked at the floor as I felt my resolve crumbling. "Britney and Becka . . . When I was in the restroom, they came in and told me."

Luke's hand tightened on my arm. "Those two little . . ." He practically growled as he fought to maintain his composure.

He lifted my chin, forcing me to look at him again. An angry flame was burning in his eyes. "Liza, is *that* what you think? That Jason *paid* me to take you to prom?" His expression was so fierce that I was almost afraid to respond.

"I don't know what to think," I murmured as tears began spilling down my cheeks.

"Come here."

Luke grabbed my hand and began leading me down the hallway. I'd never seen him react this way, and I wasn't sure what it meant. Was he mad because Britney and Becka had told me his secret, or was it because he was offended that I believed him capable of being paid to go on a date? Either way, I'd simply made him angry. I wished I'd kept my big mouth shut. I should have called my mom and bailed when I had the chance.

He pulled me through the door and outside the building. No

one was around, and Luke pressed me up against the wall, placing his hands on either side of me.

"Listen to me," he began. His face was so close to mine that I found it hard to breathe. "There's something I need to tell you and I know you probably don't want to hear it, but I'm not letting you get away again before you do." His golden-brown eyes seemed to penetrate into my very soul, and I was so electrified by his words and proximity that I couldn't move.

"Eliza Moore, I've had a crush on you from the first time I laid eyes on you." Luke's eyes smoldered with intensity, and my mouth dropped open in shock. He pulled away. "I know how stupid that must sound, but it's true."

He stepped back and sat on a bench, looking at his hands as he spoke. "Jason didn't *pay me* to take you to prom." His face twisted. "I asked him if I could take you, and he was cool enough to let me." He looked almost sheepish. "Jason said he'd had a feeling that I liked you, and after I asked about prom, his suspicions were confirmed. He wasn't even mad at me. I told him he could punch me if he wanted to, but he just laughed!" Luke smiled and shook his head. "Jason's one of the coolest guys I know. He said he'd never been exactly sure if . . ." He paused as if uncertain how to continue. "If you liked him more than a friend, and he wanted to talk to you about it."

I could tell by Luke's expression that he already knew the outcome of *that* conversation.

He cleared his throat. "I guess I kept hoping you would figure it out on your own with all the notes and stuff, but after that night on the balcony I realized you probably already knew how I felt and you didn't want to hurt my feelings."

I frowned, trying to make sense of what Luke was saying, and he misread my expression.

"I know"—he smiled wryly—"pretty lame that I still asked you to prom when I knew you didn't feel the same way, but I couldn't help myself. I hope you're not mad at me."

Crush. Notes. Balcony. CRUSH?

The words seemed to unfold slowly as my brain attempted to decipher the message it was receiving. Could Luke Matthews actually have admitted that he had a crush on me? *Me?* And what did he mean by notes? Surely not the notes I'd been getting in my locker. Those were from Jason, weren't they? Had Luke really tried to tell me all of this on the balcony at his house a week ago?

I pinched my arm to make sure I wasn't dreaming, but the resulting pain told me it must be real. I couldn't have possibly misunderstood. Luke had been too clear about everything, but my heart still struggled to accept what it wanted most desperately to believe.

After a few moments, I finally found the strength in my legs and moved toward the bench to sit beside Luke.

"Is all of that really true?" I whispered, not daring to look at him.

Once again Luke took my chin and lifted it so he could meet my eyes. "Yes."

My pulse began racing. "Why me? You could choose any girl you wanted in the school. Why would you pick me?"

Luke laughed. "Don't you see? That's exactly why I like you, Liza. You're one of the most beautiful girls in school, but you don't even realize it! You don't act like the other girls who are pretty and *know* they're pretty. There's nothing fake about you; you're completely sincere, and you stay true to yourself. Do you have any idea how refreshing that is?"

I looked at my hands in embarrassment. I never did know how to handle compliments well.

"There's something else too. Something I'm not sure I can even describe, but when I look into your eyes, it's like I'm *connected* to you somehow. I feel more comfortable with you than I do with anyone else outside of my family." He snorted. "If I didn't freak you out enough before, now you must think I'm a total psycho!"

I laughed, and the incomprehensible joy I felt made me bold. I took Luke's hand in mine. "Well, if you're psycho, then I guess that makes two of us."

Luke's eyes lit up. "Do you mean . . . ?"

I couldn't keep the smile from my face. "Yes! I've had a huge crush on you from the first day I met you too, but never in a *million years* could I have dreamed that you felt the same way!"

Luke jumped up from the bench and punched the air. "No way!"

I laughed and he pulled me up beside him, taking both of my hands in his. "But what about all the notes I sent you? I thought for sure you would have seen me dropping them off once or twice. And I was always trying to talk to you—you must have known." He raised his eyebrows as if unconvinced.

"No, I promise I didn't! I thought the notes were from Jason. And when you talked to me, I thought you were just being friendly." My eyes narrowed in playful suspicion. "Since we're asking questions, if you've liked me since the first day of school, how come it took you so long to tell me?"

Luke shrugged. "You and Jason had that health class together last semester and he started talking about you from day one. He's one of my best friends, and I couldn't tell him I had a crush on you too. But listening to him talk about you all the time while trying not to be jealous was pure torture! I felt like if I didn't do something I'd lose my mind. So I started sending you the notes.

"Once I realized we had seminary together, it was even harder for me to stay away from you. I tried to find excuses to talk to you, or just be around you. Then, last week at my house when I saw you sitting alone on my balcony, I caved and tried to tell you everything."

Luke looked guiltily at his feet. "I still feel like a jerk for trying to go after my best friend's girl, but I was so *drawn* to you." He frowned. "Jason should have punched me when I gave him the chance."

I laughed. "I'm glad he didn't! As awful as it sounds, I'll always be grateful to Jason for breaking his leg when he did, otherwise I might never have known how you felt."

Luke chuckled. "That's true. And I'd be lying if I said I wasn't totally stoked when I realized I might get the chance to take you to prom after all."

My breath caught again as his golden eyes locked with mine. "And speaking of prom, I better get you back inside before the dance is over. You'd never forgive me if we didn't dance to at least one song." He pulled me closer until our faces were a few inches apart. "And to be perfectly honest, I've been looking forward to dancing with you all night," he said in a low voice.

My heart was pounding so loudly I was sure Luke could hear it.

"C'mon." He gripped my hand, and I fairly floated as I

followed him back to the dance, blissfully unaware of anything but the feeling of his hand around mine.

We danced to several slow songs together. Each time his arms went around me, I worried that my nerves would never recover from the euphoric shock that exploded through my body!

There was nothing I could compare it to, this feeling of being so close to Luke, of knowing that he actually felt for me the way I felt for him. It was like taking my first breath of real air, as though all the air I'd breathed up to this point in my life had just been there as a standby, to keep me moving until the real stuff arrived. This new air seemed to breathe life into every cell in my body. It made my heart beat faster, and I felt alive from the top of my head to the tips of my toes. It was life-sustaining, it was incredible, and now that I'd had a taste of it, I knew I would never be the same.

All too soon the dance was over. For the first time, I noticed the people milling around us. There were many intrigued glances and some downright jealous looks as Luke continued holding my hand, but I was too absorbed in my happy place to care what anyone else thought.

"Hey, there you guys are!" Clark called as he and the rest of our group made their way toward us. I pretended not to notice Britney and Becka's eyes widen to the size of dinner plates at the sight of Luke's hand in mine, but I couldn't help but feel a little triumphant. "We're heading to Danny's house to watch a movie. We'll see you there, okay?"

Luke shook his head. "I don't think Eliza and I will make it. I made some other plans and, as cool as you guys are, I don't feel like sharing her with anyone else tonight."

My eyes widened in surprise, and I had to force back a giggle at the blatant fury on Britney and Becka's faces. Luke had been look-ing straight at them during his little speech, clearly trying to get a rise out of them, and judging by their expressions, it had worked.

He squeezed my hand once and turned slightly toward me, giving me a quick wink. A small thrill went through me as I real-ized that he cared enough for me to not want me to suffer any more at the hands of those two mean girls.

Clark laughed. "That's cool, that's cool. We understand all about 'other plans.'" He made quotes with his fingers and raised his eyebrow meaningfully at Luke. Danny and Joey caught the joke and snorted in laughter.

Luke smiled, but even though they were clearly teasing, he said, "No, not like *that!* I'll tell you about it Monday—if you can keep your minds out of the gutter until then." He punched Clark lightly on the shoulder.

We turned to leave, and to my surprise Marina came up to me and gave me a hug.

"It was so nice to meet you, Eliza!" she said sincerely. "I hope I'll see you at school sometime."

"You can count on it!" I smiled back at her as she pulled away. Marina was a true gem, and I was happy to have made a new friend. We waved good-bye to everyone before heading back to Luke's Jeep.

CHAPTER

twenty-seven

So, what do you think? Is this another good surprise?" Luke chuckled as I bounced excitedly in the seat next to him.

"It's perfect! I've wanted to ride in one of these ever since I was little!" I smiled at him in wonder. From the first visit I could remember to Temple Square, I'd been in love with the horse-drawn carriages that lined up outside the south entrance. Now, sitting beside Luke as the carriage pulled us through the city, I felt like a real princess, living the "happily ever after" before the story had even fully begun.

"I'm glad you like it." He reached over and held my hand. "I knew the guys were planning on watching a movie after the dance, and I thought that was a pretty lame activity, so I made my own plans. I was going to invite them all to join us, but after the way Britney and Becka treated you, I figured it was better this way."

I let out a huge sigh. "Thank you! I'm not sure what I did to make them dislike me so much, but I'm glad I don't have to worry about it anymore tonight."

"Don't worry about it again, *ever.* Those two are always targeting someone new to make miserable. I think they must suffer from some kind of mental problem if they could pick on someone as sweet and friendly as you." He squeezed my hand, and I wondered briefly if it was possible to die of happiness.

We watched the lights and activity of the city for a few minutes before Luke spoke again. "Eliza, there's another reason I wanted to be alone with you on this carriage ride." He looked at me intently for a moment as if gauging how to proceed. "This is something I've never told anyone outside my family, but I feel like I can trust you, and it's something you need to know."

I nodded encouragingly, my curiosity piqued.

Luke closed his eyes for a second and sighed. "My older brother, Skyler, and I are really close. I've looked up to him for as long as I can remember, and he's one of the greatest people I know."

I was caught off guard by this unexpected turn in the conversation, but tried to keep my face expressionless so as not to interrupt Luke.

"When Skyler was in high school, he had a serious girlfriend named Marcy. They were completely inseparable, and we all really liked her, but unfortunately, they ended up getting into trouble, and Marcy got pregnant just after they graduated." Luke stared straight ahead with a pained expression. "I watched Skyler go into a major depression. He'd always talked about serving a mission, and I knew it was something he really wanted to do, but because of his decisions that never happened.

"Fortunately, he really loved Marcy, and they got married. With the help and guidance of their bishop, they were able to go through the repentance process, and they were sealed in the temple after my nephew was born." Luke's face brightened at the memory. "I wasn't able to be there for the ceremony, but when they came out together as a family, I couldn't help but cry. Skyler was like his old self again, and they were all so happy—and have been ever since."

He blew out a long breath. "I learned two things from watching my brother go through all of that. First, the Atonement is *real* and it's the greatest gift imaginable and it's available to each of us. Second, I learned there was nothing more important to me than to be able to serve my mission. I vowed that I would never have a serious girlfriend before I left and that I'd do everything I could to stay clean and worthy to serve."

Luke looked at me, the golden hues of his eyes fairly burned as he spoke. "Up until now, it hasn't been a problem for me. I'd meet girls and sometimes go on a couple of dates with them, but that was it. No one ever came close to tempting me to ask them to be my girlfriend—until now."

My heartbeat quickened to a rapid staccato as the implication of his words sunk in. I felt a mixture of joy, confusion, and guilt. What exactly was he trying to say?

Luke chuckled at the expression on my face, and his posture relaxed. "Liza, you look like you're afraid I'm about to bite you or something! I'm sorry if the idea of being my girlfriend frightens you so much, but let me put your fears at ease."

I knew he was teasing me and that this was his way of softening whatever blow was coming.

He reached up and brushed my cheek softly with his hand. "I have stronger feelings for you than I've ever had for anyone—so strong it almost scares me. That's one of the reasons I waited so long to tell you how I felt. I'd ask you right here and now to be my girlfriend, but as much as I want to, it just wouldn't be fair."

I bit my lip and looked away, trying to hide the hurt and disappointment on my face.

Luke took my chin and gently turned me to face him. "Trust me, I've thought a lot about this. I'm getting my mission papers ready, and I'll be leaving in a few months. It wouldn't be fair to ask you to be my girlfriend right before I left, as much as my heart begs me to do otherwise. I can't go back on the promise I made to myself. Not when I'm so close. I know the adversary is going to be working on me harder than ever in these next few weeks and months before I leave, and as attracted as I am to you, I wouldn't trust myself to be around you too much."

Luke sighed. "That being said, I'm pretty sure I'll go crazy if I don't see you more often than I have been. So here's what I'm thinking—and you tell me if it works for you—I want to go on more dates with you, but we'll always go in a group or with a designated chaperone, like one of our sisters. I'll never do more than hold your hand and maybe hug you good night, and I fully expect you to go out with other guys if they ask you. Just please don't tell me about it." Luke's eyes searched mine. "I've been doing all the talking. I want to know what you think about all of this."

I didn't know what to say. My mind and heart were in such a state of confusion. Of course I wanted to be Luke's girlfriend! Now that I knew what it felt like to be with him, I didn't ever want him to leave my side—I would permanently attach myself to him if I could! But I cared enough for him that I wanted him to be happy, and I knew that serving a mission was the best possible choice he could be making.

It was a lot to take in all at once, but as the carriage turned a corner and the Salt Lake Temple came into view, I knew Luke was right. I committed right then and there to help him prepare for his mission—no matter what!

⸎

It was two o'clock in the morning, and although my body was exhausted, my mind was still reeling over the amazing events of the day. It was so much to process! I knew I could—and probably *would*—spend days thinking about everything that had happened. It had been a prom date from heaven; the stuff dreams were made of!

I smiled, recalling how happy Luke had been when I told him I fully supported his goal of serving a worthy mission. I was already looking forward to our next date, and it was exciting to think that I'd still get to spend time with him before he left.

I was in the middle of pondering over where he'd be assigned to serve, when an unexpected tapping on my window made me jump. It had been weeks since I'd heard that tap, and there was only one person in the world it could be.

Jill.

I quickly jumped out of bed and rushed to open the window. Jill was perched on the large branch outside of the tree she'd climbed dozens of times since we were kids. Her arms were wrapped tightly around her, and as soon as the window was open, I could hear her muffled sobs.

"Can I come in?" she whispered in a strained voice.

"Of course!" I whispered back as I helped her over the

windowsill. "What's wrong? Is everything okay?" I put my arm around her and guided her toward my bed.

"N-N-Nick and I broke up," Jill managed before breaking into another round of sobs. I pulled her head into my shoulder and held her while her body shook.

"Jill, I'm so sorry! What happened?" I'd never seen her so distraught before, and I ached for her.

After several minutes of crying, Jill sat back and took a deep breath. I grabbed the box of tissues off my nightstand and handed it to her.

"Thanks." She smiled at me weakly as she dried her nose and eyes. She took several more deep breaths, working to calm her breathing. I waited patiently, knowing that she would talk when she felt ready.

"It happened tonight, less than an hour ago," she began timidly. "Nick dropped me off right before curfew. I put on my pajamas and pretended to go to bed, but after my parents were asleep, I snuck out." She dropped her eyes guiltily to the floor. "For the past few months, I've sort of been sneaking out every now and then to go to Nick's house. We hadn't talked about my coming over tonight, but I missed him and just sort of assumed he'd be expecting me."

I tried to keep my expression sympathetic, but the sinking feeling in my stomach warned me that I wasn't going to like what I was about to hear.

Jill's face twisted. "One of his blinds was cracked open a bit. When I looked inside, I saw . . . I saw something that made me sick." She wrapped her arms around her more tightly and struggled to keep her voice calm. "He was sitting at his desk, and I could see the screen on his laptop. Liza, the picture he was looking at was awful! It makes me feel completely nauseated just thinking about it; I know I'll never be able to erase it from my mind! I was totally stunned; I couldn't believe he was looking at porn. My first reaction was to turn and run away, but then I got mad." Jill's eyebrows narrowed at the memory.

"I tapped on his window, and he hurried and snapped his laptop shut, but when he came to the window and saw my expression, he knew I'd caught him. At first he tried to act like it had just popped up on the screen by accident, but I didn't buy that for a second. He finally confessed that he's been struggling with an addiction to pornography, and he told me he needed my help to get over it." She shook her head sadly. "The thing is, I wanted so badly to believe that I could help him—that my love alone could heal his problem, but I knew that that wasn't possible. I told him he needed to see his bishop and that he was the only one who could help him through this. And then I told him it was over between us." Tears poured down Jill's cheeks again, and she rocked slowly back and forth.

I wrapped my arms more tightly about her, wishing desperately that I could ease her suffering. "Jill, I'm so sorry! I know your heart must be breaking right now, and this probably won't sound like the most comforting thing to hear, but you did the right thing."

Jill nodded numbly, and her sobs slowly began to subside. I hoped she was feeling better, but when she finally looked up at me, the pain was still evident in her eyes.

"Liza, the thing is, you haven't heard the whole story yet, and I don't know if I can tell you. I'm so ashamed!" She buried her face in her hands, and I rubbed her back. I wasn't sure what to say, but Jill suddenly lifted her head and began talking as she stared at the floor. "Nick and I have made some mistakes. We've been doing things we shouldn't have for a few months now." Her voice shook with emotion and remorse. "I kept thinking that if we just stopped that would be good enough for repentance and that I wouldn't have to tell the bishop about it.

"We would do okay for a little while, and then things would get out of hand again. I felt sick and completely empty inside. A few times, I told Nick I thought we should break up and that I was going to the bishop, but he always found a way to talk me out of it. He told me he couldn't live without me and that everything was going to work out. He even talked about wanting to marry me after we graduated.

"I was so far gone that I rationalized it was more important to be with him than it was to be in tune with the Spirit, but after tonight it was like a light turned on and I realized that I can't live like this anymore. I feel like I don't even know who I am anymore. But I'm worried that . . ." Her face crumpled as she struggled to speak. "I'm worried that I've let this go on for so long that it's too late for me now." She broke down and unleashed heartrending sobs into her hands.

The conversation I'd had with Grandma last night came back to my mind with perfect clarity, and I felt the Spirit urging me to speak.

Taking both of Jill's shoulders, I forced her to face me. Looking her squarely in the eyes, I said, "Listen to me, Jill. You are *not* too far gone for repentance. Don't you ever believe that! That's exactly what Satan wants you to believe, but it's not the truth. Christ atoned for all of us—and that includes *you*. He loves you so much, and He wants you to be happy. He wants you to go to the bishop to begin the repentance process because that's the only way you're going to be able to rid yourself of this burden."

I smiled at her reassuringly. "Bishop Howard is a good man, and he's not going to make you feel worse for what you've done. He'll lovingly help you get back on track, and believe me, you won't be the first person to have stepped into his office for this reason. I know it's scary, but I'm here to support you. I'll even help you find the number to call and make the appointment if you want."

I squeezed her hand. "Jill, you are an amazing daughter of God, and you have so much potential! The repentance process isn't easy, but that will help you to appreciate Christ's sacrifice all the more. If you follow the proper steps, you'll come away from this experience with an even stronger testimony of His atonement and love for you. The beautiful part about putting your life into the Savior's hands is that He can help you reach beyond your potential and find more joy than you ever thought possible.

"We all make mistakes, and we all need Him. Isn't it wonderful to know that His precious gift is available to all of us? You don't have to suffer forever—there is *hope*."

The words had flown from my mouth almost effortlessly, and the smile that crept onto Jill's face told me that this had been what she needed to hear.

"Thank you, Eliza!" She wrapped her arms around me in a tight hug. "I'm so sorry for the awful way I've been treating you. I've missed you so much!"

I pulled away and shook my head. "Don't worry about it. I missed you tons too, but I knew you'd come back around sooner or later. We are BFFs after all!"

Jill laughed. "You bet we are!"

CHAPTER

"Okay, girls, quiet down!"

I felt complete contentment as I listened to the buzz of chattering voices dying down around me. Jill sat on my right side and Sierra sat on my left; next to her were Courtney and Alexis, and everyone was smiling.

After the opening song and prayer, Mom began with the announcements. I found my mind wandering back to earlier that morning when I'd held Jill's hand as she called the bishop's office to make an appointment. Her hand had been shaking as she made the call, but I could already sense her relief. I was so grateful that Bishop Howard had time to meet with her after church today.

Courtney was back to her old, cheerful self, and her face positively glowed with joy. She was such a beautiful girl; I didn't envy Mom or Dad's position when she would turn sixteen and the boys would come knocking on the door!

I was also pleased that Alexis had come for the second week in a row. Her discussions with the missionaries were going well, and she even said that her mom had mentioned a desire to come back to church.

All in all, things were looking up, and it was awesome to see the lives of the people I loved improving so much.

"Sierra, will you come up to the front please?" I snapped back to reality as Sierra rose from the seat beside me and stood beside my mom.

Sierra had changed, too, in these past two weeks. Her hair was soft and shiny, pulled back with a stylish leather headband. Her glasses had been replaced by contacts, allowing her lovely eyes and delicate features to be seen. She held her head high as Mom spoke.

"As you know, we had our Young Women in Excellence program this past month, but unfortunately I didn't have enough pendants to give out that evening, and Sierra graciously agreed to receive hers later." Mom opened the box and ceremoniously handed the pendant to Sierra.

I sat on the front row, and my breath caught as I stared at the pendant. I felt as if I were seeing it for the first time—the golden medallion framing the spires of the temple seemed to gleam in the light, and suddenly it all made sense.

The last token. This was what Grandma had intended as my last token, but it wasn't something I could find. I had to earn it.

A smile slowly spread across my face and tears formed in my eyes. I said a silent prayer of gratitude, and then in my heart I added, *Thank you Grandma . . . for everything.* A warm feeling rushed over me, and somehow I knew she'd heard me.

EPILOGUE

Luke's house was fairly bursting at the seams with people coming to say good-bye and wish him luck. Since he was one of the first from his graduating class to leave on a mission, it seemed that half the school had turned out to hear him speak. They had filled the chapel overflow clear back to the stage in the cultural hall!

Luke's talk had been inspirational, and his enthusiasm to go out and serve was obvious. I knew a few of his friends who were still on the fence about whether or not they wanted to serve missions, and I hoped that after hearing Luke's talk, they'd catch the vision and commit to go.

"How are you doing?" Jill made her way to me through the crowd and touched my hand with a sympathetic smile.

It was so nice to have Jill back! These past few months had been tough for her. She'd come to me crying more than once about how much she missed Nick and how hard it was to move on. For the first few weeks after she broke up with him, he'd still call and text her, begging her to come back. I knew it was incredibly difficult for Jill to stay strong each time he contacted her, but she did it.

She blocked his number from her cell phone and deleted him from her Facebook and e-mail accounts. I admired her determination to stay on track, and I did everything I could to help distract her from her broken heart.

Now that she was sixteen, we got jobs together at a local smoothie shop. Jill was also "officially" available to date, and since things were over between her and Nick, a weekend never went by without some guy calling to ask her out. We'd been on a few group dates together, and I loved to see her happy and interacting with people the way she used to. Thanks to the help and guidance of our bishop, she was working through the repentance process, and it was incredible to see the light and joy slowly returning to the life of my best friend.

"I'm good, thanks," I answered as I put on my bravest smile.

The truth was, my insides felt like a giant volcano just waiting to erupt. On the one hand, I was so happy and excited for Luke. There was nothing better he could be doing in his life, and his strong desire to serve the Lord by preaching the gospel spoke volumes about his character and testimony. I was proud of him and elated that he would finally be able to reach the goal that he'd striven for his entire life.

On the other hand, the past few months I'd been able to spend with Luke had been the most incredible months of my life. True to our agreement, I'd dated other people and only went out with Luke once a week. Even though we always dated in a group or with a designated chaperone, I'd looked forward to those dates as if they were a lifesaving substance! Every minute in his presence was magical, and I knew from the way he looked and talked to me that he felt the same way. It was painful to know that something so special would have to be put on hold for two years. And then who knew what would happen when he came back?

I worried incessantly that he wouldn't feel the same way about me when he returned, or that some horrific circumstance would keep us from being together again.

He'd been called to the Mexico Hermosillo Mission. I knew it was in a relatively safe area, but there was always that little "what if" that haunted the back of my mind.

"Liar," Jill accused as she looked at me more intently. "Don't worry, Liza, I know this next little while is going to be tough, but I'm here for you. We're going to have so much fun the next two years that the time will simply fly by, just you wait and see!" She put her arm around me and said jokingly, "*Guys* . . . who needs 'em?"

I couldn't help but laugh as she repeated the phrase I'd been chanting to her the past few months to make her feel better. "That's right, who needs 'em?" Now the hard part was actually making myself believe it.

"Hey, Jill, mind if I steal Liza away for a few minutes?" Luke appeared from behind me, and when his arm touched my elbow, a shock wave of joy went through my body.

Jill beamed at me, then at Luke. "Not at all. By the way, you did a great job today, Lucas. You're going to be an awesome missionary!"

I smiled at the nickname Jill had given Luke. It made me happy that the two of them got along so well.

"Thanks, Jillian," Luke retorted as he winked at her.

He took hold of my arm and quickly scooted me through the crowded hallway. We had to stop every few feet because everyone wanted to talk to Luke, but somehow he finally managed to edge us close enough to the door that we could slip outside.

He took both of my hands and pulled me to the side of the house where no one could see us. "We probably only have a few minutes before my mom comes and hunts me down, but I just had to see you."

The sincerity in his eyes made my heart melt. I loved the feeling of having his hand in mine and knowing that at least for this moment, he belonged to no one but me.

Suddenly, we heard the front door open. Luke put a finger to his lips and led me down the side porch and out into the backyard.

He took me back into the old barn and slowly slid the door shut. I relished the faintly sweet scent of hay combined with leather that permeated the air. Luke's horse, Flame, nickered a gentle greeting from his stall. I went over and affectionately rubbed behind his ears.

"You did such a great job today; I'm really proud of you." I spoke to Luke but kept my attention on Flame. I was afraid that if I looked at Luke, he'd see the sadness I was fighting so hard to mask. "It's crazy to think that in no time at all you'll be *Elder* Matthews and on your way to the MTC. I'm so excited for you—"

Before I could finish my sentence, Luke gently grabbed me from behind and spun me around to face him. The gold in his brown eyes seemed to burn like embers as he stared at me. "I have something for you," he said as he reached into his pocket and pulled out a tiny velvet pouch.

"Oh, Luke, I told you that you didn't need to . . ." I started, but he held his fingers to my lips to cut me off. I'd given him a silver CTR ring and a new tie to take with him on his mission, and I'd made him promise not to get me anything in return. He was paying for his mission almost entirely on his own, and I didn't want him to spend any of his hard-earned cash on me.

"Liza, this is something I've been waiting to give you, but I don't want you to take it the wrong way." He looked a little anxious, and my stomach flip-flopped with curiosity.

He placed the pouch in my hand. I smiled at him before gently unfastening the string. I reached into the bag and pulled out a ring. It was a simple gold band with delicate filigree on top that surrounded a single red stone. It was so perfect and so beautiful that I couldn't take my eyes off it.

"Luke, it's gorgeous!" I breathed as I turned the ring in my fingers. "But you know I can't accept it. This looks like an expensive ring, and I don't want you spending your money on me."

Luke grinned at me as he took the ring from my hand and slipped it over my right ring finger. "It's a ruby. When I saw it in the store, I thought of you. I wasn't sure whether to get a silver or gold band, but then I remembered your necklace and thought they'd go well together. Do you really like it?"

As soon as he said the word "ruby," my mind went back to the last dream I'd had with Grandma and the scripture she'd quoted from Proverbs. I instinctively reached for the Young Women medallion that I now wore proudly around my neck. I'd worked at a furious pace to complete my Personal Progress and had received the medallion a few weeks ago. The fact that Luke knew how much the necklace meant to me, and that of all the rings to choose from, he'd picked a ruby, sent shivers down my spine. It was the perfect symbol for our relationship, and although my heart was already his, he won it all over again in that moment.

I threw my arms around him and felt him sigh in relief. "It's absolutely perfect," I said. "Thank you so much!"

Luke hugged me back. "I'm so glad you like it. I was worried you'd think it was weird or something."

I pulled away from him and frowned. "Weird? Why would I think that?"

He looked at the ground and scuffed his shoe in the dirt. "I don't know, I was worried that you'd think it was like a promise ring or something, and that's totally not why I bought it," he said quickly. "You know I want you to date as much as possible while I'm gone, and we agreed that we'll wait and see what happens when I get home, but these past few months have meant a lot to me, and I just wanted to leave you with something to remember me by."

Reaching up, I took his chin in my hand. "Luke, there is *no chance* that I could ever forget you. This ring is the nicest gift anyone's ever given me and I love it, but I am worried about how much it cost."

He shook his head. "No more talk about money! I've got plenty so you don't need to worry. If you really like the ring, then keep it— but you don't have to wear it if you don't want to."

I caressed the ring. "Are you kidding? I'll wear it every day! I only wish I'd gotten you a better gift; I'll have to find a way to pay you back somehow."

Luke's eyes narrowed roguishly, and he stepped closer to me. "Hmm, now that's not a bad idea. Maybe when I get home we can come up with something."

"Oh, you think so?" I smiled at him playfully, trying to keep my breathing steady. He often flirted with me in a teasing way that made me ache to kiss him, but true to his word, he'd done nothing more than hold my hand and give me an occasional hug. I admired his self-control, but sometimes I had to fight back the thought that maybe I wasn't attractive enough—that maybe he really didn't *want* to kiss me.

When the barn door slid open, we both looked up, and Luke took a step back. His mom popped her head in. When she saw us together, she gave a knowing nod. "I thought I might find you in here. Sorry to cut things short, but some people are asking for you, Luke."

"Okay, I'll be right in."

Sister Matthews smiled warmly at me. "Eliza, I'm sure Luke's already told you this, but please know that you're welcome to drop by and visit anytime while he's gone. We'd love to have you."

I smiled back at her gratefully. "Thanks, I'd like that."

Sister Matthews was such a kind woman, and I'd grown close to her over the past few months. She'd made me feel like part of the family, and it meant a lot that she would invite me to come over even when Luke wasn't there.

"Good!" She winked at us and then slowly slid the door closed again.

Luke let out a slow breath as he turned and looked at me. "Well, I guess this is it."

"Yeah . . . I guess it is." I put on my bravest smile as I gazed at him. He looked so painfully handsome standing there in his suit that I wondered for the millionth time how I'd ever been so lucky to win his attention.

I concentrated on memorizing the sight of him: the way he stood, the slight wave in his hair, and the way his eyes lit up his entire face when he smiled. I wanted to remember every detail so I could savor them for the months ahead. Besides, focusing on the present helped numb the pain creeping up inside me at the thought of the near future.

Luke took a step closer to me until his face was mere inches from mine. He brushed a strand of hair away from my face and without warning whispered, "I'm going to miss you like crazy, you know that?"

Suddenly, he grabbed my shoulders and pulled my face to his. The world seemed to stand still, and it felt like my bones had turned to liquid. Every thought in my head vanished at the thrill of his lips on mine. I'd imagined what my first kiss would be like thousands of times, but this surpassed even my wildest dreams!

He kissed me almost fiercely at first, but then the kiss softened and he gently pulled away. The kiss hadn't lasted long, but I was sure I'd never fully recover from the power of its spell.

Luke held my face in his hands. "I'm sorry that I broke my promise, but I just had to do that before I left." His eyes were suddenly intense. "I love you, Eliza," he whispered.

"I love you, too." The words came from the depths of my heart, and it felt so good to finally speak them. We stared at each other for a few more moments before Luke took my hand and we slowly walked toward the door.

I no longer felt in danger of crying. Knowing that Luke loved me just as I loved him had strengthened me, and now all I felt was excitement for the future.

I was determined to help him be the best missionary possible by writing only encouraging letters. I wouldn't distract him by telling him how much I missed him or of things that would make him miss home. I wanted these next two years to be the best two years of his life—and of mine. I wanted to grow spiritually, too, while he was gone.

As we walked hand in hand toward Luke's house, I looked again at the ring on my finger and smiled. Who knew what the future would hold?

DISCUSSION QUESTIONS

1. In the story, Eliza has powerful dreams which have an impact on her life. Have you ever had dreams or strong impressions at night that changed the way you felt the next day? Have you considered keeping a journal to write them down?

2. In seeking information about her great-grandma Porter, Eliza discovers more about herself. How much do you know about your great-grandmother? Your great-great-grandmother?

3. Which woman's story from Eliza's dreams affected you the most? Why?

4. Eliza learns about the impact of having too much technology in her life. How do you think technology affects your life? Do you think technology can interfere with the ability to receive personal revelation and feel the Spirit? Do you ever take time to "disconnect" for a while?

5. Eliza befriends Keira, a new girl in school, who asks her some questions about her beliefs. Do you think you would be prepared if someone were to ask you questions about your beliefs? How would you react if their questions were unfriendly?

6. Eliza ends up doing an act of service for someone she had once considered her enemy. Can you imagine doing something nice for someone who isn't your friend? How do you think that might alter your attitude towards him or her?

7. Eliza finds some special keepsakes that belonged to her great-grandmother. Does your family have any heirlooms passed down from past generations? What makes these items special?

8. In learning of her divine nature, Eliza realizes that she's been given special gifts and talents. What gifts do you have? Which talents would you like to develop?

9. After the series of dreams that she experiences, Eliza makes the goal that she will be married in the temple someday. Do you think having a goal can change the way you live your life? What goals have you made for yourself?

10. In a few of her dreams, Eliza sees glimpses of the lives of certain women from the scriptures. If you could choose to witness a scene from the scriptures, which scene would you choose?

11. Eliza notices two different girls who are in need of a friend (Keira Davis and Sierra Holbrook). She makes an effort to get to know them and in the process gains new friends. Have you ever noticed someone who often sits alone? What did (or could) you do about it?

12. Eliza learned to incorporate the Young Women values into her everyday life. If you had to pick one value to focus on today, which would you choose?

ABOUT THE AUTHOR

Holly J. Wood is an avid reader. She attended Ricks College and Brigham Young University, where she pursued a degree in health science. Holly has a passion for travel and has lived briefly in Israel and Mexico. True to her name, she enjoys watching classic movies and musicals. She currently lives in Mountain Green, Utah, with her husband and two young children. You can visit Holly at www.hollyjwood.com.